THE VAMPIRE EMPIRE

BLOOD OATH

DANA GRICKEN

OLIVERHEBERBOOKS

ONE

The vampires used to be strong and powerful.

That was what Levi Godfrey was thinking about as he boarded the windows and doors to the bunker, fortifying them in case of an attack. The bunker in Los Angeles was the largest in the world. If it could fall, it would mean the end of the vampires forever.

And everything they had worked for would vanish.

As he hammered away, memories came flooding back to him during his time as an architect. It was the 1970s before his brother had turned him. It was a time when the vampire world was unknown to him—new and exciting.

Back when they were fearsome predators and not easy prey.

A second later, high heels clicked behind him. He knew who it was—he could smell her familiar scent of blood and lavender.

"Need some help?" Raven asked, hovering behind him.

He glanced over his shoulder, barely looking at her. Raven was beautiful—long black hair, piercing brown eyes. But there were rumors she was with Levi's brother, Cyrus. And Levi knew better than to play with what belonged to his brother.

"No, thanks," Levi replied, bolting the door. "I'm doing just fine."

"Come on," Raven tried again. "What's the matter? Don't you find me attractive?"

"You know I do. But you're Cyrus's girl. Off-limits."

"So? I don't mind sharing." She leaned in closer to his ear. "And Cyrus doesn't have to know."

"But he'll find out. He *always* does. And his anger can be scary—trust me."

Raven scoffed. "We could all be dead tomorrow, Levi. Is this how you want to spend your last days?"

Levi shook his head, pausing his work. "We *won't* be dead by tomorrow. The Patriarch—"

"I know what the Patriarch has promised us. Eternal life and victory," Raven said, placing her hands on her hips. "But look at us, Levi—we're in a bunker hiding from the Legionnaires! We both know there's a good chance we'll lose this war."

"Don't let the Patriarch hear you say that. He doesn't like vampires who doubt his vision." Levi finally glanced back at her. "Now, if you'll excuse me, I have a bunker to secure. Go find my brother if you're looking for fun."

Raven was about to argue when a loud pounding came from the other side of the door. Levi stopped his work, glancing up in fear. Was this it? Had the Legionnaires found them after all?

Raven's eyes widened. Levi pressed a finger against his lips, signaling for Raven to be quiet. If Allegiant *had* discovered their main bunker, he didn't want to tip them off that they were inside. No—he was going to make them work for it. They wouldn't die without a fight.

"Let me in, damn it," the person from the other side said. "I may be immortal, but I ain't getting any younger!"

"It's Garth," Raven said, turning to Levi. "Hurry, open the door!"

Levi hesitated, then pulled the bolts and nails off the door, destroying his hours of hard work. He opened the door slowly, glancing around for any Legionnaires, but he didn't see them. All was quiet this time of night except for wildlife in the forest next to them.

As Levi glanced back, he finally noticed Garth. As the messenger, it was his duty to venture out into the world and report back on the Legionnaires' whereabouts. It was a dangerous job—one not even Levi's brother would volunteer for. And Levi was much happier maintaining the bunker.

Levi opened the door wider, letting Garth enter. As soon as he took a step inside, he collapsed on the floor, his black blood spewing out like tar. Raven fell to her knees, caressing Garth's face. Under the light of the bunker, Levi noticed he was badly beaten and bleeding. He closed the door and locked it tight.

"What happened, Garth?" Raven asked. "Did you find the Legionnaires?"

"More like they found me," Garth muttered, spitting blood. "They attacked me—would've killed me if I hadn't run."

Raven shook her head. "You're the best spy we have, Garth. How did they see you in the dark?"

"They're getting better, wiser to our tricks." He spat out black blood onto the floor. "But that's not all. I have information—something the Patriarch will want to hear."

"Let's get you to the infirmary first," Raven said, helping him up. "Levi, can you summon the Patriarch? Tell him Garth's hurt."

"All right—but it can't take long. If I don't fix the work I just screwed up, we might all end up like Garth."

As Raven helped Garth down the corridor, dribbling black blood onto the white tiles, Levi took a left and went down the opposite hallway. The identical red paint made the bunker feel like a maze. They had been hiding out for a little over a year now, but Levi still hadn't memorized the big place. He finally found the Patriarch's office and knocked first so he wouldn't disturb their vampire lord.

"Come in," a voice on the other side said.

Levi opened the door, noticing Patriarch Kristoff on the opposite side of the room. He stood near his desk while glancing out the window at the moonlight.

"Patriarch? Garth's back."

"Oh? And what's the latest on the Legionnaires?" the Patriarch asked, not bothering to turn around.

"Well, the Legionnaires attacked him. Beyond that, he told us he needed to speak with you."

"Did he?" Patriarch sighed. "You know...I always feared this day would come."

"What day?"

He turned silent for a moment. "Do you ever wish you could go back, Levi? Perhaps rewrite the past to alter your future?"

When the Patriarch turned around, Levi saw him now in all his glory—sharp fangs, nearly black irises, a long red cloak. He would've retired years ago if the situation with the Legionnaires hadn't worsened.

Levi gulped. "All the time."

"Yes. Me, too," the Patriarch muttered cryptically. "Take me to the messenger. I must hear what he's discovered."

Levi nodded, escorting the Patriarch to the infirmary. By now, the few dozen vampires in the bunker had heard the news. They walked with Levi, eager to hear of the messenger's condition—and what it meant for their kind.

When Levi and Patriarch Kristoff entered the small infirmary, they found Raven hovering above Garth. He lay on a long table as Raven placed healing herbs and ointments over his wounds. The bleeding was heavy, soaking through his black clothes.

Some of the others had beaten them there already. Marek, the bunker's security guard, stood near the back of the room, his dark hair hiding his worried eyes. Vikus, the tall and burly butcher, stood next to him. No one said a word. Footsteps echoed behind them, then Levi spun around.

Cyrus. His brother had a history book in his hands, probably coming from the library. His black hair was scruffy-looking and unkempt, his green eyes lifeless, and the black leather jacket he wore had faded. Hygiene and lack of clothing seemed far down on the list of worries. He was forever twenty-five—frozen in time when he became a vampire—and just two years older than Levi. But they had stopped counting.

"What the hell's going on?" Cyrus asked, entering the room. "I heard rumors the messenger got his ass kicked out there."

Garth nodded, coughing up more blood. "I did. The Legionnaires...they're coming."

"Coming? Coming where?" Levi asked.

"Here, Levi. I overheard them talking about their plans. They've already wiped out most of the country—all the other bunkers. A few vampires are still around, but they're scattered. Give it more time and they'll be dead, too."

"Hang on. Are you saying...we're some of the last vampires on Earth?"

"Yes—but we won't be for long," Garth muttered. "Not when the Legionnaires find us."

Gasps and murmurs broke out in the room. The fear in the air was tangible, sending a shiver up Levi's spine.

"Bullshit," Cyrus spat. "They won't find us here—it's too remote. We hid our tracks well."

As Garth began another coughing fit, the Patriarch turned to Raven. "Will he live?"

"I'm sorry," Raven said with a frown, "but he's lost too much blood. The Legionnaires did a number on him—hit some major arteries. It's surprising he held on this long. While staking a vampire is a definite way to kill them, they chose the slow route of making him bleed out."

"Bastards," Cyrus grumbled.

"I...had to warn you all," Garth said, his eyes boring into Levi's. "Don't let them win. Fight for...our people..."

And then Garth went still, his eyes wide open. The room turned silent again.

"Well, what's everyone standing around for?" Cyrus demanded. "We've got work to do!"

"You're right. We have no time to mourn," the Patriarch said. "Chef, get some dinner ready for everyone. When dinner's over, meet me in the conference room."

"What should I do with the body?" Raven asked.

"Burn it." The Patriarch eyed Garth's corpse. "His weakness led to this."

As the Patriarch's boots clicked away down the hallway, Levi feared they would all meet Garth's fate soon enough.

ANIMAL BLOOD just wasn't the same as human blood. Especially young blood—so sweet, so ripe. Levi would've given anything to taste it again, but times had changed. They couldn't risk going out far to hunt, so they had to stay local.

And since Allegiant had taken all the humans away to safety, it meant animals were the only creatures around to kill and drink from. It felt unfair—like a punishment. Without consistent human blood, the vampires had grown weaker.

After dinner, Levi followed his brother and the other vampires to the conference room. They took their seats, looking at Patriarch for guidance. Like usual.

The Patriarch sighed. "We've lost contact with the other

bunkers. I fear Garth's information was correct—that the other vamps are dead. We may very well be among the last on Earth."

The room broke out in murmurs again. Cyrus leaned forward. "Then we must do something. Find the Legionnaires first, organize an attack—"

"Foolish boy," the Patriarch spat. "Do you think we could win against them? A few measly vamps against an army like Allegiant?"

Cyrus growled. "We are *not* measly. Perhaps *you* are after ruling for so long—"

"That's enough," Marek said from across the room. "Don't speak to the Patriarch that way."

"I wouldn't, if the Patriarch had a plan," Cyrus shot back. "We're like lambs to the slaughter here. We can't let Allegiant get away with this."

"Then it's a good thing I have a plan after all," the Patriarch said. "Have any of you heard of blood magic?"

Levi nodded in his chair. "Sure. Well, just through rumors. It's sacrificial magic, right? By mixing vampire blood and mortal blood?"

"Very good. Perhaps you're becoming more of a scholar than your brother," the Patriarch said, making Cyrus sneer in jealousy. "Blood magic has been used only a few times in history. With its great power brings great danger, which is why we've never attempted it before. But these are desperate times, and we have no choice."

"What are you proposing?" Raven asked.

"Time travel," the Patriarch replied. "We all know the story of Emilia Rutherford, the very first Legionnaire. She began Allegiant, the organization for vampire hunters, back in 1698 at the age of twenty-three. I propose we return to that time and kill her to prevent it altogether."

The room turned silent, everyone glancing at one another.

Levi was the first one to speak up. "Is that...is that even possible?"

The Patriarch smiled, his fangs shimmering in the light. "*Anything* is possible with blood magic, Levi. That is what makes it so dangerous. This plan was a last resort—something I would consider only if our entire race was threatened. I believe it is. In my opinion, it's worth the risk."

"I like it," Cyrus said, a smirk growing across his pale face.

"And if we succeed, this timeline may have never happened," Raven said. "The vampires could be even more powerful. Stronger than our hunters!"

The Patriarch nodded. "Exactly. This could give our people another chance at freedom—at an empire. We can't pass up this opportunity."

"What do we need?" Levi asked.

"I've kept a vial of virginal, mortal blood in my safe for this ritual. We'll also require a flower and vampire blood," the Patriarch said. "Acquire everything and bring it here. I'll open the portal myself in case something goes wrong. Dismissed, everyone."

"Right away, Patriarch," the vampires said in unison.

As Levi and the others got up, the Patriarch turned to him. "Levi? A moment in private, if I may?"

Levi walked over to him as the others left. "Yes, Patriarch?"

"If anything should happen to me—either through the upcoming Allegiant attack or the blood ritual," the Patriarch began, "I want you to lead the vampires in my place."

"Me? But...why?" Levi frowned. "Cyrus would be a better choice. He's smarter—"

"Cyrus *is* intelligent, but he's too headstrong and impatient. We need a leader who won't rush into things. A leader like *you*."

Levi thought about it for a moment. If Cyrus found out the

Patriarch wanted to make Levi the leader, it could cause a rift between the brothers. But on the other hand, the Patriarch was wise. Levi couldn't refuse an order from the world's highest-ranking vampire.

Levi nodded. "All right, Patriarch. If anything happens to you—darkness forbid—I'll take your title."

He grinned, patting Levi's shoulder. "Excellent, my boy. This is your blood oath. You must kill Emilia Rutherford and save your people. Trust me, you'll make a fine—"

The power cut out, shrouding the bunker in darkness. Levi heard loud footsteps, banging, and screaming in the distance. It sounded like a battle.

"What's going on?" Levi asked.

"Allegiant. Garth was right—they've found us," the Patriarch muttered. "Hurry, get the ingredients for the ritual. We haven't much time!"

Levi could normally see in the dark, but with the lack of human blood, his night vision had deteriorated. He stumbled down the corridor, trying to feel his way around when he heard voices up ahead. He squinted, noticing the Legionnaires with their flashlights out. They were easy to recognize with the insignia on their combat outfits—the V symbol with a skull and a stake.

"Boss wants them all dead by tonight," one of the Legionnaires said. "Letting that vamp live to follow him here was genius. I would've just killed him outright."

Levi cursed under his breath. Garth had led Allegiant right to the bunker without knowing it. He knew he shouldn't have let Garth inside.

"Spread out," the other Legionnaire said. "None of them are making it out of here alive—"

The Legionnaire cried out in pain as something in the

shadows lunged at him. When Levi's eyes adjusted, he realized the man's attacker was Cyrus. He had pounced on the Legionnaire, biting his neck and drinking furiously from the human.

The other Legionnaire noticed, holding up his gun. It had a silver bullet in it—and Levi knew with one shot to the chest, Cyrus would die. A new, modern way to kill a vampire. So, Levi jumped forward, pushing Cyrus out of the way, and took the shot in his arm instead.

Both the brothers fell to the floor beside the dead Legionnaire. Levi's arm ached, but he forced himself to focus. As they looked up, they realized the other Legionnaire was still coming at them with a snarl.

"You'll pay for that, you vamp bastards!" the Legionnaire cried. "I'll enjoy gutting you all—"

With a gasp, the Legionnaire paused and fell to his knees. Raven stood behind him, her mouth red with blood. As she wiped it off, she looked down at the brothers. She had ingredients in her hands that looked like what the Patriarch had described.

"I've got everything we need," she said. "Let's get to the Patriarch before it's too late."

"What about the others?" Levi asked, rising to his feet. Cyrus did the same. "Marek and Vikus?"

"All dead," Raven said. "Shot by Allegiant."

"Who cares about them now?" Cyrus asked. "If we succeed in the past, we can prevent their deaths in the future."

Raven nodded. "You're right. We'd better—"

A single shot rang out. Black blood spurted everywhere as Raven collapsed. Levi looked down, noticing the bullet through her heart. It had killed her instantly. Levi peered across her inert body, where more Legionnaires approached.

"Come on," Cyrus said, picking up the ingredients Raven had dropped. "Let's find the Patriarch. Hurry!"

Levi nodded, running off with his brother. He wanted to look over his shoulder at Raven, but then he remembered sentimentality was a human trait. He had forsaken it long ago when he had transformed.

They made it to the Patriarch's office and slammed the door shut behind them. The Patriarch walked over, his eyebrows furrowed in concern. "Well? What's happened?"

"We're the last three left," Levi said, looking down. "The others...Allegiant got them."

"I see. That was to be expected, I suppose. Now, scatter the ingredients on the table," the Patriarch said, and Cyrus put the mortal blood, vampire blood, and flower down. "Good. Let me begin by—"

The door crashed open behind them. Several Legionnaires stood there, their guns held high. Levi looked back and noticed their leader—a tall, red-headed woman with green eyes. He would've found her beautiful if they weren't sworn enemies.

"In the name of Allegiant, prepare to die," the woman in charge said. She must've been a Rutherford—they had led Allegiant since its conception—and all had the same signature red hair and green eyes.

"Not this time, I'm afraid," the Patriarch said, pouring the mortal and vampire blood onto the flower. It absorbed the blood and turned black.

Behind them, a swirling red portal opened, making Levi's eyes widen. This was it—the blood magic had worked. A powerful wind came from the other side, sweeping across the room.

The Legionnaires murmured in surprise. The woman in charge stepped forward, her mouth opening in shock. "What is that? What have you done?"

"Go!" the Patriarch said to Levi and Cyrus, ignoring the Legionnaires. "Get out of here. I'll cover you!"

"We won't leave you, Patriarch," Levi said. "You can come with us—"

But Cyrus had already grabbed Levi, pulling him through the portal. And before their world faded to black, Levi watched as the Legionnaires unloaded their silver bullets into the Patriarch's heart, killing him.

TWO

After the blood portal shot them out, Levi and Cyrus landed on solid ground with a thud. It was pitch-black outside and pouring rain. Levi fell on the arm that had gotten shot and cried out in pain, then his brother's head snapped in his direction.

"Brother, are you all right?" Cyrus asked, helping Levi to his feet.

Levi shook his head. "No, my arm's killing me. It's that damn bullet I took for you. Think you can pull it out?"

"Let me look. Oof, it's in there deep," Cyrus said, examining the wound. "And it's silver. I touch it, it hurts me too."

"Great." He sighed. "I can't go around with a bullet in my arm! It's making me weaker by the minute. What are we going to do?"

"We'll have to find a doctor," Cyrus said, looking around. "Wherever the hell we are."

Levi glanced around. There were no cars, no skyscrapers, no technology—nothing like the world they had come from. Instead, there were huts, carts, and horses neighing in the distance. The cobblestone streets were empty this time of night, with all the shops along the walkway closed.

"Sweet hellfire," Cyrus cursed. "I think it worked!"

"You mean...we went into the past?" Levi asked. "We time-traveled?"

Cyrus nodded. "To 1698. Look around, it definitely seems like it. The Patriarch mentioned that was the year Emilia Rutherford started Allegiant. It's one thing to read about history, but it's another to see it in the flesh."

"Patriarch..." Levi hung his head. "He's dead—Allegiant shot him through the heart as we left. He sacrificed himself so we could get away."

"Did he? That's far in the future—centuries from now. If we kill Emilia first, we can save our people," Cyrus said. "I didn't agree with that old bastard on a lot of things, but this plan of his? It's genius. And we have the advantage of knowing what's going to happen. We have the chance to kill our enemy before Allegiant can even get a foothold."

"You're right." Levi craned his neck, watching as the blood portal closed behind them. He rushed over to the spot where it had swirled. "But how will we get back to our time when we're done?"

Cyrus shrugged. "I dunno. Perform another blood ritual? Look, the only thing we should focus on right now is killing Emilia. Let's find a doctor to help you and then—"

A scream echoed behind them. Levi and Cyrus turned around, noticing a woman on the street. She dressed in skimpy clothes with big hair and red lips. She looked at the brothers with wide eyes and then back at the spot where the portal had vanished.

"She must've seen the portal," Levi said. "We can't let her keep screaming. People will hear her!"

"Leave that to me, Brother." Cyrus licked his lips,

approached her slowly like a predator circling its prey. "Well, well, well...what's your name, darling?"

"M-Marcia. Please don't hurt me." The woman fell to her knees. "Please, I beg you."

"It won't hurt...much. Oh, how I've missed victims begging for their lives."

"Maybe we should let her live," Levi said. "We came here to kill Emilia, not drink blood on the side of the street—"

But it was too late. Cyrus had already sunk his teeth into the woman's neck, clasping a hand over her mouth to muffle her screams. After a few moments, she fell dead on the ground, mostly drained and pale.

Cyrus pulled back, wiping the blood off his mouth. "You want in on this, Levi?"

Levi couldn't deny it—he was thirsty. They hadn't had proper blood in years. And since she was already dead, it would've been a shame to let her blood go to waste. He stepped forward with a shrug and drank from the other side of her neck. When all the blood in her body had dried up, leaving her wrinkled and gaunt, Levi pulled back and wiped his mouth.

"Good boy," Cyrus said, patting his brother's shoulder. "Now, let's get that wound of yours taken care of. I know it's the Dark Ages, but there's gotta be someone around here who can—"

"Stop right there!" a woman cried behind them.

Levi and Cyrus spun around. A woman with red hair, freckles, and green eyes stood in front of them, holding up a dagger. She looked to be in her early twenties, dressed in a long, green robe with a satchel of herbs around her waist. The moonlight shone on her face just right as Levi noticed her beauty.

"What are you two doing out here?" she asked. "These streets are dangerous at night."

"We were looking for a doctor. Someone who understands

medicine," Cyrus explained, pointing at Levi. "My brother's hurt."

The woman looked down, noticing the dead woman on the ground. She made the sign of the cross. "Dear God! What happened to her?"

She hadn't seen them kill her. Good—it meant no witnesses.

"Someone attacked her," Cyrus lied. "They came out of the bushes. We tried to save her, but it was too late. We heard her scream and that's when we ran out here to help. But whoever killed her also got my brother before running off."

"I heard her scream too. It's why I came over." The woman leaned in closer, lowering her dagger. "Poor woman. No one deserves that fate, not even a prostitute. Did you get a good look at the attacker? Was it...human?"

"Uh, we don't know," Levi said. "It's dark out. Could've been anyone."

"True." She looked back at Cyrus. "You said your brother is hurt?"

Cyrus nodded. "Badly. He needs a healer."

"Good thing you found one then. Though, the term apothecary is more frequently used." The woman placed her dagger in her satchel. "Come with me, please."

As she led them through the village, bringing them to a shop down the path, Levi turned to her. "If you're an apothecary, why do you carry a dagger?"

"For protection," she said. "These streets aren't safe, especially at night. You've seen that firsthand."

"Are there a lot of attacks?"

The woman nodded. "All the time. It makes me so angry—especially when our village's Lord refuses to do anything about it."

"Do you know who's responsible?" Cyrus asked.

The woman paused for a moment. "Something evil. Once I treat your wound, we can speak about it. Come—my place is just over here."

She led them to a small shop where a sign read ROOTS APOTHECARY. The bell above the door jingled as they entered, then Levi got a whiff of the place. It smelled like all kinds of herbs and spices from rosemary to thyme and basil. They had no electricity back in the 1600s, so the woman lit the room with candles. In the back of the shop sat a small room with crude and archaic medical tools. Levi rolled his eyes, fearing someone so primitive wouldn't be able to help him.

"I just finished helping a late patient when I heard the woman scream," Emilia began. "If I'd hurried, maybe she'd still be alive."

"It wasn't your fault," Levi said, a strange desire to comfort her growing inside of him. "You couldn't have known what was going to happen."

She still looked sad, her eyebrows turned downward but nodded. "Thank you. Please, have a seat in the back. I'll look at your wound in there."

Levi did as she asked, sitting down on the uncomfortable straw bed. The woman brought over a candle, holding it up toward Levi's biceps. Her eyes widened when she noticed the deep bullet wound.

"What is *that*?" she asked. "I've never seen such anything like it before."

"Uh, I don't know," Levi lied. "The monster that killed the woman hit me with it. It needs to be removed—fast."

"Indeed. Here, let me fetch my tools."

When she retrieved her tools and sat back down, she used a device that looked like ancient tweezers. She reached into the wound, yanking out the bullet. Levi bit down on his lip as black blood dribbled out of his arm. Cyrus stood in the corner of the room, watching closely.

"Your blood..." She paused, wide-eyed. "It's as black as night! How is this possible?"

"Oh, that? It's a genetic abnormality," Cyrus lied, leaning forward. "It means everyone in my family has it. My people too. It's not dangerous or contagious, though. I promise."

"I hope not. We have enough plagues around here as it is," the woman muttered. "Where are you two from? Judging by your accent and strange clothes, you can't have come from the village. I'm certain I'd remember you."

"Los Angeles, California," Levi said before he could stop himself.

Cyrus glared at him.

"Los...Angeles? California?" The woman shook her head. "I've never heard of such a place."

"It's far from here—beyond the sea," Cyrus said quickly. "You wouldn't know it."

"I see. I suppose that's why you're dressed so strangely." The woman set the bloody bullet down on the table. "And what brings you here? To Osgoode?"

Levi and Cyrus paused. They couldn't admit they had time-traveled, could they? That they had come to kill the leader of Allegiant?

"For a better life," Levi said, which wasn't a total lie. "We hope to find it here."

"Well, besides the deadly night streets...I believe you'll like Osgoode. I'm terribly sorry, but I didn't get your names before."

"I'm Levi. Levi Godfrey," Levi said. "This is my brother, Cyrus."

The woman shook their hands. "Emilia Rutherford. A pleasure to meet you."

Levi's and Cyrus's mouths opened in shock. They couldn't

believe it—this was the woman who had started Allegiant. This was the woman they had traveled back in time to kill.

"What's wrong?" she asked. "You both look surprised."

"No—no, not at all," Levi lied. "It's just...we didn't expect a woman doctor...er, apothecary."

She sighed. "Yes, that's very common. Women are expected to be wives and mothers and nothing more. My parents weren't happy when I opened this place. But I love helping people—and I'll be damned if I let someone's opinion stop me."

"Well, we aren't judging you," Levi replied. "Our people have plenty of strong women, actually. They can be whatever they want in our culture."

Cyrus smiled. "And I've always found an intelligent woman extremely attractive."

Levi rolled his eyes. It was so like his brother to flirt with anything that had a pulse—human or otherwise.

Emilia blushed. "Really? Then I'm beginning to wish I could live in this Los Angeles of yours. Anyway, wait here while I retrieve the supplies to clean your wound."

As she flitted away to the other side of the shop, Cyrus leaned toward Levi, lowering his voice. "Can you believe we found her? I mean, hell, what are the odds?"

"I know. Talk about a lucky break. Did you know the famous Emilia Rutherford was like the seventeenth century version of a doctor?"

"Yeah, I read some things about her. Doctor, friend, sister. Didn't think she'd come to our rescue, though. That one's a bit ironic."

"I'll say. Maybe our luck's beginning to change," Levi murmured, watching as Emilia leaned over a box of supplies. "Look, she isn't expecting us to kill her. You could do it right now while her back's turned, then we can get out of here."

Cyrus's gaze landed on her as he grinned. "...No."

"No?" Levi asked, confused. "The hell do you mean, no?"

"I mean, we *could* kill her...but it'd be too easy." Cyrus licked his lips. "I want to hurt her—make her suffer right until the end. She deserves it for what she's done to our people. And there's only one way we can do that."

"How?"

"Infiltrate Allegiant. Make her think we're on her side, then strike. We could even find other vampires in the meantime and see if they know what she's been up to."

Levi sighed. "I don't know. I think we should follow the Patriarch's orders—"

"The Patriarch?" Cyrus sneered. "He's dead, Levi. In our timeline, at least. I'm not even sure if he was alive during Allegiant's early days. Why should we care what he wants now?"

"I still think we should follow orders. Before he died, you should know...he made me Patriarch," Levi admitted. "He wanted me to be in charge if something happened to him."

Cyrus crossed his arms. "Is that so? What, he didn't think I could handle the responsibility?"

Levi didn't want to admit what the Patriarch had said about his brother—how he was too headstrong. "I'm sure that's not true."

"Well, screw the Patriarch. Come on, Brother—where's your sense of adventure?" Cyrus smirked. "This bitch leads to the destruction of our people. We can kill her right here or have a little fun with our prey first. The choice seems obvious to me."

Before Levi could reply, Emilia walked over with a bandage and patched Levi up. "I think you'll live," she said. "I've certainly seen worse."

"How much worse?" Levi asked, sitting up. "And you never explained why nighttime is so dangerous."

"I'm...not sure if I should speak about it." She looked down. "Such things are forbidden. Even the church won't admit that they exist. The monsters I mentioned before. You're lucky you two survived, you know. I've never seen them let anyone live."

"You mean vampires?" Cyrus asked.

Her head shot up. "Is that what you call them? To me, they're monsters. Evil, unholy creatures, far from God's light."

"Yeah, our people call them vampires. Vamps for short. And we're sick of these attacks too."

Levi glanced over at Cyrus. He wasn't sure he agreed with his plan—of infiltrating Allegiant instead of killing Emilia outright—but he knew Cyrus. Once he had an idea in his stubborn head, there was no stopping him. But maybe there was some wisdom in waiting and investigating to see how far the Allegiant problem had spread.

Emilia's eyes widened. "My goodness, I didn't realize they were such a big problem—that other places had them too."

"Oh, of course," Cyrus said, leaning forward. "That's why we're here. We want to help you stop them. Whatever we can do."

Emilia turned silent for a few moments, staring out the window. "We shouldn't talk about this here. Do you two have somewhere to stay?"

Levi shook his head. "No, we just got into town. We haven't had a chance to find a place yet."

"I have my horse out back," she replied, rising to her feet. "If you'd like to stay at my family's farm for the evening, I'm sure they wouldn't mind."

"Oh, that's kind of you," Cyrus said with a smile. "Thanks."

"Of course. Take a moment to rest. I'll fetch Margaret—she's my horse—and then we can head to my family's farm."

As she exited the shop, Levi looked at Cyrus. "Why doesn't she recognize us and realize we're vamps? She's supposed to be the best vampire hunter who ever lived."

"Vampires looked very different in the past. We've evolved

—changed over the years," Cyrus explained. "It's why things like the sun and garlic don't bother us anymore. To her, we won't look like vampires at all—the ones from her time—which gives us the perfect opportunity."

Levi looked through the window, watching Emilia coming around with her horse. Levi rose to his feet and followed Cyrus to the door.

"I just hope you know what you're doing, Brother," Levi whispered. "It isn't just *us* we're risking here. It's all vampirekind."

"Oh, please, you worry too much, Levi. Everything's going according to plan. And when we take Emilia's life and destroy Allegiant forever, it'll be *that* much sweeter knowing we toyed with her in her final days."

As they exited the shop, a man in a cloak came around the corner. Emilia gasped and reached for her dagger. The man jumped back and removed his hood.

"Don't attack!" he cried. "I work at the apothecary."

Levi took a good look at him. He was short, balding on the top of his head, and middle-aged.

"Frederic?" Emilia asked, searching his eyes. "Thank goodness it's only you. What are you doing here at this hour?"

"I could ask you the same thing, my dear."

"I stayed late with a patient. Then I met these two, Levi and Cyrus, who needed my help. I was just about to head home. And you?"

"I...wanted to run a few tests," the man said, his eyes darting away. "If you'll excuse me."

He brushed past them, entering the shop and closing the door. Levi turned to Emilia. "Who was that?"

"My assistant, Frederic Bors," she replied. "He came to my shop a few months ago, begging for a job. He demonstrated his skills, and I hired him right away. In a town like this, we need all the healers we can find. And fortunately for me, he doesn't care that I'm a woman."

"Seemed like he didn't want to talk to us."

"That's just Frederic. He's been an introvert since the day I met him. He loves his science experiments and hates being bothered," she said, gesturing over her shoulder. "Anyway, come—the roads are dangerous, and it'll take some time to reach the farm. Let me just fetch a cart to carry us all."

As Frederic entered the building, Levi noticed Cyrus was still staring up at the small shop. He walked over and placed a hand on his shoulder as Emilia fetched the cart. "Cy? You okay?"

"I...I don't know. I have this weird feeling," Cyrus muttered. "I feel like I should know that man somehow. Like I've seen him before."

"From where?" Levi asked. "This is the seventeenth century, Brother. And he doesn't look familiar to me. You sure you're not just disoriented from the portal? I think it messed with my head too."

"Yeah, you're probably right. And all these peasants look the same to me. Anyway, let's head to the farm. This is a good opportunity to see where Emilia lives, whom she loves. The more victims, the better."

Levi shook his head. "You're so evil, Brother."

Cyrus cracked a grin. "And you love it."

Levi just snorted. Emilia brought the cart, then waited as the two brothers climbed in. As she flicked the reins and the horse took off into the night, Emilia had no idea the monsters she dedicated her life to fighting were only inches away.

CHAPTER

THREE

The light of dawn filled the sky as Margaret, Emilia's brown-and-white horse, trotted the back roads into the countryside. Levi noticed the endless rows of grain and old harvesting tools. Although they were there for one thing—Emilia's death—Levi hoped they'd get to do some sightseeing.

Levi was over two hundred years old. He had seen a lot of changes in his life, but nothing quite as remarkable as the Dark Ages. The Stuart era, to be exact, if Levi remembered the history books correctly. He'd never forget how untouched and pure the Earth looked back then, before the humans of the future polluted it all.

"At least I know you're not one of them," Emilia said over her shoulder, interrupting Levi's thoughts. "One of those... vampires, as you called them. They only come out at night—they're allergic to sunlight, I think. One time, I saw one hiss and disintegrate like ashes under the sun."

Thank darkness we've come a long way, Levi thought. Now sunlight only made vampires tired, but that wasn't fatal.

"Don't worry, Emilia," Cyrus said. "You can trust us."

Cyrus nudged Levi to say something, so he cleared his throat. "My brother's right. We want to help you stop these vamps."

"Thank you. I'll certainly need all the help I can get," Emilia replied. "God, so many needless deaths these days."

Cyrus chuckled quietly under his breath, but Levi started to feel something growing in his chest over how sad Emilia sounded. Was it...guilt? No, vampires couldn't feel guilt—they didn't have the conscience for that. It was most likely just a side effect of the bullet in his arm or the portal's energy. The pain was beginning to fade, thanks to Emilia's help, but maybe it was affecting his brain. Levi prayed it was nothing serious and ignored it for now.

Emilia guided her horse and cart down a gravel path that led deeper into the countryside. It brought them to a large farm in the distance. It seemed to be the biggest one around—more acres, more crops, and more farm animals.

Levi spotted rustic wagons filled with vegetables on the farm, and donkeys and horses pulling them. There were several structures set up—a barn for the farm animals, a cabin for her family, and a shed down the field to store supplies. Behind the farm sat a babbling brook and a forest that stretched on for miles. And thanks to his vampire sense of hearing, he could hear human heartbeats throughout the field. People were there tending the crops.

The strong stench of manure hit Levi's nostrils, and he grimaced. Emilia chuckled. "You'll get used to the smell, trust me. Surely you farm where you live?"

"No, not quite," Levi said. "We have...other means of getting food. We lived in a city and never saw a farm."

"Truly? That sounds like a paradise. Farming is a lot of work," Emilia said, jumping down from the cart. "Come on—

let's give Margaret a chance to rest. You can meet my family while they get things ready for breakfast."

Under the sunlight, Levi could see Emilia's features better. Her long red hair shimmered in the light, her cheeks pink and rosy, her lips full and plump. He always pictured the founder of Allegiant as an aggressive brute of a woman, muscular and taut, but Emilia was softer than that. He felt strangely drawn to her —as if there was a connection between them.

"How big is your family?" Levi asked, walking to the cabin with Emilia. Cyrus lingered behind them and scoped out the fields.

"There's me—I'm the oldest—then my brother, Peeta, and my younger sister, Dawn," Emilia replied. "They're both too young to be married off yet, so they live here and help out on the farm until then. My family owns the largest farm in town. It's been struggling lately, so we need all the help we can get. Our crops help feed the Lord and his castle. I had another sister, Sharla, but she died at birth."

"I'm sorry," Levi said, and he meant it.

Emilia nodded. "That's life. It's hard and merciless and cruel. It's why I became an apothecary—self-taught, of course —so I could help people. As I mentioned before, my parents, Loretta and Ivan, aren't too happy with my career choice. They're still insistent I find a man to marry."

"Oh. Why haven't you found one?"

"Well...I suppose my work is too important. And someone needs to do something about these monsters. If not me, then who? No one else seems eager to step up. Lives are counting on me—lives like yours."

And there it was again, guilt twisting in Levi's gut like a knife. He wanted to mention it to Cyrus but couldn't find the right words.

Levi heard the patter of feet running through the tall rows

of corn. A moment later, something jumped out and lunged onto Emilia. Levi raised a fist, preparing to strike if it was a vampire, even though he knew logically they couldn't go out in the sun during this era.

But it wasn't. Instead, it was a young girl with platinum blonde hair, in a stiffened bodice with an attached skirt. The girl couldn't have been older than fourteen. When Emilia noticed it was her, she laughed and struggled to balance herself.

"Oh, Alana," Emilia murmured. "You frightened me!"

"Sorry. I'm just so happy you're back!" the girl said, pulling away. "Was your journey into town...a good one?"

"If you're asking if I came upon any monsters, the answer is no," Emilia replied. "But there was a woman I couldn't save. A prostitute. One of the creatures had gotten to her before I arrived."

"Oh. That's too bad." The girl looked down, frowning. She straightened up when she noticed Levi and Cyrus. "Who are they?"

"These are my new friends, Levi and Cyrus Godfrey," Emilia introduced. "I found them hurt on the streets. Levi was wounded by the monsters."

"I see. My name's Alana," the girl said, shyly. "Nice to meet you—and I'm glad you escaped."

"A pleasure. Is Alana your sister, too, Emilia?" Levi asked.

Emilia shook her head. "No—Alana is an orphan who lives with us. She's close to my brother, Peeta. When she was younger...well, go on, Alana. You tell them the story."

Alana looked back at Emilia. "But...will they believe me?"

"We were attacked by those monsters last night," Levi lied. "We'll believe anything you tell us."

Alana sighed. "All right then. When I was younger, monsters killed my parents. We were out late, watching the stars when they ambushed us. I remember their eyes—yellow and frightening. Emilia saved me and brought me here. If it weren't for her, I would've died that night with my parents."

"It was good fortune I was out at that time, on my way back from attending a birth. I'm only sorry I couldn't save your parents too." Emilia patted Alana's shoulder, turning to Levi and Cyrus. "Alana was only a child when it happened. After seeing that, the frightened look in an innocent child's eyes, I became even more determined to stop these creatures. How could someone—even a monster—do something so awful?"

"They like young blood the best," Cyrus said. "It's the innocence that makes it sweeter."

Emilia gave Levi a strange look, so he stepped forward and cleared his throat. "We know a lot about these monsters. Vampires, as we said. We're historians, of sorts."

"I see. Then maybe you really *can* help me after all. Anyway, I'm sure you're hungry. Mother and Father should be around here somewhere."

Levi went to follow Emilia and Alana to the cabin, but Cyrus held him back. He waited until they were alone and lowered his voice. "I've been checking out the farm. There are so many places you can hide and stalk here—the crops, the trees, the shed."

"Then why don't we strike now while we still have the opportunity?"

Cyrus chuckled. "Patience, Brother. Once we've destroyed Allegiant from the inside, we'll be back for Emilia's family too. I think the history books mentioned she loses them all at some point. Who are we to argue with fate?"

Levi and Cyrus caught up with Emilia and Alana, following them into the small cabin. A middle-aged woman stood around a fireplace, cooking something in a giant pot. An older man and two teenagers—a boy and a girl, both red-headed—entered through the back door, carrying crops and freshly-hunted meat. The woman glanced over her shoulder at the brothers and frowned, then looked back at Emilia.

"Who are these men?" she asked. "More vagrants from your apothecary shop?"

"They need a place to stay, Mother," Emilia argued. "This is Levi and Cyrus, and they don't have anywhere else to go—"

"You think I care about that?" The woman turned to Levi's brother, crossing her arms. "If you want a place to stay, you'll have to earn your keep. We don't run no charity, and this ain't an inn."

Emilia sighed. "Mother, please. Levi was injured last night—"

"No," Levi interrupted. "It's all right, Emilia. We can help out around the farm. Whatever you need."

The woman still didn't look impressed, but she shrugged anyway. "Very well. Pull your own weight or begone."

The man—who Levi guessed was Emilia's father—glanced back at her. "Who are these outsiders? Where do they hail from? Can we trust them?"

"We don't mean you any harm," Cyrus lied. "We just need a place to stay for a little while. We're visiting from out of town."

"Levi, Cyrus, meet my father, Ivan," Emilia said, stepping forward. "You've already met Alana and my mother, Loretta. These are my siblings, Dawn and Peeta."

Dawn didn't shake their hands. She just blushed red and curtsied. When Cyrus winked at her, she blushed even harder, but Peeta stepped forward, shaking the brothers' hands with a smile.

"Nice to finally get some help around here," Peeta said. "Maybe I'll have more time for a midday nap."

"Only in your dreams, Peet," Dawn taunted.

As Peeta laughed, Levi noticed Cyrus standing back,

observing Emilia and her family. He knew what his brother was thinking—what it would be like to drink from them all. And eventually, they would.

Their mother was just about to add a few cubes of raw meat to the stew, but Cyrus stepped forward. "No—don't!"

Everyone paused, looking back at Cyrus with raised eyebrows.

"We like our meat raw," Cyrus explained. "It's a custom where we come from. It makes us sick if it's cooked."

Loretta narrowed her eyes at the brothers. "Very well. I'll cook some for us and leave yours off to the side."

"Uncooked meat," their father grumbled, glaring at his daughter. "What strange people you've brought us, Emilia."

When breakfast had finished cooking, they all sat down at the small wooden table. The brothers weren't accustomed to eating and living like this—like peasants. Levi wished they could teleport back to the bunker, sit around the glass table in their leather chairs, and sip blood from wine glasses.

But those days were gone. Their *people* were gone if they couldn't stop Allegiant. So, he and Cyrus sat there, eating raw meat without utensils and playing along.

"So, how long will you be staying with us?" Peeta asked, digging into his food.

"We aren't sure yet," Levi said. "Just long enough for a holiday. We're curious about other cultures."

"Oh, I see. Not that I'm complaining, of course. Stay as long as you'd like," Peeta said, taking another bite. "More crops harvested means more gold from Lord Tristan. We'll have double the load for him now."

Dawn laughed. "As long as he's still obsessed with Emilia, we don't need to worry about gold. He'll keep sending us gifts to impress her."

"Will he?" Levi cut into his raw, bloody steak as his eyes flickered to Emilia.

Emilia sighed. "Yes, unfortunately. Lord Tristan is quite the persistent man. He wants me to marry him."

Levi didn't know why, but a sudden surge of jealousy shot through him. Jealousy was an old human emotion—one he had discarded a long time ago. Why was he feeling it now? And over a woman he'd just met, the destroyer of his people?

"An offer you will accept soon," her father said, not even looking up from his food.

"Father, we've been over this," Emilia argued as she ate. "I don't want to marry Lord Tristan. He's a drunkard and a fool! He hasn't done anything for our people—especially the ones getting murdered in the streets. Even now, with pressure from the public, he still refuses to do anything about this plague. How can I marry such a coward?"

"Listen to your father, Emilia," her mother said. "Lord Tristan has given us a lot—nearly funded our entire farm. He expects repayment. But you must hurry, dear. You won't stay young and fertile forever."

"I don't care. I won't marry him." Emilia wiped her fingers, then rose to her feet. "I'm happy with my life at the apothecary shop. Can't you see that? Just because you threw your life away to marry Father doesn't mean I want to do the same!"

"Enough!" Her father rose and towered over Emilia. "You *will* marry Lord Tristan. Or you won't be a daughter of mine any longer."

Before Emilia could protest, her father stormed out of the cabin. Tears formed in Emilia's eyes before she left too. She slammed the door as her footsteps disappeared into the distance.

An awkward silence spread around the table before their

mother shook her head, glancing up at the brothers. "Do you have trouble with stubborn women where you come from?"

"No," Levi replied. "But we don't force them into things they don't want. Please, excuse me."

As Levi left the cabin, Cyrus chuckled at the offended look on Emilia's mother's face. Levi left Cyrus behind and followed the sounds of Emilia's crying to a nearby pond. He glanced at his reflection and winced. His black hair was disheveled, the bags under his piercing green eyes dark. He didn't look like a vampire of the Stuart age, but he *did* look like a wreck. Probably smelled like one, too, and he realized how much he missed showers and modern plumbing.

"Are you all right?" Levi asked, placing a hand on Emilia's shoulder. She sat on a rock near the pond. "I thought I'd come check on you."

"No, I'm not." Emilia kept her back turned to him, sniffling. "You heard what my father said. I'll have no choice but to marry Lord Tristan. If I don't, I could lose my family. I could lose *everything*."

"Man, I'm sorry. I wish I could help you." Levi sat beside her, feeling like Emilia was ahead of her time. She could've accomplished so much if she lived in the future. "I wish I could—"

Levi cried out in pain as he fell to the ground, his chest feeling a thousand times heavier. Emilia dropped down beside him, her green eyes twinkling with concern. "Levi, can you hear me? Are you okay?"

The pain came in waves. First it felt like a fever, then he was very cold. When he looked up at Emilia, his vision was blurry. This wasn't how he wanted to die. "Get...get my brother. I need...to see him. Please."

Emilia nodded, rushing back into the cabin. What Levi felt

was intense—more painful than getting shot with the silver bullet. A few minutes later, Emilia brought Cyrus over to him. Her parents, siblings, and Alana stood behind them and peered over.

"What's wrong?" Cyrus asked, kneeling beside him.

Levi clutched his brother's jacket. "It's...my chest. But Brother...do what must be done. Don't worry...about me..."

Just when Levi thought he couldn't hold on any longer, the pain disappeared. He sat up, breathing deeply. Cyrus's eyebrows lifted. "What just happened?"

Levi shook his head as Emilia and Cyrus helped him to his feet. "I don't know. There was pain—sharp and blinding—and then it just...disappeared."

"Perhaps I should take you back to the apothecary shop," Emilia said. "I have some leeches we could use for bloodletting. Or I could consult my herbs and make you a potion—"

Bloodletting? Potions? These people really *are* primitive, Levi thought.

"No," Levi said, firmly. "That's not necessary. Really, I'll be okay. Maybe the thing in my arm did more damage to my body than we thought. I probably just need time to recover."

Levi didn't know how to explain it—what that sensation was like. It wasn't comparable to anything he'd felt before. He thought he saw a look of recognition sweep across Cyrus's face, then it vanished.

"Perhaps it's all that raw meat you ate," Emilia's mother scolded. "I knew it wasn't good for you."

"I'm sure it wasn't the meat," Levi replied, touching his chest where the pain had spread through him. "Our people have eaten it for centuries. This was...something else."

"Well, unless you're dead, you can still work. But you better not have brought a plague with you, outsider," Emilia's father said, handing Levi a bucket. "Go on—there's plenty of grain to harvest. Emilia can show you how."

After their parents had walked away, Emilia sighed. "If you're all right, we'd better get started. Father gets angry if we dally."

"Okay, sure." Levi turned to Emilia. "Can I talk to my brother first? Alone?"

Emilia nodded, walking away with Alana and her siblings. When they had vanished between the crops, Levi looked at Cyrus. "So? Do you know what just happened to me?"

Cyrus shrugged. "I really don't. It can't be the bullet—I've never heard of that reaction before. Maybe it has something to do with the portal? The Patriarch *did* say blood magic was risky."

Levi ran a hand through his hair, sighing. "I don't know. Maybe this was all a mistake—coming through the portal, time-traveling, trying to kill Emilia. Maybe it's not a good idea to go messing with the past. We could end up making things worse."

Cyrus sneered. "Worse? Our people are all dead except for us, Brother. *Nothing's* worse than that. Look, I know you're scared, but believe me—when we save our people, they'll worship us. Our hard work *will* be rewarded."

Levi took a deep breath. "Okay, okay. You're right."

"Of course, I am. I'm a bloody genius." Cyrus reached for a wheelbarrow, turning to his brother. "Go—help Emilia. I'll keep her annoying siblings away from her while you chat her up. She seems to have taken a liking to you, anyway."

"Of course she has. All you do is stand behind us and brood."

"I'm a vampire. Brooding is what we do," Cyrus joked. "Anyway, befriend her. Make her think we're on her side. When she least expects it, we'll attack—and then get the hell outta this place. It'll all work out, Brother. You'll see."

But as Cyrus walked away, Levi wasn't so sure. The blood portal, the strange pain in his chest...something wasn't right. That was the only thing he was certain of.

FOUR

Levi followed Emilia down a row of corn and wheat. Her tears had faded, turned to rage. Levi knew the feeling all too well.

"There you are," Emilia said when she noticed Levi. "How are you feeling? Are you sure I can't do anything for you?"

"Thanks, but I think I'll be okay," Levi replied, helping Emilia remove the ears off the corn. "The pain in my chest is gone. Mostly, I'm just tired."

"Well, that's good. Should I ask Father to let you rest?"

"No, no, it's fine. I'll be okay. Besides, I wouldn't want to make your father angry. Angri*er*, I should say."

"Good point." Emilia nodded. "You've been under a lot of stress. Coming to a new town, the vampire attack, meeting my less-than-friendly parents. It's normal to feel exhausted. My parents insisting you work straight away can't be helping, but they've never trusted outsiders."

With good reason, Levi thought.

"And you?" Levi asked. "Aren't you tired of always having to do what your parents say?"

Emilia sighed, tearing off another ear of corn. "I don't want to talk about it. Their minds are already made up."

"Then let's talk about vampires. Other than Alana, who knows about them?"

"Not many people. As I said before, it can be blasphemous to even speak about them. The church denies their existence—and goes to great lengths to keep them a secret. If Lord Tristan knows, he hasn't done a thing to stop the attacks. I think the fear of acknowledging such a creature exists would cause too much panic."

"True. But if they're such a secret, how did you find out about them?"

Emilia paused. "When I was young...a vampire attacked me at the markets, much like Alana. I suppose that's why I've always felt a connection to her. I never lost my parents, though. I was fortunate."

"What happened?"

"I was out just before dawn, collecting some supplies. My parents sent me alone, figuring I'd be safe. But one of those monsters—vampires, whatever you want to call them—grabbed me and dragged me down a back street," Emilia said, closing her eyes and reliving the attack. "I was barely twelve years old. I remember running home to tell my parents, then they made me swear to keep it a secret. I suppose that's why they've become so protective of me—keep forcing me into marrying Lord Tristan. His castle is the safest place in town. Not even the vampires would trespass there."

"Sounds traumatic. How did you escape?"

"Do you remember before when I said I saw a vampire burn up in the light?" Emilia asked, and Levi nodded. "That's how I discovered their aversion. If it weren't for dawn breaking, I would've died that day. Their other weaknesses—like silver, a dagger to the chest—I discovered on my own. Mostly in combat."

"Hold on a second. You've been fighting them? Those vampires?"

"I wouldn't call it fighting...but I've been on night watch a few times, yes. You of all people should know that we desperately need guards patrolling the streets at night. I've saved a few people—barely escaped with my life. It's why I travel to my shop so often after dark. My parents think I'm treating patients, but I'm actually on lookout duty."

"Brave of you. What happened to those people? The ones you've saved?"

"Some have become recluses, but others have sent letters to Lord Tristan, demanding he take action." Emilia shook her head, shucking some corn. "A coward like him won't give in to such demands anytime soon. And besides, he'd be useless—he can't fight. The people would be better off taking matters into their own hands."

Levi could see it—the beginning of Allegiant forming as they spoke. Emilia's frustration with Lord Tristan was growing, and it was only a matter of time before she founded her own organization. He and Cyrus would have to act soon to stop her and wipe out any potential allies.

"Anyway, about before. When you thought you were going to die," Emilia continued, "you mentioned 'doing what must be done' to your brother. What were you talking about?"

Levi gulped, thinking of a lie. "To learn as much as we can about the vampires. I'm sure you'll agree that's important."

The sound of hooves clicking interrupted them. Levi turned, noticing a man dressed in expensive furs and silks sitting in the back of a carriage with several armored knights. He had no doubt this was Lord Tristan—he could practically smell his grandiosity. He rolled up to the farm with a smirk. When Emilia glanced over, she hid behind the corn stalks.

"Oh no," she muttered. "I can't let him see me. I need to get out of here."

Levi couldn't explain why, but he felt an intense desire to help her escape. He nodded toward the other end of the tall stalks. "Follow me—we can get out that way."

Levi grabbed Emilia's arm, dragging her through the field. If they could make it to the other side and into the forest, Lord Tristan might not see them.

"Your skin..." Emilia whispered, gawking at his touch. "It's freezing. Are you sure you're feeling all right?"

Levi forgot his blood was ice cold from the lack of circulation. He wasn't used to having to hide what he was. He released her arm, trying to create some distance between them. "Yeah, I'm fine. It's probably just from my injury. Come on—we're almost there."

As they reached the end of the crops, Levi heard a heartbeat coming from their right. Before he could push Emilia out of the way and hide, a man turned around the corner. Much to their relief, it wasn't Lord Tristan—but it was someone else.

Emilia's father. He frowned at them, his face stern. "Where are you two going?"

"I...was just showing Levi around," Emilia lied. Levi was impressed at how quickly she came up with an excuse. "You *did* ask us to work the field, didn't you?"

Ivan crossed his arms, glaring at both of them. "If you ask me, I think you heard Lord Tristan and tried to escape. But that wouldn't be polite, now, would it?"

Emilia and Levi remained silent.

Her father sighed. "Look, I'll forget all this if you go inside. Lord Tristan wants to see you. He came all this way for you."

Emilia stepped forward. "But Father, I told you—"

"And *I've* told *you* you'll do as you're told," he growled, glancing at Levi. "I expect your new friend to be on his best behavior too. Now get inside, Emilia. You don't want to keep Lord Tristan waiting."

Emilia sighed, looking down as she began walking to the cabin. Levi felt a pang of guilt in his heart again. Were his chest pains related to Emilia somehow? But why?

Levi moved to follow her, but Ivan placed a hand on his chest to stop him. "I don't know who you are or where you come from," Ivan began, "but if you think you have a chance at my daughter's hand in marriage, you're sorely mistaken."

Levi shook his head. "It's not like that at all, Mr. Rutherford. We're only friends."

"Good. You could never give my daughter the life she deserves—not like Lord Tristan can. Only he has the power to save our farm," Ivan continued. "So, leave her alone, boy. Or I'll make you."

Levi had to stifle his laughter, placing a hand over his mouth. Neither Ivan nor this Lord Tristan could hurt him in a million years. Ivan gave him one last hard look before following Emilia into the cabin. Alana and Emilia's siblings began walking with him, but Cyrus hung back to speak with Levi. They both kept their eyes on Lord Tristan as he entered the home with several knights in silver armor.

"So?" Cyrus asked. "Find anything out yet?"

Levi nodded. "Yeah, a little bit. Emilia's already hunted vamps—saved a bunch of people. They nearly killed her when she was a kid. It's starting, Cy. The revolution."

"Not quite. I think there's something else," Cyrus muttered. "A catalyst for what forces Emilia to start Allegiant. I remember reading about it in a history book, but it's slipped my mind. Anyway, I'm sure we'll find out soon enough. Just be ready to attack on my signal."

"You got it." As Levi walked with Cyrus back to the cabin, he turned to him. "Out of curiosity...whom does Emilia marry? The bloodline obviously continues. Her descendent looked just like her."

"I think it's Lord Tristan after all," Cyrus replied. "Guess her parents get their way."

Levi froze, balling his fists. He didn't know Lord Tristan, but he hated him already.

"Hey, you good?" Cyrus asked. "Looks like you're ready to punch someone out."

"I'm fine," Levi muttered, walking up to the door. "Let's just get this over with."

As they stepped inside the small cabin, knights and guards crowded the room. Emilia stood at attention next to her parents, her eyes focused on the ground. She didn't look at Lord Tristan as he inched closer. Everyone in the room except for the brothers gave him a little bow or curtsey. And now that he was a few feet away, Levi took a proper look at him.

The lord was young—maybe nineteen, even younger than Emilia. He looked more like a boy than a man. *His pompous ass must've inherited the title*, Levi thought. Lord Tristan had dirty blond hair with a silver crown, a cleft chin, and a lanky, slender figure.

"Emilia," Lord Tristan said with a smile. "You get even lovelier as the days pass."

Levi shut his eyes. He could feel the anger bubbling inside of him again and didn't want to lose control—not here. He didn't like this strange new emotion.

Emilia's mother nudged her to say something. She looked up at him, clearing her throat. "Thank you, Lord Tristan. You honor us with your presence."

"And I'm honored to be here," he began, grabbing Emilia's hand. "I came all this way to see you."

Lord Tristan leaned down to kiss Emilia's hand. When she winced, pulling back, he grabbed her tighter and made her hiss in pain. And Levi lost it.

He charged forward like a raging bull, punching the boyish royal in the jaw. Lord Tristan cried out in pain, falling to his knees. Before Emilia and her family could react, the royal guards had already pressed their swords to Levi's throat, holding him in place.

The swords gleamed silver—a vampire's weakness. The metal stung Levi's skin, the quiet hiss spreading around the room. He couldn't cry out and let Emilia know he was a vampire, the thing she hated so much. As long as the knights kept their swords away from Levi's chest, he'd survive. Cyrus tried to step forward to defend his brother, but the guards shoved him back.

"Please, forgive us, my lord," Ivan said, helping Lord Tristan to his feet. "If we knew our guest would be so rude, we wouldn't have invited him. He's a friend of Emilia's from the village."

"Is that so? Who is this peasant?" Lord Tristan sneered, looking back at Levi. Blood dribbled down his chin. "And why the hell did he just attack me?"

"Because you don't know how to treat a lady," Levi spat.

"You know nothing about me, fool." Lord Tristan grabbed Levi's face, angling his chin up at him. "In case no one told you, I'm the authority in Osgoode. I could have you executed for striking me, you know. Give me one good reason why I shouldn't kill you."

"Because then *I'd* have to kill *you*," Cyrus said, "and you don't want me to get involved."

Lord Tristan chuckled. "Threatening my life? Imbecile. Do you not see how many guards are in this room?"

"Please, show him mercy. I know you have compassion,

Tristan," Emilia said, stepping forward before the brothers could respond. "He's from a foreign land. He doesn't understand our way of life."

Lord Tristan scoffed. "All the more reason to teach him a lesson. Even foreigners must obey the law. We'll send him to the stocks—"

"Give him a warning," Emilia said, reaching for Lord Tristan's arm. "Please, Lord Tristan. Do it for me."

When she said that, the snarl on Lord Tristan's face faded. He looked back at Emilia and nodded. "Only for you, Emilia. Guards, release him. For now."

The guards sheathed their swords, then Levi's hand flew up to his throat. It felt like it was on fire.

"But if he tries anything else," Lord Tristan began, glancing over his shoulder, "you have my permission to kill this jackal where he stands."

"That won't be necessary," Ivan grunted. "They'll both be leaving soon."

"Good. Now, if that's dealt with, I came here on important business."

"Oh? Why are you here?" Loretta asked. "Not that you aren't welcome to stop by anytime, my lord."

"I'm throwing a ball tomorrow evening. I'd like you all to attend."

"A ball? Oh, that sounds like fun," Dawn said. "I think I have the perfect dress."

Peeta nodded with a grin. "It means the day off work, so I'm there already!"

"What's the occasion?" Alana asked.

"An engagement party," Lord Tristan said, turning to Emilia. "I'd like you to give me your answer then, my dear, and tell the guests you shall do me the honor of becoming my wife."

Emilia hesitated, then her father stepped forward. "We'll be there, my lord—and my daughter will have her answer."

"Splendid. It shall be a masquerade. I do love a good mystery—the thrill of wondering who's hiding behind the mask," Lord Tristan continued. "I've brought gowns, suits, and masks with me for all of you. No need to worry about planning a thing. I know you're very hard at work on your farm."

"Very kind of you." Ivan reached into his pocket, pulling out a handkerchief. "Here you are, my lord. Something to wipe your face with."

"Many thanks. I look forward to seeing you all tomorrow evening—especially you, Emilia," Lord Tristan said, wiping the blood off his face. "Perhaps I can show you around the castle. And my private quarters."

Levi bit his tongue so hard he felt it bleed. Something about Lord Tristan brought out the monster in him. When Levi glanced at Emilia, he noticed how forced her smile was. She hated Lord Tristan too.

Lord Tristan walked to the door, stopping beside Levi. "Now, I don't know what you tried to accomplish today, but it didn't work. You shall never show your face around me again— or at my ball. If I see you there, I'll execute you on the spot."

"Don't worry. I didn't want to go anyway," Levi spat. "I have better things to do with my time."

"Watch yourself, foreigner," Lord Tristan sneered, gesturing at the sword in his scabbard. "Or that smart mouth of yours will be mounted above my throne."

Lord Tristan turned on his heel, leaving the cabin with his guards trailing behind. They gave Levi and Cyrus glares before they followed. After they had disappeared, Ivan grabbed Levi by his collar and hoisted him up against the wall. He hit the side of the cabin so hard that it rumbled beneath them.

"I warned you to stay away from my daughter. To not ruin

this for her," Ivan spat. "I should've known scum like you wouldn't listen. I should kill you myself for your disrespect, boy. We both know Lord Tristan wouldn't mind."

"Father, stop!" Emilia cried, but her mother held her back.

"Get your hands off me," Levi said through gritted teeth.

"This is my farm, outsider. I can do whatever I want. And for starters, I want you and your brother gone. Your help isn't worth the trouble."

Cyrus glanced at Levi with furrowed eyebrows. Working on their farm was the only way they had access to Emilia. If they lost that, they might lose their best chance at killing her. They had to find a way to stay.

Levi weighed his options. Smoothing things over with words wasn't possible anymore—not since he'd punched Lord Tristan in the face. He'd have to resort to violence again to prove his point.

Ivan still hadn't let Levi go, keeping his hands around his neck. Using his superior strength, Levi pushed Ivan off him, then forced him to his knees. Staring deep into his eyes, he revealed the red hue in them, something only vampires of the future had. A flash of his bloody heritage. A warning that he was more powerful than he seemed.

"You will let us stay," Levi commanded. "Or we'll kill you."

Ivan's eyes widened in fear. "A-all right, you may stay. Just, please, don't hurt my family."

"Great, thank you. Really, we're not bad people," Levi said, making the red shade in his eyes vanish. "Emilia was hurt, and I tried to help her. Anyway, we'll live in the shed and stay out of your way." Levi turned to his brother. "Let's head back outside —there are some crops that need tending."

Emilia watched them go, her hands shaking. Levi still didn't understand why, not yet at least, but the thought of her fearing him hurt the most.

FIVE

For the rest of the day, Levi and Cyrus worked the fields, placing the harvested crops into their baskets. Ivan, Dawn, Peeta, and Alana kept their distance, working far away from the brothers. Levi didn't see Emilia and wondered if she was avoiding him.

That night, they settled into the shed at the end of the field. Supplies and harvested crops littered the small room, but Cyrus and Levi managed to find a place to lie down and sleep. Around dinnertime, a knock sounded on the door. The brothers looked at each other in confusion.

Levi rushed to open it, hoping it would be Emilia, but no one was there. Instead, a bowl of raw meat waited for them. He sighed and grabbed it, sharing it with his brother as they ate on the floor.

"Not that I'm opposed to violence," Cyrus began, "because Lord Douchebag definitely deserved it, but why'd you hit him?"

Levi shrugged. "It's just like you said—he was being a douchebag. He thinks he's all high and mighty with his cape and stupid crown. I had to teach him a lesson."

"Uh-huh." Cyrus swallowed another slice of raw liver. "You

sure it didn't have anything to do with Emilia? He kissed her hand before you lost your mind."

"I'm sure." Levi wiped the blood off his mouth. "Can we talk about something else?"

"Fine. Let's talk about the Lord's Ball," Cyrus said, lowering his voice, "and how we need to go."

Levi frowned. "You seriously want to go to a masquerade and watch a bunch of spoiled, rich people dance?"

"I'm not in it for that. I remember reading about it in a history book—the Lord's Ball of 1698. Something big is about to go down."

Levi sat forward, intrigued. "Oh? Like what?"

"I can't remember exactly. But I know it involves the vampires. So, whatever it is, we need to be there. We've got to meet some local vamps soon—tell them what we know. We have to help them."

"Why don't we just head out now? It's dark. I'm sure we'd find some down at the markets. Emilia said those streets aren't safe at night."

Cyrus shook his head. "No—the masquerade's better. It'd be easier to talk to them amidst all the chaos, and then we could prove ourselves."

"Well, sorry to break it to you, but the party is off the table. Lord Tristan told me not to come, remember?"

Cyrus smirked. "Oh, Levi. Where's your sense of adventure? It's a masquerade party, Brother. As long as we avoid attention, he won't even know we're there. And when the vamps arrive, we'll be able to slip away to talk to them."

"And how are we supposed to get masquerade outfits? There aren't any clothing stores around here, you know. And we don't have any money."

"Then we steal them." Cyrus raised an eyebrow. "Come on.

Aren't you just the least bit curious as to what's going to happen? What the vamps around here are planning?"

Levi knew what would happen at the masquerade—Emilia would have to agree to marry Lord Tristan. The thought of that made him so sick, he lost his appetite. He flung his raw meat back into the bowl. Then he reached for a twig of mint, freshening his breath.

"Whatever." Levi lay down on top of a blanket on the ground. "Steal some outfits if you want. I just don't feel like going."

"Don't feel like it?" Cyrus rose to his feet, his fists balled in anger. "We came all this way to kill Emilia and stop Allegiant. Why aren't you more on board with this? Do you want the Legionnaires to win?"

"Of course not," Levi spat, looking up at his brother. "I just don't want to go to some stupid masquerade, okay?"

Cyrus scoffed, lying down and turning his back. "Some leader you are. Can't believe Patriarch put you in charge instead of me..."

His brother's words stung. But Levi didn't want to argue with his brother anymore, so he just closed his eyes, letting his mind drift.

When he woke up again, he heard a quiet knock at the door. Moonlight seeped in through the small window. At first, he thought he was hearing things—that maybe it was in his dream —before it happened again, much louder this time. Someone stood at the door to the shed, their heartbeat thudding.

"Brother?" Levi whispered. "Do you hear that?"

Cyrus turned over, slowly rising to his feet. "Yeah. Think it's Emilia's father coming back to teach us a lesson?"

"I don't know, but it'd be his last mistake. Hopefully I scared him good when I threatened him." Levi got up, approaching the door. "Guess there's only one way to find out."

Levi ripped the door open. Instead of seeing Ivan or anyone else who wanted to kill him, it was Emilia. She wore a dark cloak to blend in with the night. She carried two sets of fancy clothes and masks.

"Emilia? What are you doing here?" Levi whispered, glancing around outside. "It's late."

"I know," she whispered back. "But I had to see you. My parents think I'm in bed, so we'll have to be quiet."

She ducked under Levi's arm, making her way into the shed. She nodded politely at Cyrus before placing masquerade outfits and masks down on the floor. When she lowered the hood of her cloak, exposing her luscious red hair, Levi remembered how beautiful she was.

"What's going on?" Cyrus asked, his eyes flitting to the new outfits.

It seemed like she had something important to say, so Levi turned to his brother. "Can you give us a moment?"

Cyrus hesitated. "Fine, fine. I'll wait outside. I'll be your lookout. But make it fast, all right?"

Levi nodded as his brother left, closing the door behind him. Then he turned to Emilia. "I'll ask you again. Why are you here?"

"I feel just awful that you're not invited to the Lord's Ball," Emilia said. "I would've argued for you, but I doubt I would've been able to convince Lord Tristan. I don't have *that* much influence over him."

Levi sneered. "Don't feel bad. I meant what I said—I don't want to go, anyway."

"Oh, I see." Emilia looked down. "I'll just go then. Sorry to have bothered you."

"Wait," Levi said, grabbing Emilia's arm before she could rush out the door. "You came here for a reason. Tell me what's going on."

"It's just…" She turned her back, sighing. "Perhaps I want you at the Lord's Ball. You and your brother, of course."

"But why?"

"We both know I have to agree to be Tristan's wife. I've been trying to deny that to myself, but it's inevitable," she replied, looking up at Levi. "You—*and* your brother—are the only ones who have made me feel like I have a choice. I need you there for support. Call me crazy, but…your presence calms me down."

In a strange way, Levi felt honored. "Oh. But…we're not allowed. Well, I'm not, anyway."

"Which is why I brought these costumes," Emilia said. "They aren't much, but they'll disguise you well enough to fool Lord Tristan. I ran out to the markets myself to get them. There's a seamstress in town who works late. Anyway, knowing you're there would mean the world. I'm not one to beg, but… please?"

Levi wanted to say no. He hated parties—even those vampire bars he and his brother used to stalk. But the way Emilia looked at him—like he was all she had left—made him feel good. And he knew it would please his brother.

"All right," Levi said, exhaling. "Cyrus and I will be there."

Emilia grinned. "Thank you so much, Levi. The evening will be painful enough with Lord Tristan pawing at me. Your presence will make me feel better about it all."

Levi felt his anger rising inside him at the thought of Lord Tristan touching her. But he forced it down, not wanting to scare her again. "Really? I thought you wouldn't talk to me after I threatened your father."

Emilia sighed. "My father doesn't care about me. He only cares about his farm—about his family name. He'd sell me to the highest bidder to keep this place. I never thought I'd say this, but…it felt good to watch you threaten him. To make him feel like the victim for once. He did look like quite the fool on his knees, didn't he?"

Levi chuckled. And when Emilia realized he was laughing, she joined, too. Levi had almost completely forgotten all his worries when a rough knock rapped on the door.

"You almost done in there?" Cyrus asked outside. "It's cold out here, you know."

"Almost done," Levi shouted back. "Hold your damn horses."

"I should go. If my parents saw me here, there's no telling what they'd do to me," Emilia said. "Wait until we're gone tomorrow evening before you follow us to the ball. It's the large castle in the distance—you can't miss it. Lord Tristan will probably be too busy with me and the other royals to even notice you, let alone suspect you'd show up after his warning. He isn't used to people disobeying him."

"And if we get caught?"

Emilia smiled. "Don't."

"Good plan. I won't mention your name if we do," Levi said. "You're in enough trouble as it is."

When Emilia nodded, Levi expected her to walk out of the shed and go home. But she did the oddest thing instead. She hugged him. He stood there, frozen like a statue before he wrapped his arms around her body. He inhaled her hair that smelled of wildflowers and raspberries.

"Thank you, Levi," she whispered, "for listening and understanding. I know we've just met, but...I'll miss you when you return home."

And then she left, letting Cyrus into the shed. He locked the door behind them and turned to Levi who was still watching Emilia from the window. Cyrus had to wave his hand in front of Levi's face to get his attention.

"Hello? Earth to Levi," Cyrus muttered. "What'd she say?"

Levi cleared his throat. "Oh, uh, we're going to the Lord's Ball. Emilia brought us costumes and everything."

"Oh, so now you're cool with it. Interesting." Cyrus crossed his arms. "Levi...are you feeling okay?"

He blinked. "Why wouldn't I be?"

Cyrus looked like he was about to explain, then he lay down. "Never mind. See you tomorrow, Brother."

"Yeah, see you tomorrow."

And as Levi drifted off to sleep, he felt that familiar pain tugging at his chest again.

THE PAIN DISAPPEARED BY MORNING. Levi still didn't know what was wrong with him, but now he knew it involved Emilia somehow. Unfortunately, that only confused him more.

When the sun rose, Levi and Cyrus worked hard in the fields all day. That evening, they watched Emilia, her siblings, Alana, and her parents get into a horse-drawn carriage that Lord Tristan had sent for them. As they disappeared down the road, Emilia's eyes flitted to her horse, Margaret. She had purposely let the horse out of the stables to graze the field. When the carriage wasn't in view any longer, Levi glanced at Cyrus and nodded.

"Let's go. Almost dusk," Levi said, gesturing at the shed. "Better put on our masks and get out of here. I just hope you know what you're doing, Cy."

"Relax," Cyrus said, putting on his dark costume and mask. "If I'm right and the vamps do attack the party tonight, we'll be safe. One bite out of us and they'll realize we're not human. Vamp blood doesn't taste as good, you know. Not as satisfying *or* nutritious."

"Didn't know you'd tried it," Levi said as he placed his mask on.

Cyrus grinned. "Well, me and Raven—"

"Don't want to know, man," Levi interrupted, making Cyrus chuckle.

They both suited up before walking over to Margaret. The brothers sat down on the horse, then Levi flicked the reins and motioned toward the path Emilia had taken. The hooves from the horse carriage in the dirt showed the way.

After ten minutes, Levi noticed the tall, silver castle in the distance. A shallow lake spread around it with a drawbridge that led inside. Levi saw Emilia's carriage nearby and knew she had arrived. Royals of all kinds—near and far, young and old— exited from their equipages and fluffed their capes and gowns.

"Any sign of the vampires yet?" Levi whispered to his brother.

"No—but it's not fully dark out," Cyrus whispered. "Be patient, Lee. Just enjoy the show, huh?"

As the brothers walked across the grass and approached the portcullis, a tall guard stopped them. He had sandy blond hair and tired brown eyes. "Halt! Who are you? Where do you hail from?"

"The Kingdom of Los Angeles, good sir," Cyrus said. "We traveled all this way when we heard about the Lord's Ball."

"Los Angeles? No, I've never heard of such a place," the knight replied. "How did you find out about this party?"

"We were invited," Levi replied. "How else would we know about it?"

The knight huffed. "I don't know who you two are, but I know you certainly didn't get an invite—"

"Is there a problem here?" Lord Tristan asked, walking over to the brothers. He wore a mask on his face, but the brothers recognized his high-pitched voice. "Is my guard giving you trouble, gentlemen?"

The brothers nodded, staying silent.

"Ah, then you must forgive Sir Anders," Lord Tristan said with a chuckle. "Dedicated, he is—sometimes, too much. Go on, Sir Anders. Leave our poor guests alone."

"But my lord," Sir Anders began, "what if they're—"

"Dangerous? They won't be," Lord Tristan interrupted. "No one would dare to hurt me here—not in my own castle with dozens of guards around. Please, enjoy yourselves tonight, you two."

Levi and Cyrus bowed at him before pushing past the guard, walking into the ballroom. A band stood off to the left, playing a medieval tune. Hundreds of royals stood around, chatting while sipping ale from fancy glasses. A large throne sat in the middle of the room with five chairs around it, one for each of the Rutherford family.

Emilia sat down directly next to the large throne. She looked miserable, Levi realized. Her lips were pressed together in a thin line, her leg bouncing up and down. She avoided talking to anyone and focused on her drink instead. None of her family members talked to her, too busy schmoozing with the royals.

When Emilia's eyes met Levi's, she grinned. And for some reason, Levi couldn't help but return the smile. She wore a strapless red gown with her hair up in a bun. He thought she looked beautiful, but he much preferred her in normal clothes.

"Probably best if we mingle," Cyrus whispered to him. "Talk to some people, try to look like you belong here. I'll come find you if I see any vamps."

As Cyrus walked away, Levi realized he wasn't even listening. His gaze focused on Emilia. She rose to her feet, nodding her head to the left. It led to the balcony. She began walking to it and didn't look back.

Levi knew he probably shouldn't be alone with her—not here—but he felt compelled to follow her. As he walked out onto the balcony, he noticed the view. He could see the entire village of Osgoode from up here—all the little homes and forests. But he was more impressed by the ravishing woman in front of him.

Emilia turned around, her lips spreading into a wider grin. "I'm so pleased you came. I know we're not supposed to be talking, but…I couldn't help myself. And there wasn't anyone interesting to talk to in there, anyhow."

"Yeah, I get that," he said, glancing over his shoulder at the snooty royals. He turned around and looked back at her. "You look beautiful, by the way."

She blushed, her cheeks turning the same color as her hair. "Thank you, Levi. That suit fits you quite well—in all the right places."

A gust of wind blew by, pulling a piece of hair out of Emilia's bun. Levi reached a hand out to tuck it behind her ear. That was when he realized how close they were—close enough to kiss. And Levi also realized he wasn't opposed to the idea.

This is crazy, Levi thought. *This woman and I are enemies. She may not know it, but I do. I couldn't kiss her…could I?*

To test the waters, Levi reached out, touching her hand. Emilia blushed. She didn't pull away, making Levi figure it was as much of an invitation as he was going to get.

Just when he worked up the courage to lean in, going for a kiss, loud footsteps echoed behind them, When Levi turned around, Lord Tristan stood in front of him. His hard gaze flitted between the two. "What's going on here?"

"Nothing at all, my lord," Emilia said, bowing. "Just chatting about the ball."

Lord Tristan's gaze remained on Levi. "We must return to the ballroom, my dear. The engagement will be announced any minute now."

Emilia nodded, linking her arm with Lord Tristan's. As they walked back to the ballroom, Emilia didn't look back—it was too risky. But Lord Tristan did. His eyes searched the visible part of Levi's face, looking like he was trying to recognize him, but he couldn't place him. He eventually gave him one last glare before looking away.

As Levi turned from the balcony, he saw something dart below. When he looked again, he noticed shadows moving in the darkness before they disappeared. He could smell it in the air—their pheromones.

These were the vampires Cyrus had told him about. And in a few minutes, they'd reach the castle for whatever they had planned.

CHAPTER

SIX

Levi returned to the ballroom, still in a daze over how close Emilia had stood to him. She'd wanted to kiss him too—he'd felt it. He brushed a finger against his lips, wondering how she would taste. How it would feel to run his fingers through her hair, to hold her close. Just touching her hand made him feel electrified.

It was a forbidden daydream, but Levi couldn't stop himself from fantasizing anyway.

Cyrus walked over to him. "Hey. Where have you been? I've been looking for you for the past ten minutes."

"Huh?" Levi asked. "Oh, I was out on the balcony."

Cyrus raised his eyebrows. "Why?"

"Uh, for the vantage point." He didn't know why he felt he had to lie to his brother, but it was just another strange thing to add to the growing list. "And I could smell them, Cy. The vampires you're looking for. They're coming this way, moving through the forest behind the castle."

"Really? Then I was right." Cyrus grinned, patting Levi's shoulder. "And here I thought this night would be a disappointment."

Levi heard the clinking of glasses and turned his head. Emilia had returned to Lord Tristan's side like a loyal pet, sitting next to him on his big throne. The lord raised his glass and tapped it again as the room turned silent.

"If I could have your attention, please?" Lord Tristan asked. "Dinner will be served now. Please find your seats."

Levi and Cyrus didn't have assigned seating, so they grabbed two extra chairs and pulled them up to a table of royals. They were old and haughty, paying no attention to the brothers as they sipped from expensive glasses. Cyrus picked up a glass and chugged.

"Bleh." He spat his wine back into the glass. "I'd kill for a victim right about now. Nothing beats freshly squeezed blood."

"Well, we can't let the others know that," Levi whispered. "So, play along."

As the royals ate their dinner, Levi caught Emilia glancing over at him. It was hard to resist, but he managed to avoid her gaze. He didn't want to draw any more attention from Lord Tristan. He glanced around the room instead, checking for any vampires, but he didn't see any. Not yet.

"I know I saw them out in the forest," Levi whispered. "Where the hell are they?"

Cyrus chuckled. "Not all of us are like you, Levi. Some vampires like the element of surprise—the thrill it brings. Some like the theatrics."

Levi rolled his eyes. Sure, the vampires had evolved physically, but mentally, they were still up to their same old tricks.

As the servants took away their plates, Levi and Cyrus stuffed the food into nearby potted plants to make it look like they'd eaten. When everything had gotten cleaned up, Lord Tristan rose to his feet.

"I'm sure you're all wondering why I've summoned you here," Lord Tristan said, "and the occasion we're celebrating tonight. As many of you know, my father, Lord Gregoris, passed away last month. His dying wish was that I take over Osgoode and marry a fine woman to continue our bloodline."

Levi knew what was coming. The proposal. He clenched his hand around his wine glass so hard it surprised him when it didn't shatter.

Everyone in the Rutherford family grinned—all but Emilia. Her face looked lifeless, deflated. Levi hated it. Her father, Ivan, beamed like he'd just won the lottery.

But Lord Tristan didn't get to pop the question. A middle-aged man wearing dress clothes who had a birthmark on his left cheek stood up, ripping the mask off his face. Levi noticed how grimy and dirty he looked. The man smoothed down his shaggy brown hair and turned to Lord Tristan, clasping his hands in prayer.

"Excuse me, your lordship, but my name is Edmund Doyle. I represent the Peasant's Guild," he began. "While you celebrate in your castle, our people are dying out on the streets!"

"Your people? What are you blathering on about?" Lord Tristan rolled his eyes. "I don't recall inviting you—"

"You didn't. I had to sneak past the guard. What else was I supposed to do? You won't do anything to help," Edmund interrupted. "There are beasts among us—monsters! They attack at night, preying on children. Surely, you've heard of the dead bodies—their necks bitten and blood drained. How long before nowhere is safe?"

The royals in the room murmured in concern, so Lord Tristan turned to them with a smile. "I assure you, Osgoode is perfectly safe. This man is insane. Guards, remove him from my castle."

"I'm not crazy!" Edmund shouted as guards dragged him out the door. "You could be next!"

The door closed with a loud slam. The room turned silent,

people's glances shifting from one to another. Lord Tristan smoothed down his hair as he tried to compose himself.

"The man's right, my lord," Emilia spoke up. "Yesterday I had a patient who survived a monster attack. We must do something."

"Quiet, girl," her father snarled, glaring at Emilia. "Do *not* ruin this moment!"

"There are no monsters. They exist only in fairy tales," Lord Tristan said, sternly. "You'll drop this at once, Emilia."

Levi shook his head, watching Emilia sink down in her seat. He hated the way Tristan spoke to her.

Cyrus chuckled, nudging his brother's shoulder. "Man, this place is like a ticking time bomb. Wonder when it'll explode?"

"As I was saying before that rude interruption, I think I've found just the woman I've been looking for," Lord Tristan said, reaching for Emilia's hand. "I knew when I first glimpsed her beauty that she must be mine. Emilia Rutherford of Osgoode, will you do me the honor of becoming my wife?"

The glass in Levi's hand finally shattered, soaking the tablecloth with red wine.

Everyone in the room gasped, looking over at Levi. When he glanced up, he noticed Lord Tristan's glare. The room broke out in murmurs when people spotted how black his blood was. He sat there, stunned he'd gotten angry enough to break the glass as servants rushed over to clean up.

"Bloody hell!" Lord Tristan cried, walking away from Emilia. "Can we not go five minutes without an interruption?"

Levi glanced at Cyrus, wondering what he should say. If they spoke, Lord Tristan would recognize their voices. If they didn't, it would look suspicious. Levi reasoned he couldn't win —that the Lord would find out eventually.

But luckily for him, Levi didn't have to respond. A thud echoed from the side of the castle near the balcony. Everyone in the ballroom diverted their attention from Levi to the location of the sound. He sighed in relief and wiped up the red wine that had spilled on his clothes.

"What was that?" Lord Tristan asked, turning away from Levi.

"Oh, I think I know," Cyrus whispered to Levi, grinning. "This party's about to get a *lot* more interesting."

"Guards, investigate," Lord Tristan demanded. "Find out what's going on—"

People in the room screamed as more than a dozen vampires entered through the balcony. Levi counted fifteen and realized they must've climbed up the side of the castle. The guards hesitated when they noticed their sharp fangs and gleaming, yellow eyes.

The vampire in front of them grinned, leading the others forward. "Having a party, are we? We heard rumors it was taking place tonight. An engagement celebration, it seems. How come we weren't invited?"

Levi took a moment to study him. He wore a long black cape and leather boots and had dark hair and golden eyes. A knife scar stretched across his mouth and chin. His lips twisted upwards, constantly smirking.

"Sweet darkness," Cyrus muttered. "I think that's... Slaughter!"

"Who?" Levi asked, as the people in the room murmured.

"The most lethal vampire in history." Cyrus stared at him, grinning. "And he's only a few feet away from us. What an honor."

A vampire woman sauntered in after Slaughter, placing a hand on his shoulder. She had long blonde hair to her waist, a cloak that accentuated every curve, and a violet necklace. Her black heels clicked as her yellow eyes roamed the room, sniffing the air. The fear was palpable. Behind them, several other vampires crept up.

"Don't start without me, Brother," she said, grinning. It exposed her rows of jagged teeth. "You know I love a good party."

"Recognize her?" Levi whispered to his brother.

Cyrus nodded. "Only from ancient drawings. That's Night Temptress, Slaughter's sister. She mostly preys on men while her brother attacks children—and she's the most gorgeous thing I've ever seen. Goddamn."

She's got nothing on Emilia, Levi wanted to say, but kept his mouth shut. "What happens to the two of them? Do they die?"

Levi nodded. "Yeah—Emilia stakes them both at one point. Good thing we're here to stop that, huh?"

"You don't frighten us," Lord Tristan said as guards flocked to his side. He stood in front of Emilia, shielding her. "Leave my castle. Right now."

Night Temptress laughed. "And why would we do that? The night's just beginning."

"Because I'll order my knights to attack you," Lord Tristan said. "But if you leave on your own, I'll let you live. The choice is yours, creature."

Slaughter laughed, glancing at Night Temptress. "If they want a fight, let's give them one."

Night Temptress glanced around at the crowd. "Gladly, Brother."

As the guards and vampires crashed into one another, stabbing and clawing and biting, the room turned to madness. Some royals tried to run, but the vampires pounced on them and drank their blood.

"I'll talk to the legendary Slaughter himself—try to convince him we're one of them," Cyrus said. "Go, get to Night

Temptress and convince her. Just be careful, Levi. I hear her claws are sharp!"

As Cyrus rushed off, ducking through the swordfighters, Levi wanted to obey him and find Night Temptress. But the voice in the back of his head was too strong—the call to protect Emilia. He had to find her.

He slid under the legs of a snarling vampire, rushing over to the place where Lord Tristan, Emilia, and her family sat. They had gotten cornered by a rabid vampire who growled at them, the guards too distracted by their own fights to notice. It was only Lord Tristan, Emilia, and her family left standing. The boyish ruler pulled out his sword, trying to protect them. The rest of her family shivered in fear. Emilia looked like she wanted to fight, reaching for a scabbard that wasn't there. Her dress had no place for weapons.

"Stay away from us," Lord Tristan said, his voice wavering. "Don't...don't come any closer!"

"Ah, what's the matter?" the vampire taunted. "Is the little lordling afraid? Going to soil your golden drawers?"

As the vampire stalked closer, Lord Tristan jutted his sword out. He had terrible aim—missing the vamp altogether. The vampire grabbed the sword, chucking it across the room. It slid across the floor.

"Pathetic," the vampire taunted. "Let me show you how a real warrior fights!"

"Not today," Levi said, grabbing the vampire by his collar.

Levi threw the vampire up against the wall, punching him in the face. The vampire staggered back and took a moment to recover.

"You," the vampire said, locking eyes with Levi. Violet blood trickled down the vampire's face, their old blood color before their evolution, Levi recalled. "You're not like the others," the vampire mused. "No...you're something different, aren't you?"

Levi growled, tossing the vampire across the room. He crashed into a nearby table, landing on the floor with a thud. He groaned and staggered while clutching his head. Levi looked back at Emilia who had wide eyes, the rest of her family shocked too.

"Are you all right?" Levi asked them all.

"Levi, watch out!" Emilia cried, pointing over his shoulder.

Levi felt strong arms reach for him, pulling him back. Vampire teeth sunk into his neck and he cried out in pain.

"Ugh," the vampire muttered, spitting out Levi's black blood. "That doesn't taste right."

With the vampire distracted by the foul taste, Levi pushed his attacker off and spun around—coming face-to-face with Night Temptress. She wiped off her scarlet-colored mouth, looking at Levi with surprise and delight.

"Well, well, well," she murmured, eyeing him up and down. "Looks like we aren't the only surprise at the ball tonight."

"No!" Emilia cried behind Levi. "Get off my sister!"

Levi craned his neck. He noticed a male vampire biting Dawn's neck, ferociously drinking her blood. Before Levi could spring into action, Emilia grabbed a silver fork off the table and stabbed the vampire in the chest.

The creature went motionless, then fell to the floor, dead. But it was too late for Dawn. She lay on the ground, her eyes open in shock and her neck wound gushing blood. Levi could see the deadly bite mark and knew there was nothing they could do for her. Alana, Emilia, Peeta, and their parents hunched over Dawn's body.

"No, no, no," Emilia said, caressing her sister's cheek. "This can't be happening. My darling sister, no."

A kaleidoscope of emotions burst inside of Levi. Anger, sadness, grief. He wanted to skin all the vampires alive for hurting Emilia.

"Get out of here if you want to live," Levi said, turning back to Night Temptress. "I mean it."

Night Temptress looked at Levi one last time. He feared she'd reveal his secret—expose him in front of Emilia. But she didn't. Her eyes scanned the ballroom, grinning when she noticed dozens of dead royals on the floor. Then they landed on Slaughter who was talking to Cyrus.

Levi noticed too. It looked like Cyrus and Slaughter had fought. Cyrus's mouth gushed black blood and Slaughter's coat was rumpled. But then Cyrus grinned, and Slaughter returned to Night Temptress's side.

"Come," Slaughter said to his sister. "I think we've had enough fun for one night. And we have something exciting to talk about."

"Very well. We'll meet again, stranger," Night Temptress said, looking at Levi. She turned toward Lord Tristan. "Thanks for the party, my lord."

Night Temptress curtseyed with a smirk. Slaughter then whistled and all the vampires rushed to his side, even the one Levi had injured. They strolled back to the balcony and vanished down the castle walls. Levi wanted to chase after them, but Cyrus rushed over and grabbed his arm.

"Don't. We'll meet up with them again soon," he whispered. "I spoke with Slaughter. He's not fully convinced we're real vamps, but he's going to give us a chance to prove ourselves. We're supposed to meet him tomorrow night in the markets."

Levi glanced across the ballroom. Many were dead, others dying. Most of the guards had gotten wiped out except for Sir Anders who limped over to them. He bowed before Lord Tristan.

"I'm sorry, my lord," he said. "We couldn't stop those monsters—"

"Useless," Lord Tristan spat. "All of you, so very useless. I could've been killed!"

Levi scoffed. Is that all Lord Tristan cared about? His own safety? He wished he could've killed him right there.

Levi turned to Cyrus, his blood boiling. "What was the point of that? All that bloodshed?"

Cyrus raised an eyebrow. "The point? The point is we're vamps, Levi. Bloodshed is what we do. You always enjoyed it before."

It was true—he used to. All the fighting, hunting, and drinking. It felt like a game, a deliciously evil hunt. Now it just bothered him.

Levi walked over to Emilia who sobbed over her sister's dead body. He placed a hand on her shoulder, sighing. "I'm so sorry, Emilia. I wish I could've done something to save her."

"It wasn't your fault, Levi. You had your own life to worry about," Emilia said, wiping her tears away. She pointed at Lord Tristan. "I don't blame you. I blame *him*."

"Me?" Lord Tristan frowned. "What have I done?"

"It's what you *haven't* done that's going to kill us all," Emilia said, standing up with a snarl. "That man, Edmund, was right. The monster threat is growing, and you haven't done a damn thing about it. Look at my sister's body if you don't fucking believe it!"

"Watch your tone, Emilia," her father scolded. "Don't speak to a lord like—"

"Oh, hush, Father! If Lord Tristan had taken action to protect these streets, we wouldn't be here. And you know it!"

Her father's jaw clenched, but he said nothing.

"Listen, I'm very sorry Dawn's dead," Lord Tristan began, calmly, "but there's nothing I can do. You saw my knights get slaughtered—we're helpless against these fiends. That's why I haven't done anything."

Emilia crossed her arms. "Then maybe someone else needs to take the job. Someone more capable."

"Such as?"

Emilia didn't reply, glancing down at her sister's dead body. "We'll bury her in the morning. I want her body returned to our farm at once."

"It will be done," Lord Tristan said, turning to Levi and Cyrus. "And you two. You saved us—persuaded the vamps to leave. Who are you?"

Levi removed his mask. He wanted Lord Tristan to know it was him—to realize Levi was better at protecting Emilia than he was. "Oh, we've already met."

"*You*," Lord Tristan muttered. "I should have you executed for trespassing. But...seeing as you saved our lives, I suppose I can forgive and forget. This time."

"How generous of you," Levi taunted.

Emilia pulled her mother, brother, and Alana away from Dawn's body. "We can't stay here, weeping all night. We must get home."

"And your answer, Emilia?" Lord Tristan asked. "Will you be my wife?"

"You'll have my answer soon, my lord," she said, "after the funeral. I need time to grieve."

At least he didn't argue with that. As Emilia and her family walked out of the castle, Cyrus and Levi followed. Lord Tristan's servants began repairing and cleaning up the castle immediately. As Cyrus jumped onto their horse and rode home with Levi, he had the widest smirk.

"I told you we had to come tonight. Aren't you glad we didn't miss all that?" Cyrus asked. "Shit, it's got my blood pumping. Can't wait to meet up with Slaughter again."

Levi faked a smile and nodded, but in his heart, he suddenly knew none of this was right.

SEVEN

They buried Dawn the next morning.

Ivan and Peeta dug a hole in the far end of the field as Emilia's mother cried onto Emilia's shoulder. After they placed Dawn in a makeshift coffin, Levi and Cyrus walked over to pay their respects.

Ivan glared at them but didn't say anything. It seemed Levi saving his life had changed his opinion of the brothers. He let them stay without a fight—for now. After twenty minutes of silence, it started to rain. Alana and Peeta brought their tearful mother inside as Ivan turned to Emilia.

"Lord Tristan will be here soon," her father said. "Clean yourself up and wait for him."

"And why should I?" Emilia asked. "He should be helping our people, not pestering me."

"He already told you he can't do anything. He's waiting for your decision, Emilia," Ivan replied. "You promised you'd give it soon."

Emilia chuckled dryly. "My decision? Is it, truly? You've never cared about *my* decision, Father. Don't pretend like you do."

"Look, I don't know what's gotten into you lately," Ivan spat, "but I suggest you think of someone else for a moment. You need to marry Lord Tristan, Emilia. During these hard times, he's the only one who can help us—help our farm. You know it's in trouble, Daughter. Our crops have had a rough spring."

Emilia turned her head. "Go, Father. I wish to be alone."

Ivan scoffed, walking off toward the cabin. Emilia didn't turn around.

"I'll be in the shed if you need me. No need to water the crops today," Cyrus said, pointing up at the rainy sky. "My condolences, Emilia."

Emilia said nothing as Cyrus walked away. Levi knew Cyrus wasn't truly sorry—that he couldn't feel guilt or grief. But it surprised Levi how much his own heart ached for Emilia. It had been so long since he'd felt his humanity.

Levi waited for Emilia to say something first, but she didn't. She continued to stare down at the fresh pile of dirt that had Dawn's body underneath. Raindrops fell on her face, caressing her rosy cheeks and soaking her clothes.

Levi was about to speak up when Emilia looked up at the depressing, gray rain clouds and screamed. It stretched on for a good ten seconds, scaring the hummingbirds out of the nearby tree before she stopped.

"I, uh, should leave you alone," Levi muttered. "Excuse me."

"No." Emilia turned to him. He noticed her bloodshot eyes and shaky hands. "Stay. Please."

He nodded and stepped forward, placing a hand on her shoulder. But she turned and pulled him into a hug, crying on his shirt. He returned the hug before he removed his jacket to place over her shoulders so she wouldn't catch a cold. Humans were such fragile things, Levi remembered.

"Thank you," she murmured, sinking into his warm coat.

"God, Levi...everything's gotten so complicated. My sister's murder, Lord Tristan's proposal, the deaths on the street. When will it end? Who will be next? I'm just so sick of it all."

"Me, too," Levi said. "My brother and I meant what we said before, Emilia. We want to help you."

"And I *did* say at the castle that someone more capable needed to take care of things. Lord Tristan won't be the one to save us. I was a fool to think he would be."

"If not him, then who?" Levi asked, though he knew the answer from the history books.

"Me," Emilia replied. "*I* will lead the revolution. I want to track down this Peasant Guild. Edmund Doyle, I believe his name was. He's their leader, it seems, and I know there are more of them. They'll agree to help us. They have to."

Levi felt giddy for some reason, a shiver of delight rising up his spine. "Where do you think we'd find him?"

"The markets, perhaps? One of the poorer houses in the villages? We should ask around. But the Peasant's Guild's tactics were flawed, you know. They never should've come to the castle."

"Oh? What do you mean?"

"Going to Lord Tristan was a mistake—I see that now. He can't help us, and even if he could, I doubt he'd risk his life. We need our own militia. People working together to stop these monsters. A...coalition of sorts."

Emilia reached down, plucking a flower out of the ground. She laid it on the wet dirt above her sister's grave. She took a deep breath before she turned around, her eyes narrowed.

"We'll be called Allegiant," she said. "And we'll be the thing vampires fear."

"Look at you," Levi said with a grin. "A woman taking charge. I like that."

Emilia smiled too. This was the moment Levi and Cyrus had

time-traveled for—what they eagerly awaited. Emilia had no idea of it yet, but Allegiant would change the world. Vampires *would* fear them one day.

And in that moment, they should've killed Emilia. Ended it before it all began. But since that thought made Levi sick to his stomach, he vowed to keep it from his brother.

The familiar sound of hooves echoed in the distance. Levi looked over his shoulder, sighing. "Not him again. Want me to get rid of Tristan? Tell him you left?"

Emilia shook her head, looking down. "No, Levi. I must tell him I've agreed to marry him."

Levi snapped his neck toward Emilia, his mouth opening in shock. "But...you don't want that. You just said you planned to take care of those monsters without his help."

"And I will. But this Allegiant of ours won't be free," Emilia said, sadly. "We'll need a stronghold—a well-fortified castle to train recruits. I plan to teach them all about vampires and their weaknesses. Like a school, almost. What better place than Lord Tristan's castle? It already has barracks and everything we need."

"But...Lord Tristan has no interest in helping you or anyone else," Levi said, closing the gap between them. "He'll never agree to this. Especially in his own castle."

"No—which is why I won't tell him. It'll be our secret. I'll marry him for his money and castle, all so I can start Allegiant."

"But why not here?" Levi gestured around the farm. "You can put in some training dummies behind the shed. You could use the cornstalks for target practice."

"Oh, please. My parents would never approve of such a thing. They're as stubborn and foolish as Lord Tristan," she said, looking up at Levi. "I know you don't want me to marry him, but I have no choice. For the sake of Allegiant, I must make this sacrifice."

As Emilia turned, Levi grabbed her arm. "Wait. It's gold you're after, right? To pay for a place—and some supplies?"

"Well, yes," she said, looking at Levi strangely. "But I don't have any. The gold Lord Tristan gives us goes straight to Father who spends it on the farm. If I married him, I'd have access to the household fund. I could reallocate some gold for Allegiant without him knowing."

"Then I'll get you gold—whatever it takes. We'll find a stronghold together. We can do it without Lord Tristan," Levi stunned himself by saying. "I know we can."

Emilia paused. "You would do that? For me?"

"Yes, no matter how far I have to travel," he said, suddenly knowing it was true. "My people have found resources before— made a home out of nothing. I could do it again."

"Hmm. And you truly think you could make enough gold?" she asked, her green eyes hopeful. "Purchasing land isn't cheap. And then we'd need to pay for supplies, upkeep, food..."

"I'll figure it out, Emilia. The markets seem like a good place to start. Just promise me you won't marry that pompous Lord Tristan?"

Emilia flung her arms around Levi, hugging him tight. "I promise. And thank you, Levi. But what if he and my parents try to force me?"

"Then I'll show them why that's a bad idea," Levi said, pulling back. "You'd better get inside. Give Lord Tristan your answer and send him off for good."

"All right. Now, not that I'm not grateful you're doing this... but why do you care so much about me? If it were anyone else in your position, they would've let me marry him. Like my father."

Levi shrugged. "I guess I'm not like everybody else."

"No, you're not." She gave him a small smile. "Can you come with me? I've faced vampires before, but I'm not sure I have the strength to face my family right now. To see them so disappointed in me. I don't want to do it alone."

"Of course." Levi turned, walking with her through the rain. "But you're doing the right thing. Your family might not see or respect that, but I do."

Emilia nodded and took a deep breath. The horse and carriage sat near the cabin, empty. Levi knew Lord Tristan must've been inside already. When he and Emilia entered the cabin, they noticed Loretta sitting at the wooden table, crying softly. Alana and Peeta tried to comfort her as Ivan spoke with Lord Tristan and his knights. There weren't many left after the castle attack.

"I'm sorry to intrude during this time," Lord Tristan said to Ivan, "and you have my sincere condolences. But I must get Emilia's answer. I've waited long enough."

Levi's anger began to bubble in his chest again. Lord Tristan had no compassion for Emilia or her family—not even now in the aftermath of her little sister's death.

"And you'll have your answer right now, my lord," Ivan said, noticing Emilia over his shoulder. "There she is."

Lord Tristan turned around, that unsettlingly grin spreading across his face again when his eyes landed on her. "My goodness, you're soaked! Don't worry, my dear—you won't need to do any farming or run your little shop any longer. You'll be safe inside my castle, living like a lady."

"It's not a *little shop*," Emilia hissed. "I've saved many lives, you know. Taught myself medicine and alchemy too."

"Yes, yes, whatever you say." He waved her off, then turned to Levi. "Levi, was it? I'm disappointed you're still here."

Levi crossed his arms. "Are you? I thought we were on good terms after I saved your life. I could've let those vampires tear you apart, you know. Lord knows it would've been more entertaining than your party."

Lord Tristan sneered. "You might've saved my life from those fiends, but I'll never forget how you treated me when I first arrived. One wrong move and I *will* strike you down, foreigner."

Levi wanted to hit him again, but he had something better to wound the lord. Emilia's rejection. He only smirked, saying nothing.

Ivan cleared his throat, stepping forward. "I've already had some of your clothes packed, Emilia. Although I'm sure the seamstresses at the castle will sew you a dress worthy of a lady—"

"I'm not marrying him, Father," Emilia interrupted. "I'm refusing his proposal."

The room became silent except for Loretta's sobs. Ivan turned to Emilia, a snarl on his face. "What did you just say?"

"You heard her," Levi said. "She doesn't want to marry Lord Tristan. She's been saying that for a while now, but you haven't been listening."

"Did you bump your head last night?" Lord Tristan asked Emilia, blinking. "Our marriage will be the best thing for your family, Emilia. I could give you everything—gold, prestige, luxury. You need me!"

"I don't want any of those things." Emilia crossed her arms. "If you bothered to take the time to get to know me, you'd know what I want."

"What is it?" Lord Tristan asked. "I'll give you anything. Diamonds, rubies?"

"No. I want something done about these vampires. I want you to train your knights to hunt them all down."

He sighed. "You frustrating woman. As I've told you before, I can't. You saw what happened last night. We can't possibly take on those monsters."

"Then you have nothing I want, Lord Tristan. I must bid you goodbye."

"You!" Ivan stepped closer, glaring into Levi's pale face. "You did this, didn't you? Convinced her not to marry Lord Tristan?"

Levi shook his head. "Not at all. This is Emilia's choice, Ivan. I just encouraged her to follow her heart."

"I don't need to stand here and listen to this!" Lord Tristan said, removing his sword. "*I* am the Lord of Osgoode, the law around here! You have been promised to me, Emilia. I don't intend to leave here without you—"

Levi kicked the sword out of Lord Tristan's hand, then it clanged on the floor. Before the few guards could swarm him, Levi grabbed the royal by his throat, making him groan. The guards reached for the weapons in their scabbards.

"Come any closer and he dies!" Levi warned Lord Tristan's entourage.

The knights paused.

"Foreigner scum," Lord Tristan choked in Levi's grasp. "You'll regret defying me. You *and* Emilia!"

Levi dropped Lord Tristan onto the floor. "And *you'll* regret ever coming around here if I see you try anything."

To prove he was serious, Levi made his eyes flash red again. Lord Tristan gasped before his eyes returned to normal.

"This...this isn't over. Be glad I don't call in my allies to destroy this puny farm," Lord Tristan muttered, turning to Emilia. Her parents murmured behind her. "Perhaps in time I'll be thanking you. I don't want a whore like you as my wife, anyhow."

"That's enough," Levi hissed, shoving Lord Tristan and his guards out the door. "Get on your carriage and piss off. For good!"

He slammed the door in their faces, his jaw tight with rage.

He glanced back at Ivan, thirsty for a drink of the man's blood—anything to take the edge off. But his rage faded when Emilia placed a hand on his arm.

"Thank you, Levi," she said. "Tristan would've kidnapped me if you hadn't stopped him. And my father would've let him."

Levi relaxed, breathing in and out before he nodded. Something about Emilia always calmed him down.

But Ivan wasn't calm. He stepped forward, his face red and scrunched. "I want you out of this house, Emilia. Pack your things and leave!"

Emilia glanced back at her sobbing mother. Peeta and Alana watched, their mouths wide. "You've lost one of your daughters already, Father. Do you honestly want to lose another?"

"You stopped being my daughter when you refused Lord Tristan's proposal," Ivan snarled. "You doomed this family and our farm, all because of your own selfishness. Now, get out of my sight!"

"She stays," Levi said, stepping forward. He stood right in Ivan's face and stared long and hard at the man. "And so do we."

"Is that so? And why do you care so much about where she lives now?" Ivan asked. "You already got what you wanted."

"Where I come from, you don't abandon your own people. Ever. So let her stay or I'll break your arms and shove them up your ass. Do you understand?"

Ivan paused, his Adam's apple bobbing. He glared back at Emilia. "She can stay—but our relationship is over. I'll never speak to you again, Emilia."

And then he stormed out of the cabin, slamming the door behind him. Loretta only sobbed harder. Emilia walked over to her, bending down to hug her, but Loretta pushed her away and rose to her feet.

"No, don't!" Loretta cried, her cheeks wet with tears. "Don't you see? Marrying Lord Tristan could've saved this family. Now you've ruined it all!"

Before Emilia could argue, Loretta fled the cabin. Emilia sighed and looked back at Peeta and Alana. "Are you two mad at me as well?"

"Honestly?" Peeta asked. "Lord Tristan was an idiot. I'm glad he won't be my brother-in-law."

Alana nodded, shyly tucking a loose strand of hair behind her ear. "And I would've missed you too much if you left, so maybe this is a good thing."

"Well, I'm glad I still have some support," Emilia said, turning to Levi, "and yours as well. Prepare yourself for a trip to the markets. I want to find that Peasant's Guild leader. The one from the party last night."

"What for?" Alana asked.

"I'm starting a militia," Emilia told them. "We must do something about these monster attacks. And since Lord Tristan won't, I have no choice but to take it upon myself. I'm calling it Allegiant."

"Really? Then...I want to join," Alana said, nervously playing with her hands. "I know I'm small, but I'm fast and quiet. I can't sit by on the sidelines—not while they murder my friends."

"Yeah, me too," Peeta said. "It's stupid that Lord Tristan won't help us, especially after last night. I think if anyone can save us, it's you, Emilia."

"You will fight? I have to warn you both, it could be danger-ous," Emilia said. "You saw how fierce those monsters were last night. Levi and Cyrus call them vampires. And they show no mercy."

Peeta shrugged. "Then we'll be careful. It's a small price to pay to avenge Dawn."

"Looks like you've found your first two members," Levi said, leaning against the wall. "Other than me and my brother, of course."

Emilia grinned. "So I have. I hope recruiting others goes this smoothly. Hurry—take whatever you need for the journey, Levi. I'll fetch Margaret from the stables."

"What about us?" Alana glanced between them. "Can we come too?"

"No, it'd look too suspicious. Stay here with Mother and Father and tend to the farm until I can get things arranged. Lord knows they'd never approve if they found out what we're doing."

As the teenagers and Emilia went their separate ways, Levi walked to the shed to tell Cyrus what had happened. His brother stood by the door, eagerly awaiting him with a smirk.

"There he is," Cyrus began. "Loverboy's returned."

"Huh?"

"Don't act coy. I saw how close you were with Emilia," Cyrus replied, stepping closer. "Call me crazy, but it looks you've got a crush on her. I mean, she's hot and all, but she'll be dead soon, Levi."

"I *don't* have a crush on her," Levi said. "I could never fall for a human—especially not the leader of Allegiant. That'd be an insult to me *and* my people. And I'd never disrespect the Patriarch's memory like that."

"Right. Just making sure. So, what's going on?"

"It's starting. She mentioned Allegiant, Brother. We're heading to the markets to find that peasant from last night to recruit him."

"So it begins. Go ahead without me for now. You have better luck getting information out of her, anyway." Cyrus shrugged. "And besides, I have to save my energy for tonight."

Levi frowned. "Tonight?"

"Did you forget? Come on, Levi—I thought you'd be excited

about this. We're meeting those vamps at the markets after sundown, remember? Slaughter and Night Temptress will be there. This is our chance to help them."

"Oh, right," Levi muttered. "Yeah. Great."

"So, whatever business you have with Emilia, be back before dark so we can leave. Vamps hate to be kept waiting." Levi nodded, turning to the door before Cyrus called out his name. "Levi?"

He turned around. "Yeah?"

"We're doing the right thing," Cyrus said, his eyes boring into his. "By infiltrating Allegiant. Remember that."

Levi said nothing, closing the door to the shed behind him.

EIGHT

Levi and Emilia traveled to the markets on her horse, the hot sun beating down on their heads. The rain had stopped, leaving the roads muddy and dirty. Levi hadn't seen the markets at this time of day. Busy peasants purchasing food, animal furs, and supplies they needed for their families flooded the streets.

He felt a pang of sadness in his chest when he noticed how impoverished and starved they were. The children coughed into their cloaks, much too thin and pale. Their parents' clothes were dirty, and their faces were long. Some didn't even have enough gold to buy all the food they needed.

Three of Lord Tristan's constables patrolled the crowds, looking for any thieves or brawlers. They glared at Levi and Emilia when their eyes locked, but stayed silent. As they trotted along, Levi considered Cyrus's words. Did he have a crush on Emilia? How could that be possible? Vampires didn't get crushes—they didn't experience love.

Cyrus is wrong, Levi thought. *He's just messing with me.* And yet, why was he feeling this tug in his chest? Why was he helping her?

"Ah, the markets," Emilia said, interrupting Levi's thoughts. "Deserted at night, but bursting with life during the day. Look at these people—so happy and unaware. Any of them could be the next to die."

"Not if we can help it," Levi lied, jumping off Margaret. "Where to?"

Emilia tied Margaret to a post, then the horse began chewing on the grass. "Let's ask around. The Cauldron's a good place to start."

"The Cauldron?"

"Right, I forgot how little you know about Osgoode. The Cauldron's our most popular tavern. Come, I'll show you."

They pushed through the crowd, knocking shoulders with people from all walks of life. The smell of alcohol filled Levi's nostrils as they neared the tavern, then he noticed the CAULDRON sign above the door. He also spotted a *Wanted* sign for a group of bandits hanging on the wall.

Emilia sneered, noticing the bulletin. "We have vampire threats at night, and still, criminals roam our streets. You'd think we'd all come together at a time like this, but I suppose not. Unbelievable."

Emilia pushed the door open and entered, with Levi close behind. The Cauldron was busy in the afternoon. People sat around tables, drinking merrily while laughing and clinking their mugs together. Levi's vampire hearing went into overdrive, the loud sounds hurting his ears. But then a soothing melody started.

A beautiful bard stood to the right of the tavern, playing an upbeat melody on her lute. It helped to drown out the laughs and belches of the sailors. She had wavy blonde hair, a green cape tied around her shoulders, and shoes with pointed toes. Some of the drunken customers tossed gold at her and she bowed her head in thanks. Her eyes briefly flitted toward Levi and Emilia, but when Levi looked back at her, she diverted her attention to her lute again.

He tried to concentrate as Emilia turned to him. "We should talk to the barkeep, Mickey. I helped him out a year ago. Well, I hope he sees it that way. He could have some information on where to find—"

"Well, aren't you pretty?" a drunken sailor asked, staggering over to Emilia. He eyed her up and down, his mug spilling sticky beer onto the floor. "You don't come here often, do you? I'd remember a red-headed beauty like you."

"Um, no, I don't. Please, excuse us," Emilia muttered, pushing past him. "We're here on important business."

"Yeah, me too." The drunken man grabbed Emilia's arm. "And my business right now is *you*."

"Back off," Levi snarled, pushing his hand away. "The lady already told you she doesn't want to talk."

The drunken man sneered at him. "Yeah? And who are you? Her husband?"

"I'm someone you don't want to mess with." Levi towered over the man. "So, piss off before I put your head through that wall."

"I'd listen to him if I were you," Emilia said, glancing between the men. "His temper can be scary."

The man waved them off, chugging his beer. "Ah, you aren't worth the trouble. Stupid tavern wench..."

As he left, Emilia smiled at Levi. "Thanks for that. I don't like the tavern—too many grabby hands. Let's just ask the bartender about Edmund and get out of here."

As Levi nodded and they pushed toward the bar, he heard a commotion coming from the left side of the tavern. Several pirates sat around a wooden table while playing a card game.

Mermaids, pirate ships, and pictures of treasure chests decorated the cards. They were the loudest patrons in the tavern—laughing and slamming the cards on the table. But no one dared to ask them to quiet down.

"Who are they?" Levi whispered.

"Oh, them? They're a pirate guild called The Black Flag," Emilia explained. "They're playing Raging Tides, a popular card game. Believe me when I say they aren't people you want to cross."

"No? Why not?"

"They're pirates—that's reason enough to stay away from them. I hear they kill their enemies by tossing them to the whales. Even Lord Tristan is afraid of them, so he warns people to stay out of their way when they dock here. He wouldn't dare force them out of town. Too dangerous."

The woman wearing a pirate outfit howled in laughter. She had short black hair, piercing brown eyes, and a golden front tooth. An orange parrot squawked on her shoulder while several swords and daggers sat on her hip. She dragged a pile of gold across the table toward her as the other pirate players groaned.

"Who's she?" Levi asked.

"Oh, that's their leader—Captain Gem," Emilia replied. "It's probably a fake name. None of the pirates use their real ones. She's got a bad temper, I hear, so it's best to stay out of her sight. In many ways, I admire her. Her leadership, the way her men follow her orders. And I bet she doesn't have drunken sailors pawing at her all the time."

Levi looked away when Emilia tugged him toward the bar. They had to fight to get a seat, pushing away a drunken man who had passed out.

"Hello, Mickey," Emilia said to the bartender. "Remember me?"

The bartender turned around, wiping off a dirty glass. He had a long gray beard and wore an apron over his plain clothes. "Oh, erm...Emilia Rutherford, right? The apothecary?"

"That's me. Do you remember when that bar fight broke out a year ago? And I treated the wounds of those involved, free of charge?"

He shrugged. "Vaguely. Why?"

"Well, I prevented people from dying in your bar. That would've been bad for business. That has to be worth something, right? A favor?"

The barkeep sighed. "Everybody wants something. What is it *you* want?"

"Information," she replied. "I'm looking for a man named Edmund Doyle. Ever seen him around?"

"Can't say that I have." He wiped down the bar, scrubbing the beer and blood stains away. "But most people who come here aren't looking for conversation. They don't tell me their names, just their orders."

"Well, he has brown hair, looks a little dirty," Emilia said. "And I think he has a birthmark on his left cheek. Ring a bell?"

The bartender shrugged. "Nothing stands out about that description, no. So many people come in here every day that it's hard to keep track of them. It's possible I saw him, but I just don't remember."

"Is there anyone who might know?" Levi asked, leaning on the bar.

The bartender shrugged. "You're welcome to ask, but again, my patrons aren't the talking type. Just don't get yourself killed with your questions, all right? Blood's the worst stain to get out, and I'm short on bar wenches around here."

As the barkeep scurried away, filling more mugs, Emilia sighed. "I suppose we could wait for this Edmund fellow to show up. People like to drink after work."

"But that could take forever," Levi muttered, "and I'm getting sick of this place."

"You're right. We need to find Edmund Doyle now—before sundown."

"Perhaps I could be of assistance," a mysterious voice said behind them.

When Levi and Emilia turned around, the blonde bard stood in front of them. She had a sly grin on her face, plucking absentmindedly at the lute on her hip. Levi noticed the same birthmark on her cheek that Edmund had.

"Who are you?" Emilia asked.

"Allow me to introduce myself," the woman said, holding out her hand. "My name's Samantha Doyle, local bard."

Emilia shook her hand. "Samantha Doyle? As in, related to Edmund Doyle?"

She nodded, then shook Levi's hand next. "The one, the only. I'm his daughter. Why are you looking for my father? Is he in some kind of trouble?"

"No, not at all. Let's talk outside—it's too noisy in here."

Once they were outside, Emilia turned to Samantha. She continued to play her lute as people passing by threw coins at her feet. Around her neck, Levi spotted a silver necklace, one chiseled in the shape of a lute. "Thank you, thank you very much," Samantha said, grinning. "So, about my father? Why are you looking for him?"

Emilia lowered her voice, looking over her shoulder to make sure the constables weren't listening. "He's in charge of the Peasant's Guild, right? People who want justice for all those killings by monsters?"

Samantha frowned. "You aren't here to charge him with anything, are you? Forming a guild isn't against the law—"

"No, of course not. We want to help him," Levi said. "We're

starting a group—well, Emilia is. It's called Allegiant. We know all about these monsters and how to kill them."

Samantha sighed in relief. "Well, why didn't you just say so? I'm sure my father would love to help. Come on, I'll take you to him."

"Where is he?" Emilia asked as she and Levi followed.

"At work," Samantha said. "But don't worry, he won't mind the interruption. Finding people to help him is all he's ever wanted. He hates these creatures more than anything."

"They're a big problem at night for sure," Emilia began, "but why does he care so much? He seemed very passionate."

Samantha shook her head. "It's probably best if he told you. You know, I wasn't even going to admit he was my father. I wasn't planning on helping you at all."

"What changed?" Emilia asked.

"You chased off that drunken sailor. He had his hands on me all day," Samantha muttered, scoffing in disgust. "Now, come on—before it gets late. We both know it's not safe to be out after dark."

LEVI AND EMILIA followed Samantha outside the markets, taking a dirty back-road path. It led them to a mine in the distance. Miners dragged cartloads of gold, silver, and bronze out of the mine, then placed them in the back of a horse cart to bring into town.

"He works here?" Emilia asked. "In the mines?"

Samantha nodded. "Not my first choice of job for him, but yes. Someone has to bring Lord Tristan his precious gold. My father's in charge of the miners, so he shouldn't be too hard to find."

Levi, Emilia, and Samantha walked into the mine's

entrance, ducking through the small hole. Specks of dirt fell from above and Levi blocked his nose at the foul stench of dirt and sweat. A group of miners stood near the wall, hacking away at the large chunks of rock.

"Hey! You can't be in here," a miner said, walking over. "It's too dangerous—especially for such lovely ladies."

"I'm here to see my father, Edmund," Samantha said. "And if you're implying I'm weak, you're sadly mistaken."

"Feisty. You really must be Edmund's daughter," the miner said with a laugh. "Follow the path and take a left. He's back there working on some of the harder rocks. But don't tell him I let you through—he'd kill me for letting his daughter in here."

The three nodded and followed his directions, taking a left down the path. A group of miners hacked at the walls, sweat dripping down their necks. Emilia and Levi recognized Edmund immediately.

"Working hard or hardly working?" Samantha joked, playing a riff on her lute.

The other miners noticed her first, whistling at her in approval. Her father, Edmund, zipped his head around, staring at her with wide eyes. Once the miners realized it was his daughter, they shut their mouths and returned to work.

"Sammy? What are you doing here?" Edmund asked, putting his pickaxe down. "You know I don't want you in the mines! What if you get hurt? What if a rock falls—"

"Relax, Papa. We won't be here for long." Samantha gestured at Emilia and Levi. "I've got two friends here who want to meet you. Their names are…?"

"Levi Godfrey and Emilia Rutherford," Emilia introduced. "Nice to meet you."

"Emilia Rutherford?" Edmund's eyebrows furrowed. "That name sounds familiar. Weren't you supposed to be betrothed to Lord Tristan?"

Emilia nodded. "Well, yes—"

"You have some nerve coming 'round here," Edmund said, crossing his arms. "What kind of lord refuses to help his own people? Royals make me sick. I don't want to talk to any of them—especially you. You ain't got a clue what we go through or how hard life is out here."

"Actually, she *does* know. And she's not marrying Lord Tristan," Levi said. "Emilia's here to help you fight the vampires, what we call the monsters who kill people at night."

"Yeah, right. I know this is all some trick to get me arrested. I ain't falling for it. Tell Lord Tristan he can go to hell."

"Papa, I don't think this is a trick," Samantha said. "Would you just listen to them?"

Edmund sighed. "All right, I'll play along. How do you plan to stop these vampires?"

"Well, we don't have everything figured out yet," Emilia said, "but I want to buy some land and start a training school. We'll call ourselves Allegiant—people working together to stop the vampires. My friend, Levi, knows all about them."

"Really?" Edmund asked, glancing at Levi. "And how do you know so much?"

"We have them where I come from, too," Levi said. "I've killed many in my time. I could help you make the streets safer at night."

"You were a brave man to stand up to Lord Tristan at his party," Emilia said. "We need people like you—people who aren't afraid to do what's right."

Edmund scoffed. "And who's to say I need you? The Peasant's Guild already has plenty of members."

Samantha snorted. "I wouldn't say *plenty*, Papa. And anyhow, inexperienced miners and worried midwives from the village don't count."

"And no offense, but the vampires are still out there. They're a lot more dangerous than you realize," Levi said. "Your Peasant's Guild will need all the help it can get."

Edmund sighed, looking down. "I fear you're right. It's been tough trying to rally people, you know. Most are too afraid to do anything while some fear retribution from Lord Tristan. Others just think I'm a crazy old man."

"Well, you need people—as do we," Emilia said. "I have some influence. I'm sure I could recruit the right people. Allegiant could save the world, Edmund. And I want you there, someone with your spark. You truly hate the vampires, don't you?"

"I do. And for good reason. They took my wife—Lilia, Samantha's mother. Killed her in her home at night while I was out working." He took a second to compose himself, clearing his throat. "Good thing Sammy was sleeping over at a friend's house, or they would've killed her too."

"Then join Allegiant, Papa. Stop trying to do it all by yourself," Samantha said. "I'm saying yes. I want to help them—I want to help Emilia and Levi. It's more than what Lord Tristan has ever tried to do. And we can get justice for Mama this way."

Before Edmund could give them his answer, a scream echoed from down the mineshaft's corridor. All the miners around them paused, looking in its direction. Edmund dropped his pickaxe and rushed forward.

"That sounded like Arthur," he said. "I sent him on a deep cave expedition. Quick—we need to find him!"

Emilia, Levi, and Samantha chased after Edmund, following him even deeper into the mines. The ceilings became less sturdy and the four avoided falling rocks and debris. As Levi looked down, he noticed the red blood on the ground. He could smell the death in the air—the pheromones of his own people.

"Vampire," he whispered.

"What?" Emilia's eyes widened. "Where?"

A second later, a vampire turned around the corner. He wiped the red blood off his face; flesh stuck between his sharp fangs. Levi could barely see him under the dim torches of the mines, but he had silver hair and wore a long black cloak. Levi didn't recognize him as Slaughter, Night Temptress, or any of the other vampires from the castle attack. Who was he?

Samantha gasped, pointing at the ground. A fellow miner laid dead, his neck bitten and drained. "Dear God...poor Arthur."

"You!" Edmund snarled at the vampire, standing in front of his daughter to protect her. "What did you do to Arthur?"

"Arthur? Was that his name?" the vampire asked, shrugging. "I didn't stop to ask."

"You killed him, didn't you? You're a monster," Emilia spat. "Where did you come from?"

"That doesn't matter," the vampire said, walking toward her. "What matters is that I can take whatever I want from you—and you can't do anything to stop me."

Time seemed to stop for a moment. Levi felt bound to his duty to his own, to protect the vampires and complete his mission. But when he looked at Emilia, seeing the horror on her face, he knew he couldn't let this vampire hurt these people.

His stomach twisted, his hands shook. And then he made his decision.

"Think again," Levi said. "Anyone got any silver? Hurry!"

Samantha yanked at the chain around her neck. She handed it to Levi who used his sleeve to grab it out of her hands, then picked up the ax on the ground. Placing the necklace over the ax, he thrust the tool into the vampire's heart and the creature paused, his yellow eyes blown wide.

He looked down at the ax through his chest and then back up at Levi. It looked like he recognized Levi—what he was. But he couldn't speak with the violet blood pouring out of his mouth.

"Silver," Levi panted as the vampire fell dead. "It kills them instantly. Made the ax deadlier. Thanks for that, Sam."

"Jesus Christ," Edmund said. "You...you killed him!"

"It wasn't a person," Emilia corrected. "That was a vampire."

"Damn. I've never seen one before—just heard about them from witnesses. The one who killed my wife was long gone when I got home," Edmund whispered. "So bloody, so brutal..."

"These are the fiends that walk our streets," Emilia said, "that we need to protect our people from. We can make things right, Edmund. Allegiant can."

Edmund stared at the vampire's dead body. "To think one of these butchered my Lilia...I'm in. I want them all dead, Emilia. Every single last one of them."

"Good," Emilia said, still staring at the dead vampire. "Now let's get out of these mines before more show up. From wher-ever they're sneaking in."

"Edmund, burn the body. That's the proper way to dispose of a vampire," Levi said. "The stench from his corpse will only attract more of them."

Edmund nodded, dragging the vampire's body out of the mines. Levi and the others followed and watched as he set the corpse ablaze with a nearby torch on the wall. As he turned away, Levi felt a pang of guilt in his chest. He doubled over, clutching his heart. It was different from the pain he'd felt after meeting Emilia.

"Levi, are you all right?" Emilia asked, placing a hand on his shoulder. "The vampire didn't hurt you, did he?"

Levi shook his head. "No...no, he didn't. I'll be okay."

He craned his neck at the pile of ashes the vampire had been reduced to. He finally realized why he felt so awful—he had remembered the Vampire Commandments. The worst sin a vampire could commit was to kill their own. Some even considered a vampire who killed another cursed forever, but he had done it to save Emilia.

Levi sighed, knowing he couldn't tell his brother. If Cyrus found out...

He'd have to strike Levi dead in punishment.

NINE

As the miners fled—terrified more vampires would arrive soon—Levi and Emilia followed Samantha and Edmund outside. Except for the bustle of the miners and their worried chatter, all was quiet. Levi couldn't smell any more vampires in the distance.

"Nowhere is safe anymore," Edmund told them. "These monsters—vampires, you call them—show up everywhere, just like the plague."

"The safest place is outside in the sun," Levi said, pointing up. "The vampires can't handle the sunlight. It kills them."

"A fat lot of good that does at night," Edmund muttered. "And in the mines, it's always dark. Ain't no one to save us in there if more show up. But you—you protected us. Risked your own life to kill that vampire. Why?"

Levi shrugged. "It was the right thing to do. He would've killed us too if I hadn't."

The right thing to do. Levi felt a little funny saying those words. Vampires worried about their next victim and rising through the ranks, not doing the right thing. It went against everything he had learned—all the Vampire Commandments.

"Levi's a hero," Emilia said, looking up at him with a smile. "We all owe you our lives."

Levi looked away, unable to meet her gaze. The guilt crept up his spine like spiders. He was no hero—he knew it deep down inside. But the way Emilia had looked at him made him want to be one for the first time in his unnaturally long life.

"What are we going to do?" a miner in the crowd asked. "What if more of those things show up? Those royal bastards ain't going to protect us!"

The miners loudly agreed. Emilia glanced at Levi, knowing what she had to do.

"Perhaps we could look at offering protection to the miners. Allegiant, I mean," Emilia said, turning to the working men. "We're starting a revolution against the vampires. We'll train you to become a Legionnaire, a vampire hunter. That way, no one else will end up like Arthur. Are any of you interested in joining?"

The crowd remained silent. The miners looked around at each other, hesitating.

"Will it...will it be dangerous?" a miner asked.

Levi nodded. "Very. But so is working the mines without knowing how to properly defend yourselves. If one vampire found you, more will. They always do."

The miners glanced around at each other. Just when Levi thought they'd refuse, they all nodded.

"We'll join you," a short, balding miner said. "We don't want to live in fear—and we don't want to end up like Arthur. We've got families depending on us. On our salaries. If you can teach us anything at all, something that could save our lives, it'll be worth it."

Emilia grinned. Levi glanced at her, unable to hide his smile. He liked seeing her happy.

"Glad to hear it," Edmund said, glancing around at his

fellow miners. "I'm in too. I've got a wife to avenge and a daughter to protect."

"I have someone to avenge too. I lost my sister recently to a vampire attack," Emilia said. "So I know how you feel, Edmund. Let that rage empower you."

"Then you understand. I'm damn proud to have someone sympathetic leading us," Edmund said. "I have a few people I'd like you to meet—people I think would join us, other than the miners. The more Legionnaires the better, right?"

"Absolutely. Where to?"

"Our cabin," Samantha replied. "It's just behind the markets. We've opened our home to vampire victims—and it's not pretty, we have to warn you."

EMILIA, Levi, Samantha, Edmund, and the horde of miners rode their horses back to the markets. The miners kept looking over their shoulders, expecting vampires to jump out at them, despite Levi promising they were safe in the sunlight.

Emilia shook her head, gesturing at the miners. "You see that, Levi? How nervous everyone is? These vampires don't just take our lives from us—they take our sanity too. Our sense of security. Everyone's overly wary."

"We'll crush these vampires," Edmund said, "one at a time, just like the one you killed back there. It felt good to see one of them dead for a change. Who would've thought silver could kill one of them freaks?"

By telling them that, Levi realized he'd just signed the death warrant for more of his people. Whether he liked it or not.

"About that," Levi said, leaning toward Emilia. "Can you not tell Cyrus I killed a vampire today?"

Emilia frowned. "Why not? Won't he be happy? He isn't too crazy about vampires either, as I recall."

"It's just, um...all that blood and violence scares him. I don't want to cause him any more stress. Let's keep what happened between us, okay?"

Emilia nodded. "I understand. I want to shield Peeta and Alana from it too. We'll go to great lengths to protect our family, won't we?"

"That we will."

More than Emilia knew.

"I didn't want them to join Allegiant, but we need everyone we can get," Emilia said with a sigh. "We don't know how many vampires are out there, just waiting in the shadows."

Levi tensed. There were many, many more—and he wasn't sure for how long he could play both sides.

Half an hour later, they arrived at the markets. It was nearly dinnertime now. Levi could tell from the way the markets were thinning out, and the sun was dimming. He only had a few hours left before they'd all have to get off the streets.

"This way," Edmund said, pointing at a row of shacks in the distance. "Our home's back here."

Everyone got off their horses, following Edmund into his cabin. As soon as they entered, Levi smelled tea brewing and a stew cooking over the fire. There were dozens of people inside, scattered throughout the kitchen and living area. They ranged in age and background—from babies and children to adults and the elderly. They looked up at Levi, Emilia, and the miners with frowns.

"Edmund, back so soon?" an elderly woman asked, walking over to them with a giant stick for a cane. She had short, snow-white hair and age spots covering her face. "Did you have a good day at work?"

"We had to vacate the mines, Gwendolyn. Don't tell Lord

Tristan," Edmund began. "A creature known as a vampire sneaked in and attacked us. It killed Arthur."

The crowd of people sighed, then began murmuring. They all took a moment of silence before Emilia spoke up again.

"Who are all these people?" she asked.

"Our guests," Samantha replied. "They have nowhere else to go. And we're safer in numbers, so it makes sleeping at night a little easier."

"Smart," Levi said. "So, these people are homeless?"

Edmund nodded. "They are. You could call them refugees. The vampires took everything from them—their families, their homes. It's a miracle they survived."

"We've turned our home into an inn of sorts," Samantha continued. "A shelter. All my tips from the tavern go to buying food and clothing."

"So does my gold from the mines. But don't tell anyone," Edmund said, turning to Levi and Emilia. "Technically, you're supposed to buy a license to run an inn, then pay taxes to Lord Tristan. We ain't got the gold for that—neither do these people. So, if any of the guards ask, they're just family visiting from out of town, you hear?"

Emilia nodded. "Your secret is safe with us. Lord Tristan doesn't know about Allegiant, either—and that's the way it'll stay. It's kind of you to open your home, you know. You should feel proud."

Samantha and Edmund smiled.

"Stew's ready," Gwendolyn said, peeking inside the pot. "You folks hungry?"

Emilia nodded. "We could eat. Levi likes his meat raw, though."

"No problem," Gwendolyn said. "We accommodate all of our guests. Why don't you set the table?"

As Gwendolyn, Samantha, and Edmund placed the stew in

the bowls, saving a chunk of raw meat for Levi, he and Emilia set the large wooden table. They placed a cloth over the table, gathered enough utensils for everyone, then beckoned everyone forward. They let the children and elderly sit first, then pulled over extra chairs for the new guests. It wasn't easy fitting everyone at the table—especially the burly miners—but they made it work.

As Levi ate his bloody carcass raw—bear, it tasted like—Emilia turned to the elderly woman. "Gwendolyn, was it? How did you come to be here?"

"A vampire killed my son and husband right in front of me," the elderly woman began, "before setting fire to my house. I only escaped because I stabbed the bastard with a knife. Good to know they can be killed."

"Silver is a vampire's weakness," Emilia explained. "The knife must've been silver, and you probably stabbed them in the heart."

Levi put the raw meat down, feeling nauseous. He wondered—which vampire had killed Gwendolyn's family? Slaughter? Night Temptress? The one he had killed in the mine? It could've been any of them.

"And you?" Emilia asked, looking down at a young boy. He couldn't have been older than six or seven. He had dirt and grime on his face, his overalls torn. "Why are you here, sweetie?"

The boy shook his head, hiding his face in his hands. Gwendolyn leaned over and placed a hand on his shoulder. "Billy doesn't like to talk about it. In fact, he hasn't said a word since he lost his parents."

"Do you know what happened to him?" Emilia whispered.

Edmund scoffed. "What's happened to all of us here, Emilia—the vampires came for us. We managed to escape, but...our loved ones weren't so lucky. Or maybe they were the lucky ones while we suffer."

Groaning came from the corner. Levi and Emilia craned their necks, noticing a teenage girl sitting in the corner. She rocked back and forth, mumbling words underneath her breath. They were too low to understand.

"You really must eat, Margot," Gwendolyn said, getting up and placing a bowl at the girl's feet. "Try to have a nibble, all right, dear?"

"What's wrong with her?" Levi asked as Gwendolyn sat down again.

"A vampire nearly killed her," Samantha said, biting into a piece of bread. "They tortured her for days, but she managed to escape. I knew Margot before the attack—she was lively, happy. A sweet girl. She wanted to become a nun. Now, she's too traumatized to speak."

"Vampire bastards," Edmund muttered, shoveling more stew into his mouth. "They love to break us—play with our minds. Sometimes I think they like it more than the bite."

Torture? Kidnapping? Burning homes? Most modern-day vampires drank and left. No funny business. But these vampires were sadistic—they enjoyed toying with their victims. It was like Cyrus wanting to play with Emilia. Levi hated it, he realized.

He glanced around the table. All the other faces looked the same—a similar depressed gaze, some even sniffling and drying their eyes as they picked at their food. Their faces, both young and old, blended together in a sea of sorrow.

And for a moment, Levi swore he could feel their pain like it was his own.

Levi couldn't take it any longer. He began to feel dizzy as though his entire world had collapsed around him. He stood up, rushing toward the door. Everyone watched as he left, slamming the door shut behind him. He paced outside and breathed in the fresh air.

My people did this, Levi thought. *They've tortured, killed, and destroyed homes. How can I justify this? How can I go back to Cyrus and help him kill Emilia after hearing their stories?*

He felt his cheek get wet and thought it was raining. But when he looked up at the sky, it was clear. He touched his cheek and pulled his hand away, realizing it was a tear.

He brushed it away. If his brother saw him showing emotion...

"Levi, are you all right?" Emilia asked, exiting the home behind him. She placed a hand on his forehead and checked for a fever.

"No," Levi replied, honestly. "I don't think I am."

Emilia sighed. "It's hard to hear their stories, isn't it? To see what the vampires have done? It was difficult for me too. But we can make things right—I know we can. It'll just take some time. Are you ready to go back inside yet, or do you need a moment?"

"I'm all right. Let's go back inside—only so the others don't worry."

When they had returned inside, walking toward the crowded table, Samantha looked up at them. "You two okay?"

"I'm fine," Levi lied, taking his seat.

Emilia clinked her glass as she turned to the others. "If I could have your attention, please. I'm sure you're all wondering why we're here, yes? Why we've brought the miners with us?"

The crowd nodded.

"Levi and I have come with a proposition," Emilia began, "one that could change the world. We're starting Allegiant—a militia against the vampires. We plan to buy some land and teach about the vampires while training recruits. To fight and kill them all."

"My father and the miners and I have already joined. How could we not?" Samantha said, glancing around the table. "Emilia and Levi are confident they can train us—teach us how to protect ourselves against these vampires. And after Levi killed a vampire today, saving our lives, I'm confident they can."

The room turned silent. Levi could tell they were afraid to join—afraid to get hurt. The smell of fear and despair was so strong, it nearly made him dizzy again.

"Will you kill them all?" Billy asked. "Can you...can you make them pay for what they did to my Momma and Papa?"

Emilia bent down beside Billy, placing a hand on his shoulder. "Every last one."

"Then it's settled," Gwendolyn said. "We'll join you—not just because it's the right thing to do, but because we have nothing left to live for. I don't know how much help I can be as an old woman, but I'll do whatever you ask."

"We'll need a chef," Emilia said, "and the children can do some chores to help out. In Allegiant, everyone has a place."

"To Allegiant," a miner said, lifting his glass, "and to giving these vampires a bloody death."

Everyone raised their glasses, clinking them together. Emilia looked at Levi and grinned.

A young girl with pigtails turned to Samantha. "Will you play for us?"

Samantha smiled, pulling out her lute. "You know, I've had a melody spinning in my head all day. Let's see if I can put something together, hmm? For Allegiant."

As Samantha started plucking her lute, everyone listened to the words of her song:

"Hush, little child, don't you cry
I've come to tell you something that'll dry
*   your eyes.*
Hush, little child, don't despair
Hope has been born, a hero is there.
It's a name they'll sing forevermore
Until the end of time, after the last war.
Our lands, we will reclaim
We will heal the grief and pain.
In the darkness, a revolution came
Allegiant is the name.
Allegiant is the name..."

Soon, all the miners had joined, singing the Allegiant song at the top of their lungs. Even Emilia and Levi began to sing, unable to resist. It suddenly hit Levi—the irony of singing a song about his people's downfall. Cyrus would've thought he'd gone insane if he could see him now.

Samantha continued to play the lute, humming the tune under her breath after the singing had stopped. Levi and Emilia helped Gwendolyn clear the table and wash the dishes. It was getting late so some of the children went to bed, sleeping on cots in the back of the cabin. The adults stayed awake, chatting about Allegiant and sharing their hopes for the future.

Edmund walked over to Levi and Emilia. "Can I speak to you both? In private?" They nodded, following Edmund outside. When they were alone, the old man sighed. "I don't mean to dampen spirits around here, but...someone has to say it. How will you train these people? And where? Nothing's free in our world, you know. We'll need land, equipment, food, supplies...there's a lot to do."

"There is. And Levi promised he'd get us the gold to do it,"

Emilia said, her eyes sparkling when she looked at him. "I know he'll find a way."

"Oh, will he?" Edmund glanced at Levi. "And how does he plan to do that?"

Levi shrugged. "Well, I'm not sure yet—"

"Lovely," Edmund muttered sarcastically. "I knew this was all too good to be true. You just gave those people in there false hope, you know. You promised them protection without a damn plan."

"We're not without a plan," Levi argued. "It'll all work out."

"I hope so," Edmund said, turning toward the door. "Because those kids in there are counting on us. And if we can't fulfil our promise, I ain't gonna be the one to break it to them."

He walked back into the cabin, leaving Emilia and Levi alone in the silence. They stared out at the markets as the sun began to set. People scurried home, dragging their children along.

"Edmund's right, you know," Emilia said quietly. "All we have is an idea with no gold to back it up. Oh, I knew I should've married Lord Tristan. It would've been a surefire way of making this happen."

"Don't say that," Levi said, turning to Emilia. "You wouldn't have been happy with him, and you know it."

Emilia scoffed. "Who cares about what I want right now, Levi? Sacrificing my happiness is a small price to pay for saving the world. Give me one good reason why I shouldn't go back to Lord Tristan, throw myself at his feet, and beg him to marry me to get access to his gold?"

Levi took a moment to think, looking across the way at The Cauldron. Despite the threat of nightfall, he could still hear the sounds of beer tankards clinking, people laughing and talking, and cards getting dealt.

And that was when it hit him.

"What do you know about Raging Tides?" Levi asked. "Do you know the rules?"

Emilia nodded. "I do. I had a patient who was very good at it, and he taught me as payment for treating his wounds. Why do you ask?"

"Because," Levi said, dragging Emilia toward The Cauldron, "I just figured out how we'll get the gold to start Allegiant."

CHAPTER

TEN

The tavern had mostly cleared out for the night, with peasants scurrying home before they could become the next meal for the vampires. But as Levi and Emilia entered, they found the pirates still sitting at the table, playing cards and drinking.

Mickey the bartender walked over, carrying empty tankards. "You folks should get going now, don't you think? Head on back to your ship? These streets ain't safe at night, not even for pirates."

Captain Gem scoffed. "We'll keep playing as long as we want, barkeep. Just keep those drinks flowing."

If it were anyone else, Mickey would've argued. But seeing as it was Captain Gem and the very dangerous Black Flag pirate group, he just sighed and returned to cleaning up the bar.

"You two can't be in here," he said, noticing Levi and Emilia. "It's closing time."

"We'll be quick, I promise," Levi told him. "We're here to gamble. We'll give you a cut of the profits if we win."

"You'd better," Mickey muttered. "I ain't risking walking home at night without a big incentive."

As Levi tried to walk over to the pirate table, Emilia grabbed his arm and held him back. "You can't be serious," she whispered. "You'll never win—especially against them. You've never even played before!"

"It's why I have you," Levi said with a wink. "You can give me some pointers. Maybe we'll get lucky."

"Look, the pirates haven't seen us yet," Emilia said, glancing over Levi's shoulder at them. "We should leave while we still can. If we piss those pirates off, the vampires will be the least of our worries. Trust me."

"Well, we can't leave. The only other option to get gold is you marrying Lord Tristan—and I won't let that happen. Besides, I've fought vampires. These pirates can't be any harder."

"You'd be surprised. I heard they killed a man for looking at them the wrong way." Emilia shook her head. "Levi, it's getting late. We should get back to the farm. If we get stuck on these streets at night..."

"I'm not afraid of the night streets. If we get ambushed, I'll protect you—don't worry."

Emilia looked skeptical, raising an eyebrow, but Levi's voice didn't waver. When Emilia realized he wasn't backing down, she sighed and nodded. "Fine. But I still think this is a bad idea."

"Noted."

The tavern door opened behind them. Mickey's head shot up from the bar, frowning. "Hey, no more customers. We're closing up."

Samantha entered, still plucking at her lute with a grin. "Make an exception?"

"Only for you, Sam," Mickey said, cleaning the bar. "You're lucky your music brings in so much gold, girl."

As she walked over to them, Levi frowned. "Samantha? What are you doing here?"

"I overheard what my father said to you," Samantha replied. "Although he can be crude at times, he has a point. You two look like the kind of people who won't give up, so I had a feeling you'd come to the tavern to gamble. It's the only place to make fast gold. Gold we need for Allegiant."

"Do you think Levi can win?" Emilia asked.

Samantha shrugged, reaching for another stack of cards behind the bar. She began shuffling them. "Guess we'll find out soon enough, huh?"

Levi took a deep breath and walked up to the pirate table. They paid no attention to him, fully immersed in their alcohol and card game. He cleared his throat and leaned over their table.

"Excuse me, Black Flag?" he asked. "Can I have a moment of your time?"

They paid no attention to him. Levi looked back at Samantha and Emilia, frowning.

"They can be a little selective with whom they talk to. Prideful, even," Samantha whispered. "You might have to prove yourself."

"That's insane," Levi muttered, tapping Captain Gem on the shoulder. His other hand rested on the table. "Excuse me, but I need to talk to—"

Captain Gem removed her dagger, stabbing it onto the table. It missed Levi's hand by an inch. She turned, her eyes falling on Levi with a glare. Their table turned quiet as the pirates waited for Captain Gem's orders.

"Yeah? What do you want?" she asked. "Why the hell are you touching me?"

"I want to join your game," Levi said. "I need to make some gold."

The entire table laughed. It burned Levi's ears, angering him.

"And what makes you think we'd want to play with you?" Captain Gem asked, turning her back on him. "I'm only gonna tell you this once, stranger—piss off. I'm not in the mood."

Levi removed the dagger from the table, then cut his hand with it. Black blood dribbled down his palm. His face twisted into a grimace, the silver from the dagger burning like acid.

"I'm not from around here," Levi said, showing the pirates his strange black blood. "I come from a faraway place you've never heard of. That pique your curiosity?"

"Hmm," Captain Gem muttered, glancing at his blood. "Never seen someone bleed black before. You got some kind of plague or something?"

Levi shook his head. "No plague—I'm clean. My apothecary, Emilia, can confirm that. As I said, I come from faraway. My people are...different. *Very* different."

Captain Gem shrugged. "All right, I'm intrigued. Take a seat, foreigner. What are you betting?"

Levi had no money, only a gold ring on his finger. One given to him by Cyrus long ago. The pain of parting with something so sentimental tugged at his heart, but he had no choice. These were desperate times.

"I'll wager this," Levi said, gesturing at the ring. "Is this enough?"

"You're off to a good start." Captain Gem's eyes raked over the ring. "Got anything else to sweeten the pot?"

With nothing else, Levi glanced at Emilia. She looked hesitant to hand over her gold, but sighed and reached into her pocket. She pulled out a few measly gold coins and placed them on the table. The pirates looked around at one another, blinking.

"Sorry," Emilia muttered. "Most patients can't pay me for

my services, and all the gold from the farm goes to Lord Tristan."

"That's it?" Captain Gem asked. "You'll need a bigger pot to play with us, foreigner. Where's the fun if the risk isn't high?"

"It's all I have," Levi said. "But I promise you, it'll be a good game—"

"No deal," Captain Gem muttered. "Now get out of here before I stick my dagger someplace else."

Levi sighed, rising to his feet when Samantha stepped forward. "Allow me."

She reached into the pocket of her green cloak, removing several pouches of gold. She placed them down on the table and the pirates' eyes went wide. Even Emilia and Levi couldn't believe it.

"Where did you get all that?" Emilia asked.

"From working the tavern and playing songs for the villagers," Samantha replied, shrugging. "This is everything I've been saving. I was planning to spend it on the people back home."

"You should. Think of all the food you could buy for the needy," Emilia said. "Don't your people need it more?"

"Relax, Emilia." A mysterious glint twinkled in Samantha's eyes. "I have faith in Levi that he'll win this and make our gold back. Double, in fact. Don't you?"

Emilia looked hesitant as Captain Gem snorted. "Whatever you say. But all betting is final—you can't take it back when you lose. Sure you still want in?"

Samantha nodded. "Levi will play."

Captain Gem shuffled the cards, grinning as she placed them down on the table. "Haven't played with a foreigner in a long time, but gold is gold, as they say. Can't wait to add a new sail to our ship. Maybe it'll be coated in diamonds?"

The pirates chuckled. *The captain's smug*, Levi thought. *Now I have to beat her.*

"This is my first time playing," Levi said as he sat down. "Is it okay if my associates tell me the rules?"

Captain Gem shrugged. "Sure, why not? You'll still lose anyway."

Levi noticed Captain Gem was only dealing for two players. "What about your pirates? Aren't you going to deal them in, too?"

"No, I've decided I want you all to myself. I'm going all in and upping the stakes."

Levi's eyes widened as Captain Gem dragged a large stack of gold coins to the center of the table. There was more than enough to feed their army and buy a large section of land, maybe even some luxuries.

"I see those greedy eyes," Captain Gem teased. "Don't fool yourself, foreigner—this gold won't be yours."

Levi bit his tongue, holding back a taunt of his own. Samantha winked at him as she took a seat to his left and Emilia sat to his right.

The card game began. Emilia and Samantha whispered the rules in his ears—all about the seven unique cards. Levi learned about the pirate, sea monster, mermaid, ship, tsunami, parrot, and the rare treasure card. There was only one treasure card in the deck, and Levi doubted he'd get lucky enough to see it, but it meant an automatic win.

It reminded Levi a lot of poker. They even had something similar to flushes and a full house. You played with seven cards in your hand, and if you drew all pirate, ship, parrot, or sword cards, you would win—in that order. The sea monster, mermaid, and tsunami cards had negative impacts, and you could lose the entire game if you acquired more than four of each. Every time Captain Gem looked at him, Levi flashed his eyes red, trying to distract her. She narrowed her eyes at him and continued playing.

"Your turn," Captain Gem said. "We're almost at the end. Can't wait to take all your gold, foreigner."

But when Levi drew the next card, his eyes widened. The rare treasure card was looking up at him. He placed it on the table and looked up at Captain Gem. She was speechless, just like the other pirates.

"I guess I won," he said, laying his hand down. "The treasure card is rare, right? An automatic win?"

Captain Gem glanced at the pot of gold coins on the table, then back up at Levi. She slammed her cards down, removing the sword from her scabbard. As she rose to her feet, aiming her sword at Levi, the other pirates did the same. Emilia, Levi, and Samantha took a step back with wide eyes.

"You cheated!" Captain Gem cried. "There's no way you could be this lucky—not on your first game."

"Ever hear of beginner's luck?" Levi asked, holding up his hands. "I didn't cheat. I followed all the rules. And besides, don't you think you would've seen me cheating?"

"I don't care how you did it, but I know you rigged the deck somehow," Captain Gem growled. "I won't let you take my gold —not like this. Black Flag, get these cheaters. Make 'em all bleed!"

Mickey ducked behind the bar, hiding as a brawl broke out. Levi shoved Emilia and Samantha back, shielding them as he grabbed a sword from a nearby pirate that swung at his face. With his vampire strength, he wrestled the sword away, kicking the pirate to his knees.

One by one, the pirates came at him—jabbing their swords in his direction. Levi dodged every attack, turning them on the pirates instead. No one could overpower him. When every pirate had fallen, panting and bleeding on the floor, Captain Gem approached Levi with her sword held high.

She glanced down at the pirates, her eyes wide at how fast Levi had taken them down. Captain Gem hesitated. Levi knew he could kill her easily, but he was sick of all the fighting.

"I didn't come here to kill anyone," Levi said. "I came here to win gold. You know why?"

"I don't care what you peasants spend your gold on," Captain Gem muttered.

"You should, though. We're starting a militia called Allegiant. You know about all those strange attacks at night?"

"Of course. How could I not? It's all the townspeople talk about."

"And for good reason. Everyone's scared," Levi continued. "I have a proposition for you. If you're willing to listen, that is?"

Captain Gem raised an eyebrow. "What kind of proposition?"

"One you should take if you value your life," Levi replied, gesturing at the floor. "Look at your pirates. I took them down and barely broke a sweat. I've fought those night creatures—vampires—the same way. You know I could kill you right here, don't you?"

Captain Gem lowered her sword. "I'm listening. You still haven't told me your proposal."

"It's simple. Join Allegiant," Levi replied. "It could be worth your while. Once people realize how good Allegiant is at protecting this city, they'll be generous with their donations. We might be willing to share some of the profits. You're obviously talented fighters, and we need people like you if we want to stop these beasts."

Captain Gem glanced down at her wounded pirates again, pausing. "Get up. All of you."

With groans, the pirates rose to their feet. Levi could smell their blood oozing from their wounds. But for the first time, their blood repulsed him. He found it odd. *Maybe I'm just getting used to animal meat instead,* he thought.

"You're a good fighter. A true warrior," Captain Gem said, looking back at Levi. "And you play a mean game of Raging Tides. Perhaps *I* should be the one offering *you* an invitation to join my crew. You ever think about sailing?"

Just another thing he had never done. There were so many possibilities, so many paths in life that were cut off when he became a vampire. It made him want to scream.

Levi shook his head. "As fun as that sounds, Allegiant needs me. What do you say?"

Emilia and Samantha held their breath behind him. However they expected the card game to play out, they certainly didn't foresee Levi offering an invitation to the most dangerous gang of pirates. But with the Black Flag on their side, it'd only make them more formidable—much more than the miners and villagers.

"You drive a hard bargain. Promises of gold, fame, and fighting?" Captain Gem cracked a smile. "How could we refuse?"

The pirates laid their weapons down in a show of good faith. Emilia and Samantha sighed in relief. Even Levi smiled, then a strange feeling tugged at his chest. When Cyrus turned against Allegiant, Black Flag would die—just like everyone else they had just recruited. The smile disappeared from Levi's face at the thought.

"Here, take it," Captain Gem said, dragging the tower of gold coins toward Levi's side of the table. "You're lucky I'm feeling generous. Now what happens?"

"We'll need to buy land for a stronghold," Emilia said, stepping forward. "We can demand an audience with Lord Tristan tomorrow morning. But for now, I think it's best if we return home before it gets dark."

Captain Gem nodded. "Very well. My crew and I will be on our ship, the *Marauder*, if you need us. We're the giant red vessel at the docks. Tomorrow morning, we'll meet here before we proposition this Lord Tristan. Oh, and my name's Rosalie Reyes, by the way. Only my friends know my real name, so you should feel honored. I'm looking forward to working with you, foreigner. To seeing if betting all my gold was worth the adventure. If not, well...this is what I've got this for."

Rosalie patted her sword before leaving the tavern with her men. Once they had vanished, Emilia threw herself into Levi's arms. He smiled and hugged her back.

"You did it, Levi," she cried. "I wasn't sure it could be done, but you won us gold *and* got the Black Flag on our side. Gosh, it sounds insane to say it out loud."

"I had nothing to do with it, really. You two coached me through the card game." Levi pulled back, glancing at the table. "And it was sheer luck I pulled that rare treasure card."

Samantha chuckled. "Don't know if I'd call it that."

Levi crossed his arms. "What did you do?"

Samantha pointed at the underside of the table. When Levi looked, he realized there was a hole there, large enough to slip a card through. As Levi turned back to Samantha, she had the widest grin on her face. He sighed at her and waited for an explanation.

"I stole the rare treasure card from another deck," she began, "then added it to the bottom through the hole to match your turn. I had to let the game play out at first—I couldn't make you look too lucky. Don't worry, this wasn't my first time cheating. Working here's made me think of all kinds of creative ways to win."

"Are you insane?" Emilia asked, glaring at Samantha. "Your cheating could've gotten us killed!"

"It all worked out, didn't it?" Samantha shrugged. "Besides, do you honestly think I'd part with my gold that easily? I had to make sure Levi would win."

"Well, don't tell the pirates that," Levi muttered. "We need their support."

Mickey lifted his head from behind the bar, glancing around at the three of them. "Is it...is it safe to come out now?"

Levi nodded, placing a few gold coins down on the bar. "It's safe. Here's some gold for your trouble."

Mickey's eyes lit up when he noticed the coins, pocketing them immediately. "Hey, thanks. And good luck with Allegiant. I hope to God you can make our streets safe again."

"So do I." Samantha glanced out the window at the darkening sky. "Well, it's getting late. I'd better get home. I'll tell my father and the others what happened. They'll be so happy to hear about your winnings. See you tomorrow, you two."

As Samantha left, Emilia and Levi collected their coins and followed. They got onto Margaret and wasted no time galloping down the street. The markets were empty now—vacated for the night. Levi didn't sense any vampires in the distance, but he didn't want to take any chances for Emilia's sake.

"I'm happy we got the gold, but...something's been bothering me, Levi," Emilia began. "At the ball...those vampires said some strange things to you."

Levi tensed. "Oh?"

"One said you didn't taste right. Then that female vampire said she wasn't the only surprise at the ball, implying you," Emilia murmured. "And I've been watching your fighting skills. You fight well. Almost like the vampires."

"Well, it's, uh, like I told you before. We have vampires back home," Levi stammered. "I've studied them—learned to fight as they do. And I'm just as confused about what they said. Maybe my blood tastes different because I'm a foreigner?"

"Perhaps," Emilia said, yawning. "I don't mean to sound as

though I'm accusing you of anything. I was only curious. You've been a good friend, Levi. I don't think I could've started Allegiant without you."

"Oh, I'm sure that's not true."

"I think it is. Thank you, Levi. Truly."

What have I done? Levi briefly wondered. *I created the very thing I was sent to destroy.*

It was certainly a funny turn of events. But any twinge of worry or regret were drowned out by his growing feelings for Emilia.

They said nothing for the rest of the ride, making it back to Rutherford Farm. When Levi directed their horse into the stable, Emilia jumped off. "Anyway, I'm glad we made it home in one piece. Some aren't so lucky. You should get your rest for tomorrow, Levi—it'll take lots of strength to face Lord Tristan again. In the meantime, I'll tell Peeta and Alana what happened. They'll be so happy to know we'll be getting vengeance for Dawn."

"So will Cyrus," Levi lied. "Goodnight, Emilia."

As soon as Levi walked away from Emilia and entered the small shack he shared with his brother, Cyrus jumped to his feet from the blanket on the floor. "There you are! I've been waiting all afternoon. Where the hell have you been? And what's with all that gold?"

"I helped Emilia get enough to money to buy some land," Levi said, placing it down on the nearby table. "She thinks it's for Allegiant,"

Cyrus whistled. "Damn. You've been busy, haven't you? Whatever makes Emilia think we're on her side, I guess. Can't wait to see the look on her face when she learns who we really are."

Levi didn't say anything. The idea of betraying Emilia didn't sit well with him, but he kept his mouth shut.

Cyrus gestured at the door. "Anyway, we'd better get going. Time to meet Slaughter and the others. What an honor it'll be to work with our ancestors. Shit, I'm so excited."

As Cyrus opened the door, Levi sighed and followed. He realized that, for the first time in his life, he dreaded meeting more of his people. More vampires.

It was like Emilia and the humans were starting to feel more like his own.

CHAPTER

ELEVEN

Levi borrowed one of the horses from the stables for their journey into town. He hushed the horse when it began to neigh, not wanting to wake anyone in the cabin. The sun had long set and left the sky shrouded in darkness.

As they trotted to the edge of the field, Levi sensed someone's presence—a human heartbeat approaching. It was Emilia's scent. It was too late to hide, so all Levi could do was prepare an excuse.

Emilia stood behind him, her face twisted in confusion. She wore her nightgown and slippers with her luscious hair cascading onto her shoulders. "Levi? Cyrus? What are you two doing?"

"Going for a midnight ride," Cyrus lied. "We couldn't sleep."

"Sorry if we woke you," Levi added.

"Oh, I see. Here I thought you were leaving with the gold," Emilia said with a little laugh. "I couldn't sleep either. I'm worried about tomorrow—about asking Lord Tristan for land."

Levi shook his head. "He won't refuse us, Emilia. We've got enough gold to persuade him."

Emilia sighed. "I suppose you're right. Still…I can't help but worry. We both know he's a very stubborn man."

"We'll find a way. We got the gold, and we thought that wasn't possible at first, right? We can do this too."

Levi could feel Cyrus's gaze on him.

Emilia nodded. "I hope so. Anyway, you know it's dangerous to go out during the night. Where are you going? There won't be any shops open now."

"We're heading out for some air," Cyrus lied. "We won't be long."

"Can I come with you?"

Levi looked back at Cyrus, his eyebrow raised in concern. But his brother didn't miss a beat. "No offense, but taking a ride after dark is a brotherly tradition."

Emilia nodded. "Oh, I understand. Family time is so important. I should get back to bed and try to rest anyway. Have fun on your ride. And please, don't get hurt."

After the brothers bid Emilia good night, and she walked inside the cabin, Cyrus sneered. "Nosy bitch. She'll get what's coming to her soon enough."

Levi cleared his throat, flicking the reins. "Let's just find these vampires before we draw more attention to ourselves."

"And if we're lucky, recruit them to our mission," Cyrus added. It made Levi's stomach twist.

As they rode into the markets, the streets were empty, dark, and quiet. All the townspeople had returned home, boarding their doors and windows. Cyrus sniffed the air.

"Can you smell that? The fear?" Cyrus grinned. "It's my favorite scent. That's the power we have over mortals, Brother."

It made Levi ill. His stomach churned, his hands trembled. He cleared his throat. "Right. See any of the vampires yet?"

"Not yet." Cyrus jumped off the horse. "But we're supposed to meet behind the shops. More secluded. Follow me."

As Levi followed Cyrus behind a row of shops, he looked over his shoulder. "Is this even safe? How do we know these vampires won't kill us?"

"Because it goes against the Vampire Commandments," Cyrus shot back. "Vampires know better than to kill their own. We're teammates—family. No vampire would ever harm another."

Guilt ate away at Levi like a mouse nibbling on cheese. He *had* killed a vampire—and realized he enjoyed it. Although he hated keeping secrets from his brother, he had no choice.

"You sense that?" Cyrus whispered. "Movement. Their heartbeats are too irregular to be humans."

Before Levi had a chance to reply, he heard footsteps approaching. When he turned around, there they stood—the vampires from the castle attack. Night Temptress and Slaughter led a dozen vampires. They had their fangs out, sharp and gleaming under the moonlight. A terrible feeling twisted in the pit of Levi's stomach.

"Hey, glad you showed up," Cyrus said to the vampires. "We've got some important business to discuss."

"Not here," Slaughter said. "Anyone could see us. Let's talk in our lair—if you are who you claim to be."

"We are." Cyrus nodded. "No doubt about it. So, where's your lair?"

Slaughter chuckled. "You think we'd tell you—complete strangers we don't trust yet? Too risky."

Night Temptress turned to the vampires behind her. "Bloodborns, restrain them. Take them back to our lair."

"Restrain us?" Levi scoffed. "Now, wait a second. I didn't agree to—"

Before he had time to react, the vampires lunged at them. They placed dark sacks over their heads, blocking their sight. Levi couldn't see a thing and started to panic.

As he swung a fist, one vampire kneed him in the chest. Levi groaned and collapsed, falling to the ground. He felt the vampire grab him and pull him to his feet. Levi prepared to attack again, but they clasped shackles around his wrists. He heard the shackles tighten on Cyrus and feared for their lives.

"Don't fight them, Brother," Cyrus whispered. "They need to know they can trust us."

"But Cyrus—"

"It's okay, Lee. I know what I'm doing."

"No, he's smart to be concerned," Night Temptress said. "I wouldn't want someone to restrain me either. In combat, at least. But we must be certain you are who you say you are."

"Put them on the back of their horses," Slaughter ordered. "The more time we waste, the more the sun has a chance to rise. Hurry, let's get moving."

Levi felt himself ushered down the street, the vampires pushing him along. He could sense Cyrus beside him, which brought him a little comfort, but not much. He hated feeling so helpless—especially around primitive vampires. They were unpredictable.

A vampire helped him onto the back of his horse, then put Cyrus on another. Once they were ready, a vampire swung up behind him and Levi felt the animal starting to move. As the horse took off down the street, Levi hoped his brother hadn't led them to their deaths.

Levi listened to the hooves of the horses galloping down the street, trying to calm his shaky breathing. He couldn't do anything—not with his hands tied. When the horses came to a stop, he sighed in relief.

The vampire grabbed him and his brother, dragging him

through a muddy field. A chill ran up his spine as the breeze faded. When the bag lifted from his head, he looked around.

He and his brother stood in a dark, dingy cave. Water droplets fell from the ceiling and the entire place looked dirty. He spotted several coffins for the vampires in the back of the cave with pints of blood and raw meat.

"Where are we?" Levi asked, the shackles digging into his skin.

"Our lair," Slaughter said, entering the cave with Night Temptress by his side. "Welcome to the Bloodborn Order. This is where we hibernate during the day. I'm Slaughter, and this is my sister, Night Temptress."

"Hello," Night Temptress purred, looking at Levi. "A pleasure to meet you. And you are?"

"Levi. Levi Godfrey," he replied. "This is my brother, Cyrus."

"Levi." Night Temptress grinned. "I like that name."

"Thanks." Levi glanced outside the cave, noticing only one horse. "How did you all make it here so fast?"

"We're quick runners," Night Temptress said, standing inches away from Levi's face. "If you're a vampire as you claim, you should have that ability as well. Why would you even need a horse?"

"We're different from your kind," Cyrus said. "We lost speed as a power centuries ago. We gave it up to look more human— to help us hunt better. We even gained the ability to go out in the sun."

"Is that so?" Slaughter walked toward them, taking a long look at the brothers. "Is that why you look so different from us? The eyes, the blood? Even your fangs aren't as sharp. It's like you're a different breed of vampire altogether."

"We are. We're from the future," Cyrus replied. "The year 2130."

The vampires turned silent for a moment. And then they all broke out into hysterical laughter.

"Hey! We're telling the truth," Cyrus said, his face red with anger. "In the future, vampire hunters called Legionnaires have killed all our people. We traveled back in time using blood magic to kill Allegiant's leader. You know, to stop them from winning."

"We'd like to believe that," Night Temptress said, running a hand across Levi's face. Her sharp fingernails scratched his skin lightly. "But it sounds so far-fetched, doesn't it, Slaughter?"

Slaughter nodded. "It does. And we don't like liars. We're busy people, you see—we don't like when someone wastes our time. You're lucky we didn't kill you when we attacked the castle."

"I think you knew deep down inside that we're one of you," Cyrus said. "Come on—think back to the ball. We fought together and I kept up with you. It's because we *are* you—your descendants."

Slaughter shrugged. "So? Your fighting skills don't prove anything."

"Wait," Night Temptress said, looking back at Levi. "Perhaps there *is* some truth in what they say. When I bit this one, he tasted...different. I could sense something inside of him. A hunger that only vampires have."

"Hmm." Slaughter paused. "If you truly are vampires, why haven't you killed this Allegiant leader yet? Why haven't you returned to the future already?"

Cyrus laughed. "You really don't know why? Like I told my brother, killing her would be too easy. And a waste. We plan to infiltrate Allegiant and make it crumble in front of her eyes. Play with our victim before the kill. Like a spider would."

Slaughter nodded, a smirk growing. "All right, that does

sound like fun. But what do you want from us? Why did you want to meet?"

"We want to join you—the Bloodborn Order, you called ourselves. That way, you get to have a little fun with the woman who kills all our people too."

"Wait a moment. There's something I don't understand. We're vampires—creatures of the night," Night Temptress said, glancing between them. "We have power, strength, immorality. If you're like us, why did you allow Allegiant to gain power? You future vampires sound weak."

Cyrus sighed. "It wasn't our fault. You don't understand the future—how widespread Allegiant is. They had training schools all over the world, even technology to help them. Our only hope of winning the war was to travel back in time. To kill Allegiant before it has a chance to grow."

"Hmm. And the leader of this Allegiant," Night Temptress continued, looking at Levi, "was she the one you were with at the castle? The red-headed human?"

Levi didn't say anything. Something inside of him didn't feel right telling the Order anything about Emilia.

"That's her," Cyrus said. "Her name's Emilia Rutherford. We've done well so far—we're staying on her farm. I think she even sees Levi as a friend. The betrayal will be as sweet as blood. So, what do you say? Will you help us?"

Night Temptress looked back at Slaughter. "We need some time to discuss this. Excuse us for a moment."

As the vampires sauntered away, talking quietly in the corner, Levi turned to Cyrus. "So? Do you think they'll help us?"

"I don't know," Cyrus whispered back, his eyes on the group. "I'd hate to kill our own, but...if they turn against us, we'll have to fight our way out of here. Our mission is too important to screw up."

As the Bloodborn Order continued to whisper, Levi heard

footsteps approaching. Someone in a long cloak stepped through the entrance to the cave. Both Levi and Cyrus feared it was someone in Allegiant—that one of the recruits had seen and followed them. Or maybe it was Emilia herself who had lied about going back to bed.

"Intruder!" Cyrus cried.

The visitor lowered their hood, revealing Frederic Bors—the other employee at Emilia's apothecary shop.

"Relax," Night Temptress said, glaring at Cyrus over her shoulder. "He's one of us. Come in, Doctor."

"One of us?" Levi frowned in confusion.

Frederic glanced at Slaughter. "What are they doing here?"

"They claim they're vampires from the future," Slaughter replied, "and that they've come to kill Emilia Rutherford, the one who destroys the vampires in the year 2130. Can you believe that?"

Frederic paused. "Emilia? Hmm. She was always passionate about protecting people. Their story isn't as impossible as you think, Slaughter."

"Wait a second," Levi said, blinking. "You're a vampire?"

Frederic nodded. "In the flesh."

"But...I've seen you in the sunlight. You didn't burn up like the others. How is that possible?"

"Through my experiments, of course," Frederic replied. "It's taken me many years to make progress. I'm finally getting results. But my serums still have a long way to go—sunlight makes me weak after a while, and I'm not satisfied with it yet to give it to the other vampires."

Cyrus gasped. "You wouldn't happen to be the Bloody Doctor, would you?"

Frederic grinned. "Indeed. That's what they call me. How did you know?"

"Yeah. Who's the Bloody Doctor?" Levi asked, glancing at his brother.

"I read about him in a history book. He's the one who evolved the vampires. His serums make us immune to sunlight."

Frederic walked over to Levi and Cyrus, removing the shackles from their wrists. Slaughter rushed over, his face twisting into a snarl. "What are you doing? We haven't decided if we trust them or not!"

"I do," Frederic said, tossing the shackles aside. "They're telling the truth—they're from the future. How else would they know my nickname? How else would they have evolved?"

"Exactly. And sorry to break it to you," Cyrus began, "but Emilia kills you herself after you evolve the vampires."

"Then it's a good thing you're here," Frederic replied. "Please, take a look around. This is as much your home as it is ours."

Levi walked over to the coffins, running his fingers along the fabric. He'd heard only rumors of coffins but had never seen one in his life. They didn't need them in the future—they had no reason to sleep during the daytime anymore. Everything was so different here, so foreign.

At the end of the cave, Levi noticed a long tunnel. He turned to Frederic in confusion. "Hey, where does this lead?"

"To the mines," Frederic replied. "We dug that tunnel ourselves to get around town easier. I'm mostly immune to sunlight, but the others aren't. Not yet."

So that's how the vampire got in, Levi thought. *He had a secret entrance. The miners need to know about this.*

"A vampire went through there yesterday," Slaughter said. "His name is Loner. As the name suggests, he likes to keep to himself. He never really fit in among the Order. Anyway, we haven't seen him since. You know what happened to him?"

Levi shook his head. "Uh, no clue, sorry."

Cyrus glanced at his brother, raising an eyebrow. Levi avoided his eyes.

"Too bad. Anyway, can you tell us about the future?" Frederic asked, leaning against the wall of the cave. "I'm curious."

"Well, we don't live in caves anymore," Cyrus replied. "We lived in a bunker, hiding from Allegiant. But our world was war-torn—dangerous for vampires. We didn't see much of it after we went into hiding."

"A pity," Frederic muttered. "I thought I evolved the vampires to strengthen them. Not for them to go extinct. What a bloody tragedy. Pardon the pun."

"Who knew we became such weaklings in the future?" Slaughter asked, glancing at Levi and Cyrus. "If the Bloody Doctor believes you, we do too—but you still have to prove yourselves."

Levi scoffed. "How? We're clearly vampires."

"Shut up," Cyrus muttered at his brother. "Their lair, their rules. We need their help, remember?"

Slaughter nodded. "Precisely. We put every vampire through a ritual—a way to demonstrate their abilities. Are you ready?"

"Of course." Cyrus stood up straighter. "What do you need us to do?"

"Find and kill a human. Embrace your legacy—embrace what you are. And maybe we'll believe you."

"That doesn't sound too hard," Cyrus joked. "You sure this is a test?"

"It's difficult at night when the streets are empty," Night Temptress said. "And vampires can't go out in the sun. You can, but you can't risk killing someone during the day. Emilia might find out."

"Okay, you have a point. When do we leave?"

"Tonight," Slaughter said. "We've still got time before sunrise. We'll go with you—we could use a snack along the way."

"All right then. Me and my brother are in. Despite what you think about future vampires, we aren't weaklings. We'll show you."

"I'll come, too," Frederic said. "It'll be fascinating watching how the vampires of the future hunt."

As Levi followed his brother and vampires out of the cave, his stomach churned again. Could he really hunt down an innocent human and kill them? He had done it so many times before, but now? Now it just felt wrong.

As he went to get on his horse, Night Temptress grabbed Levi's hand. Her skin felt cold on his, not warm like Emilia's. She had long, black nails and veiny hands. He resisted the urge to recoil.

"Good luck," she purred. "Can't wait to see you in action."

She vanished down the street, following the other vampires in a blur. Levi almost wished he could move that fast. As he hoisted himself onto their horse, he heard Cyrus scoff behind him.

"Night Temptress seems to like you," Cyrus murmured. "I didn't get any credit for the fact that it was *my* idea to toy with Emilia first."

Levi chuckled. "Jealous?"

"No. Well, maybe a little."

"I'm not interested in Night Temptress, Brother. I wasn't interested in Raven either. You want her, go after her. She's not my type."

"But Emilia is, isn't she?"

"What?" Levi's head snapped back to look at him.

"Nothing, nothing," Cyrus muttered. "Let's just get this over with. The faster we impress these vamps, the faster we can get back to destroying Allegiant from the inside."

The vampires—or Bloodborns, as they preferred to call themselves—had already beaten Levi and Cyrus to the markets. As expected, the streets were still empty.

"Glad you made it," Night Temptress said to Levi when they arrived. "Now the real fun can begin."

"Doesn't look like there's much fun to be had," Cyrus mumbled, jumping off their horse. "What a ghost town."

"We told you it wouldn't be easy," Slaughter said. "We like it better when a helpless victim's walking down the street, but we'll have to switch things up tonight."

When Slaughter pulled out some matches from his pocket, Levi frowned. "What's that for?"

"For burning down someone's home, of course," Night Temptress purred, caressing Levi's bicep. "It's not enough to take a life—that's too easy. The fun part is watching everything they've worked for go up in flames, then luring them for the kill."

As the vampires grinned, Levi tried not to throw up.

"So, hurry up and choose a place," Slaughter said. "I'm getting antsy."

"There are so many to choose from," Cyrus murmured, glancing around the village. "So many sleeping, unsuspecting victims. Hmm."

Levi's eyes flicked to Cyrus. Would his brother agree to this savagery? Levi saw Edmund and Samantha's home in the distance and prayed they wouldn't choose that one.

"I think Levi should have the honor of choosing a target," Night Temptress said, much to Levi's relief. "Consider it a gift."

Cyrus turned around, growling. "Now, wait a second—"

"What happened to playing by their rules?" Levi asked his brother.

Cyrus glared at him but kept his mouth shut.

"Anything catch your eye, Levi?" Slaughter asked. "Which unlucky mortal should we drink from and burn tonight?"

Levi glanced at the vampires. They had all turned quiet—waiting to hear Levi's answer. He realized he couldn't do it, couldn't let an innocent die at their hands. He knew Emilia would hate him for it.

But he also knew they had to kill someone tonight. If he refused altogether, they'd know something was wrong with him—especially Cyrus, who already suspected something was up. So, he made his choice.

"Those bandits on the wanted sign," Levi said. "I want them dead."

"Who?" Cyrus asked, raising an eyebrow.

"We know who Levi's talking about. They're a mercenary group we've helped a few times," Slaughter replied. "They're humans—they steal from travelers and villagers. Why would you want them dead?"

Night Temptress nodded. "Yes, we've grown quite fond of those troublemakers. Why don't you choose someone else?"

Levi had to think of a lie—and fast.

"They...they attacked me," Levi said. "Robbed me too. I've been wanting revenge on them ever since."

"They did?" Cyrus looked surprised. "You never told me that. And we've been together this whole time—"

"It happened without you," Levi lied. "Then they ran off."

"Why didn't you kill them when it happened?" Fredric asked. "I would have."

"I couldn't. I was with Emilia at the time."

"Hmm. Perhaps the bandits had no idea you were a vampire," Frederic said, tapping his chin. "You were out in sunlight, weren't you? It's possible they thought you were a human. If they would've known you were a vampire, they would've left you alone. We have...an agreement, of sorts."

"Well, agreement or not, I've made my decision. They die tonight."

Slaughter crossed his arms over his leather duster. "I understand the need for revenge, but they're valuable to us. Pick someone else."

Cyrus nodded. "All right. May I suggest—"

"Night Temptress said I could choose," Levi interrupted, glaring at his brother. "Will she honor her promise or not?"

The vampires turned quiet again. Night Temptress sighed, looking back at Slaughter. "He's right, I did say Levi could choose."

"You don't need the bandits, anyway," Levi continued, trying to convince them. "With our help, we'll bring this village to its knees. And besides, they're mortals. They don't deserve your protection."

Slaughter thought for a moment. "You're right—we don't need them anymore, not with your ability to go out into the sunlight. Let's show them that our little partnership is over."

"Good. Now, do you know where they are?"

Night Temptress nodded. "They live down by the docks. Come—they won't be expecting us."

Levi and Cyrus got onto their horses again, following the vampires that sprinted down the road. As they made it to the docks, Levi noticed the red ship that belonged to the Black Flag pirates. He kept his head down, hoping that if they were still awake, they wouldn't recognize him.

The vampires came to a halt outside a small cabin. Levi could hear the sounds of cards shuffling and tankards clinking inside, reminding him of the tavern. The brothers hopped off their horses and waited for the vampires to make the first move.

"They're in here," Slaughter whispered. "I can hear their heartbeats. You ready?"

Everyone nodded, eager for the bloodshed to begin. Cyrus was already licking his lips.

Slaughter kicked the door down, sending it flying across the room. Levi and Cyrus followed the vampires inside the cabin, noticing the bandits sitting around playing a card game. There were less than a dozen men and women. They wore black leather jackets and gloves, trinkets and treasures lining the room. They looked up with wide eyes before they smiled.

"Slaughter," one of the bandits said, rising to his feet. "To what do we owe the pleasure?"

"We've come here to take revenge, Rocco," Slaughter said. "You attacked one of my kind."

As Slaughter gestured at Levi, Rocco narrowed his eyes at him. "What? That's crazy. I'd never attack one of you. I value our partnership."

"Hmm. You sure it was him?" Slaughter asked Levi, glancing back.

Levi didn't like lying, but he had no choice. A human had to die tonight—the brothers had to prove themselves. And killing criminals was the only way Levi could live with himself when it was over.

"Yeah, it was him," Levi said, working up the courage to look at Rocco. "He took my gold and beat me up."

"Hang on a minute. We steal from a lot of people, that's true," a female bandit said, rising to her feet. "But we'd remember you. I think you've got the wrong guys."

"Are you calling my own kind a liar?" Slaughter asked, balling his fists.

"No, of course not," Rocco said, backing up. "But—"

"Then, if you're not calling him a liar, you *did* attack him," Slaughter said, turning to the vampires. "Let's get 'em."

The vampires pounced on the bandits, taking chunks of flesh out of them and drinking from their necks. Some bandits tried to fight back, using their daggers and arrows, but the vampires moved too fast. Even Cyrus joined the fray—drinking from one of the burlier bandits. Levi stood off to the side, frozen.

He didn't want to feed. He didn't want *any* part of this.

While the vampires had their feast, Rocco watched the carnage with wide eyes. Then he turned, sprinting out the back door.

"He's getting away, the coward," Slaughter said, looking up from a dead bandit. He had red blood smeared across his mouth. "Levi, stop him!"

Levi forced himself to move. He chased the bandit through the back door, running along the empty docks. Rocco sprinted, panting heavily as he kept looking over his shoulder. Levi could feel his fear—it was palpable. He increased his speed to stay on Rocco's tail.

While looking back, Rocco tripped over a rock near the row of ships. He plummeted on the sand, landing with a thud. He groaned and looked back up at Levi who had finally reached him.

"You're...you're a vampire, too, right?" Rocco stammered. "One of Slaughter's people?"

"Yes," Levi replied, sadly. "Yes, I'm a vampire."

"Please," Rocco whispered. "Please don't kill me. I'm so sorry we ever attacked you. I'll do anything..."

Levi glanced over his shoulder, looking back at the cabin. The vampires and his brother were still inside, drinking blood to their heart's content. He glanced back at the bandit.

"Get up," Levi told him.

Rocco rose to his feet, his hands shaking. "What...what are you going to do to me?"

"Get out of here, Rocco. Now."

"You...you mean that?" Rocco hesitated. "This isn't some trick?"

Levi shook his head. "No trick—just start running and don't look back. But on two conditions."

Rocco nodded. "Anything, anything at all."

"No more criminal activities," Levi replied. "Leave the humans alone. Get a real job and make gold that way. And leave town—never show your face around here again."

"Sure, you got it. Anything you say."

"Good. Now, get going—hurry."

Levi watched as Rocco turned, attempting to run. But then he paused and looked back over his shoulder.

"If you're a vampire," Rocco began, "why did you spare me?"

"Hey, I told you to start running," Levi snarled. "Don't make me regret this."

Rocco nodded, disappearing beyond the forest that connected to the docks. Levi looked back at the cabin. Everyone inside was dead. He could smell their blood—once intoxicating, but now it made him feel queasy.

Levi leaned over the side of the docks and threw up into the water.

"Brother?" Cyrus asked, approaching the docks. "Are you all right?"

Levi wiped his mouth, struggling for an explanation. He could smell the death on his brother's breath, and it nearly made him sick again.

"The blood portal," Levi lied, still keeping his back turned to his brother. "I think it messed me up. I haven't felt good since we got here."

"Huh. Well, I feel fine," Cyrus said, placing a hand on Levi's shoulder. "Maybe your body just needs time to adjust. Come on, let's catch up with the others. They're waiting for us inside."

"No," Levi said, looking at his brother. "I...I don't want to go back inside that cabin. Not again."

Cyrus furrowed his eyebrows. "Why not?"

Much to Levi's relief, the door to the cabin opened. The vampires exited, drying their bloody mouths on their sleeves. The vampires noticed Levi and Cyrus by the docks and walked over with grins.

"What a night!" Slaughter said. "You chose well, Levi. Those bandits were delicious. A bit sad they aren't still alive to cause trouble, but I'm sure we'll manage just fine without them."

Night Temptress sniffed the air. "What's that smell?"

Levi didn't know what to say. He couldn't admit he had just vomited after smelling human blood.

"It's Rocco, the bandit," Cyrus lied. "He vomited on himself when he saw Levi chasing him. It was pretty funny, actually."

Levi gave Cyrus a sidelong glance. Why was his brother lying for him?

"Disgusting." Slaughter shuddered. "Glad I didn't drink from him. But where is his body?"

"I tossed him into the water," Levi lied, mustering the

courage to look Slaughter in the eyes. "Had to get rid of the evidence. If this was traced back to us, it'd look suspicious. We can't have Emilia finding out what we are. Not yet, anyway."

"Hmm. That's a good idea." Slaughter turned to the vampires. "Everyone—grab a body. Throw their remains into the ocean before someone comes sniffing."

Levi looked away as the vampires dragged all the dead bodies toward the water, tossing them over with loud splashes. Red blood decorated the ocean like food coloring. They placed rocks on top of the bodies, letting them sink to the bottom.

"Well, we both had a lot of fun tonight," Cyrus said, gesturing at his brother. "So, did we pass?"

Slaughter, Night Temptress, and Frederic looked at each other. Levi feared he and Cyrus had done something wrong. Did the others know he had thrown up? That he had let Rocco go?

"Let's head back to our cave where it's safer," Frederic said. "We can discuss it there."

As the vampires took off into the night, Levi and Cyrus got on the back of their horses. When they rode off toward the markets, the only way to get to their cave, Levi looked over his shoulder. He didn't see Rocco anywhere—the bandit had kept his promise of disappearing.

But Levi knew what this meant. Rocco was proof he was changing—finding his humanity again. If anyone found out, the vampires would kill him for sure. And his brother might not defend him next time.

As they passed through the markets, Levi smelled blood again. Swallowing the bile rising in his throat, he feared the worst. Had the vampires killed an innocent anyway?

But as they galloped closer, Levi looked down and gasped. It wasn't an innocent—it was a dead vampire on the ground. A beautiful one with blonde hair and sharp fangs.

"Belladonna," Night Temptress murmured, lingering above the vampire woman. "No, not you..."

"What happened?" Cyrus asked. "Who's Belladonna?"

"A vampire we know. You see, some of the vampires prefer to work on their own. They're still in the Bloodborn Order, just independent," Slaughter explained. "Belladonna was one of them—much like Loner. And now she's dead."

Levi jumped off the horse, looking at her violet-spattered body closer. He thought maybe Emilia was responsible for the vampire's death, but then he noticed the silver bullet glittering in the woman's chest wound. As the vampires mourned one of their own, Levi stepped back, pulling his brother aside.

"Belladonna wasn't killed by a primitive weapon," he whispered. "She was killed by a silver bullet—something that hasn't even been invented yet."

Cyrus nodded. "I know, I saw. How is that possible?"

"I have no idea. It doesn't make any sense."

"We can't leave the body here," Night Temptress said, glancing around at her people. "A foul human might tamper with it. Vampires—take her back to the caves. We'll lay her to rest there."

Levi and Cyrus followed the vampires back to the caves, watching as they sprinted while carrying the dead woman. Levi worried about the murder the entire way—who her killer was, where they had vanished to, and how they had a silver bullet from the future.

Something wasn't right.

Slaughter gestured for Levi and Cyrus to enter the cave. The vampires placed the woman's body in one of the coffins, then closed the lid. They decorated the coffin with human blood to honor her memory.

"We must find the human who did this," Night Temptress said. "Belladonna was a good friend and a fine hunter. She needs to be avenged."

"All in good time, my dear," Frederic said, patting her shoulder. "The vampire hunters will die soon enough. That's what Levi and Cyrus have come here to do, yes?"

Cyrus nodded. "Yeah—and more vampires will die if you don't help us. We can stop the genocide of our people. But we can't do it alone."

"Then you've been accepted into the Bloodborn Order," Frederic said with a smile. "Congratulations. We were very impressed by what we saw tonight—especially you, Cyrus."

A year ago, Levi would've been jealous of his brother becoming the favorite. Now Levi found it a relief that he was so different from him and the others.

Cyrus grinned. "Thank you. You know, it's been a while since I drank human blood. All Emilia feeds us is raw animal meat."

Frederic placed a hand around his shoulder. "Well, no more of that. Things are about to change, Cyrus—for the better. Now, for my experiments, would it be all right if I took some of your DNA? You come from the future. It could save me a lot of time with my research."

"If it'll help you speed up our evolution, absolutely," Cyrus said with a nod. "We'll be unstoppable when all the vampires are immune to sunlight."

Cyrus held out his arm for Frederic to take some blood, then the doctor stabbed his syringe into his vein. Levi realized he had no choice, so he allowed Frederic to take his DNA too.

"By the way," Cyrus said to Slaughter, "I'm a huge fan of yours. You've killed the most humans in history, you know. You're something of a legend."

Slaughter grinned. "Always nice to meet a fan. With your help, I'll kill even more."

Levi looked at his brother in disgust. How could he worship a ruthless killer like Slaughter? He needed to get out of the cave, needed to clear his head.

"We should head back to the farm," Levi said. "It'll be morning in a few hours."

"Leaving so soon?" Night Temptress purred, caressing Levi's bicep again. "I was hoping you would stay a while."

"Uh, as flattered as I am," Levi began, trying not to insult her, "we've already been gone too long. If Emilia finds out—"

"Yes, yes—everything will be ruined. I get it," Night Temptress huffed. "But whenever you have some free time... remember that my coffin can fit two."

Levi gulped. "I'll, uh, keep that in mind."

"In the meantime, we'll be awaiting more information," Frederic said. "Please let us know if we can help you. You're not alone in this fight—we want to stop Allegiant too. I'd sign up to fight on the frontlines, but my experiments at the apothecary shop are too important."

"Just focus all your energy on our evolution," Cyrus said. "When the time comes to destroy Allegiant, your experiments will help."

"Let's go, Brother," Levi said, growing impatient. "We need to get back."

As Levi left the cave with his brother, he never felt so relieved to get away from vampires. But an unsettling feeling crept up his spine.

He didn't really belong anywhere. Not with the vampires, not with the humans. And that made Levi the loneliest he'd ever been.

CHAPTER

THIRTEEN

When they returned to Rutherford Farm, Levi was relieved Emilia wasn't waiting for them. He didn't know how to explain what had taken so long.

"You can't keep avoiding her forever, you know," Cyrus said, putting the horse back in the stable. "You can't resist her. You have to give in."

"Huh?" Levi asked.

"Night Temptress," Cyrus replied. "In case you didn't get the not-so-subtle hint, she's into you. And a little piece of advice? Night Temptress isn't good at taking rejection. She's right behind Slaughter in the number of human kills, you know."

"Oh. Damn. You think she'd kill me for rejecting her?"

"Nah, not you. That's not her style. But something—or someone—you care about. As much as a vampire *can* care, of course."

Levi's mind flitted back to Emilia. He hated the thought of any vampire getting their hands on her—especially Night Temptress or Slaughter.

"Well, I'm not interested in her," Levi said with a shrug.

"Our mission is too important. We can't afford any distractions. Women or otherwise."

He immediately regretted saying those words. These days, he wasn't too sure about their mission. About the morality of it all.

Cyrus grinned, patting his shoulder. "Glad to hear you say it. I was starting to think you were going soft spending time with these humans. But for our sake, try to let Night Temptress down gently, okay?"

Levi nodded as Cyrus turned, heading back to the shed. "Will do. Hey, Cyrus?"

He glanced over his shoulder. "Yes, Brother?"

"Thanks for not telling the vampires about my throwing up. That was nice of you."

Cyrus shrugged. "They'd only see it as a weakness—and we've got enough trouble already. They don't truly understand us, you know. They don't get how Allegiant could overpower our people. But with their help, it'll never happen."

As Cyrus walked to the shed, Levi didn't follow. He walked over to the small pond, rinsing his mouth out with water. When he had finished, the evidence was gone, but the doubt inside his head wasn't.

I need guidance, Levi thought. *I can't talk to Cyrus about this— he'd never understand. And maybe he'd turn against me. No, I need to look inside myself for answers.*

Levi sat down on the grass, crossing his legs. Vampire meditation was a forgotten art—lost centuries ago since no one had the time anymore. But Levi was desperate. He forced himself to close his eyes, focusing on his breathing. And then, through the darkness, he asked himself the question he had tried to ignore all this time.

Can I really kill Emilia when I'm falling in love with her?

There it was—something so forbidden that he couldn't say

it out loud. Levi didn't know how or if vampires could love, but he couldn't deny the fierce desire to protect her. And maybe he was crazy, but he swore Emilia was beginning to have feelings for him too.

Levi remembered what love was like before he was a vampire. It was strong, pure, and good. He'd had plenty of girl-friends—some he even loved—so the emotion wasn't completely forgotten. But when he was with Emilia, the feeling was so strong.

As though he couldn't live without her.

He sat there for another twenty minutes, considering every-thing. And although it brought him pain, he made his decision. The voice in the back of his head knew what he had to do.

He couldn't kill Emilia. Which meant one thing.

He'd have to stop his brother and the vampires from ending her life. He knew the other vampires were a lost cause, but he hoped his brother would listen to reason. And in the meantime, he'd help Emilia make Allegiant as strong as he could to protect her and her people.

He rose to his feet, returning to the shed to find his brother fast asleep. What would Cyrus say if he found out Levi loved Emilia, he wondered? That he was planning to help Allegiant? He knew it would lead to war.

Levi lay down on his blanket and went to sleep, his dreams only of Emilia. But then they changed into something darker. A memory. His father, drunk and belligerent as always, stood over him, yelling and striking him with a belt. Cyrus rushed over to protect Levi, but he was struck too. Both boys cried in pain.

When he awoke, he was clammy and shaken. Cyrus was already awake and eyeing him. "You all right? You were mumbling in your sleep."

"Yeah." Levi ran a hand through his sweaty hair. "Just had a nightmare. Of Dad. Do you remember what he did to us?"

"Of course I do." Cyrus sneered. "That bastard got what was coming to him. Mom, too, for not doing anything to protect us. But that was a long time ago. Anyway, the sun's up now. Aren't you and Emilia supposed to be buying land today or something?"

Levi sat up, yawning. "Yeah, that's right—if Lord Tristan even says yes."

"Well, I'm coming too. I want Emilia to think she can trust me. You shouldn't get to have all the fun with her, Brother."

Levi faked a smile. "Sounds good. Let's go wake her."

Levi grabbed all the gold off the table and put it in his pocket. They didn't see Emilia or the others plowing the field, so they entered the cabin. The family sat around the breakfast table, eating eggs and fruit. Although a vampire's diet consisted of flesh—either human or animal—Levi felt like his tastebuds were coming back. The smell of fresh eggs and strawberries almost made his mouth water for the first time in forever.

"Hello, Levi," Emilia said, looking up with a smile. "Glad to see you two made it back after last night. Did you have a good time?"

"Uh, yeah," Levi lied. "We didn't go far. The streets are too dangerous at night."

When her parents noticed the brothers, they got up and left the room. Levi and Cyrus only shook their heads, eating the raw meat Emilia had left out for them. Peeta looked over his shoulder and made sure his parents were out of earshot before he leaned over the table.

"Did you bring the gold?" he whispered. "Is it official?"

Levi nodded, reaching into his pocket to pull out the coins. Peeta and Alana's eyes widened as he placed the gold on the table.

"I can't believe it," Alana whispered. "Allegiant's finally coming together. I can avenge my parents."

"And Dawn," Peeta added.

"About that," Emilia said, glancing between them. "We need to set some rules. You're young, so I don't want you out on the frontlines, you hear me? That's a job for the adults."

"What?" Peeta frowned. "Come on, we'd be good Legionnaires. You promised you'd let us help!"

"Help, yes. But I won't put you in harm's way," Emilia argued, "and that's final. I'll teach you how to fight, but I want you two to stay back. To help with more menial tasks. We need cooks and farmers as badly as we need Legionnaires."

Alana sighed. "But Emilia—"

"No." Emilia rose to her feet. "I won't let Dawn's fate happen to you too. We've lost enough already."

Levi noticed the gleam in Cyrus's eyes. He would kill Emilia and her family in an instant—with no hesitation. And the time to strike was growing closer.

Would his brother kill him too, he wondered? For getting so close to Emilia? Only time would tell.

"Anyway, come on," Emilia continued. "We should get going. Lord Tristan has a small window in the afternoon when he hears petitions, so we'd better hurry."

When Levi tried to follow Cyrus, Peeta, and Alana to the stables, Emilia grabbed his arm and held him back. "Levi, can I speak to you for a moment? In private?"

He nodded, growing nervous in her presence. "Of course. What's wrong?"

"Nothing, actually. I just wanted to let you know our talk last night helped. No matter what Lord Tristan says, I know everything will be all right because you're with me."

Levi didn't know how to reply. He wasn't usually this speechless around women—vampire or otherwise.

Emilia looked down, clearing her throat. "Anyway, I just thought you should know that."

"Well, I'm happy to help." Levi glanced out the window. "I have something to say to you too. It's about last night—what my brother and I discovered."

Emilia looked concerned. "Oh?"

"We found a dead vampire along the side of the road. It looked like a professional kill—like someone knew what they were doing. Was it you? Or one of the others?"

Emilia shook her head. "No, I was in bed all night. We can ask Edmund and the Black Flag about it, but I'm almost sure they couldn't have done this. They don't know the first thing about killing vampires. Not yet anyway."

Levi grew silent again. If it wasn't Emilia or anyone she knew, then someone else was killing vampires. But who? And how did they know so much about the creatures of the night?

Emilia grinned. "But this is great, Levi. Perhaps there's a whole legion of vampire killers out there that we don't know about. If we can find them, we could have new allies!"

Levi forced a smile, but he had a bad feeling in his stomach —especially when he remembered the silver bullet in the vampire's chest. But he didn't want to say anything and burst Emilia's bubble. She looked so happy at the thought of more Legionnaires. He pocketed the gold coins and followed her to the stable instead, grabbing a horse to ride to the markets.

THE MARKETS WERE ALWAYS busy in the daytime and today was no different. Townspeople rushed to get their chores and shopping done to vacate the streets at night. Levi and the others rode to Edmund's house first, waking everyone. The miners still hadn't returned to work—too afraid of what they might find inside.

When Levi showed them the gold coins, the old ladies nearly passed out.

"Well, I'll be damned," Edmund said, his eyes wide. "When Sammy told me you won the game, I believed her, but...I didn't think you'd won *this* much. We ain't ever going to have to go hungry again."

When the people congratulated them—even Billy, the boy who rarely spoke—Levi felt his heart burst with something. Was it happiness? He couldn't tell, but it felt good. His smile faded when he remembered his brother standing next to him.

Cyrus narrowed his eyes at Levi. "A game?"

Levi nodded, clearing his throat. "Uh, yeah—Raging Tides. A card game. It was pretty fun, actually."

"It's only fun when you're winning. Good thing you had me," Samantha replied, winking. She turned to Cyrus. "I don't believe we've met. I'm Samantha Doyle."

"Cyrus Godfrey," he replied, shaking her hand. "Levi's brother."

"Ah, then I see good looks run in the family."

"You're not too bad yourself," Cyrus flirted back. "Samantha's a gorgeous name, you know. It suits you."

Levi wanted to grab Samantha by the shoulders and shake her—to warn her to stay away from the monster she was flirting with. But he couldn't. He could only watch helplessly as they bantered back and forth. Levi introduced Cyrus to the others when he had finished wooing Samantha, and then they left their small cabin to head to the tavern.

When they entered, they found the Black Flag pirates playing another game of Raging Tides near the back wall. Captain Gem—now known as Rosalie—laughed in triumph as she collected all her earnings from an unsuspecting peasant.

Her head snapped up when she recognized Levi. "Ah, the foreigner's back! Is today the day?"

Levi nodded. "We're heading to Lord Tristan's castle. You coming?"

"Of course." Rosalie stood up, downing her ale. She showed Levi the number of daggers and swords attached to her body. "And if he doesn't agree, we'll just have to persuade him, won't we?"

"Wait a second," Peeta said, his jaw dropping. "Are you... Captain Gem? The leader of the Black Flags?"

Rosalie grinned. "The one, the only. Nice to meet you, kid. This here is Scrooge, my second-in-command. He doesn't talk, but he *is* damn good with a sword."

She pointed at a man with long black hair and an eyepatch. He grunted at them, tipping his hat to be polite.

"Is that his real name?" Samantha asked.

"Who knows?" Rosalie asked. "Scrooge suits him, so we go with that."

"Hang on—who's the Black Flag?" Cyrus asked, glancing around.

"The most notorious pirate gang this side of the ocean," Alana whispered, turning to Emilia. "Are they on our side?"

Emilia grinned. "Yes—thanks to Levi."

Samantha cleared her throat.

"All right, Sam, too," Emilia added, laughing. "They've agreed to join Allegiant."

"Impressive," Cyrus muttered, glancing at Levi. "It must not have been easy to make this alliance."

Levi said nothing. Judging by the look on his brother's face, he wasn't happy. As the others cleared out of the tavern, heading to their horses, Cyrus tugged on Levi's arm and held him back.

"Are you crazy?" he whispered. "You convinced pirates to join Allegiant? Are you trying to make our mission harder?"

Levi racked his brain for a lie. "Hey, don't get mad at me. I'm trying to make Emilia think we're on her side. If you recall, I told you we should've killed her in the first place. You're the one who wanted to screw around first."

Something Levi now regretted ever suggesting. He couldn't believe he had once wanted to kill her.

Cyrus let him go, sighing. "I'm beginning to think you were right. After you, Brother."

As Levi nodded, walking off ahead, an alarm sounded in his head. What if his brother decided to kill Emilia anyway? And what if he couldn't stop it?

Those worries would *definitely* keep him up at night.

THEIR SMALL ARMY rode toward Lord Tristan's castle in the distance. As they approached, the remaining knights and guards in his service were still making repairs from the vampire attack.

As Levi approached the door, Sir Anders limped over to them and withdrew his sword. "What are you doing here?"

"We're here to petition Lord Tristan," Emilia said. "It's very important."

Sir Anders narrowed his eyes at her. "Wait a moment... aren't you Emilia Rutherford, his betrothed?"

"We were *never* betrothed," Emilia shot back. "He only thought we were."

"Well, I doubt he'd want to see you. And besides, the castle requires repairs. It's closed to the public for now."

"Something tells me you'll let us pass," Rosalie said, removing her sword. "Sure would be a shame if you didn't."

Sir Anders wanted to argue, but when he noticed all the weapons the pirates carried, he sighed. "Fine, you have five minutes. Make it quick."

As they entered the throne room, the castle looked much worse on the inside. Servants scrubbed away old bloodstains, builders repaired tables and chairs, and guards were still bandaging each other's wounds. The dead royals had been dragged away already.

Lord Tristan sat on his throne, speaking with one of his advisors. When he noticed Emilia and Levi, he sat up with a snarl. "You. Get this scum out of my castle!"

"Not so fast," Samantha said at the approaching guards. "Your knight said we could pass. And take a look at us—do you think you could overpower everyone here?"

Lord Tristan ignored her when he noticed the miners, rising to his feet. "I've heard work has stopped in the mines. Care to explain why?"

"There was a vampire attack," Levi said. "Not like you'd care. The miners are too scared to go back to work."

Lord Tristan laughed. "Too scared? They work in the mines —they don't sell candles on the street corner. What did they expect? If they wanted safety, they should've chosen a different profession. Look, I won't hear any excuses. Just get back to work."

"No," Edmund said, stepping forward. "We ain't gonna do that, your Lordship."

Lord Tristan sneered. "No? What do you mean, *no*?"

"You can't change their minds, but there *is* a way this could work out for all of us," Levi said, pulling out his gold. "See this? We want to buy some land to build a vampire hunting militia, one called Allegiant. Emilia's starting it."

Lord Tristan chuckled. "Emilia? How amusing. Does she honestly believe she has what it takes to stop these attacks?"

Emilia glared at him. "I do. Allegiant will help people, Lord Tristan. And by training these miners, they'll feel more confident to return to work. Isn't that what you want?"

"I don't want your gold," Lord Tristan spat. "Now, get back

to work, miners—or I'll force you myself. As for the rest of you, I suggest you get out of my sight."

As guards swarmed them, the pirates held up their weapons. Even Samantha, Edmund, and the miners removed knives from their pockets. Cyrus grinned, most likely eager to see more bloodshed. Levi knew he had to do something before someone got hurt.

"Wait! Look, I saved your life at the Lord's Ball," Levi said. "You told me you owed me a favor. Don't you remember?"

"I do. And here is my favor," Lord Tristan said, walking closer. "I'll let you all live if you forget this Allegiant foolery and walk out of here. That's more than generous, no?"

"You're making a huge mistake," Emilia said. "We've got gold. What more do you want?"

Lord Tristan shook his head. "If you would've agreed to marry me, perhaps I would've been a little kinder. But you rejected me, Emilia. And I can't just forget that."

"Well, shit," Rosalie muttered, glancing at their group. "What now?"

Levi had no answer. This wasn't the way things were supposed to go. As he tried to think of a solution, the door to the castle flung open behind them. A tall, muscular man with a shaggy black beard walked inside, carrying a silver sword. He wore long furs and looked like a barbarian.

"Lord Tristan!" the man bellowed, swinging his sword around. "I am here to seek vengeance for my daughter. As she died in your castle, under your protection. The blame falls onto you."

The room turned silent. Lord Tristan gulped, his eyes widening as he stepped back. Levi had never seen the royal look so terrified.

"Who's that?" Levi whispered to Emilia.

"King Brutus of Kelgat," Emilia whispered back. "His

daughter, Axa, was visiting the kingdom to cement relations between our people, but she died in the vampire attack. I completely forgot about it until now."

Lord Tristan gulped. "Please, King Brutus—don't be so hasty. Let's talk about this, hmm?"

"No talk," Brutus said, inching closer. "I won't be satisfied until I see your head on a spike!"

The guards tried to swarm Brutus, but he looked at them and growled. It was enough to make them back off. He glared at Lord Tristan, stalking toward him. Lord Tristan backed up, banging into the wall behind him.

"Prepare to die, Lord Tristan," King Brutus said with a hearty laugh. "Oh, it will be a glorious death."

Lord Tristan looked over Brutus's shoulder at the crowd. "Help—someone, please help!"

FOURTEEN

Levi had a choice to make.

He weighed his options—all of them. He could let King Brutus kill Lord Tristan, making way for another lord. That one could be better, more determined to protect his citizens. But they could also be worse.

The other option was to spare Lord Tristan's life—even though he didn't deserve it—in the hopes that he would grant them their request. He risked making an enemy out of King Brutus, and that seemed dangerous.

Levi sighed and stepped forward, his mind made up. He grabbed King Brutus's arm and yanked back. "Step away from him. I won't ask you again."

"You're really going to save him?" Cyrus asked, amusement dancing in his eyes. Emilia and the crowd murmured behind them.

Levi glared at him over his shoulder. "Not now, Cyrus."

King Brutus sneered. "And who the hell are you? Look, I'm here to get vengeance for my daughter. He let her die!"

"I didn't *let* her die," Lord Tristan stammered. "The vampires attacked us—"

King Brutus growled. "Vampires? Now you sully my daughter's name by lying?"

"He's not lying," Levi said. "There really were vampires here—monsters that drink blood and kill humans. They only come out at night. And the reason we survived is that I fought them off. I saved Lord Tristan's life, but I couldn't save your daughter's. For that, I'm sorry."

"He's telling the truth," Tristan added. "He saved my life and drove the vampires out of my castle. As much as it pains me to admit."

"Well, if these vampires are such a problem," King Brutus said to Lord Tristan, "then what are you doing to stop them? To prevent this from happening again?"

Lord Tristan looked down. "Well, you see…"

"He's done nothing, King Brutus," Emilia said. "Our people are being slaughtered by these vampires every night. I've pleaded with Lord Tristan to put more guards on patrol—to do anything at all—but he won't lift a finger."

King Brutus shook his head, turning back to Lord Tristan. "Then explain why I shouldn't kill him right here—for what he allows to happen on your streets *and* for my daughter's death?"

"I don't *allow* anything!" Lord Tristan cried, glaring at Emilia. "The truth is, I'm helpless to stop these vampires. Look around at my castle—how destroyed it is. My guards aren't doing any better. To fight the vampires would be suicide. We simply don't have the resources for it."

"But that is your duty as a lord, is it not? To protect your people? There is nothing I wouldn't do for my kingdom. If you're too afraid to take action you're not fit to lead. By killing you, I'd be doing your people a favor, coward."

"Wait," Levi urged. "We have a solution to stop the vampires without Lord Tristan's help. It's why we're here. Emilia, tell him. It's your idea."

"Very well. We're calling ourselves Allegiant," Emilia said to King Brutus. "We plan to purchase land to begin a school for Legionnaires—trained warriors who hunt these vampires. We even have enough gold to do so, but Lord Tristan won't sell us the land we need."

"And with Allegiant, we could avenge your daughter, King Brutus," Levi added. "That's what Allegiant's all about. Fighting for the ones we've lost."

Levi gestured at the miners, peasants, and pirates behind them. They all nodded. King Brutus paused for a moment, turning back to Lord Tristan.

"Then you will grant them this land," he said. "To do otherwise would be to spit on my daughter's memory."

"Yes, fine, fine! I'll give you whatever you want," Lord Tristan said, falling to his knees. "Please, just don't kill me."

King Brutus shook his head, stepping back. "Cowardly fool."

"Not to interrupt, but what spot would be best for our operations?" Emilia asked Lord Tristan. "We'll need land big enough for a training yard, barracks, stables..."

"Hmm...well, past the farms, there's an old, abandoned keep," Lord Tristan said. "It was used a long time ago for a royal family, but they've since died out. Is that good enough for you?"

Emilia nodded. "Yes—it will be, once we make some alterations to it."

"Rise to your feet, Lord Tristan," King Brutus ordered. "You look pathetic on your knees."

As Lord Tristan rose, Levi tossed some of the gold coins at him. He made sure to save enough for supplies and food. "Here—and a little extra for your trouble."

"How generous," Lord Tristan sneered, looking back at his servants. "Collect the gold. And if I see any of you stealing, I won't hesitate to hang you for theft."

As the servants collected the gold, King Brutus turned to

Levi. "I think your cause is noble. And in the event these vampires should spread to my kingdom, I want to send some of my guards to help you."

Emilia's eyes lit up. "Really? You have no idea what that means to us, King Brutus. Thank you."

"On one condition," King Brutus replied, his eyes still on Levi. "Lord Tristan said you saved his life by fighting off these so-called vampires. You must be strong then? Formidable?"

Levi shrugged. "I guess. What are you getting at?"

"A duel," King Brutus said. "I want to fight you—to see how strong you are. If you defeat me, I'll do everything in my power to support your battle against the vampires."

"In my castle?" Lord Tristan gawked. "Surely you can take this outside—"

"Right here," King Brutus snarled. "I came all this way for a fight in this castle, and I intend to get it."

"Very well," Lord Tristan muttered. "Just leave me out of it, thank you."

"And if Levi loses?" Samantha asked.

"Then I'll know he's not strong enough to start this Allegiant," King Brutus said, "and I'll take pleasure in striking down someone so weak. But then I would have to kill Lord Tristan for having no solution to the vampire crisis."

The room turned silent.

"Please, King Brutus—there's no need to include me in this," Lord Tristan began, nervously playing with his crown. "I already granted your request. Why not take this outside and settle it on your own terms—"

When King Brutus glared at him again, Lord Tristan shut up.

"One second, please." Emilia pulled Levi aside. "Do you think you can win this?"

Levi shrugged, looking back at King Brutus. He was stronger

—taller than Levi. But Levi had supernatural powers that the barbarian king lacked.

"I don't know," Levi whispered, "but I'll try my best. If his barbarian friends look like him, then we need them on our side. More people to fight the vampires is always good, right?"

"Yes—but not if it means sacrificing your life." Emilia sighed. "Be careful, Levi. I don't want to lose you."

When she said those words, Levi felt like he could do anything. He wanted to make Emilia proud.

"Your answer?" King Brutus asked behind them.

"I agree to your duel, King Brutus." Levi turned back toward him. "May the best fighter win."

"Win this, Levi," Lord Tristan said, his eyes desperate. "For the love of God, win this."

"Hang on a moment. I should be fighting alongside Levi," Cyrus said. "I also defended the castle from the vampires."

"I've already chosen my dueling partner," King Brutus said. "The rules have been set. One-on-one, I'll see how strong he is myself."

Cyrus gave Levi an apologetic look.

King Brutus removed one of the swords from his scabbard, throwing it at Levi. He caught the handle and swung it around a few times. The silver on the blade gleamed in the candlelight, catching Levi's eye.

If King Brutus stabs me in the chest, it's all over, Levi thought. *And in my death, Emilia would know exactly what I am and never forgive me for it. I have to win this.*

Levi stood across from the barbarian, staring him down. Emilia, Cyrus, and the crowd moved back, giving them space to duel. Even the servants and guards fled the hall, murmuring and whispering. Levi could hear Lord Tristan's pounding heart a few steps away.

"What are you waiting for?" King Brutus asked, circling him. "Come on, show me how strong you are!"

Levi stepped forward first, swinging his sword. King Brutus dodged, swinging low to strike Levi in the knee. He hissed, black blood trickling down his leg. The silver from the blade felt like it had seared his skin. Emilia and Cyrus in the crowd gasped behind them.

"And you were strong enough to stop these vampires?" King Brutus laughed. "Pathetic. They must be equally weak then!"

I'm no good with a sword, Levi thought. *I need to shift this fight in my favor.*

Levi pretended to approach King Brutus again with his sword. As he dodged, distracted for a moment, Levi slammed into the barbarian with all his strength. He wasn't expecting a fistfight. The barbarian felt as sturdy as a brick house, but it was enough to trip him up.

Levi copied his fighting technique—swinging his sword low. King Brutus plummeted to the floor, his sword flying out of his hands. Levi kicked it away and aimed his sword at King Brutus's throat. The barbarian looked up at him, frozen and panting.

"I didn't fight the vampires with a sword," Levi told him, tossing his weapon aside. "I fought them with my hands, with my strength. I was trained to conquer—to stalk my enemies. A true warrior relies on the power inside of him, not any weapon."

"That he does. Well done," King Brutus said, glancing up at him. "You've impressed me. Not many can, you know."

Levi held out his hand, helping the barbarian to his feet. "I've had years of fighting experience, believe me. And you were a strong opponent."

The crowd swarmed them with Emilia pushing through to

the front. "Thank goodness all this fighting is over. Does this mean you'll send some reinforcements, Your Majesty?"

King Brutus nodded, looking back at Lord Tristan. "I will—and it means your lord can live. For now."

Lord Tristan breathed a sigh of relief as the crowd congratulated Levi on his victory. Emilia smiled up at Levi, and he felt himself grinning too. But there was one person in the crowd who wasn't. Cyrus.

Emilia's smile almost made Levi forget about the throbbing pain in his leg. He looked down, wiping some of the blood away. Emilia glanced down and noticed.

"Here, allow me," Emilia said, wrapping Levi's leg in a bandage that she kept in her pouch. "The sword...it burned you. I saw it. Why did that happen?"

"It's our physiology," Cyrus lied. "Where we come from, our skin reacts differently to things. Don't worry, he'll be okay. My brother's strong."

Emilia nodded, though she still looked concerned. Levi feared she'd make the connection between the silver and his wound and realize he was a vampire soon enough.

King Brutus sheathed his sword, turning to Levi. "I must return to Kelgat. I wish I could join Allegiant myself, but my people need me—especially after losing our princess. I'll send some of my finest barbarians on a ship when I return."

"Thank you, King Brutus," Emilia said, bowing. "I lost a sister to the vampires, so I'm sorry for your loss."

"Then may we both find peace in vengeance," he said, turning to Levi. "But fail your mission...and I'll return to kill you myself. All in Axa's name. Good luck, Allegiant."

After King Brutus had left, Lord Tristan's scowl returned. "If you're finished dueling in my castle, then we're done here. I sold you your land—so get out of here. And I expect the miners back at work soon."

"They'll return to work when it's safe," Emilia said, "once they learn how to fight. If you'd taught them already, you wouldn't have this problem."

The miners nodded in agreement. Lord Tristan just rolled his eyes.

Levi stepped forward. "I don't understand why you're so angry with us. Allegiant could solve all your problems—it could make your streets safe again."

"You don't understand?" Lord Tristan asked, eyes wide. "You stole my betrothed, disobeyed my laws, and humiliated me here today. I won't ever forget what you've done. I can't. Would you?"

Levi hesitated, but honestly? Probably not.

"Come on, Levi," Emilia said, glaring at Lord Tristan. "We have what we came for. Let's leave."

"Finally, we can agree on something," Lord Tristan mumbled. "Watch yourself, Levi. Vampires aren't your only enemy around here."

As they left the castle, the crowd continued to celebrate. But Levi feared Lord Tristan would try something—not against him, but against Emilia. It was something else he had to protect her from.

Sir Anders rushed over to them. Levi prepared himself for another fight, but the guard wasn't armed. "So, that's it, then? You're starting Allegiant? I overheard what happened."

Emilia nodded. "That's right. Why?"

"I want to join. It sounds like you'll need all the help you can get."

"Hang on a second," Levi said. "How do we know you weren't sent after us to spy for Lord Tristan? What's your reason for joining, anyway?"

"Lord Tristan doesn't care what you do now. He never wants to see you lot again," Sir Anders replied. "And in case you forgot, those vampires hurt me too. And killed my friends last night. Don't deny me the pleasure of taking my revenge."

Emilia nodded. "Makes sense. As you said, we could always use more help. Welcome to Allegiant, I guess. But will Lord Tristan let you join?"

The guard shrugged, getting on one of the nearby horses. "Who cares? He won't know. And since I'm still working for him, I'll be able to warn you if he tries to retaliate."

"Deal," Levi said. "That'll be helpful, thank you."

"It really will be. Isn't this wonderful?" Emilia asked, turning to Levi. "Dozens of recruits, land, *and* enough gold left over for supplies. Allegiant will be unstoppable. All thanks to you, Levi. I can't sing your praises enough."

Emilia threw herself into Levi's arms and hugged him tight. He noticed his brother eyeing them, shaking his head. Levi faked a smile and hugged her back. "Yeah, it's wonderful, Emilia. I'm so happy for us."

She pulled away without a clue of what evil things were running through Cyrus's head. That innocence inside of her—that goodness—is what Levi wanted to keep safe.

"About time the damn Lord's saying yes to something," Edmund muttered. "We've lost enough of our people."

Samantha nodded, still plucking away on her lute. "We have. So, what are we still standing around here for? We've got the land. Let's go check it out!"

The crowd cheered at that, getting on their horses. Emilia glanced at the brothers. "You two coming?"

"In a second," Cyrus said, his eyes flickering to Levi's. "I just need to talk to my brother."

Emilia nodded, riding off ahead. Cyrus's smile vanished as he turned to Levi. "Well, well, well. Barbarians, pirates, miners, peasants. What an army you've built, Levi. As Emilia said, you'll be unstoppable—and it's all thanks to you. The irony."

"Hey, like I said, this was your idea," Levi argued, trying to cover for himself. "Don't forget that."

"You're right—and now I think this game's coming to an end. We strike soon, Levi. Right after Frederic makes the vamps immune to sunlight. I hope you're ready. That is, if you're not too busy getting close to the enemy."

Before Levi could reply, his brother had already mounted his horse and rode away.

Levi sighed, following his brother and the other riders into the distance. He was the last one to arrive, joining the group of horses and villagers. But the keep was nothing like Levi had pictured.

It lay in ruins, the left side of the castle completely collapsed. It was nothing but a heap of rubble with bricks and wood everywhere. The disheveled castle sat in a long, dirty field without anything around except for a forest.

The crowd murmured, dismounting their horses. They walked around the field with frowns.

"Well, this isn't what I pictured. Now what?" Emilia asked, her hands on her hips. "This place won't give us much safety from the vampires. Oh, I knew Lord Tristan wouldn't give us something without a catch!"

Levi paused for a moment, glancing up at the castle. He could see it now—all the possibilities. His old life returned to him, memories of fixing houses worse than this. For a split second, he almost felt human again.

"I never told you this, but I was an architect a long time ago," Levi said. "I built a lot of homes. It's been years since I've done any work, but there's potential here. If we work together, we can fix up this keep."

Emilia's eyes lit up. "You mean that? You aren't just saying that to cheer us up?"

Levi shook his head, passing gold coins to some of the

recruits. "No, I really believe it. Here, go to the markets and buy some materials. We'll need tools—axes, hammers, stone, that sort of thing. And don't forget to buy seeds for our garden. In the meantime, the rest of us will clean up around here. Look for anything salvageable, all right?"

Cyrus stood off to the side, watching as Levi took charge. He could feel his brother's eyes on him, but he didn't have time to worry about it. He needed to get this castle fixed—fast. The peasants nodded, getting on their horses and riding off to the markets. The others got to work immediately with the clean-up. Even the children helped, sweeping the grounds and tossing out garbage.

Rosalie stepped forward with her pirates. "What about us, Levi? What do you need us to do?"

"You're the strongest fighters we have," Levi replied. "I want you to patrol the perimeter. Not a glamorous job, but when night falls, we can't have any surprise attacks. When we get our barracks up, I want you to be our commander."

Rosalie grinned. "You got it. We'll get started right away."

As she and the pirates had walked off, Cyrus looked at Levi. "And me, Brother?"

Levi didn't want to give his brother *any* job. He would've preferred him to stay away from Allegiant instead of seeing their vulnerabilities and hearing their secrets. But he knew his brother wouldn't leave, so he had to give him a menial task.

"You can help Emilia and me with the clean-up," Levi said. "We've got a lot to do, so let's get started—"

"Someone's coming!" a peasant said behind them, pointing in the distance. "Look!"

It was still sunny out, making it unlikely to be a vampire, but Levi prepared himself anyway. When the figure stepped closer, he realized it was Frederic Bors. And he had brought science supplies with him.

FIFTEEN

"Fred? What are you doing here?" Emilia asked, pushing through the crowd. "I didn't expect to see you today."

"I heard you were hunting vampires," Frederic replied. "I wanted to join. My experiments could help Allegiant."

"That's very generous. But how do you know about Allegiant?"

"This is a small town, Emilia." Frederic's eyes flitted to Levi and Cyrus. "Word gets around."

"I guess it does. Say, I didn't even know you knew about the vampires. Some deny they exist."

"Well, those people are naïve. I know better. I work at the same shop you do—I've seen things that are strange. And the attacks have everyone riled up," Frederic replied. "Any one of us could be next. I'm no fighter, but I *am* good at science. If I can help—even in a small way—then I'd like to."

Levi didn't know what Frederic was up to, but he knew the vampire had no intention of helping. And he couldn't let another double agent join the ranks.

"What about the apothecary shop?" Levi asked. "With

Emilia spending her time here, someone needs to take care of the patients."

"Oh, that's right." Emilia frowned, looking back at Frederic. "Do you think you could watch the apothecary while I'm gone?"

Frederic glared at Levi. "I can, but I'd like to spend some time here too. There's an experiment I've been working on that I think will really help."

Levi shook his head. "I really don't think that's necessary—"

"We'd love to have you, Frederic," Emilia said, grinning. "As you can see, the keep isn't ready yet, but when it is, we'll ensure you have a space to do your experiments. In the meantime, let me take your equipment."

Emilia took the microscope, vials, and tools, walking across the field to place them on a wooden table that had gotten cracked in half. As she set up, Frederic looked at Levi and crossed his arms.

"What was that about?" he snapped. "Were you trying to get Emilia to turn me away?"

"I...no. Emilia still thinks you're human—but the more time she spends around you, she might find out the truth. If she discovers me, then you were my back-up. A second chance to stay in Allegiant. If we're both here and get caught, it's all over."

"Hmm. I suppose that makes sense," Frederic muttered. "But don't worry—I've been fooling Emilia for months. She has no idea what I am. And this way, I can spy on Allegiant too."

"About that," Cyrus began. "What about your experiments for us?"

"They're coming along well," Frederic replied. "By taking a sample of your blood, it's sped up the process. I think I'll have the evolution serum soon—which gives me the chance to work on other projects. Any weapons and equipment I make for the Allegiant will be tainted, given a weakness our people can exploit. And since Emilia trusts me, she won't suspect a thing."

As Cyrus and Frederic shared a smile, Levi started to panic. It was one thing to fool his brother, but how would he explain why he's helping Allegiant to Frederic? And could he protect them from all the tampering the Bloody Doctor prepared to do?

He wished he'd never given him a sample of his blood. He wished he had killed them all in their lair when he had the chance.

Levi couldn't warn Emilia about Frederic, but he *could* warn her of something else. He excused himself and walked over to her table, making sure his brother and Frederic were out of earshot.

"Got a second?" Levi asked her.

Emilia nodded, still setting up Frederic's equipment. "Sure. You know, it's wonderful Frederic's agreed to help. He's a genius."

Levi bit his tongue. "Uh, right. Look, there's something you should know about the mines—why it isn't safe for the miners to return to work just yet."

Emilia turned around, her eyes landing on Levi. "What is it?"

"A vampire lair connects to the mines. It's how they're able to reach it in the daylight."

Emilia's eyes widened. "My goodness. No wonder one got in and killed Edmund's friend. This isn't good, Levi. What are we supposed to do?"

"Train the miners as hard as we can," Levi said, watching them clean the field. "It's all we *can* do."

"Yes, I suppose so. But how do you know about the vampire lair?"

"Uh, my brother and I found it the night we went out. Dumb luck, I guess. Don't worry—the vampires didn't see us."

"That's a good thing. Anyway, I'll warn Edmund and his miners right away. This will save a lot of lives, you know. Even prevent another ambush."

"I know. But again, don't tell my brother. He was pretty traumatized when he found the vampire lair."

"Of course. There's nothing more terrifying than knowing a monster is in your midst," Emilia said, and Levi's smile faded. "Now that Frederic's brought some medical supplies, I can take a look at your leg again."

"Really, it's fine," Levi said, but Emilia had already pulled off the bandage to reveal smooth skin.

"It's...healing." She blinked. "Incredibly fast. There isn't even a bruise."

Damn that regenerative vampire healing, Levi thought.

"Guess I'm just a fast healer," Levi joked, hoping Emilia wouldn't press him for details.

He turned around when he heard footsteps approaching. He feared it was the vampires again, but it was Emilia's parents, Ivan and Loretta. Their horse munched on grass nearby while waiting for them. Emilia noticed them right away, then rushed over to her parents.

"Mother? Father?" Emilia asked. "What are you doing here? Are you joining Allegiant?"

"Certainly not," Ivan snapped. "It wasn't enough leaving us? You had to force your brother and Alana into it too?"

"She didn't force us into anything, Father," Peeta said, pushing through the crowd. "We chose to join Allegiant."

Alana nodded, rushing over. "You remember what those monsters did to Dawn. Don't you want justice?"

"Yes, of course we do," Loretta said, "but not at the cost of your lives. We consider you family, Alana. It would destroy us if we lost you and Peeta."

"You won't. This I promise you," Emilia said. "I've already

told them I'm keeping them here to cook and clean. I don't want them fighting. Not this young."

"How nice for you," Ivan muttered, "but what about the farm? Your mother and I can't work the fields all by ourselves."

Levi reached into his pocket, pulling out some leftover gold coins. "Here—take this to hire some farmhands."

Ivan sneered, shoving the gold away. "I don't want your coin, foreigner. You caused this. You stole my children from me!"

"No—the vampires did that when they killed Dawn, Father. You can't expect us to sit back and do nothing. We're not like Lord Tristan," Emilia replied, crossing her arms. "Now, take Levi's coin and leave. Be grateful he's agreed to give you that much after everything you've done to him."

Ivan scoffed, grabbing the gold coins out of Levi's hand. "I regret ever letting you stay with us, foreigner. Let's go, Loretta."

Ivan stomped away to the horse, but his wife stayed behind. She pulled Emilia, Peeta, and Alana into a big hug. Levi felt like he was intruding on something personal, so he gave them some space.

"Your father is just upset—and worried. As am I," their mother whispered. "But I know you, Emilia. You wouldn't commit to something unless it was important. Fight the vampires if you must—but be careful. I'm praying for you, my brave girl."

Emilia smiled. "Thanks, Mama. Take care of yourselves."

After her mother had nodded and galloped away with Ivan, Peeta and Alana returned to help the others clean up. Emilia looked at Levi. "That was a kind thing you did, helping my father. He's been an asshole to you. Why'd you do it?"

Levi shrugged. "Seemed like the right thing to do."

Just like letting Rocco go. He hadn't forgotten the bandit—

or how that was the day he decided to ignore his vampire instincts. Something had changed inside him.

When the peasants returned with supplies—more than enough to fix the keep—Levi got to work right away. The miners were fast learners, but some of the peasants needed to learn how to hold a hammer and lay the bricks. Levi had no experience with medieval architecture, but he did his best.

Cyrus and Frederic only pretended to help, cleaning up some debris from the field. Levi knew they had no intention of building Allegiant—not like he did. Levi knew the weaknesses of the vampires, so he designed the castle with hidden alcoves to protect innocents in case an attack came. The watchtower gave them the perfect view of the road, so they'd be able to see an army of vampires coming.

Samantha played the lute as they worked, day and night—occasionally flirting with Cyrus, which angered Levi. They only took breaks to sleep and eat. They sang Allegiant's song at the top of their lungs, and Levi couldn't resist joining in. Emilia's siblings, Peeta and Alana, were helpful and cooked for the recruits. The pirates continued to guard the perimeter, but no vampires showed up. Frederic must've told them to stay away —for now. Even Sir Anders helped, trading in his sword for a hammer.

By the third day, the keep was nearly finished. There were already rooms inside from the previous owners—a kitchen, bedrooms, a chapel, a watchtower—so all Levi needed to do was fortify the castle. He had done it many times to the bunker, and this was no different. He added a science lab for Frederic even though he didn't want that vampire anywhere near them. But it was Emilia's request—and Levi couldn't say no to her without explanation.

Emilia, who had stayed by his side to help, stepped back

and looked at their work. "I can't believe it. The keep finally looks like it can protect us."

"That it does," Cyrus said, walking over. "Well done, Levi."

"Yes, well done," Frederic added. "You've made it very... secure."

Levi feared they were on to him, but they wouldn't say anything. Not in front of Emilia.

Before Levi could respond, horses galloped toward them in the distance. Levi watched as several dozen barbarians rode toward the keep. They jumped down from their horses, walking toward them. Cyrus and Frederic's eyes widened in fright, knowing these barbarians would be difficult in battle, even for vampires. The two in front—a man and a woman—wore heavy furs and leather boots, their scabbards adorned with swords and daggers. Even the woman was muscular, her red hair in a ponytail. The man had dark hair and scars across his body.

"This is Allegiant?" the barbarian man asked, and Levi nodded. "It looks formidable. King Brutus sent us here to help."

"And we're sorry our journey took so long," the woman said, her voice as gruff as the man's. "The sea gave us some trouble. My name is Vana. This is my husband, Novak."

Emilia rushed forward, bowing. "Thank you for coming. I know you're skilled at fighting, but do you have any other talents?"

"Not to brag, but we're good at a little bit of everything," Vana said, one hand on her scabbard. "Building, cooking, plant-ing. Kelgat has a harsh climate, so we need to be well-rounded to survive."

"Good, that'll help us greatly. Anyway, Levi's finished building the keep. It looks much better than it did a few days ago," Emilia replied, gesturing at the castle. "But there are always repairs and other work to do. My brother, Peeta, can show you around. In the meantime, Levi, can I speak with you? In private?"

Levi nodded, following Emilia away from the crowd as the barbarians entered the keep. "Did you warn Edmund and the miners about the vampires' secret entrance yet?" he asked.

"I did—and now they're even more afraid to go back to work," Emilia said, sighing. "But Edmund and his miners are willing to learn how to fight. I just wanted to thank you for all your hard work."

Levi shrugged. "It was nothing."

"It wasn't *nothing*," Emilia said, reaching for his icy hand. She held it in hers. "Thank you, Levi. If you ever need something from me, don't hesitate to ask."

Just forgive me, Levi thought, *if you ever find out what I am.*

The image of her finding out the truth flashed across his mind. The pain in her eyes, then the anger. The disgust.

He had to take a deep breath to avoid throwing up.

"The keep is looking beautiful. We have barracks, training grounds, a kitchen—everything we need to live here and train our recruits," Emilia continued, interrupting Levi's thoughts. "But there's one thing missing."

Levi frowned. "Oh? I thought I covered everything."

"A priest, Levi. It'll help improve morale. I have no doubt the days ahead will be difficult, and people will need something to believe in—a higher purpose. Do you think you could ride into town and get Father McGregor to stay with us? I've met him before. He's a nice man."

"Sure, I guess so."

"Thanks." Her smiled faded. "I'd do it myself, but...I'm not religious anymore."

"Oh. You used to be before?"

She nodded, sighing. "Oh, yes, I used to attend church all the time. But when the vampires attacked...my faith waned.

How could any God allow something so evil to exist in our world? How could a God let people die on the streets?"

Levi didn't have the answers. He'd only recently started asking himself those questions too.

"I keep up the façade that I'm religious so I don't get accused of heresy, but the truth is...my faith is conflicted these days." Emilia sighed. "Do you believe in God, Levi? Are you religious?"

He thought of the Vampire Commandments, but that was hardly religious. Then he remembered his life before becoming a vampire.

"I used to be," Levi replied, honestly. "A long, long time ago, but not anymore. Same reason as you, I guess."

"So, you understand. Anyway, it's best if I don't go. The last time I did, I...might've yelled at Father McGregor. Because I was angry at God," Emilia said, looking down in shame. "We already have a chapel—all we need is a priest to bless our Legionnaires and pray with them."

"Well, I can ask him, at least. Do you think he'll agree?"

"I don't know. His work in town keeps him busy, but we need him. He'll bring the others some comfort. Anyway, I'll finish setting up the keep while you're gone. See you soon."

Levi nodded, walking over to Margaret to saddle up. Cyrus and Frederic followed.

"So?" Cyrus asked. "What's the latest?"

"I'm heading into town to get a priest," Levi replied. "Emilia thinks he'll be able to inspire the Legionnaires."

"Yikes. You sure you want to step foot inside a church?" Cyrus shivered. "One touch of anything there—the cross, the holy water—and it'll hurt you. Badly."

"I know, but I've already promised Emilia I would. I can't let her down."

The words came out of Levi's mouth before he could stop

them. Frederic looked puzzled, frowning in confusion, but Cyrus didn't look as surprised.

"Of course not," Cyrus said. "Anything to make Emilia think we're on her side, right? Good luck, Brother."

As he rode away, he feared he had said too much—especially in front of Frederic.

Levi galloped through the markets, taking the dirt trail to the church. When he got closer and swung off Margaret, tying her up outside, a wave of nausea hit him. *Must be the church's effect on me,* Levi thought. *I shouldn't waste time here.*

He entered anyway, pushing those feelings down inside. The church was quiet and empty in the afternoon, sunlight trickling in through the stained-glass windows. A balding, older man—who Levi assumed was Father McGregor—stood near the aisle of pews, sweeping the floor. Nuns scurried around, getting ready for mass later on. Levi spotted the crosses and religious décor and swerved around them.

"Oh, welcome!" Father McGregor said, looking up from his cleaning. "My sermon begins later, but you're welcome to pray in the meantime. Our church is a safe place for all."

Was it safe for the vampires, he wondered? For the evil creatures of the night? He felt like a fraud, like an imposter.

"That's, um, nice, thank you. But actually, I've come here to talk to you about something important," Levi said. "It's about Allegiant."

The priest froze. "I see. I've already heard about them—one of the guards in the castle told a peasant about it. You know how gossip spreads in a small village."

"Right. Anyway, Emilia wanted—"

"Ah, Emilia Rutherford. I hear she's leading Allegiant now. I haven't heard from her in years. The last time we spoke, it wasn't pleasant. Does she still practice her faith?"

"Uh, you'd have to ask her," Levi lied, not wanting to offend him. "She wants you to join Allegiant, Father. We already have a chapel, and those risking their lives to fight the vampires could use your guidance. Your moral support too."

Father McGregor sighed, setting the broom aside. "Ah. It isn't that I don't want to help, but the church needs me. I'm the only priest in this town, you see, and I already have a lot of duties. There are many sick and needy people here."

"I understand that, Father," Levi said, stepping closer, "but Allegiant is important. We could get rid of the vampires forever —and you could play a role. Don't you see how much you're needed?"

"I'm sorry, but I can't help you. Not right now, at least." Father McGregor reached for the broom again, turning his back to sweep the floors. "Best of luck to you and Allegiant, though. I really do wish you the best. May the Lord grant you the strength to fight the evil in this world. And win."

Levi couldn't let the priest walk away—not when it meant so much to Emilia. He realized he had only one option left to persuade him.

"Wait," Levi said. "I have another question. Do you do confessions here?"

"Of course," the priest replied, turning back around. "Are you in need of absolution?"

"I am. Can we speak in private?"

"Of course. Follow me."

The priest led Levi to a small section of confessional booths. He entered the left side of the confessional while Levi entered the right, and he could barely see the priest through the mesh. Levi took a seat on the bench inside the booth as his heart hammered.

"So, what's bothering you, my child?" Father McGregor asked. "What can I help you with?"

"First off...everything said here is confidential, right? You won't run off and tell anyone? Not even Emilia?"

"Of course not," Father McGregor replied. "What is said here is between you and God. I am merely the mediator."

Between him and God. Levi hadn't felt close to a higher power in years—not since becoming a creature of darkness.

"Good. No one can know what I am, but...I feel the need to tell someone." Levi sighed. "And it might just convince you to join Allegiant."

"Oh? How so?"

"Well, Emilia means a lot to me. I think...I think I'm falling in love with her," Levi murmured. "My brother would laugh if he heard me say that, but it's true. I want to help her and Allegiant, but...she has no idea what's inside of me. Sometimes, what I am makes me sick. And it's only since I arrived here, in this time."

"I don't understand." Father McGregor frowned. "Are you confessing a sin of lust?"

"No, no—not lust." Levi took a deep breath. "Father...I'm a vampire."

CHAPTER

SIXTEEN

The priest's confessional booth creaked, but he didn't say a word. The terrible truth had eaten Levi up inside —and just telling someone made him feel like a weight had lifted off his shoulders.

"A...vampire?" the priest whispered. "One of those foul creatures that's been attacking people at night?"

"Yes—that's exactly right. But you see, Father, that's not the full story. I actually traveled through time to get here..."

Levi told him everything—how the vampire population had dwindled in the future, Allegiant's role in their demise, blood magic, and his growing feelings for Emilia. The priest didn't interrupt, not even once.

"I think I'm becoming more human," Levi said, finishing the story. "Normally vampires can't experience love, but I know I love Emilia. She represents everything good in this world, everything pure. Kindness, bravery, intelligence. She makes me want to be human again. Anyway, I don't know if the change happened because of the blood magic's side effects or what, but I'm also remembering my past life. Bits and pieces, anyway."

"Your past life as a human, you mean?"

"Yeah, before my brother turned me," Levi replied. "I've never told anyone this, but...my brother was in with the wrong crowd in the 1970s. Drinking, drugs, theft. That's when he met a group of vampires and they turned him—initiated him into their ranks. It's pretty rare for a vamp to turn a human into one of them, but I guess they saw something dark inside of him. He was always up to no good—even before he became a vampire. Maybe it was his fate."

"Hmm. And how did *you* become a vampire?"

"I wasn't like my brother. I didn't care for partying or drugs. I went to school and became an architect," Levi replied. "Anyway, I got home one night...and my parents were dead. My brother had killed them both. There was so much blood everywhere..."

The scene came flooding back to Levi. Their normal lives before Cyrus became a vampire. It wasn't perfect—their father drank a lot during their childhood and would strike them from time to time, something their mother would ignore. But then Cyrus became a vampire and killed them both, then turned Levi. Into a monster, an abomination.

"And did you get the authorities?" the priest asked, pulling Levi out of his thoughts.

"I couldn't. My brother had disconnected our phone. He didn't want anyone calling for help," Levi said, knowing the priest wasn't familiar with that technology. "He was supposed to kill me. The other vamps didn't think I had it in me to cause evil, and they feared I'd hold Cyrus back. But my brother couldn't kill me—we'd always been close—so he turned me into one of them instead. I tried to run, but...he overpowered me. The next thing I knew, I had changed forever. I'd become one of them, losing my conscience in the process."

Levi felt a tear slide down his cheek. He hadn't thought

about his parents in decades—or their painful, unnecessary deaths. Levi wiped his eyes and cleared his throat.

"I see. Did you ever resent your brother for what he did to you?" Father McGregor asked. "For killing your parents and stealing your humanity?"

"No, not until now. Vampires love evil, depravity. When I became one, I loved it, too. But now that I'm becoming more human...I'm beginning to wish Cyrus would've killed me that night. That he would've spared me from this life. It's evil."

"My goodness," Father McGregor murmured. "What a terrible burden to carry."

Levi exited the confessional, needing to see him face-to-face. Levi ripped open the curtain to Father McGregor's side and entered. The priest looked frightened for a moment, his eyes wide as he backed away. For once in Levi's life, a human's fear bothered him.

"It's okay. I won't hurt you," Levi told him. "Do you believe what I told you, at least?"

Father McGregor sighed, dropping his tense shoulders. "While most people would think you've gone mad...there's something honest about you that makes me believe your story. I don't think you would make up something so horrific."

Levi breathed a sigh of relief. "Thank you. It feels good to get that off my chest. But now do you see why we need your help? Our Legionnaires need all the moral support they can get. And you could inspire them, Father."

Father McGregor rose to his feet, looking down. "I still don't know, Levi. I have so many obligations as it is..."

"Father, please," Levi urged. "The future of humanity is at stake here. Pardon the pun. If we don't help the Legionnaires, the vampires will kill them all. And I'll have to live with the guilt."

Father McGregor nodded. "I see your point. Very well—take

me to Allegiant Keep. I'll send a letter to the monastery to have another priest handle my sermons while I'm gone."

"Great, thank you," Levi said, breathing out. "I have a horse outside. I'll take you to the keep."

As Levi turned around, the priest's voice stopped him. "Wait a moment, Levi. There's something we must do first."

"What is it?" Levi asked.

He made the sign of the cross. "May God grant you forgiveness and peace. I absolve you of your sins in the name of the Father, the Son, and the Holy Spirit."

A priest would pray for him? A wicked creature, devoid of everything good and holy? It was a nice thought, but Levi shook his head. "Thanks, but I don't think God would forgive me. You wouldn't either if you knew half the things I'd done in my life. I've killed, Father. Time and time again. And I've liked it."

"But that was in the past. And God is more forgiving than us," Father McGregor said, placing a hand on Levi's shoulder. "Our religion teaches us that no one is above forgiveness—no matter how much pain we've caused—as long as we repent and do better. The fact that you stepped into that confessional booth proves you wanted to change. That's a start."

The priest was right—he *had* come here looking for guidance, for forgiveness. Levi just didn't expect it would be that easy.

"There can be forgiveness for me...a creature of evil?" Levi asked. "Are you sure?"

Father McGregor nodded. "Yes. It isn't too late to change, Levi—to do what is right. I pray Emilia will forgive you when she learns the truth. You *do* plan to tell her soon, correct?"

"Yeah, I have no choice. When the Bloodborn Order evolves and attacks, she'll find out about Cyrus, then she'll realize I've been lying to her. You won't tell her, will you?"

"No, of course not. Everything we said here was private. And besides, I think you should be the one to tell her. I'll keep your secret as long as you promise to protect Emilia and Allegiant. You seem to be the only thing standing in the way of their deaths right now."

"You're right. And I'll do my best, Father," Levi said firmly. "This, I swear."

LEVI RODE with the priest back to Allegiant Keep. The man didn't fear Levi any longer—didn't recoil as he had in the confessional. Levi was glad, really needing a friend right now. A confidant.

"When you told me you already had a keep, I didn't expect it to look this good," Father McGregor said, glancing up at the castle in awe. "You've done well, Levi. You're on the road to redemption."

"Thanks," Levi murmured. "I sure hope so. Well, here we are. Make yourself at home."

As Levi and the priest jumped off the horse, Emilia ran over to them. "Levi, you did it! You got the priest. You *are* staying with us, right, Father McGregor?"

The priest nodded. "For now. How long do you plan to run this operation, Emilia?"

"Until every last vampire is dead and gone." Her eyes narrowed. "I'll make sure of it."

Father McGregor glanced at Levi, raising an eyebrow in concern. Would Emilia spare Levi's life when she learned the truth? Or would she demand his death too?

"Anyway, you were gone a long time," Emilia continued, turning to Levi. "Did you run into any trouble?"

"No, no trouble," Levi stammered. "The priest and I just had a good talk."

"Well, I'm glad it all worked out. Now, how about I give you a tour of the keep, Father?"

"I'd love that, thank you. Lead the way."

Sir Anders, Edmund, Samantha, and the other miners practiced their sword fighting in the training yard. Levi nodded politely at them as they led the priest into the foyer. While Levi was out, Peeta, Alana, and some of the others too young to fight had decorated the keep. They placed flowers and banners around to make it homier. Rosalie, Scrooge, Vana, Novak, and the others guarded the castle, still on patrol. Levi noticed Cyrus and Frederic whispering in the corner and worried about their plans.

Emilia led Levi and the priest to the small chapel in the back of the keep. She had decorated the room with religious items—crosses, paintings of God, and holy water. The others had found an old desk that the priest could work at and carried it into the chapel.

"Here we are, Father. Your office. I wanted to make this the safest room in the keep," Emilia explained. "We don't want anything to happen to you—and we wanted to make you feel at home."

Father McGregor smiled. "That's kind of you, thanks."

Levi spotted a memorial stone near the back of the room. As he walked over to it, he realized it read: DAWN RUTHERFORD, TAKEN TOO SOON.

"You found that, huh? I couldn't forget about her," Emilia said, sadly. "She's the reason we started Allegiant, after all."

"Dawn passed away?" Father McGregor asked, wide-eyed. "My goodness."

Emilia nodded. "She did. You haven't heard? She was killed by one of the vampires when Lord Tristan's castle was attacked. It feels like a lifetime ago."

"Dawn will be the last to die," Levi said. "You have my word."

The priest looked proud, giving him a half-smile. Levi didn't want to let him down.

"I hope so. Well, I think everyone's eager to get started," Emilia said. "Why don't we begin our first lesson in here?"

Levi nodded, rushing outside to round up everyone. They crammed inside the small chapel, then Levi watched Cyrus and Frederic wander in after them. Levi hated that they were there, listening in on them. Learning all their secrets. He wanted nothing more than to expose them both.

"Levi, you should start this lesson," Emilia said, turning to him. "You mentioned you've dealt with vampires in the past. Why don't we talk about their weaknesses first?"

The crowd stared at Levi. He felt nervous as he stepped forward—another human emotion he didn't anticipate. Cyrus and Frederic watched Levi, hoping he'd give the Legionnaires false information, but he couldn't do that.

Levi thought about this era's vampires. "Well, sunlight is a big factor. The vampires can't survive under it. But don't be fooled—vampires are constantly evolving. Don't be surprised if sunlight doesn't affect them one day."

As the Legionnaires murmured in fear, Cyrus and Frederic shared a glance.

Alana raised her hand. "If they become immune to sunlight, how else can we identify them?"

"Many ways. Silver—it burns their skin like acid," Levi replied. "Religious items too, like the cross. Stab it right through their heart to kill them. Anywhere else—like the arm or leg— isn't good enough. Since vampires have no emotions, you can also identify them by their evil deeds. Serial killers, thieves, kidnappers. They follow that sort of behavior."

Levi felt nauseous to think about it—that he was once just

like them, without remorse or a conscience. Becoming human again was painful.

"That's helpful, Levi, thanks. Now that we know how to kill them," Emilia began with a smile, "let's practice, shall we? Follow Levi, everyone, and we'll get started."

Levi led the group outside to the training yard. Emilia had set up a row of dummies—with pointy, drawn-on fangs—so they'd have something to attack. The Legionnaires each grabbed a silver sword and swung them around.

Emilia glanced at her recruits. "All right, we're ready now. Sir Anders was kind enough to borrow some weapons for us from the castle. Luckily, Lord Tristan hasn't noticed. Now, I know fighting can seem daunting, but really, it just takes some practice..."

Emilia demonstrated a few moves, then the others followed. The Legionnaires began practicing as Levi watched from a distance. He gave them advice but made sure not to touch the silver. Some of the miners were naturals, but others needed some work. Levi helped them correct their form and hoped they'd be powerful enough when Frederic's formula was perfected.

Samantha swung her sword, beating the dummy with rapid strikes. Cyrus walked over, standing behind her as he placed his hands on hers.

"Your stance is a little off," he said. "Here, I'll guide you."

Samantha smiled as Cyrus helped her swing. His teeth were inches away from her neck, and he could've killed her in the blink of an eye. Levi looked away, his fists balling.

Emilia walked over to Levi, panting. "Well, training is going well, I'd say. The miners should be able to return to work soon. I warned them about the vampire's lair, and they'll block it off as soon as they get back."

"A smart idea," Frederic said, walking over to them. "We

wouldn't want the vampires too close for comfort, now, would we?"

Levi gulped as Frederic sauntered away, watching the Legionnaires practice their sword-fighting. He was studying them—learning their weaknesses. Levi knew he was. Despite his nonchalance, it worried him. Especially when he had gone to great lengths to keep Cyrus out of the loop.

They practiced until sundown, and Levi started to see some improvements—especially with the advice he had given them. Cyrus hadn't said anything to the others, spending the entire day getting closer to Samantha. Levi didn't know what Cyrus was planning, but he *did* know it wouldn't end well for her. Every so often, Cyrus would glance over at Levi, making him wonder if his brother was growing even more suspicious— especially since there was a priest on the premises now.

By nightfall, the training had stopped so the new Legion- naires could eat and sleep. Sir Anders said goodbye, needing to return to the castle. Alana and Peeta served them their meals, making sure to include some raw meat for Levi, but he didn't want it anymore. For once, human food was starting to taste good. After he had finished his dinner—slipping in some rice and vegetables when Cyrus and Frederic weren't looking—he searched for Emilia, but he couldn't find her anywhere.

On a beautiful night like this, there's only one place she could be, he thought.

He climbed the staircase to the watchtower, gazing out at the farmland under the darkness. Emilia stood near the edge, the cool night breeze swaying her red hair. It cascaded down her shoulders, free from the confines of the ponytail she usually wore.

"There you are," Levi said, standing beside her. "I was looking for you."

She looked back at him. "Sorry, I just needed some alone time."

"Oh, I get it. I'll be downstairs—"

"Stay," she said, grabbing his arm. "Please."

That brought a smile to his face. They stood in silence for a few moments, with Emilia staring out into the distance. Levi cleared his throat and leaned toward her, nudging her elbow. "So, what are you thinking about?"

"Allegiant. Seems that's all I think about nowadays," she murmured. "Everything is going well. The keep, the training, Father McGregor joining us..."

"But? I sense a *but* coming."

"*But* I feel like something terrible is going to happen," she said, looking at Levi. "Maybe I'm just afraid, but...our luck can't be this good, can it?"

This is it, Levi thought. *A chance to come clean and warn her about the vampires. I need to tell her the truth about me, no matter how hard it is.*

Levi sighed. "Emilia, I need to tell you—"

"What is that?" Emilia asked, pointing in the distance.

Levi looked at what had caught her eye. His vampire vision let him see through the darkness, noticing the fire. It spread around a large area of crops before creeping toward a cabin. It took Levi a moment to recognize it from so far away.

"Rutherford Farm," Levi cried. "It's on fire!"

Emilia wasted no time. She sprinted down the stairs, rushing to Margaret whom she had left tied up outside. Everyone in the dining hall watched, murmuring in fear. Levi chased after her, wanting to find out what had happened.

After he stepped outside, Sir Anders approached on a horse and jumped down. Emilia paused, confused. "Sir Anders? I thought you went back to the castle. What are you—"

"I was too late. I couldn't stop it!" he cried, panting. "I'm so sorry, Emilia. So very sorry."

Emilia frowned. The people inside left the keep, rushing over to see what was going on. Peeta and Alana pushed through to Emilia's side while Cyrus and Frederic kept their distance, just watching like always.

"Stop what?" Levi asked. "Why are you sorry?"

"Lord Tristan," Sir Anders began, still trying to catch his breath. "He set fire to Rutherford Farm. He was still angry with you for rejecting him. Anyway, by the time I got to the castle, he'd already left to set the blaze himself. When the guards told me where he was going, it was too late. I couldn't talk him out of it."

The crowd gasped. No one wanted to believe Lord Tristan could do something so horrible—but Levi could. He had threatened them time and time again. Levi felt like he should've seen this coming.

"Shit, this isn't good. I need to find my parents," Emilia said. "I have to make sure they're all right."

"We're coming too," Peeta said, helping Alana onto Margaret.

"Count me in as well. If you run into any vampires, you'll need back-up," Levi said, grabbing another horse and pulling himself up. "Let's go!"

Emilia nodded. Sir Anders followed the four of them, galloping behind on his horse. By the time they'd made it to the farm, the fire had enveloped the property. The little shack where Cyrus and Levi had slept had disintegrated, the crops burned to a crisp, and the roof on the cabin had collapsed. Everything was a bright sea of orange and red under the starry sky.

Emilia jumped off her horse first. "I'm heading inside to find my parents. I need to make sure they're all right."

Levi grabbed her, holding her back. "Are you crazy? It's too dangerous. Stay here with the others. I'll head inside and look for your parents."

"But—"

"You're too valuable to Allegiant, Emilia," he interrupted, looking into her eyes. "If we lost you, everything would fall apart. But I'm not important."

"But you *are* important, Levi. To me."

And then she pulled him in for a quick kiss, leaving Levi stunned. Her lips on his stirred something inside of him. In that moment, he felt alive again—like he wasn't a monster anymore. Like he really was the man she thought he was.

"Come back alive," she whispered, "and get my parents out safely."

The crackle of flames behind him snapped him out of his daze. Levi nodded, leaving Emilia with Peeta, Alana, and Sir Anders as he rushed inside the blazing cabin. He didn't know if he'd find anyone alive, but he had to try—for Emilia's sake.

SEVENTEEN

The smoke was thick as Levi rushed through the door of the cabin. The fire had torn through the home, destroying everything in its path.

"Hello?" Levi called out. "Is anyone in here?"

No response. Levi closed his eyes, listening carefully. He heard only one heartbeat nearby—human, but it was faint.

Levi rushed through the kitchen, the flames nipping at his skin before he tripped over something solid. He looked down, realizing it was Emilia's father, Ivan. His face looked badly burned from an explosion.

When Levi bent down to check his pulse, he couldn't find one. Although he hated the man, he felt sorry for him. And Emilia's loss.

But it meant one thing—her mother was still alive. That must've been her heartbeat Levi had heard. And if he could get to her, maybe something good could still come out of this.

Levi stepped over Ivan's body, sprinting to the bedrooms. He knocked down the doors of two rooms before making his way to the third. When he entered, he noticed Emilia's mother lying on the floor. It looked like she had tried to escape through the window, but the smoke had knocked her unconscious.

When Levi checked her pulse, he could feel it beating against his hand—but it was growing weaker by the second. He picked up the woman, holding her in his arms as he walked toward the window. But the wall collapsed, trapping the two of them in a ring of fire. With the flames creeping closer, Levi had one option left.

He had to run through the fire.

He took a step back, then sprinted as fast as he could through the broken wall. The fire licked his skin—not as bad as silver, but painful enough to make him cry out. He kept Emilia's mother close to him, shielding her body from the spitting flames.

When he'd made it outside, taking shelter in the field, his sleeve was on fire. He placed her mother on the ground, then patted the flame out. Emilia, Peeta, Alana, and Sir Anders rushed over with wide eyes.

"Mother!" Emilia cried, feeling for a pulse. "Can you hear me?"

The woman didn't respond. Emilia tried hard to save her mother, placing different herbs on her chest, but nothing helped. It was a primitive way of trying to save her life. Levi pushed her aside gently so he could perform chest compressions and mouth-to-mouth on her mother as the fire burned behind them. Alana led the animals out of the stables, keeping them safe. After a few attempts at CPR, Levi pulled back, the woman lying still.

Emilia checked her mother's pulse again, hanging her head in shame. "She's...she's gone."

Tears welled in Peeta's eyes as he looked at Levi. "What about our father? Did you get him out too?"

Levi shook his head. "I'm sorry, but he was already dead when I got there."

When the house collapsed behind them in a sea of burning rubble, Emilia wailed. Levi pulled her into his arms as Alana and Peeta cried together. Even the animals seemed distressed behind them, attempting to burst through the fenced, grassy area while moaning loudly at the destruction of their home.

"How could Lord Tristan do this?" Alana asked. "He's no better than the vampires!"

"Jealousy can make people do crazy things," Levi said. "And some people just have evil in their hearts."

"The last time I saw my parents," Emilia said, sniffling, "we argued about Allegiant—about Peeta and Alana joining. Now they're gone..."

"Hey, none of this is your fault," Levi said, pulling back to look her in the eyes. Their green depths drowned in tears. "Your parents knew you loved them, and in the end, that's what mattered. Besides, your mother came around—she said she supported you. Don't blame yourself for what Lord Tristan did."

Levi glanced back at the cabin. Sir Anders kept trying to put the fire out, using the water from the stables, but it was barely helping.

"Sir Anders, take them back to the keep," Levi said, rising to his feet. "Take the animals, too."

"Why? Where are you going?" Emilia asked, drying her eyes.

Levi balled his fists. "I'm going to find Lord Tristan. He'll answer for this."

"I'm coming with you."

"No, I don't think that's a good idea. He might try to kill you, too. Let me handle this. I'll make him pay. I swear it."

Emilia nodded, but Sir Anders stepped forward with concern. "I don't think that's a good idea. Lord Tristan has a lot of power—"

"I don't give a damn," Levi snapped. "Royal or not, what happened here was wrong. Now, go—take everyone back to the keep. I've got a score to settle."

Sir Anders nodded, escorting Emilia, Peeta, and Alana onto the back of his horse. He herded the animals, gesturing for them to follow him, as Levi got on his horse and galloped down the dusty country road. The farm continued to burn behind him.

When he made it to the castle, he noticed Lord Tristan's carriage out front. There was no knight on duty outside the castle, so Levi kicked the door down, entering the throne room. Lord Tristan was still awake, speaking with several advisors while sitting on his throne. Their heads snapped toward him at the sudden noise.

Lord Tristan sneered at Levi. "You! I thought I told you never to show your face around here again."

Levi shoved the guards and advisors to the side before pushing Lord Tristan to the floor. The royal fell with a thud, looking up into Levi's eyes. As the guards swarmed them, ready to attack, Levi reached forward and grabbed the sword from Lord Tristan's scabbard. The silver stung his hand, but he barely felt it.

He swung the sword at the guards. "Come any closer and I'll kill you. Now, outside—go on. This is a private meeting."

The guards looked at Lord Tristan, waiting for orders. The throne room turned silent.

"I mean it," Levi continued. "Outside—now. Go!"

The guards, servants, and advisors fled the castle. After they had closed the front door, Lord Tristan scoffed. "Goddamn cowards. They're all fired—"

Levi pressed the sword against Lord Tristan's neck, shutting him up by drawing blood. "I didn't come here to talk about your guards. I came here because you burned down Rutherford Farm and killed Emilia's parents."

"I did no such thing," Lord Tristan spat. "You're mistaken, foreigner."

"Sir Anders says otherwise. You can't lie your way out of this one."

He blinked. "Sir Anders? When did you speak with him?"

"A few minutes ago. He joined Allegiant. He's been spying on you for us."

"Blasted fool," Lord Tristan muttered. "I'll have him hanged for this!"

"It isn't him you have to worry about," Levi continued, "it's yourself. Why shouldn't I kill you for this?"

"Because it could be very lucrative for you." Lord Tristan gestured around the castle. "Think of all the gold I could offer—"

Levi kicked Lord Tristan in the face, then the royal groaned and rolled over. "You can't bribe me—not after what you've done. Monster!"

Lord Tristan reached a hand up, wiping away the blood on his face. "Stop, stop! Surely, you've been rejected by a woman before. Haven't you ever wanted revenge?"

Levi paused. As a vampire, revenge came naturally to him—like drinking blood. But Lord Tristan was a human. He had no excuse.

"I have, but we're not talking about me. We're talking about *you*. I should've let King Brutus kill you when I had the chance. Emilia's parents would still be alive if I had," Levi muttered. "I thought you needed Rutherford Farm? That it was the largest in Osgoode?"

"I did at one point, but we have other suppliers," Lord Tristan said, spitting blood onto the floor. "We can do without one bitch and her family."

Levi growled, picking Lord Tristan up and slamming him

into the wall. "Don't talk about her like that, asshole. She's a better person than you'll ever be."

"My, my...you really care for her, don't you?" Lord Tristan searched his eyes for the truth. "No. It's more than that, isn't it? You love her?"

Levi scoffed. "What business is it of yours?"

"Because she's not worth killing me for. Believe me, you'd find better company down at the brothel."

His words only antagonized Levi further, pushing him completely over the edge. He tossed Lord Tristan across the floor, his fangs protruding in anger. Levi wanted to feast, to drink from Lord Tristan right there, to make him die slowly.

When Lord Tristan rolled over and looked up at Levi, his eyes widened. "You're...you're one of them. Those monsters. Aren't you?"

"Yes, I am," Levi said, his fangs giving him a lisp. "And I'm sure you know all the ways I could kill you."

"No, no, no. Please," Lord Tristan said, crawling onto his knees to beg. "Don't kill me. I'll give you whatever you want. I'll...I'll build Emilia a new farm!"

"No—she lives at the keep now. And a new farm couldn't bring back her parents." Levi hoisted Lord Tristan up by his cape. "The only thing I want is you dead."

"No...someone, help!"

But as Levi prepared to sink his fangs into Lord Tristan's neck to kill him, something inside of him snapped. He realized how fragile humans looked when they were begging for their lives.

Levi knew one thing—he couldn't do it. Killing was wrong, no matter what the vampires had taught him. He tossed Lord Tristan to the floor again, turning his back on him. Everything became quiet in the throne room.

Lord Tristan scrambled to rise to his feet, his eyes wide. "You...you won't kill me?"

"No," Levi said, forcing his fangs to disappear. They faded back into his gums. "Be glad I showed you mercy. Be glad I'm not like the other vampires. And if you tell anyone—especially Emilia—about what I really am..."

"I won't, I swear it. Thank you." Lord Tristan exhaled. "Is there any way I can show my gratitude?"

An idea flashed across Levi's mind as he turned around. "Yes—you'll publicly come out and support Allegiant. You'll supply us with everything we need, even use your castle for parties in its honor. In fact, I think you should invite those foreign royals over again—recruit their armies for Allegiant. We could always use more Legionnaires."

Lord Tristan nodded without hesitation. "Yes, yes, of course—anything you need. I'll get started on that right away. But what if the royals don't want to return after the last attack?"

"Then convince them," Levi said. "Allegiant will be there, and if another surprise attack happens, we'll be better prepared to stop it. Maybe the vampire attack will inspire them to be generous—with their coin *and* soldiers."

Lord Tristan nodded again, gulping. "Indeed. Indeed, I can do that."

"Good. And one last thing. If you ever come near Emilia again," Levi said, getting in his face, "I *will* kill you."

"Understood—believe me." Lord Tristan swallowed hard. "May...may I ask you something?"

"What is it?"

"If you're a vampire...why are you helping Allegiant?"

Levi paused. "It's...complicated. You wouldn't understand—"

"Watch out!" Lord Tristan cried, pointing behind Levi.

Levi jumped out of the way as a silver sword swung toward him. When he looked back, he saw Sir Anders coming at him. The front door was open an inch where the knight must've sneaked inside.

"What the hell are you doing?" Levi demanded. "You could've killed me!"

"Good. I know what you are, Levi. I overheard everything," Sir Anders replied, holding his sword high. "Does Emilia know?"

Levi said nothing, glancing down at the floor.

Sir Anders scoffed. "Of course not. If she did, she'd kill you. You've been fooling everyone, only pretending to help her so she'd let her guard down. Haven't you? Answer me!"

"You really shouldn't be here, Sir Anders," Levi said. "I told you to take Emilia and the others back to the keep."

"And I did. But after I made sure they were safe, I decided to come to the castle in case you needed my help." Sir Anders shook his head. "My God. A vampire—right under our noses this whole time."

"Look, I may be a vampire," Levi began, "but I've changed. I want to help Allegiant. And I care about Emilia, so put the sword down—"

"He's right," Lord Tristan said behind him, much to Levi's surprise. "Levi could've killed me for what I did, but he let me go. He's not like the others. Sir Anders, I order you to put your sword away."

"No—no, I can't trust you. Either of you," Sir Anders said, glaring at them. "You're both murderers. And while I can't kill a human—not even one as despicable as Lord Tristan—I *can* kill a vampire. It's what you trained me for, remember?"

Levi still had Lord Tristan's sword in his hand, so he held it up to block Sir Anders's attack as the knight leaned forward. Their swords clanged together, making a crisscross. Sir Anders grunted as he tried to get the upper hand and force his sword into Levi's chest, but Levi was too strong.

Lord Tristan moved out of the way, rushing back to his throne as the two men fought. Levi and Sir Anders went back and forth, one sword swinging at a time, and the knight groaned in exertion.

"I don't want to kill you," Levi said, dodging another swing. "And you know I could—easily. So just put the sword down and we'll talk this through. You're a good fighter, Anders. I don't want Allegiant to lose someone like you."

"No—no, I can't. You warned us that vampires were cunning, and I know what you're planning," Sir Anders snarled. "I won't listen to you. Perhaps Allegiant won't kill all the vampires, but at least I can start with—"

Sir Anders gasped, then went still. Levi's eyes widened when he noticed the bite mark on his neck and the familiar tuft of brown hair over his shoulder. Cyrus stood behind him, his fangs burrowed into the knight's neck. After a few seconds, he released Sir Anders, who then fell dead on the floor.

"You're welcome," Cyrus said, wiping the blood off his mouth. "Ah, fresh blood. Delicious."

"What the hell did you do that for?" Levi demanded. "He was an innocent!"

Cyrus laughed. "Killing innocents is what we do, Levi. In case you forgot. Sir Anders wouldn't have stopped, you know. You would've had to kill him. Why's it matter if it was with a sword or my fangs?"

Maybe Cyrus had a point. Still, Levi looked down at the dead body, ashamed. "What are you even doing here, Brother? I thought you stayed at the keep."

Cyrus shook his head. "I decided to follow you to find out what was going on. When I saw you say goodbye to Emilia outside the farm, I knew you'd come here. For revenge. Because

I know I would have. And when I spotted all the guards outside, I sneaked up the side of the castle in case you needed back-up."

"Well, I *don't* need back-up," Levi snapped. "I can handle this by myself, thank you very much."

Cyrus turned away and ignored him, directing his attention toward Lord Tristan. "There's just one witness left. And we both know we can't have that."

Lord Tristan was too injured from Levi's beating to run, so he staggered toward the door. But Cyrus lunged on him, dragging him back over to Levi. Lord Tristan squirmed in his grasp as Cyrus chuckled. It made Levi feel sick again, his stomach churning.

"Should I do it, or do you want the honors?" Cyrus asked Levi, gesturing at Lord Tristan.

"No, please," Lord Tristan cried, his eyes wide in fear. "Levi, do something. I'm begging you!"

Cyrus laughed. "Levi isn't going to help you—"

Levi lunged forward and pushed Cyrus off Lord Tristan. He moved in front of the royal, shielding him from his brother. When Cyrus regained his balance, he looked at Levi, his eyes wide.

"What the hell are you doing? We both know we can't let him live, Brother," Cyrus argued. "He'll tell everyone what you are! And besides, you've hated Lord Tristan since day one. I thought you'd want this."

"No. I won't kill him," Levi said firmly. "And he's already agreed to keep our secret. Isn't that right?"

Lord Tristan nodded, his eyes briefly flitting to Sir Anders's dead body. "Yes—yes, your secret is safe with me. Please, just let me go!"

"Get out of here, Tristan," Levi ordered, his eyes never leaving his brother. "Return to the guards outside. When they ask what happened in here, lie."

Lord Tristan nodded, limping out of the castle. Cyrus sneered when it was just the two of them. "All right, time out. I don't know what the hell's gotten into you, but you've been acting weird since we got to Osgoode. And don't think I didn't see you kiss Emilia! That's right, I followed you. I've been concerned about your behavior."

Levi's heart clenched in fear. "Hey—she kissed me, not the other way around! And if I hadn't run inside, she would have—and the fire would've killed her. Why would I want her dead when we haven't had the chance to sabotage Allegiant yet?"

"God damn it. That better all be true," Cyrus said, getting closer. "Because if I find out you aren't just playing around with her, and you're serious..."

"You'll do what?" Levi asked, crossing his arms.

"You don't want to find out. Trust me."

And then Cyrus turned and fled the castle.

Levi looked down at Sir Anders's body in the silence, shaking his head. Another needless death at the hands of a vampire. As he dragged the body out of the castle, he wondered how he would explain his death to Emilia and the others.

EIGHTEEN

As Levi placed Sir Anders's body on the back of his horse, he didn't see Cyrus anywhere and assumed his brother had left. The guards headed back inside, but Lord Tristan stayed behind. Levi was just about to leave when the royal stepped in front of his horse.

"You didn't have to spare my life back there, you know," Lord Tristan said. "You could've killed me—or let your brother do it. Maybe I would've deserved it. Why didn't you?"

Levi glanced out into the distance, noticing the stars in the sky. He was about to say Emilia as his reason, but it was more than that. Sure, she had awakened something inside of him— but he wanted to change.

Maybe there's still hope for my redemption, Levi thought. *Maybe Father McGregor was right.*

"Does it matter?" Levi asked, not wanting to tell Lord Tristan more than he needed to know. "You're alive. Don't waste it."

"Right. I know this doesn't mean much, but...be careful, Levi. I wish you great success in stopping the vampires. And I *will* keep my promise to Allegiant about getting more recruits."

Levi nodded and galloped toward Allegiant Keep in the distance, passing Rutherford Farm. Everything the Rutherfords had worked for all these years had vanished with one fire. With the rain, Levi hoped it would put out the flames. It had already started to extinguish the old shed.

As he neared Allegiant Keep, Levi spotted the pirates patrolling the grounds. The pirates and barbarians worked in shifts, and tonight, it was the pirates' turn. Rosalie lifted her silver sword but lowered it when she made out Levi through the darkness.

"You made it," Rosalie said. "Your brother's inside, too—he just got back. He spoke with Frederic for a little while before heading to bed."

Levi wondered if Cyrus had told Frederic what happened. He was running out of excuses to justify his traitorous behavior.

Rosalie's eyes widened in shock when she noticed Sir Anders's body. "Dear Lord. What happened to him?"

"Vampires," Levi said. "I need to talk to Emilia. Where is she?"

"In the training yard," Rosalie replied, still looking at the knight's body. "Poor son-of-a-bitch..."

As Levi entered the training yard, shielded by a thick wall of stone, he spotted Emilia practicing on a dummy. She was soaking wet from the rain, aggressively stabbing it with groans of exertion. Levi felt even guiltier for Sir Anders's death now. He had safely gotten Emilia and her family back to the keep, and Cyrus had killed him anyway. The knight deserved better.

As Levi put his horse away in the stables, he spotted Peeta and Alana taking care of the animals they had brought from Rutherford Farm. They laid down some hay for the animals to eat and made sure their troughs had enough rainwater. Levi walked over, poking his head inside the stables.

"Hey, what's Emilia doing out there?" Levi asked them. "It's late."

"Getting out her anger," Peeta replied, watching her from the window. "She's done this before. I'd just leave her alone if I were you. As for us, we couldn't sleep, not after…"

Levi didn't say anything. He could feel their grief—something the humans called empathy.

"Did you…did you make Lord Tristan pay?" Peeta asked, quietly.

Levi nodded. "Don't worry. He learned his lesson."

Alana's eyes widened when she noticed Sir Anders's dead body at Levi's side. "What happened?"

"Oh, uh, vampire attack," Levi muttered. "Keep his body here. We'll give him a proper burial in the morning."

Levi fled the stables, walking over to Emilia. He stood behind her, thinking she'd talk to him, but she only continued hitting the dummy. As she raised her arm again, lifting the sword, Levi grabbed her hand.

"I think you've practiced enough," Levi said. "It's been a long night. You need your rest, Emilia."

Emilia wiggled out of his grasp, returning to the dummy. "I don't want to stop. It's the only thing taking my mind off everything."

"Are you still blaming yourself?"

She paused, her head low. "Yes. A bit. I should've told my parents to stay here. I shouldn't have given them a choice. Now look at them. They're fucking dead!"

"If you have to blame anyone, you should blame *me*," Levi said. "I promised you Dawn would be the last to die. And I failed. I should've known Lord Tristan would do something."

Emilia shook her head. "I could never blame you, Levi. You've been Allegiant's biggest supporter—*my* biggest supporter. Besides, Dawn was killed by the vampires. This was different. I should blame Lord Tristan for this. Nobody forced him to set fire to my farm. He made that decision alone, out of jealousy and anger."

"Well, if it's any consolation, Lord Tristan got what was coming to him."

"You...you didn't kill him, did you?" Emilia asked, fear in her eyes as she glanced at Levi. "I know he did something evil, but still."

The way she looked at him—as though she thought he was a murderer—made him realize she might not forgive him for his past. He hated that look in her eyes. He wanted her to go back to seeing him as a loyal friend, maybe something more. Whatever that kiss had meant.

"No, I didn't kill him," Levi eventually said. "But I *did* leave a few bruises."

"You didn't have to do that. Probably best if you hadn't," Emilia muttered. "What if he sends his guards after you?"

Levi shook his head. "I don't think he'll do that. Trust me— he learned his lesson. You should've seen him begging for his life."

"Good." Emilia tossed her sword to the ground. "Now I wish I could've been there."

"*And* he offered his support to Allegiant. He's inviting royals from all over the world. He's agreed to tell them about Allegiant —to get more recruits for us."

"Really?" Emilia asked, cocking an eyebrow. "If we would've had his help a long time ago, perhaps things would've been different. In any case, thank you for convincing him, Levi. Lord Tristan has a lot of influence—he could help us build an army. Think of what we could do if we had hundreds of soldiers instead of a few dozen. Perhaps something good *will* come from this."

"It just might." Levi nodded. "Did you bury your mother yet?"

"No—we're waiting until morning when the rain stops." Emilia sighed. "I wish I didn't have to bury her at all. Or my father."

"I know. And I'm sorry," Levi said, wincing. "I have some more bad news, actually. Sir Anders came to the castle to help me, but...he was attacked by a rogue vampire. He...didn't make it."

"Lord have mercy." Emilia placed her head in her hands. "When will it end, Levi? All this death and suffering? What if Allegiant can't stop the vampires?"

"I don't know," Levi mumbled, pulling her into a hug. "Let's just get inside. I don't want you to get sick."

As Emilia sniffled and entered the castle with Levi, the warmth of the nearby fireplace hit them immediately. Emilia looked beautiful in the orange glow, and Levi wanted to ask her about the kiss. What had it meant? Was it just a heat-of-the-moment thing? So many questions ran through his head, but he thought it might be inappropriate to bring it up while she was still grieving.

"I know I've said it before, but thank you for all your help," Emilia began, looking up at him. "Not many people would've confronted Lord Tristan for me."

"You're welcome." Levi noticed Emilia glance down at his hand, wide-eyed. "What? What's wrong?"

"Your hand," she said, reaching for him. "Just like your leg..."

Levi had completely forgotten about the burn mark on his hand from wielding the silver sword. He ripped it away from Emilia, shrugging. "It's nothing—don't worry. I must've burned my hand while pulling your mother out of the fire."

Levi knew it would begin to heal quickly, and he didn't

want Emilia to see that. It was bad enough she had noticed how fast his leg had healed. He stuffed his hand inside his pocket, hoping she'd forget about it.

"You're incredible, you know that?" Emilia asked. "Rushing in to save my parents, teaching Lord Tristan a lesson. You've got to be the kindest man I've ever met in my life. A real breath of fresh air around here."

Levi squirmed, uncomfortable hearing her say that. He knew it wasn't true—that she'd take it back if she knew what he had done.

Levi hesitated. "I'm not as kind as you think I am, Emilia. Trust me."

Emilia frowned. "What are you talking about?"

"Emilia, listen." He leaned in, struggling for the words. "There are some things you don't know about me—"

"I've done it!" a familiar voice cried, their footsteps rushing into the room.

Levi spun around, scowling over the interruption. He noticed Frederic standing there with dozens of swords in his hand. He placed them on the nearby table as Cyrus stood behind him, smirking.

"What *is* all of this, Fred?" Emilia asked, looking down at the swords.

"My latest experiment was a success, Emilia. I fortified these blades with extra-strength silver," Frederic explained. "The vampires won't know what hit them."

Levi couldn't believe it. Why would Frederic give Allegiant something so powerful? And why was Cyrus awake when Rosalie had said he'd gone to bed?

Emilia beamed. "Thank you, Frederic. Tomorrow, we'll let our recruits test them out. I'm so glad you decided to join us. I can tell you're going to do a lot of great work for Allegiant."

"Count on it," Frederic said with a wink.

"Wonderful." Emilia yawned, turning to Levi. "Anyway, I should get to bed. We have long days ahead of us. See you tomorrow, Levi."

After she had walked upstairs, Frederic raised an eyebrow. "What's going on with Lord Tristan?"

Levi's heart pounded. "Emilia, uh, managed to get Lord Tristan on Allegiant's side. Who would've thought? I guess humans *can* change."

Cyrus and Frederic said nothing. Their silence wasn't good. And Levi could sense it.

Levi cleared his throat, lowering his voice. "Anyway, what's the deal with all these weapons? Are you really helping Allegiant?"

Frederic snickered. "Oh, please—don't make me laugh. These weapons are useless against the vampires."

"But...that's not what you told Emilia."

"Of course not! We want Allegiant to think we're on their side, right?"

"Exactly," Cyrus said, his eyes boring into Levi's. "And that's the plan we're going to follow."

Levi gulped. "And when do you plan to do that? Uh, when do *we* plan to attack?"

"Soon," Frederic said, glancing back at Cyrus. "Once the sunlight serum is ready, this town will be ours for the taking. And with little acts of sabotage like this one, letting everyone believe these swords can kill vampires when they really can't, it'll be too easy to destroy Allegiant. From within."

Levi tried to keep his hands steady, but he knew he was shaking.

"And another thing," Frederic continued. "Our vampires are getting hungry again. They need to hunt—and I'm sure you and Cyrus are starving too. All that raw animal meat Emilia's been feeding you just isn't the same. We were thinking of attacking the orphanage tomorrow night. Slaughter's idea."

"The...orphanage?" Levi asked, his stomach queasy.

Cyrus nodded. "Yeah—I heard from Samantha they've got a lot of children living there. She and her dad send a lot of gold to help out. We've been getting closer lately—she feels comfortable sharing more things with me now. Just like you and Emilia."

It's nothing like that, Levi thought.

"How nice," he said through gritted teeth.

"It's almost dawn, so we'll head out later tonight," Frederic said. "And if any of the Legionnaires find out and try to stop us, these swords won't do them much good. There's no silver in them at all. They're practically props."

When Frederic looked down at the sabotaged swords with pride, something inside Levi snapped. He picked up all the weapons, snapping them in half before chucking them inside the nearby fireplace. They all burned up, broken and bent.

"No!" Frederic cried, falling to his knees. "What the...why did you do that, Levi?"

Cyrus slammed Levi up against the wall, pinning him there. "A good question. What do you have to say for yourself, Brother?"

"It's a waste of time," Levi lied, struggling against the wall. "All these petty tricks and mind games, I mean. You should be working on the sunlight cure instead. *That* will be Allegiant's downfall, not some faulty weapons. Besides, if they found out there wasn't real silver in there, it'd look suspicious, wouldn't it?"

"I hope that's the truth, Brother," Cyrus muttered, pulling back.

"Why wouldn't it be?" Levi asked. "Look, I want Allegiant to die just as much as you do—to avenge those we lost, like Patriarch. You know how close I was with him. He made me his replacement, after all. Did you think I'd forget it was Allegiant who killed him?"

That seemed to persuade Cyrus. His gaze softened.

"I know we can focus our efforts on better things," Levi continued, "like the sunlight cure. That's more important than anything else. We should focus on sabotage while Frederic gets to work. He's the brains here."

Frederic sighed. "Perhaps you're right. Let him go, Cyrus. I'll get back to work on the sunlight cure. But if you destroy my experiments again...I'll stake you myself."

Levi gulped. "Noted."

A minute later, Emilia rushed down the staircase. "What happened? I heard shouting."

He knew he had to tell her about the weapons. She'd find out eventually when Frederic had nothing to give her tomorrow.

"An accident," Levi said, motioning toward the fireplace. "The weapons were destroyed. I'm so sorry, Emilia."

"What? How did it happen?" she demanded.

"Frederic, he...he tripped," Levi lied. "We tried to salvage them, but they burned up too fast."

She looked disappointed, the curves of her mouth turning downward. "I see. Well, I'm confident we can carry on. Would you be interested in making us more, Frederic?"

"Of course," Frederic lied. "I'm also working on a...secret project. I think it'll really help."

"Are you? Good, I can't wait to see it." Emilia turned back toward the staircase. "Well, goodnight again—and be careful around the fire. Everyone at Allegiant is family, and I don't want to see anyone get hurt. We've already lost Sir Anders."

As Emilia left, Levi felt so guilty, he thought he might burst.

"See you tomorrow evening, Brother," Cyrus said, patting

his shoulder. "Remember all those hunts we used to go on in our younger days?"

Levi nodded sadly. "I remember."

"It's been too long," Cyrus replied, cracking his knuckles. "I can't wait to get back to it. See you later."

When Levi said goodbye, then returned to his private room, he didn't sleep at all. He kept thinking about Emilia's kindness and how that would get her killed if he didn't save her. But then his mind drifted to the orphanage, and he knew one thing.

He couldn't let the vampires kill those children. Like the swords, he'd have to find a way to sabotage their plans—but without them knowing this time. He was on thin ice as it was. He lay awake all night, dreaming up a devious plan that only a vampire could think of.

The next morning, Levi joined the others at Sir Anders's funeral. They had dug a little spot near the training yard to bury Emilia's mother, father, and Sir Anders. And although Levi knew Cyrus and Frederic were watching, he still pulled Emilia in for a hug, unable to resist.

"We may have lost some of our own, but take heart," Father McGregor said, as they lowered the bodies. "This is not the end. I can feel it in the air—God is with us, and Allegiant is the way forward. When we destroy the vampires, these souls will be avenged."

That seemed to cheer everyone up—even Emilia.

After the funeral, Edmund approached them. "Very sorry for your loss, Emilia. Just letting you know that the miners and I are heading back to work today. Although Lord Tristan sent us a letter telling us to take our time—generous, I know—we want to get back. And we plan to block off that entrance into their lair when we get in."

Cyrus walked over to them. "A lair? What lair?"

Edmund nodded. "One that leads right into the mines. No

wonder that damn vampire sneaked in! Good thing Levi was there to—"

"Good luck heading back to work," Levi interrupted, clapping a hand on Edmund's shoulder. "You don't want to be late now."

Edmund nodded, turning to leave the keep. Levi watched the miners go with him and hoped he hadn't said anything too incriminating in front of Cyrus. It looked like his brother wanted to say something, his mouth opening, but he couldn't in front of Emilia.

Levi turned to Cyrus. "Anyway, you'd better get back to training. Emilia and I need to go over the keep."

"We do?" Emilia asked, frowning.

Levi nodded, dragging her inside the castle while leaving his brother outside. "Yeah—we needed to talk about fortifying the place some more, remember? I've got some ideas."

Levi turned his head, relieved when his brother didn't follow. He led Emilia up to the watchtower, then they glanced down at the peasants, pirates, and barbarians practicing in the training yard. He spotted Cyrus and Frederic whispering by themselves again, but he couldn't worry about that—not right now. The orphanage was more important.

"Levi, what's going on?" Emilia studied his face. "You seem distraught."

This is it, Levi thought. *I need to tell her and stop this carnage.*

"Emilia, listen to me. There's going to be a vampire attack on the orphanage," Levi whispered, turning to her. "And if you don't do everything exactly as I say, a bunch of kids are going to die."

NINETEEN

Emilia gasped, her eyes widening. "What...what are you talking about? Why an attack on the orphanage?"

Levi looked down, ashamed. "Vampires love young, pure blood. And children are easier targets than adults. I've...heard some stories."

"Oh my God." Emilia turned silent for a moment. "How do you know this is going to happen?"

"Rumors," Levi lied. "Even if I'm wrong, I still think we should evacuate the children. We need to go now—before it gets dark and the vampires come out."

Emilia nodded, glancing over the side of the watchtower. "You're right—better to be safe than sorry. We'll head to the orphanage right now. Sister Tess—from Father McGregor's church—runs it, so we'll have to get her out too. Too risky to keep any of them there."

"Agreed. Does she run the orphanage by herself?"

"Yes—and she's done a wonderful job. She gets gold from the church's donations to help, of course. But if she's the only one there, she won't stand a chance. I'll organize a group of Legionnaires to come with us to evacuate everyone—"

"No," Levi interrupted. "It has to be us—alone. No one can know. Especially not Frederic or my brother."

Emilia frowned. "Why not? They could help us."

Levi thought of another lie, worried his nose would grow soon from all the secrets. "Think about it, Emilia. Too many Legionnaires would draw attention—then the vampires would know we moved the children. And we don't want that."

"Hmm," Emilia said, pausing to think. "All right, I see your point. If too many people know, it could ruin the element of surprise."

"Exactly. And another thing—we can't bring the children here. Before you protest, the keep is a target. The vampires know we're here. They could even be watching us at night, studying our movements."

Emilia gasped. "You believe that? That they'd risk spying on us at night—even with guards on duty?"

Levi nodded. "I *know* that's what they're doing. I don't think they fear us, Emilia. I think they believe they're going to win."

Especially with Cyrus and Frederic sabotaging Allegiant from within.

Emilia sighed, rubbing her temples. "Okay—we won't bring the orphans here. But where else can we put them? Nowhere is safe, it seems. Not the markets, not the mines..."

Levi's eyes lit up. "The Marauder—Rosalie's ship. We can keep the children there. I don't think the vampires will check the ships."

"But then we'd have to tell the pirates what's going on. I thought you wanted to keep this a secret?"

"We don't have to tell them the whole truth," Levi said, "just that we think getting the children out of the markets would be safer for them in the event of an attack. We can get Rosalie and some of her pirates to stay on the ship and protect them. They're strong fighters—I have faith they'll keep the orphans safe."

"But this could be our chance, Levi," Emilia urged. "After getting the children out, we could get the Legionnaires and wait at the orphanage. When the vampires show up, we can attack—"

"No."

She gawked. "No?"

"You heard me," Levi said. "Sorry, Emilia, but Allegiant isn't ready yet. And like I mentioned before, they'll know it was us who moved the children if we're waiting for them. They might retaliate. And believe me, hungry vampires are even angrier than regular ones."

"Goodness me. While I wish you'd let us fight the vampires head-on," Emilia said, sighing, "I'll respect your plan. As long as the children survive, I'm satisfied. Let's head to the orphanage now. And Levi?"

"Yeah?"

"You just saved a lot of lives, you know." She smiled. "If it weren't for you overhearing those rumors, those kids could've died a terrible death. This is what Allegiant is all about, Levi. Protecting the innocent. Thank you."

"Don't mention it," Levi muttered, hating all the praise she gave him. It made him feel like a fraud.

As they walked down the stairs, Emilia and Levi spotted Frederic in the small lab they had built for him. When Levi noticed the vials of black blood—the same blood he and his brother had given him—his heart beat a little faster.

He was working on the sunlight cure. And getting closer by the minute.

"Look at him working," Emilia whispered to Levi. "So dedicated to our cause. I can't wait to see what he comes up with next."

Levi said nothing, swallowing the bile in his throat.

They left the keep, heading for their horse in the stables. All the recruits had woken up by now, spending another long day practicing in the training yard. Levi and Emilia nodded politely at Peeta and Alana, who collected fresh eggs and milked the cows. As Levi placed the saddle on Margaret, he heard footsteps behind them and spun around.

Cyrus. Levi feared he was following them.

"Hey, where are you two going?" Cyrus asked, glancing between them.

Emilia froze, so Levi spoke. "We're heading to the markets to pick up a few supplies. We won't be long—don't worry."

"The markets?" Alana asked, rushing over. "Can me and Peeta come? We need a new brush for the horses and—"

"No," Emilia interrupted. "We'll leave in shifts. Although it's still daylight out, large groups of us shouldn't be away from the keep for too long. All right?"

Alana sighed. "That's fine, it isn't that important, anyway. We'll head out next time."

As she walked away, Cyrus was eyeing the two of them suspiciously. Levi could tell. "Well, I hope you find those supplies, Brother. See you later."

As he left the stables, Levi breathed a sigh of relief. "Come on, Emilia. We still need to talk to Rosalie."

They found the sea captain and Scrooge on the far ends of the perimeter, guarding the keep with eyes like hawks. Levi rode over to them, explaining—or lying, more like—about the situation. Thankfully, Rosalie didn't get suspicious, not like Cyrus.

"That's fine by us. We'll go wherever you need Allegiant," Rosalie said. "But who will guard the Keep with most of us gone?"

"Some of your pirates can stay, then we'll divide the barbarians up to give more support on patrols," Emilia said. "It might spread us a little thin, but I think it could work. We need to protect that orphanage, and we believe your ship is the safest place for those children."

Rosalie nodded. "All right, sounds good. I'll get some of my pirates to come with us right away. Scrooge will come, too. He never leaves my side."

"Do it discreetly," Emilia said. "We're trying to keep this quiet."

Levi looked over his shoulder, relieved when he didn't see Cyrus or Frederic standing there. He and Emilia jumped on horses, then flicked the reins, guiding their mounts toward the markets.

"I hate lying to them," Emilia said. "It just doesn't feel right."

"I know, but it's for a good reason. Everything will work out —you'll see."

He didn't know if he was trying to convince her or himself.

They made it to the markets in the sweltering heat, tying up the horses outside the orphanage. Some of the children were outside, playing tag and laughing. While pushing through the large crowds of little ones, Emilia smiled at them, watching them run before her expression turned into a frown.

"I used to want to be a mother," she said, "but then I learned about the vampires. I didn't want to raise children in a world of monsters. After you helped me reject Lord Tristan, I didn't need to worry about having them anymore anyway."

"Smart. I can't blame you."

"What about you, Levi?" Emilia asked. "Did you ever want children?"

Levi almost chuckled. The vampires had children rarely, only when their population dwindled. When he thought of his child born as a bloodsucking monster, he shuddered.

"Never," Levi said. "For the same reasons as you, I guess."

"I see. Well, we'd better head inside," Emilia said, gesturing at the orphanage door. "It'll take some time to explain everything to Sister Tess, and then we'll need to move them all—"

Levi froze when he heard shouting coming from one of the market huts. Emilia and Levi glanced at each other in confusion, then rushed toward the loud voice. They found a middle-aged woman speaking with a constable. She had dark hair with an apron on, and several young children circled her while chasing each other and playing games.

"I know you're upset," the constable said, "but there isn't much we can do, ma'am."

"What's going on here?" Emilia asked. "Patricia, what's with all the shouting?"

"You know this woman?" Levi asked.

Emilia nodded. "Yes, her name is Patricia York. She's a midwife. I helped her deliver a few babies when she needed an extra pair of hands."

"Oh, Emilia, I'm glad you're here. This constable isn't listening!" Patricia cried. "Maybe you can help me."

"With what?" Levi asked.

"A week ago, a red-headed woman showed up on my doorstep. She looked dazed and confused, then I noticed she was bleeding."

Levi froze. That would've been right around the time when Cyrus and Levi stepped through the blood magic portal.

"Then what happened?" Emilia asked.

"I treated her wounds and took care of her, of course. She wasn't a vampire—I didn't see any fangs or yellow eyes—so I thought it was safe."

Good thing vampires in my time have red eyes, Levi thought, *or Emilia would have me identified in no time.*

"It was nice of you to give her shelter. But why didn't you

tell me?" Emilia asked. "I could've treated her and found out what was wrong."

"I figured you were too busy. Life of an apothecary and all that." Patricia shrugged. "And then you started Allegiant, and I didn't want to bother you. I thought I had it under control."

"Well, where's the woman now?" Levi asked.

"That's the problem. She left when I turned around, and she's been gone for a few days. I thought she'd return at some point—for food or rest—but it's been a while and I'm getting worried about the poor thing. I summoned a constable here to tell him, but he won't help me."

"Ma'am, calm down," the constable said. "As I mentioned before, there's nothing we can do. We'll put more constables on patrol to look for her, but we need to accept the inevitable."

"And what's that, constable?"

"That perhaps she wandered off and was killed by the vampires."

Patricia wailed at that. Her children looked over, frightened and wide-eyed because of their mother's cries. The constable just bowed his head and left. Emilia wrapped her arms around Patricia, helping her to her feet.

"Take heart—it'll be all right. This is why I started Allegiant," Emilia said. "Now, did the woman say anything to you before she left?"

Patricia shrugged, drying her teary eyes. "Bits and pieces. Most of it was gibberish, but she did mention the word vampire a few times."

"So, she knew about them," Emilia murmured. "Interesting. Have you ever seen her around before? Was she a foreigner, I mean?"

"Yes, I think so." Patricia sniffled. "In fact, she didn't seem to recognize anything. Perhaps she was a traveler who'd gotten lost."

"And what was she wearing?" Levi asked. "It'll help us identify her."

"She had armor on—like a knight. And she had a strange weapon, one I've never seen before. You know, she resembled you, Emilia. Red hair, green eyes. You two could've been twins."

The more Patricia described her, the more Levi felt like she was familiar, but he couldn't put his finger on it.

"A strange weapon, speaking of vampires…" Emilia glanced over Levi. "Do you think she could be a vampire hunter? Another one, I mean, besides us?"

Levi shrugged. "It's possible. But why was she bleeding and confused? What happened to her before she arrived?"

"No idea," Patricia replied. "I tried to get answers out of her, but she wouldn't tell me. She was too disoriented. Perhaps she was mentally ill—or suffered a concussion. You'd think someone would've seen her by now, though. This is a small town. Not many places to go."

"You really should've come to me, Patricia," Emilia said. "In the future, don't hesitate, okay? I may be with Allegiant, but I'm still a healer."

Patricia sighed. "You're right—it was foolish of me. If you find her, will you let me know?"

"Of course. But can I ask a favor in return?"

Patricia nodded. "Absolutely."

"Tell everyone in the village to lock their doors tonight— board the windows too," Emilia replied. "Just trust me. I want this place to be a ghost town. And don't let anyone inside—no matter how injured they look. You have children to think about."

After Patricia agreed and closed the door, Emilia turned to Levi. "I hope we find that woman soon. It sounds like she needs help—and with her weapons and armor, she could be valuable. Perhaps we'll find another ally in her."

"Maybe," Levi said, thinking for a moment. "And maybe... no, I'm not sure."

"About what?"

"Do you...do you think she was the one who killed that vampire? The one named Belladonna?" Levi asked. "It was right here—in the markets. It would've been around the same time Patricia claimed the woman left."

Emilia shrugged. "Possibly. If so, she sounds formidable— just who we need. Now I really hope the constable's theory is wrong. Vampire hunter or not, let's pray this woman gets to safety before nightfall again."

"Pray?" Levi started walking with Emilia over to the orphanage. "That doesn't sound like you."

Emilia paused. "Yes, well...perhaps I'm starting to believe again. That's your effect on me, Levi. You've given me hope."

When she smiled at him, Levi returned it. But deep down, her words weighed on him. He wanted to confess what he was, but he felt dirty—sinful. If Emilia knew, she wouldn't think he was a ray of hope anymore.

Emilia knocked on the door to the orphanage as Levi peered over her shoulder. "Hello? Sister Tess, are you in there? It's Emilia Rutherford, the apothecary from the local shop. I'm here with my friend, Levi."

Friend? Levi wondered. *Is that all I am to her? After that kiss?*

Levi heard footsteps on the other side of the door that interrupted his thoughts. Then he heard the screech of metal before the door opened. A nun appeared in front of them—a woman in her mid-fifties with dark hair and wrinkles. She wore a long black robe with a traditional headpiece.

"Emilia, good to see you again," she said, smiling.

"You know her, too?" Levi asked. "I suppose I shouldn't be surprised. You take care of people and try to help. You're well-connected."

"I am. I know many people in town," Emilia replied. "I even cured a few of the orphans' coughs."

"And I'm still very grateful for that. You've saved a lot of these orphans. Most won't lift a finger unless there's some incentive," Sister Tess said, shaking her head. "Anyway, how can I help you today?"

"Well, I don't know how to tell you this, Sister Tess," Emilia began, "so I'll just say it plainly. You and the orphans are in danger."

Sister Tess's mouth opened in shock. "Danger? How?"

"I'm sure you know the markets are dangerous at night with the vampires on the loose. You're lucky you've survived this long," Levi said. "But we know for sure the vampires are planning an attack on the orphanage. The targets are the children—and they'll have no problem killing you to get to them."

Sister Tess gasped, looking at the children playing in the yard. "Vampires? Yes, I've heard of those terrible creatures. Father McGregor teaches that they're evil incarnate—the embodiment of sin. We try not to speak of such things, especially in front of the orphans. How could they want to kill children?"

Levi felt ashamed. He couldn't speak, so Emilia answered. "Because that's what they are, Sister. Evil. You said it yourself. Now, will you let us take you to safety?"

"But...this orphanage is all these children have known. Some were babies when they came to me," Sister Tess replied, gesturing at the door. "And I *do* take precautions to keep us safe."

Levi poked his head inside the orphanage, noticing the lack-luster bolts on the door. He shook his head. "It's a good effort, but that won't hold the vampires back—believe me. They'd knock down this door and kill you all without batting an eye.

The old rumor that vampires can't enter a place uninvited isn't actually true, you know."

Sister Tess sighed. "Very well. Although I don't like it, I won't disagree—not when it comes to the safety of the orphans. Where will you be taking us?"

"A pirate ship, Sister Tess."

The nun's eyes widened. "A...pirate ship? Oh, my. What kind of people are you associating with, Emilia?"

"Don't worry," Levi said. "The pirates are friendly—and they'll defend you with their lives. I'm sure the vampires won't look there for you."

"If you say so. How long will you keep us there?"

"We don't know," Emilia replied. "As long as it takes to kill every last vampire. As long as it takes to make this world safe for children again."

Sister Tess nodded. "I see. Wait here—I'll round up the orphans. They won't be happy to leave, but I'll tell them they're going on an adventure at sea. That'll pique their interest."

As Levi and Emilia waited outside, watching the nun gather the orphans, Levi kept looking over his shoulder. He feared Levi or Frederic might be listening.

"Who are you looking around for?" Emilia asked, noticing Levi's fidgeting. "You look nervous."

"Vamps," Levi replied. "You can never be too careful."

"In the sunlight?" Emilia shook her head. "That's impossible."

"Don't be so sure of that," Levi muttered. "I believe one day vampires will be immune to sunlight. Then they could strike anytime—any place."

"Really? That would be an utter disaster. Then...nowhere would be safe."

Levi nodded. "I know."

Emilia gulped, saying nothing.

When the nun had gathered the children, they took them in carts, just a handful at a time, covering them with blankets so no one would notice as they transported them to the docks. Some of the children cried as they said goodbye to the orphanage, dragging their ratty dolls and teddy bears along, but Emilia promised them sweets if they were quiet. Naturally, the kids obliged.

When they'd finally all made it to the docks, Rosalie and a few pirates were already waiting for them. The other pirates remained at the keep so as not to stir up suspicion. The last thing Levi wanted was his brother to know anything was amiss, putting their lives in jeopardy. The children perked up when they noticed the ship, rushing up the gangplank and touching everything. Sister Tess shook her head and followed while smiling apologetically at Rosalie.

Rosalie sighed. "They're going to make a mess of my ship, aren't they?"

"Sorry," Emilia said. "They *are* children, after all."

"Good point," Rosalie replied, watching them play. "I'm a bit sad I won't be at the keep anymore. I didn't expect to grow so attached to it. I never thought I'd admit it, but...losing *Raging Tides* to you was the most exciting thing to happen to me and my crew."

Levi laughed. "Then you're welcome. And don't worry about food and supplies—Emilia or I will deliver some regularly."

"Great. We've got some reserves on the ship, too. And if you ever need us, we're always ready," Rosalie said, patting her sword's scabbard. "Good luck with everything, you two. Give the vamps hell for us."

"Will do." As Rosalie, Scrooge, and several pirates boarded the ship with the orphans, Emilia turned to Levi. "We'd better get back to the keep. Let's pick up a few supplies so no one suspects anything."

As Levi jumped back onto his horse, something dark crept up inside of him when he thought about tonight. When the vampires realized the orphanage was empty, what would they do? And would Cyrus suspect Levi had warned them? Too many coincidences had occurred lately, so it was likely. One more suspicious thing would collapse it all like a house of cards.

Levi counted on his brother believing in his loyalty to their people. It was flimsy, but he hoped it would last for now.

It was getting harder and harder to protect Allegiant. Levi realized it was all leading up to one thing.

He would have to kill his brother soon if he turned against him, no matter what the Vampire Commandments said. His brother. His flesh and blood.

Which side would Cyrus choose, Levi wondered?

TWENTY

Levi and Emilia returned to the keep, carrying supplies they'd picked up from the markets. Although they didn't really need them, it was always a good idea to stock up on extra food, bandages, and tools. As Levi put the horses away in the stables, he noticed Cyrus leaning against the wall, watching him and Emilia.

"Have a good trip?" Cyrus finally asked, eyeing the bags of supplies.

Levi nodded. "It went well."

"Good. I noticed Rosalie and some of the pirates are missing," Cyrus continued. "It isn't like them to abandon the keep—they seemed pretty loyal to you. Where did they go?"

Emilia glanced at Levi, hesitating. Levi didn't miss a beat this time. "They decided to start patrolling the streets. Eventually, Allegiant will have nightly patrols."

Emilia nodded, following the lie. "Yes, exactly. Rosalie and the pirates are better fighters than most here, so we figured they were ready."

When Cyrus didn't reply, Levi feared he could read his mind

—that he knew exactly what he had done. Emilia had no idea why there was so much tension between the brothers.

"Anyway, I should get back to the others," Emilia said, turning to Levi. "We can't afford to skip out on training. Whenever you're ready, Levi, the Legionnaires could always use another lesson."

After she left, Cyrus stepped closer. "Remember—we leave tonight after sundown. Everyone should be asleep so we can sneak out. And by the way, don't be late like last time."

Before Levi had a chance to reply, Cyrus turned and left the stables. *At least he isn't accusing me of anything,* Levi thought, as he left and joined Emilia in the training yard. They went over vampire fighting tactics again with Levi giving a demonstration. He practiced with Emilia, wrestling her to the ground to show the Legionnaires how to stake a vampire.

When some of the male Legionnaires whistled, Emilia blushed and rose to her feet. A grin spread across Levi's face until he realized his brother was nearby—and he didn't look amused, his face long and scrunched up.

Cyrus didn't join the sparring—he only watched from afar. He was doing that a lot lately, Levi realized. He didn't spot Frederic in the crowd and assumed he was still working away in his science lab. Levi still didn't know how, but he knew he needed to destroy the sunlight cure.

One thing at a time, Levi told himself. *Just get through tonight.*

The miners returned after a long day of work, grateful to have a safe place to rest their heads. Samantha rushed over and hugged her father when she noticed he had returned. She and Edmund headed toward Levi and Emilia as the Legionnaires practiced on the dummies behind them.

"Good news. The mines are safe," Edmund said. "No sign of any vampires. But you were right—there *was* a tunnel. God only knows what evil stuff the vamps are doing on the other end, but we sealed it off for good. Gave Arthur a proper burial too, the poor bastard."

A wave of relief washed over Levi. The last thing he wanted was another vampire coming through the tunnel to catch the miners off-guard.

"What Papa's trying to say is that he's grateful you saved his life," Samantha began, "and the lives of the miners. I am too. You've changed all our lives—for the better."

"And I, uh," Edmund began, glancing down, "I wanted to apologize to both of you."

"Us?" Emilia raised an eyebrow. "Why?"

"I was the one who yelled at you—accused you of not having a plan," Edmund said, his cheeks red in embarrassment. "I was rude and out of line."

"You were just worried about your people, Edmund," Emilia replied. "I would've done the same thing in your place."

"Well, you sure proved me wrong. I believe Allegiant has a good shot at killing all those damn vamps now. And when we win this war, the world will be singing your names for all eternity. Sammy will make sure of it."

Samantha plucked at her lute, nodding.

Emilia smiled at Levi. "I'd love to take the credit, but it was Levi who won the gold for us. It was Levi who promised a solution when I thought I'd have to marry Lord Tristan. He's the true leader of Allegiant. The true hero."

"Oh, please," Levi said. "You were already killing vamps before I came into town. And it was your idea to call us Allegiant—to get Edmund and his people on our side. I didn't do much, really."

Emilia snorted. "Always so humble. It's what I like the most about you, Levi."

It was Levi's turn to blush.

Edmund cleared his throat. "Anyway, I'd best get back to training. No such thing as being too prepared."

After he had walked away, Samantha turned to Levi. "I'm glad you came to Osgoode, Levi—and I'm sure Emilia feels the same way. If you hadn't, I never would've gotten to meet you. And that hunky brother of yours."

"Hunky, hmm?" Emilia giggled. "Are you courting each other?"

"Well, he hasn't officially asked me to be his yet," Samantha said, glancing at Cyrus who stood across the yard, "but we *have* been spending a lot of time together."

Cyrus noticed Samantha's stare and winked. Samantha giggled and waved.

Levi didn't want to upset her, but he knew he had to say something. "Look, Samantha...I don't think dating my brother is a good idea. Or, uh, courting. Whatever you people call it."

Samantha furrowed her brows. "Why not?"

Levi struggled to think of a lie. "Because...he just got out of a long-term relationship. It was messy, and I wouldn't want you to be the rebound."

She blinked. "The...rebound?"

"Yeah. You know, the person someone bounces back with just to get over an ex. What I mean is, I don't want you to get hurt."

Samantha seemed to understand that. And really, it was a half-truth. Cyrus had an on-again, off-again fling with Raven. And although she was a vampire, Levi had seen how emotionally abusive and unhealthy their relationship was.

Samantha shook her head. "I don't think Cyrus is that kind of person. He's kind, thoughtful, attentive. Even gentlemanly. Everything I've ever wanted in a man."

Levi almost laughed. "Really, Sam, he's not what you think—"

"Maybe I don't have to be his rebound, as you called it," Samantha continued, not evening listening to Levi. "I could help him heal and move on. We won't know unless we try, right? Wish me luck."

As she walked away, making her way over to a smirking Cyrus, Emilia smiled. "Aw, I think they're cute together. Don't you?"

Levi gritted his teeth. "Yeah, real cute."

"Anyway, do you have plans tonight, Levi?"

"Uh, no. Why do you ask?"

"I was wondering if you'd like to meet in my room after sundown," she said, blushing. "To talk. No one will be around—it'll give us some privacy. If that's all right with you, of course."

Levi thought of the orphanage attack and what his brother had said. *Don't be late like last time.* But he couldn't refuse Emilia. The thought of being alone with her made him as giddy as a teenager, eager to hear what she had to say.

"Tonight," Levi agreed. "I'll meet you in your room."

Emilia grinned. "Perfect. See you then, Levi."

As she walked away, Levi felt butterflies in his stomach. *Whatever Emilia had to say, it needs to be quick,* Levi thought.

Because if I'm late for another vampire meeting, it might just be my last.

As SOON AS he saw dusk fall, Levi grew nervous. His hands shook like a leaf in the wind.

The keep's main level cleared out with the Legionnaires heading upstairs to sleep. Most shared rooms, but some of the higher-ranking members—like Levi, Emilia, Cyrus, and Frederic—had private quarters. With Rosalie and some of the pirates gone, the barbarians nodded at Levi and Emilia and left to patrol the keep's perimeter.

Frederic left his lab, walking over to Cyrus in the main hall. As they waited for everyone to fall asleep and for darkness to overtake the sky, Levi assumed they wouldn't notice if he hurried upstairs to talk with Emilia for a few minutes. He slipped through the crowd and made his way up to her room.

He knocked on the closed door twice, lowering his voice. "Emilia? It's me. What did you want to talk—"

When she opened the door, Emilia was scantily clad in a white nightgown. Levi's eyes widened. She opened the door a little further, gesturing for him to come inside.

"Hello, Levi," she said. "I've been waiting for you. Come on in."

Levi entered, closing the door behind him. The room was small —only a single bed with a wardrobe and some supplies from downstairs. Emilia sat on the edge of the bed, patting the spot beside her.

"Have a seat," she said. "Please."

"Okay. You...look beautiful," Levi sputtered, sitting next to her. "Just...wow."

She blushed. "Thank you. I...was afraid you wouldn't come tonight."

"Why wouldn't I?"

She lowered her eyes. "It's just...I wasn't sure if you felt the same way."

"The same way? What do you mean?"

Emilia laughed, nervously. "Don't make me spell it out for you, Levi. I have feelings for you—strong feelings that I thought would go away. And when I kissed you before you ran into my burning cabin, you never spoke of it again."

"Well, I just assumed it was a heat-of-the-moment thing. A way to say goodbye, if I'd died."

Emilia shook her head. "No—no, it meant more to me than that, Levi. I don't make it a habit of kissing men I don't care about. You know, I wasn't sure if it was a good idea to pursue this or not..."

Levi forced himself to speak. "Why not?"

"Because the vampires should be our main focus. Allegiant comes first," she replied, leaning in closer. "But...I can't stay away from you, Levi. No matter how hard I try. And Samantha told me life is too short to not say how you feel."

Levi rose to his feet, turning his back on her. "Look, I told you before, Emilia—you don't want to love someone like me."

"And why is that?" Emilia stood and approached him. "Levi, look at me. Please."

He turned around, unable to resist. He could melt in those emerald-green eyes of hers.

"You're one of the greatest men I've ever known—and I'm not just saying that to be nice," Emilia said. "You're kind, strong, smart. And I'll never forget how you saved me from Lord Tristan."

Levi shook his head as Emilia inched closer. "I mean it, Em. You don't know what you're getting involved with."

"I think I know exactly," she whispered.

And then she kissed him—and he found himself reciprocating like it was the most natural thing in the world. He kissed back ferociously, their lips and tongues intertwining. It was nothing like the kiss they had shared when the farm was on fire. This was intense, passionate—full of desire and love. Levi didn't want it to end.

And although Levi knew Cyrus would never approve, it felt right. Levi knew in that moment Emilia was the one—that this was his destiny. It almost broke his heart when he remembered it couldn't happen.

Emilia pulled away first, looking up at Levi. "Tell me you feel the same way. Tell me I'm not crazy."

"You're not," Levi replied. "I *do* feel the same way. More than you know."

Levi was already in love with her—that much he knew for sure. He just didn't want to tell her and break her heart when she found out the truth.

Emilia grinned. "Then stay here with me tonight, Levi. Show me how much you care."

He wanted to say yes—to stay in her room and hold her body close to his all night long. But he knew Frederic and his brother were expecting him, so he forced himself to take a step back.

"I can't, Emilia," he whispered. "I'm sorry."

The look of hurt on her face was something he'd never forget. She looked down, biting her lip. "Oh...all right. I understand."

"No—you really don't," Levi murmured. "I want to stay here with you, but...I can't. Not tonight. I don't want to rush you into anything you'll regret."

Emilia shook her head. "I have no regrets, Levi—not with you. But if you can't stay, I'll respect that. You know where I stand now. Whenever you're ready, I'll be here."

Levi nodded, the familiar chest pain returning as he exited her room and closed the door behind him. He hadn't felt the pain in such a long time that it surprised him. Luckily, it disappeared as he walked down the stairs, his mind still on Emilia—on her kiss, her touch, and how badly he wanted to turn around and go back to her.

"Brother, you ready to go?" Cyrus asked, walking over to him. Frederic stood at the front door. "We've been waiting forever. What the hell took you so long?"

"Sorry," Levi muttered, forcing himself out of his daze. "I

had to go over a few plans with Emilia."

"I see," Frederic said, eyeing Levi.

"Well, I'm glad you're here now. We're meeting the vamps near the orphanage," Cyrus said, smirking. "I haven't been this excited in a long time. Sure, the bandits were fun, but this? *This* is about to take the cake."

"Right," Levi lied, forcing a smile. "Let's get going."

As they left the keep and walked over to the stables, Vana, Novak, and some of the other barbarians on duty noticed them. They rushed over, their swords and other weapons held high underneath the dark sky.

"Shit, the guards," Cyrus whispered, and Levi could feel his brother itching for a fight. "Either they let us go...or we kill them to get past."

"Wait. Let me handle this," Levi whispered. "No fighting— it'll look suspicious."

"What are you three doing out here so late?" Vana asked, pausing in front of the men. "It's dangerous."

"Frederic made a new serum. He wants us to test it out on the vampires, which means we need to leave and find one," Levi said. "Look, I know you're worried, but we'll be fine."

"We should accompany you," Novak said, standing next to his wife. "For extra protection."

"That isn't necessary, trust me. We fought vampires before we came to Osgoode. We'll be all right, I promise."

Novak and Vana glanced at each other. Levi feared they would say no, but the barbarians parted to let them through.

"Very well," Vana said. "Don't be gone too long."

"We won't. But don't tell Emilia or the others where we went, okay? They'd just worry—and we don't want to let them down if Frederic's serum doesn't work."

The barbarians nodded, returning to their patrol. Levi

sighed and put a saddle on Margaret, hopping onto the horse. Cyrus and Frederic mounted their own horses.

"Smooth talking, Brother," Cyrus said, as they galloped into the distance. "I was ready to kill them all."

"There doesn't always have to be a fight," Levi said over his shoulder. "There are other ways to get what you want."

Cyrus shrugged. "Yeah, but where's the fun in that? I wanted to see some blood."

"All in good time," Frederic said, holding onto his horse. "Once the sunlight cure is perfected, we'll destroy them all. From the inside."

Levi said nothing, his stomach twisting into knots.

When they had made it to the market area, it was empty for the night. They jumped off the horses and tied them up outside the orphanage, glancing around the quiet town square.

"I don't see any vampires," Levi said. "Do you?"

Frederic shook his head. "No, not yet."

"You don't think they went ahead without us, do you?" Cyrus asked. "I swear, if they drank all the blood and left none for us, I'm going to be *so* pissed—"

The bushes rustled behind them. Slaughter, Night Temptress, and the other vampires in the Bloodborn Order popped out.

"Come on," Slaughter teased. "You don't think that low of us, do you?"

"Well, when we didn't see you, we just assumed the worst," Cyrus replied with a nod. "Good to see you waited."

"Of course. What a pleasure to see you again, Levi," Night Temptress purred, walking over to him. "I always look forward to our conversations."

Levi shivered in disgust when she placed a hand on his cheek, caressing it. It didn't feel as good as Emilia's embrace. It was wrong, corrupt.

"It's been a while," Slaughter said, ignoring his sister as he turned to Frederic. "Have you made any progress with Allegiant?"

"I believe they trust us," Frederic said with a nod. "And I've gotten further with my experiments. Be patient, Bloodborns— we'll attack soon. Sunlight will no longer be your enemy in a few days."

A few days? Levi thought, fear spreading through his body. *Shit, I thought I'd have more time than that.*

"Until then, we'll have to find another way to satisfy our hunger," Night Temptress said, gesturing at the orphanage. "Go ahead, Levi. You do the honors."

Levi nodded and kicked the door down with a loud slam. He prayed no one would come to investigate, but the townspeople knew better than to leave their homes at night.

"I've been looking forward to this," Slaughter said, licking his lips. "Follow me, everyone."

Levi, Cyrus, Frederic, and the vampires entered through the kicked-down front door. It was pitch-black inside with clothes, toys, and furniture left behind. But as they poked their heads inside the bedrooms, no one was around.

"Where the hell are all the orphans?" Slaughter demanded.

Cyrus turned to Levi. "Any ideas?"

Levi shrugged. "No clue. Maybe they're sleeping somewhere else tonight."

"Maybe," Cyrus began, "or maybe someone moved them."

"Who could have done such a thing?" Night Temptress asked.

Cyrus said nothing, glaring at his brother. Levi scoffed. "You aren't accusing me, are you?"

"Should I be?"

"No," Levi lied. The vampires turned quiet behind them. "I

wouldn't betray the vampires. And besides, if I rescued the orphans, wouldn't you have seen them at the keep?"

Cyrus stepped back. "All right, maybe you didn't take them. Where else could they be?"

"Who knows? All that matters is that they're not here," Slaughter said, his nostrils flaring, "and I'm starving."

"You won't have any luck in the village," Levi said, hoping to stop them. "The townspeople have gotten smarter. I hear they're boarding their windows at night and keeping silver by their beds."

Slaughter growled. "Then give me one good reason why we shouldn't go to the keep and rip everyone there to shreds?"

Night Temptress nodded. Even the other vampires seemed on board, snarling and drooling in anticipation.

"Because that's not the plan," Levi said. "We need the sunlight cure first before we—"

Slaughter picked up a chair, smashing it against the wall. "You think I give a damn about that right now, when I'm starving?"

"No, Levi is right," Frederic urged. "We can't be too rash. Everything is coming together, and we must be patient for the final attack."

"Then what do you propose we do for food?" Night Temptress rubbed her stomach. "We're killing something tonight. We have to. I'm itching for some blood."

"The forest," Levi said. "I know it doesn't compare to human blood, but it's something. It's what my brother and I have been living off of. Better than nothing, right?"

Levi feared they would say no—that they'd decide to attack the keep anyway, despite Frederic insisting otherwise. Slaughter puffed his chest in anger, but Night Temptress glared at him.

"Settle down, Brother," she said. "We'll try Levi's idea first. To the forest—before we all pass out from hunger."

TWENTY-ONE

As they left the orphanage with the vampires snarling in hunger, Slaughter reached into his pocket. Levi's eyes widened when he pulled out two sticks and rubbed them together. When they caught on fire, he waved them around first, transfixed by the blaze.

"This," Slaughter began, "is for our troubles."

Before Levi could stop him, Slaughter tossed the burning sticks toward the front door to the orphanage. It burst into flames and spread inside within seconds. Slaughter and the vampires howled in laughter behind Levi, but he didn't find it funny.

"Let's get out of here," Slaughter said. "The forest is close."

"Won't it spread to the village?" Levi asked. "It could burn down the whole town!"

Slaughter snorted. "And?"

Levi said nothing. The vampires grinned back and turned, walking toward the forest in the distance. Levi made Cyrus, Frederic, and the others think he was coming by trailing behind, but then he turned and rushed back to the orphanage when they were busy with their conversations.

He knew he didn't have much time—one of the vampires would notice he was missing, and the flames would encroach the homes soon. He found a bucket outside—probably used for the children to bathe in—and filled it with water from a nearby well. He then rushed inside the orphanage, trying to put out as much of the fire as he could.

He stopped the fire before it could spread inside the bedrooms, sparing some of the children's toys. After he had finished spraying the blaze, Levi surveyed the damage. One of the orphanage's walls had collapsed and the place smelled like smoke. The orphans wouldn't be able to return—not now, not ever, but at least the village was safe.

He tossed the bucket aside, sprinting to catch up with the vampires. He rejoined them as they neared the forest. They were still chatting and didn't seem like they had noticed Levi was gone. But Cyrus wasn't as distracted. He raised his eyebrows when he noticed Levi rushing up behind them, panting.

"Where were you?" he asked.

"I, uh, thought I saw someone from Allegiant poking around. Emilia *did* ask the pirates to patrol at night."

"And? Did they see you?"

Levi shook his head. "It was just a shadow."

"Don't worry, Brother. It'll get better soon." Cyrus patted Levi's shoulder. "The Day of Sunlight is coming."

"The...Day of Sunlight?" Levi asked, confused. "Should I know what that is?"

"Crap, right. We didn't tell you yet. It's what Frederic's calling it," Cyrus explained. "Our day of reckoning—when he finally figures out the sunlight cure. Then we kill everyone in the town and burn it all down before getting back to our time."

Levi gulped. "Oh. That's...a plan, all right."

"Are you coming or not?" Night Temptress purred up ahead, turning back to Levi.

"Of course," Levi said, faking a smile. "Right behind you."

Night Temptress smirked. "Good. You'll be my hunting partner, Levi. Cyrus—leave us. You can hunt with Slaughter and Frederic. I want Levi all to myself."

Cyrus looked a little jealous, narrowing his eyes at his brother, but nodded anyway and moved beside Slaughter and Frederic. Like wolves on the prowl, the vampires descended upon the forest that stretched around Osgoode. They divided themselves into groups of two and three, then went their separate ways. Levi looked back at Cyrus, not wanting to leave him, but he had no choice. Disagreeing with Night Temptress didn't seem like a smart idea.

Levi followed Night Temptress as she took a left, leading him away from the other vampires. He glanced up, noticing the full moon as the pitter-patter of hooves sounded in the distance. Something was close—an animal. Levi could smell their scent.

"This is my favorite part of the hunt," Night Temptress whispered. "The stalking. It's such a thrill—to lure your victims, get them alone...then strike."

"Uh, yeah," Levi muttered. "Mine too."

Night Temptress grinned at him. Levi remembered a time when he would've shared that grin, but it felt like a lifetime ago.

"Get ready," Night Temptress whispered. "I sense something's coming our way."

True to her word, a deer scampered ahead of them, popping out of the bushes. The creature walked to the creek, taking slow, small sips. Night Temptress gestured at Levi, then started to creep toward the animal. The deer hadn't made any movements yet—it didn't seem like it knew they were there.

Levi watched as Night Temptress bared her fangs, ready to attack. But Levi couldn't—it just didn't feel right. He picked up a rock off the ground, then threw it ahead of him. It hit the target—a tree near the creek—and the deer's head snapped up. The animal then took off running into the forest, vanishing.

Night Temptress growled. "What the hell? I should've had that!"

"Maybe it heard us," Levi said. "Deer are skittish creatures."

Night Temptress growled again but didn't chase after the animal. She turned to him, a look of fury, hunger, and desire in her eyes. For a second, Levi thought she might eat him.

"No humans, no animals," she muttered, her eyes still on his. "What a long night. I need something to turn this hunt around."

And then she pounced on him, kissing his mouth, his neck, his face. Levi didn't kiss back—he froze like a statue. He didn't want to upset Night Temptress, but she was nothing like Emilia. She was the one he wanted—not some murderous vampire.

"You know, no one's around," Night Temptress said, pulling away to look at Levi with a smirk. "What do you say? I'm sure you've got some built-up tension from being around that Allegiant bitch all day."

When she tried to caress his face again, Levi grabbed her hand and stopped her. "Uh, I don't think this is a good idea, Night Temptress."

"And why not?" she demanded.

"I think we should just stay friends," Levi said, although he didn't even want that from her. "I don't want to mix business with pleasure. Our goal should be stopping Allegiant."

"And that's *still* our goal," Night Temptress said, smirking. "But who says we can't have a little fun along the way?"

When she reached for him again, tugging on his pants, Levi's temper got the best of him. He pushed Night Temptress as hard as he could, then she went colliding into the nearby tree. She hit her head with a yelp, looking up at Levi in surprise.

She wiped away the violet blood from the back of her head and licked it like a cat lapping up milk.

"I'm sorry," Levi said, taking a step back. "But I don't want to be with you. Not like that."

The truth seemed to sober her up. The emotion in her eyes switched from passion to anger, her eyes hardening. He feared she might try to kill him. She rose to her feet, using the tree to help her stand.

"Nobody rejects Night Temptress," she hissed. "Before you start something you'll regret, you might want to rethink this."

"I don't need to rethink anything," Levi replied, growing angry. "I don't want you, Night Temptress. Go find someone else to seduce. Try my brother—or Frederic. I don't care, really."

"You asshole," she snarled. "When I kissed you, I could taste her, you know. The human's scent. You've been intimate with the vampire hunter, haven't you?"

Levi froze. He didn't want to admit it, but he couldn't lie. She already knew his secret.

"It's all right, Levi. I'm not judging you," she said, then smirked. "I know how fun it is to play with your prey before the kill."

Levi crossed his arms, staying silent. He knew he shouldn't have gone to Emilia's room. Had his love for her put her in danger?

"But I'm a little hurt. A human is good enough for you, but not me?" she continued, adjusting her hair that had gotten dishevelled from the fall. "I could show you a great time."

Levi scoffed. "You just never quit, do you? I gave you my answer, Night Temptress. I don't want you."

"Fine." She sauntered past him, glancing over her shoulder. "You're a vampire, Levi—so you should know how serious we take revenge. You'll pay for rejecting me. In a way that hurts you the most."

"You can't hurt me. Vampires don't attack each other—it goes against our laws."

"Not you," she said with a grin. "But everyone else is fair game."

Levi grabbed Night Temptress's arm hard enough to leave a bruise. "Like who? What are you planning?"

Night Temptress snatched her arm away from him. "You'll just have to wait and see."

As she walked away, Levi contemplated picking up a stick and staking her through the heart. But if she didn't return, Slaughter and the others would get suspicious—and Levi's head already spun from all the other lies he had told today.

He only hoped Night Temptress wouldn't tell the others he had kissed Emilia. He knew sooner or later, his story would stop adding up, and everything would fall apart. He just had to make sure he kept the upper hand—that he stayed one step ahead of everyone else. No pressure.

As he followed Night Temptress's trail back to the others, he noticed smoke rings in the sky. He feared it might be from the orphanage, but it was coming from deep inside the forest. It looked like a campfire.

Levi followed the smoke, delving deeper into the trees. He reached the campfire, but no one was there. It looked recently lit judging by how strongly it was burning. The owner had left all their stuff behind as if they had rushed off in a hurry, likely overhearing the vampires. But who would be out there camping —especially at night when the vampires could attack? The villagers knew better than that.

Levi bent down, rummaging through the stranger's belongings. He found the usual things—a blanket for warmth, a dead rabbit roasting above the fire, and a hand-drawn map of the area. But one thing caught his attention.

A gun. The weapon that was out of place in the primitive world.

Levi thought he heard footsteps and the crunch of a tree branch nearby, but when he glanced around, he didn't see anyone.

"Levi?" Cyrus called out in the distance. "Levi, where are you?"

"Over here, Brother!" Levi shouted back.

He heard footsteps approaching and spun around. Cyrus stood there, looking down at Levi with a frown. "There you are. Why'd you set up camp?"

"I didn't. This isn't mine," Levi replied, rising to his feet. "I just found it. But look at that weapon, Cyrus. It's a gun."

Cyrus's eyes widened. "Holy shit, you're right. Is it loaded with silver bullets? Has it been fired?"

"I don't know. I don't want to touch it in case it misfires."

"I get it. But Levi...there's only one kind of person who carries a weapon like this."

"A Legionnaire," Levi answered, "and one from our time. I know—I watched them kill Raven and the Patriarch with a gun like this."

The brothers turned silent. Levi's brain whirled with possibilities, each one more troubling than the last.

"Do you think the person who set up camp here killed that vampire in the markets?" Levi asked. "Belladonna, the one with the bullet holes?"

"Could be. Anyway, come on," Cyrus said, gesturing over his shoulder. "Slaughter caught a few deer and he's ready to leave. Let's head back before it gets light out. We'll deal with this shit another time."

"All right, if you say so." Levi followed Cyrus, lowering his voice so the vampires wouldn't overhear them in the distance.

"There's another vampire hunter out there, Cyrus—and they're not involved with Allegiant. Not this one, anyway."

"I know that," Cyrus muttered. "Let's just pray there's only one and we can find them soon. If not..."

Cyrus shivered, not finishing his sentence, but Levi caught his drift. This new hunter made things a bit more complicated.

They walked back to Slaughter and the others who carried dead animals. Levi forced himself to look away, nearly barfing in disgust. The smell of death sickened him like nothing else.

"It's not a human, but at least it's something," Slaughter said. "It won't keep us full forever, but it'll last until Frederic works out the sunlight cure."

Frederic nodded. "And these streets are full during the day. We'll never go hungry again."

The vampires murmured in agreement, giddy at the thought of causing more deaths. Levi glanced over at Night Temptress who kept her distance. She glared at him, clearly still angry about the rejection.

"You two find anything?" Slaughter asked her.

"Nothing at all," Night Temptress muttered. "Perhaps I should've picked a stronger partner."

As she sauntered away, walking back to the village, the vampires followed. Cyrus shook his head as he hung back with Levi. "Wow, she sounds pissed. What did you do to her?"

"She came on to me in the middle of the forest," Levi mumbled, "and I rejected her."

Cyrus chuckled. "Rejected the proud Night Temptress? I told you you're gonna pay for that—and it won't be pretty. But anger's good. We can channel it against Allegiant."

Levi didn't say anything.

"Do you think we should tell the others what we found? That a Legionnaire from the future might be among us?" Cyrus continued. "Because that's pretty disturbing."

"No," Levi replied, not wanting to give them a heads-up. "We don't know anything for sure. Maybe someone in the village is capable of making a gun and just hasn't shared it yet."

"That seems far-fetched. Remember what era we're in, after all. These people don't even have lighters for cigarettes, let alone guns," Cyrus mumbled. "What if you're wrong?"

"Then we'll deal with them," Levi lied. "Just like we're going to deal with Allegiant."

"There's my brother," Cyrus said, grinning as he patted Levi's shoulder.

When they returned to the markets, everyone ate ravenously, then Cyrus, Levi, and Frederic said goodbye to the vampires. Frederic vowed to keep working on the sunlight cure and would keep them in the loop. Night Temptress was still ignoring Levi—which was just fine with him.

As the three arrived back at the Keep and put their horse in the stables, Novak walked over to them. "Did it work?"

Levi frowned. "Did what work?"

"The experiment you were testing. You said Frederic wanted to try out something on the vampires tonight."

"Oh," Levi said, hoping he hadn't made them suspicious. "No...no, it didn't."

Novak looked at the three of them for a moment, then nodded. "I see. Glad you returned in one piece."

As the barbarian walked away, Cyrus scoffed. "I don't like him—he and his wife are too nosy. They're worse than the peasants."

"They may be strong, but we can beat them," Frederic said, his eyes on Novak's back. "Just give me some time."

The three said goodnight and Levi returned to his private room. He debated knocking on Emilia's door—mainly to beg for forgiveness for turning her away earlier. He could see candlelight under the crack of the door and knew she was still awake, but he couldn't bring himself to do it.

Maybe forgetting her was better. Maybe denying his emotions was what he needed to do to protect her. Or maybe he should've spurned her harder to prevent her from falling in love with a vampire, the very thing she hated.

He tucked himself into bed, dreaming of her instead of going to her side. It was easier for both of them that way.

The next morning, Levi woke up and walked past her bedroom. The door was open, and Emilia wasn't inside. He feared Night Temptress had done something to her until he glanced out the window, noticing Emilia practicing in the training yard below.

She grunted and panted, beating the dummy with her sword. Levi realized she looked upset. She was frowning, her eyebrows turned downward. He wanted to go down and talk to her, but he wasn't sure what to say.

I can't let her out of my sight—no matter how painful it is to be around her now, Levi thought. *Even in the sunlight, Night Temptress could try something—like set a trap for her. And if anything were to happen to Emilia...*

Levi knew he would murder every vampire out of revenge.

A few seconds later, he heard galloping in the distance and looked down. A carriage approached with several guards. In the backseat sat someone Levi had told to stay away.

Lord Tristan. *What does that pompous royal want now?* Levi wondered. He rushed down the stairs to find out, hoping to keep him far from Emilia.

TWENTY-TWO

When Levi reached the entrance, Lord Tristan was already stepping out of his carriage with his guards. Had he come to arrest Levi? To expose his secret and finally get the woman of his dreams? This could've been some elaborate trick.

Then Levi looked over his shoulder, noticing the garments on the back of the horses. He must've brought enough evening wear for the entire keep.

As Lord Tristan smoothed out the wrinkles in his golden cape, Levi took the time to properly look at him. He still had bruises on his face from where Levi had beaten him, but they were healing. It looked like he hadn't slept, judging by the bags under his eyes. Levi wasn't sure how the royal had explained his injuries to the guards, but Levi knew he had lied for him. If not, the guards would've arrested him by now.

"What are you doing here, Tristan?" Levi asked, crossing his arms. "I told you to stay away for good. If Emilia sees you…"

"Forgive me," Lord Tristan began, bowing, "but I wanted to tell you the good news in person. The ball you requested for the royals is happening this afternoon at my castle. I'm holding it in the daylight so it's safer."

"And people agreed to come?"

"They did. When I told them of Allegiant, they seemed interested. King Brutus wasn't the only royal who was upset about the many deaths."

"Hmm. And what are those?" Levi asked, pointing at the garments.

"Evening wear for you and your Legionnaires. Free of charge, of course."

"How generous," Levi muttered. "You won't be at the ball, will you?"

"No, I'll remain in my bedchamber until it's over. I understood you before, Levi. I'll stay out of Emilia's sight."

"Good, smart choice."

Levi heard footsteps behind him and spun around. It wasn't Emilia as he feared, but Edmund. The old peasant wiped the dirt from his brow and smirked at the royal.

"Now I'm glad I have the day off," Edmund began, "to see the look on your stupid face. You tried to stop us—even kicked me out of your precious castle—but we started Allegiant anyway."

"Yes, you did. I was stubborn," Lord Tristan admitted. "I should've seen the dangers the vampires pose. Levi...he helped changed my mind."

When Lord Tristan and Levi's eyes locked, Levi had to look away. He hated that the lord knew his secret—but the royal had kept it, much to his surprise.

"Yeah, right," Edmund said, rolling his eyes. "You're still the same arrogant, spoiled noble you were before. No good deed you do now will change my mind about you. Ever."

As Edmund walked away, Lord Tristan sighed. "I know no

one here likes me, but I really want the best for Allegiant. And everything is set up already. The food, the tables. I recommend making a speech to your guests to convince them to send soldiers to your keep—"

Emilia walked around the corner, her eyes landing on them. Then she balled her fist and punched Lord Tristan in the jaw. Levi watched in surprise as the lord fell to the ground, his guards surrounding him with their blades drawn. Emilia stood over him, her fist red and probably aching.

"That was for my parents, you bastard!" Emilia snarled.

The guards moved to apprehend Emilia, their weapons drawn, but Lord Tristan held up his hand. "Don't! Don't harm her. It's all right, gentlemen. I'm fine."

The guards moved back but kept their weapons in hand. One of the guards helped Lord Tristan to his feet as he massaged the cheek Emilia had struck.

"Look, I know you're still upset with me for what I did," Lord Tristan began, "and I know nothing I can say will make it better—"

Emilia spat on him, shutting him up. The guards glanced at Lord Tristan, waiting for his order to retaliate, but it never came.

"Save your words, Tristan," Emilia hissed. "I don't want to hear them. What is this bastard doing here, Levi?"

Levi cleared his throat. "He came to tell us about the ball. I asked him to set it up. We needed some way to recruit more soldiers into our army, ones from different kingdoms. Anyway, it's happening this afternoon."

"Good," Emilia said, turning back to Lord Tristan. "I'll never forgive you for what you did to my family. But maybe you can make amends for the vampire attacks. Just maybe."

Lord Tristan nodded. "Yes, I'd like that—"

Emilia gestured at her sword. "But if I see your face again, I won't hesitate to kill you—your guards be damned. Do you understand?"

Lord Tristan said nothing but nodded again. Emilia huffed one last time before she walked back to the training yard.

"I suppose I deserved that," Lord Tristan muttered, looking back at Levi. "And to think I almost married a woman of her... tenacity. You were always a better match for her, Levi—which is why I hated you from the beginning."

"You really think so?" Levi asked, cocking an eyebrow.

"Of course—and you're courting her, aren't you? Anyone can see the way you look at each other. It's the same way my father looked at my mother when they were still alive. A look of true love. I've dreamed of finding a love like that, but alas, it never happened for me."

If Lord Tristan could notice it, had Cyrus noticed too? Of course he had. His brother was no fool. The question was what would he do about it?

"You deserve a lot worse than what Emilia did to you, you know," Levi said as he changed the subject, grabbing all the evening wear. "If you had met me a few years ago...you wouldn't have survived that night at the castle, Tristan."

"I know," he murmured. "And although it pains me to admit it...I *am* grateful. I'll tell the royals this afternoon that Allegiant has my full support. And about Sir Anders..."

"Keep your voice down," Levi hissed, glancing over his shoulder. "I didn't tell the others what really happened to him. They can't know. Not yet."

"I won't tell your secret then," Lord Tristan began. "But I wanted to tell you that what happened to him wasn't your fault. You tried to save him—and that's what counts. Despite what you are, Levi...you're a much better man than I."

"Save the pep talk," Levi muttered. "I don't want it from you. Just get out of here."

Levi watched Lord Tristan nod before he and his guards got back into the carriage and disappeared down the road. Levi heard footsteps again and craned his neck to see Father McGregor approaching. But the priest wasn't looking at him—he was watching Lord Tristan fade.

"Bah, I never cared for Lord Tristan," Father McGregor began. "I found his love of gold repulsive—his disregard for his own people even more so. But there *is* something different about him now."

"Like what?" Levi asked.

"He's becoming a different man," Father McGregor said, turning to Levi. "Anyone can change, you know—we're not bound to the person we were yesterday. There is hope of redemption for everyone, Levi. Even those who have committed terrible sins."

And then he walked away, leaving Levi wishing that was true.

When Levi brought the outfits to the main hall, Emilia entered from the training yard. She placed her weapon on the rack and walked over to Levi with a sigh.

"Hey. I'm sorry you had to see that," she began, patting her sweaty forehead from all the training. "I've tried to distract myself after my parents' death, but seeing Tristan...that anger spilled just came out. I couldn't control myself."

"You don't have to explain yourself to me," Levi began. "If I were in your place, I probably would've done the same thing. Just leave some of that anger for the vampires, all right?"

Emilia nodded. "Oh, don't worry. I have enough to spare."

She hadn't mentioned her feelings for him again—or what had happened last night—and Levi wondered if she would. But the Legionnaires entered the main hall next, ruining any chance of a private conversation. Their eyes widened when they saw the outfits.

"Good timing. Get ready, everyone," Emilia explained. "The ball is this afternoon—with dignitaries and nobles traveling to see us. This is our chance to recruit more soldiers to our cause. Although I don't want to step foot inside that damn castle again, it's for Allegiant. We need to do this."

"But we can't let everyone go to the ball," Levi said. "I know it's still light out, but we should keep some people here to watch over the keep."

"Good point. Legionnaires, divide yourselves up—half of you will accompany us and half of you will stay here. As a precaution."

As half the Legionnaires took their outfits to their quarters to get dressed, Cyrus walked over to Levi. "I'll stay here. Don't worry—I'll make sure nothing happens to Allegiant while you're gone."

Emilia smiled. "Thank you, Cyrus."

Levi narrowed his eyes. Cyrus wasn't the generous kind—and he wouldn't do any favors for Allegiant. What was the real reason he was staying behind?

"Where's Frederic?" Levi asked.

"Oh, he wanted me to tell you," Cyrus began. "He left for the markets—said he had some experiments to do back at the shop. Plus, he wanted to help any patients that might come in."

Emilia nodded. "That's Frederic. Always thinking of other people."

Levi wanted to tell her how wrong she was, but Novak and Vana burst through the door.

"Oh, there you two are," Emilia said. "We were just getting ready for the ball, and we'd love it if you came—"

"We heard news the orphanage burned down last night,"

Novak said, panting. "One of the villagers noticed it this morning and spread the word."

The Legionnaires gasped and began murmuring.

Emilia glanced at Levi, then back at Novak. "That sounds like something those vampires would do. Were any of the children hurt?"

"No. Strangely enough, there was no one found inside," Vana said. "If the vampires kidnapped those children, we *will* make them pay. Harming a child in Kelgat is punishable by death."

"Well, vampires would've left the bodies behind, drunk from and withered," Levi said. "I think it's a safe bet none of the orphans were there in the first place."

"Good," Novak said, his grip tightening around his sword. "I hope the vampires starved to death then. Shall we send out a search party?"

"If you'd like," Levi said, knowing they'd never find them. The barbarians nodded and divided themselves up.

Cyrus glanced at Novak and Vana, trying to hide a growing smirk. "What about the markets? Any houses burn down too?"

"No," Novak replied. "It looked like someone had already put the fire out before it could spread. Lucky for the villagers, hmm?"

Cyrus glanced in Levi's direction, but he refused to meet his brother's gaze.

"That's good. If not, it could've destroyed the whole village. Whoever put it out is a hero," Emilia said. "When you're in town next, question the people. Perhaps they'll know what happened. Anyway, excuse me. I need to get dressed now."

Emilia grabbed a dress, returning to her room. As Levi chose some clothes to wear, Novak and Vana walked over to him and Cyrus.

"You two were out last night," Novak said, narrowing his eyes. "We saw you."

Cyrus shrugged. "Yeah. And?"

"Did you see anything suspicious? Like the vampires around the orphanage?" Vana glanced between them. "Anything at all?"

"Uh, no," Levi lied. "If we had, we would've stopped them."

"Right." Novak blinked. "Well, I suppose we'll see you at the ball."

As they walked away, Levi had a bad feeling in the pit of his stomach. Cyrus seemed to feel it too, judging by how his eyes narrowed.

"You think they suspect us?" Cyrus whispered.

"I hope not," Levi whispered back. "For barbarians, they're very perceptive. Here I thought they were all brawn and no brain."

"Same here. Well, if they keep asking questions, we might have to kill them," Cyrus said, glancing in their direction with a smirk, "before everyone else. In the meantime, I'll be here, practicing in the training yard. I haven't had the chance to practice in a while—and if Allegiant gets more Legionnaires, I'll have to be on top of my game. Thanks to you. You're sure making our job more difficult, you know that?"

"Hey, the ball wasn't my idea," Levi lied. "Tristan must've changed his mind about supporting us. Don't worry, Brother. It'll all work out."

"Yes, it will," Cyrus said, a mysterious gleam in his eyes. "Oh, and we're not allowed in Frederic's lab while he's gone. Tell the others that, all right? He doesn't want any of them touching his stuff. The last I heard, he was super close to the sunlight cure."

"Really?" Levi asked, nervously playing with the hem of his shirt.

"Really. I'd say Allegiant has a few days left, if that. And it can't come soon enough. Well, I'll see you later, Brother."

The lab—Levi had almost forgotten. With Cyrus outside, Frederic gone, and the Legionnaires distracted, this was Levi's only chance.

He had to destroy the sunlight cure.

After putting on a suit that Lord Tristan had brought, he tip-toed over to the lab, looking over his shoulder to make sure no one was around. Most were getting ready for the ball while the others were busy training and patrolling. It was the perfect opportunity.

Levi entered the lab, looking around. There was a lot of equipment he didn't recognize, but he noticed one thing as clear as day—several vials of a yellowish, orange liquid. Frederic had left it out on the table.

Levi took all the vials he could find, stuffing them in his pocket. He walked outside the castle, taking a left into the nearby field. He tossed each vial on the ground and shattered them with his boot. He rushed back inside to grab a bucket and filled it with water, then returned to wash away the cure that had stained the field. After he had finished, he sat down on the grass, admiring his work.

"Levi? Are you coming?" Emilia asked, walking over to him.

Levi jumped to his feet, taking a good look at her. She wore the most beautiful blue gown he'd ever seen, accentuating her curves. Her red hair was bouncy and thick, and her eyes shimmered like the stars.

"Yeah, I'm ready," Levi said, nervously.

"Good. What are you doing out here? You could've ruined your clothes by sitting on the grass, you know."

"Just soaking up the sunshine," Levi lied, holding out his arm for Emilia to take. "Come on—we don't want to be late."

They rode to the castle with the Legionnaires on horses

trailing behind. Levi craned his neck and noticed Cyrus was watching them disappear down the street. When Cyrus questioned him on what had happened to the vials—and that seemed likely—Levi hoped he'd have a good answer, one that could deflect blame. As difficult as it was becoming to point the finger elsewhere.

Every time the vampires were thwarted, Levi had previous knowledge. Cyrus was bound to piece it together soon enough.

Emilia sighed, bringing Levi back to reality. "The last time I was at the castle, I was about to marry Lord Tristan. I don't talk about it much, but...I'm grateful you saved me from that life. Look at how much we accomplished since then."

Levi shook his head. "It's all because of you, Emilia. I'm just following your lead."

"Oh, that's not true. You've been a big help, Levi—especially this afternoon. I'm not sure I could've return to Lord Tristan's castle if it weren't for you. Not after..."

"Hey, it's okay," Levi said, after she'd trailed off for a few seconds. "He can't hurt you anymore—or anyone you love. He'll be locked away in his room, so you won't even have to see him."

Emilia took a deep breath. "You're right—it's foolish to still be afraid of him. We have bigger things to worry about. And Levi...you were right about the orphanage attack. I'm guessing the vampires burned it down when they couldn't find the orphans. They're petty, aren't they?"

"Very. I guess the rumor I heard was right," Levi muttered, not wanting her to grow suspicious. "My intel was good."

"It worked out that time, but what about the next? What if they attack someplace else? Someplace bigger?" Emilia shook her head. "We need more information, Levi—straight from the vampires themselves. I need time to figure out a plan, but I have a few ideas in mind already."

Levi gulped. Her rushing into action was going to get her hurt—and Levi couldn't stand the thought.

As they approached the castle, Lord Tristan had kept his promise. Levi didn't see him anywhere. His guards ushered the foreign royals inside, spinning a lie that Lord Tristan was ill and resting in his room. It sounded believable enough.

"Oh my God. Do you see how many people are here?" Emilia asked, her eyes widening. "So many kingdoms...and imagine the armies they have! If they give us even a quarter of their soldiers, we may need a bigger keep. But it means we might just succeed."

"We will," Levi promised. "I believe that."

The guards gave them the side-eye, but let Allegiant enter. The ballroom was busy and crowded with royals chatting and servants carrying platters around. As they paused to take it all in, Edmund and Samantha walked over.

"Hey, there you two are. I agreed to play for the royals tonight," Samantha said, strumming her lute. "If you can't win them over, perhaps my songs can."

"Oh, I don't think Emilia and Levi will have any trouble. These lot are royals—they'll believe anything if they think their precious kingdoms are in danger," Edmund said. "Good luck tonight, you two. With more Legionnaires on our side, those damn vamps won't stand a chance."

As they walked away, returning to mingle and drink, Emilia turned to Levi. "We'd better greet everyone and thank them for coming. When I give the signal, I'll start my speech. And I want you up there with me."

Levi frowned. "Me? Why? I'm not good at speeches. And besides, you're in charge of Allegiant, not me."

"Your modesty is endearing, Levi, but unnecessary. You'll do fine if you follow my lead. Be ready, okay?"

As she sauntered away, Levi went to approach a nearby

royal in the crowd when he spotted two people he didn't think he'd find. Frederic and Cyrus. They spoke in hushed whispers in the corner, wearing formal clothes to blend in. It looked like a tense conversation. But what were they doing there after Cyrus had said he wanted to train while Frederic was busy at the shop? His heart fluttered with panic.

Levi walked over to them, needing to find out.

TWENTY-THREE

Frederic and Cyrus hushed as Levi approached. "Hey guys. I thought you weren't coming?"

"I finished up at the shop early," Frederic said, "and figured I deserved a break. I've been working hard on the sunlight cure, and I've almost got it."

"Uh, right. And you?" Levi turned to his brother. "You told me you were hanging back to train."

"And I did for a bit," Cyrus replied. "But if we're getting new Legionnaires, I thought I should be here to see them—to spot their weaknesses. And besides, who doesn't love a good party?"

There was something about their tone that Levi didn't trust. Why had they been whispering before he walked over? It had to be about the shattered vials. In the back of Levi's mind, he knew it was only a matter of time until they fully pieced it together.

Tick tock, tick tock, tick tock...

"You'd better get back to the party," Cyrus said. "Wouldn't want Emilia to think you're not on her side, right?"

"Right," Levi muttered. "Excuse me."

As he walked away, he could feel their eyes on his back. It sent a chill up his spine. He rejoined the party, grabbing a glass of ale to blend in. He mingled with some of the royals, mentioning Allegiant, Emilia, and the vampires here and there to pique their interest. They seemed both curious and impressed, something Levi hoped would help them win over more Legionnaires.

When he felt a tap on his shoulder, he turned around. King Brutus stood in front of him with an axe attached to his back. "Levi," the barbarian lord began. "Do you remember what I said to you the last time we met?"

Levi nodded. "That if I didn't avenge your daughter, you'd kill me yourself."

Levi feared for a second that he hadn't satisfied King Brutus's wish. But the burly barbarian wrapped a large, muscular arm around Levi's shoulder and grinned. "You've done well so far—even managed to get Lord Tristan on your side. I didn't think it could be done."

"Me either," Levi replied, "but he came around. He just needed a little incentive."

"Indeed. And I saw Allegiant Keep," King Brutus continued. "Very impressive. You already have my full support. If I could spare any more of my own, I would, but Kelgat needs its army too. I decided to come today as a show of good faith—to convince people your fight is a worthy cause. When the time comes to make your speech, I will support you."

"Thank you, we appreciate that. Enjoy the party."

As King Brutus walked away, vanishing in the crowd, Levi spotted Cyrus flirting with Samantha as she played the lute. She wasn't singing, but strumming the tune to *Allegiant is the Name*. Cyrus was smirking and saying something to her. Frederic leaned against one of the castle's walls nearby, his eyes roaming over the party.

When Levi turned away, unable to watch Samantha flirt with a monster and Frederic lick his lips at the crowd, he noticed Emilia across the room. She wasn't talking to the royals but staring at a spot on the floor near the throne.

"Emilia?" he asked, walking over. "Are you all right?"

"Yes. Or...no. It's just, Dawn died right there," she said, pointing near the wall. "The vampires had us cornered, and... and then..."

Emilia grew silent. Levi wrapped his arms around her, hoping Cyrus and Frederic wouldn't notice.

"Thanks. I never want to feel that helpless again," Emilia said into his arms. "And I don't want to lose anyone else again. Especially you."

"You won't," Levi lied, but he wished he could mean it. "I'm not going anywhere."

Emilia pulled away, wiping the tears from her eyes. "Good. Well, it's time to do what we came here for. Shall we?"

Levi nodded. "Let's do it."

Emilia walked over to their table, banging her fork on a glass. "If I could have your attention, I have something important to say. Please, take a seat."

Emilia waited for the royals to sit and quiet down. She looked back at Levi, gesturing at him to join her. When he did, he felt everyone's eyes on him—including Cyrus and Frederic's. He tried not to look in their direction.

"As many of you know, monster attacks have plagued Osgoode for a long time," Emilia began. "We call them vampires. Levi, can you explain what they are?"

"Yes, of course." He cleared his throat. "Vampires are blood-sucking creatures. They can't survive out in the sun, their eyes are bright yellow, and silver and holy objects can kill them. Worst of all, they have no conscience—no way of determining right from wrong." Levi glanced at Cyrus who was still staring at him. "That's what makes them despicable. Evil."

Emilia nodded. "Yes, exactly. The last time you were all

here, the vampires attacked—killing some of the guests. King Brutus's daughter was among them. We want to extend our deepest sympathies for all the lives taken."

The royals glanced at the barbarian lord. He hung his head, tears welling in his eyes. A pang of sorrow shot through Levi's body.

"But we have a plan to stop them. Levi and I have started Allegiant—a militia dedicated to hunting vampires," Emilia continued. "We've already foiled some of their plans. Our keep is strong, and we have dozens of Legionnaires. But we need more."

"That we do. And we know the vampires will intensify their attacks—they won't stop after the last massacre here," Levi said, growing more confident. "Any of you could be next. We have to stop them before they attack again. And we'll do that by uniting."

The room began to murmur. Emilia reached back for Levi's hand, squeezing it gently. This was it.

"Excuse me, but isn't it dangerous?" a royal in the crowd asked. He was an older, overweight man with a graying beard. "Is it worth risking our soldiers' lives?"

"And there haven't been any vampires spotted outside Osgoode," another royal said. She was younger, with dark hair and a pink ballgown. "What makes it our problem?"

"Because they attacked you when you came here," Levi said. "They've killed dozens. And just because you haven't seen them in your kingdoms doesn't mean they aren't there. Or won't visit at some point. Believe me, they spread like the plague. Don't you want justice?"

"Not if it costs us our lives," an older woman in the crowd said. She wore a golden tiara, her dark hair graying. "Look, we're all very sorry for what's happening in Osgoode, but our kingdom's safety comes first."

The crowd murmured again. Even some of the royals that seemed enthusiastic before were skeptical now. Emilia glanced back at Levi, worried.

King Brutus slammed his fist on the table, then rose to his feet and glanced around the room. "And what's to stop the vampires from invading our lands? You saw them at the castle—they were intelligent creatures. I wouldn't be surprised if they had a ship halfway across the ocean by now!"

The crowd stopped murmuring.

"Look, I've already sent some of my finest barbarians to Allegiant. I would advise you all to do the same," King Brutus said. "I've lost a daughter. I know what the vampires are capable of—and when they do come after your kingdoms, perhaps Allegiant won't offer to protect you at all. Then what? Do you honestly believe you can stop these vampires on your own? You can barely wipe your own asses without a servant. So don't be foolish, people. Unite with Allegiant—it's our only chance to wipe out these beasts and survive."

The crowd of royals glanced around at each other again, gasping. Then, after thinking it over, they nodded and lifted their glasses to show their support.

"Very well," a stuffy royal in the crowd said. "We will each spare some of our soldiers—but we expect updates on your progress."

"We can do that," Levi said with a smile. "Thank you. We won't let you down."

The Legionnaires that Emilia and Levi had brought cheered. Emilia squealed with joy, throwing her arms around Levi. As he hugged her back, he spotted Cyrus across the room. His face was hard, red with anger. But Frederic wasn't. He was smirking, looking amused. Levi wasn't sure he wanted to know what was going through their heads.

"Well, this calls for a toast," Emilia said, picking up her

glass. "To Levi for his support and encouragement. When I say I couldn't have done this without you, I mean it—and don't be modest. You know how special you are. To Allegiant, to Osgoode. And to me."

Levi blushed. Everyone raised their glasses, toasting to him. He downed his drink and thought of the irony.

If Patriarch Kristoff had known I'd do this, I'm sure he would've chosen Cyrus as his successor, Levi thought. *If only he could see me now.*

Emilia took a sip of her drink and turned to Samantha. "Sam, let's liven up this party a little bit. Play something inspiring!"

Samantha played *Allegiant is the Name* on her lute, and the Legionnaires sang the words loudly. Emilia looked away from the crowd, smiling at Levi. But then her smile faded into a frown, and she dropped her glass. It shattered on the floor, sending shards flying everywhere. When she collapsed, the crowd gasped and swarmed her. Samantha stopped strumming and rushed over.

Levi fell to his knees, hovering above Emilia. "Em? What's going on?"

She could barely speak. Sweat gleamed across her face, her skin paler than usual.

"We need a healer," Levi said, turning to the crowd. "Is anyone here an apothecary?"

No one stepped forward, not even Frederic.

"Poison," Emilia whispered, glancing up at Levi. "I...think I've been poisoned. I have all the symptoms. Weak, nauseous, sweaty..."

"Poison? But...but how?" Levi asked. "Who would poison you?"

Emilia's eyes flitted to her glass on the table. Levi noticed her gaze and realized someone must've spiked her drink. A risky, desperate, and cowardly thing to do.

Levi ran through the suspects in his mind as he lifted Emilia, holding her in his arms. He couldn't let her die—not like this.

"Where are you taking her?" Samantha asked.

"To the apothecary shop," Levi replied, looking over his shoulder. "Cyrus, Frederic—come with me. Now."

"What about the rest of us?" Edmund asked, following Levi out of the castle. "What should we do while you're gone?"

"I don't care," Levi said, placing Emilia on the back of his horse. "I only care about making sure Emilia survives."

The crowd watched as Cyrus and Frederic pushed through to Levi. They got on their horses as Levi flicked the reins on his animal, then he and Emilia disappeared down the road.

When they had made it to the markets, the villagers passing by stopped to stare at Emilia. Levi made the horse stop in front of the apothecary shop, then picked up Emilia who couldn't walk. He carried her inside, placing her down on one of the tables. Cyrus and Frederic sauntered in behind them. Emilia looked delirious as she lifted a hand, placing it on Levi's cheek.

"I should've told you before, Levi," she slurred. "How I felt. Long, long before. Then we could've had more time..."

"Shh," Levi said, caressing her cheek. "Just relax—don't strain yourself." When she fell unconscious from the poison, Levi turned around, glancing at Frederic and Cyrus. They hadn't moved or made a noise. "What are you just standing there for?" Levi asked Frederic, approaching them. "You're supposed to be one of the smartest scientists in history, right? Help her."

Frederic crossed his arms. "And why should I? It seems it would end our problems if we let her die."

Levi paused for a moment. "You did this to her, didn't you? Poisoned her drink?"

"And if I did?" Frederic asked.

"Why?" Levi demanded. "We agreed to wait to kill Emilia until the end. It isn't the right time yet!"

"It was Night Temptress's idea, actually," Frederic began. "I must confess, I didn't go to the shop this morning. Instead, I returned to the lair to tell the vampires about the ball. Night Temptress suggested poisoning her drink to settle a score. Since she can't come out in the sun yet, she asked me to do it in her place."

"What score?" Cyrus asked, raising an eyebrow.

Frederic shrugged. "She wouldn't say. But who am I to argue over causing a little chaos?"

Levi knew it—this was Night Temptress's revenge on Levi for rejecting her. He was sure he would've killed that vampire if she were there instead.

"For me rejecting her," Levi muttered. "She mentioned something like this would happen."

Cyrus shook his head. "Should've just bedded her, Levi."

Levi glared at Cyrus. That was a suggestion he wasn't even going to entertain.

"Why poison?" Levi eventually asked. "That doesn't seem like the kind of thing a vampire would do."

"She wanted Emilia to suffer slowly. Can you blame her?" Frederic glanced over at Emilia, sneering. "This bitch will kill our people. She deserves no less."

Levi growled, pointing at the lab in the back of the shop. "I mean it—heal her. This wasn't the plan."

"Why, Levi," Frederic began, stepping closer, "if I didn't know better, I'd say you want the woman to live. The same woman who's responsible for killing all our people in the future."

Levi's eyes narrowed at Frederic. "That's...no, that's not it at all. I just want things to go according to plan. It was Cyrus's idea to befriend her—to make her think we're on her side. I'm just making sure we stay on script."

"It's true," Cyrus said. "Maybe you should save her, Frederic. If anything, it'll make her angrier—feistier. And I like my humans with a little spirit."

Levi hated leaving Emilia's life in someone else's hands. He thought Frederic might refuse as he stared at him, but then he sighed. "Very well. This better be worth it in the end, Levi."

Emilia was still unconscious on the table, looking worse by the minute. Her skin was paler; her breathing had slowed. As Frederic worked in the background, mixing potions, Levi wanted to reach down and grab her hand. But with Cyrus nearby, he resisted the urge.

"Hey. During Emilia's speech," Cyrus whispered, "she said she'd already foiled some vampire plans. What did she mean by that?"

Levi feared Cyrus suspected that they had saved the orphanage. "Uh, I dunno. Probably by starting Allegiant. That's what leads to our downfall."

Before Cyrus had a chance to reply, Frederic walked over with a strange-looking concoction. The vial was bright blue and smelled like feet.

"What is that?" Levi asked, making a disgusted face. "God, it smells awful."

"The cure," Frederic said. "I made the poison for Night Temptress, so I know the antidote."

Frederic leaned beside Emilia, pressing the vial up to her mouth. He tipped it, letting it flow down her throat gently. When the vial was empty, he placed it down and stepped back. But nothing happened.

"What did you do to her now?" Levi demanded, glaring at Frederic. "Did you poison her again?"

"No, of course not. I did what you asked. The cure needs

time to work," Frederic said, staring at Emilia's body. "I'd suggest taking her back to the keep and letting her rest."

As Levi picked her up bridal style, Cyrus stepped forward. "She deserves a much bloodier death than that, anyway. I look forward to it."

"Speaking of which," Frederic said as Levi turned to the door, "you should be the one to kill her, Levi. After all, she trusts you the most. That much is evident from her little speech."

Levi said nothing. He wasn't about to swear to be her killer. And with a little luck, maybe he could dissuade them from killing her too.

"It'll be harder to kill her, you know," Levi finally said, "with more Legionnaires coming. How do you expect us to win against Allegiant now? We've let it go on too long. We should've killed them all when we had the chance. Maybe it'd be better if we ran and tried to repopulate somewhere else."

Frederic shook his head. "Don't be so hasty. You think more Legionnaires will stop us? We're vampires, Levi. We don't back down from a challenge. And besides, we have...reinforcements of our own."

Well, damn, at least I tried to get them to stop, Levi thought.

"What are you talking about?" Levi eventually asked. "What kind of reinforcements?"

"There are some vampires who have traveled outside Osgoode for us. We like to know what's going on out in the world," Frederic replied. "One day, we hope to invade other countries. But with the Legionnaires coming, we had no choice but to call on them. We can't let Allegiant get the upper hand."

Levi said nothing, though he was worried. More vampires meant more trouble. And they had enough of that these days.

"You'd better get her back to the keep, Brother," Cyrus said, his eyes on Emilia. "She needs her rest before Frederic figures out the sunlight cure. And then it's *go* time."

"Right," Levi said, turning his back.

As he placed Emilia on the back of his horse and galloped away, he shook his head. More vampires, Night Temptress's revenge, Frederic's request of Levi to kill Emilia. It was all spiraling out of control. Levi wasn't sure how much longer he could go without both sides growing suspicious of him. He had to make a stand soon—to prevent the vampires from killing more people.

But first things first, Levi thought. *It's time to kill Night Temptress for this and get her out of the way.*

With his fists firmly balled, he vowed to make her pay for this.

TWENTY-FOUR

When Levi arrived at the keep, carrying an unconscious Emilia in his arms, the Legionnaires they had left behind rushed over to him.

"What happened to her?" one Legionnaire asked.

"Poisoned," Levi mumbled, carrying her up to her room. "But she's been given the cure. She just needs to rest and get better."

"My God. Was it the vampires?" another Legionnaire asked, following him. "Did they do this to her?"

"If the strongest Legionnaire can be poisoned," another one began, "what hope do the rest of us have?"

Levi turned around, sighing. "Look, Emilia needs her rest. She'll live—but you need to give her some space, all right? I'll let you know how she's doing soon."

They nodded, heading downstairs. When Levi reached Emilia's room, he placed her on her bed, pulling up the blankets around her. He shut the door behind him to give them some privacy and then kneeled beside her.

He reached for her hand. Hers were small and warm—much

different from Levi's. As Emilia slept, Levi had only one thought on his mind. Night Temptress's death.

I've already killed one vampire, he thought. *It's all been coming down to this. Either the vampires kill Emilia and stop Allegiant...or I kill all of them. Including Cyrus, my own brother, the one I've known longer than anyone. As much as it will destroy me to stake him, I can't let Emilia die.*

That echoed around in his head for a little while. *I can't let her die, can't let her die, can't let her die...*

When Emilia didn't stir, a thought crossed his mind. To save her...would it be possible to turn her into a vampire? Her neck looked so inviting, so open. One bite would make her stronger.

But it would also change her completely. And Levi liked the way she was. Oh, who was he kidding?

He *loved* her. She was perfect already, even in her human form. She needed to survive this poison attack. She just had to.

A knock sounded on the door. Levi growled, not bothering to turn around. "Go away!"

The door opened. Levi turned, ready to yell at whoever it was when he noticed Edmund and Samantha.

"Oh, it's you two," he grumbled. "You left the ball?"

Edmund nodded. "Damn straight. Didn't feel right celebrating while Emilia was ill."

"And we had to know how she was doing," Samantha began, walking over to her bedside. "Will she be okay?"

"I hope so. I gave her the antidote," Levi replied, watching Emilia's chest rise and fall with her light breathing. "There's nothing else I can do. I...I just hope she lives. I don't know what I'd do if I lost her."

Samantha placed an arm on Levi's shoulder, glancing down at his hand in Emilia's. "You love her, don't you?"

Levi only nodded.

"I know she feels the same way," Samantha whispered.

"Because of that love you share, I believe it'll save her. She'll wake up—you'll see."

"You really think love is that powerful?" Levi asked, trying not to choke up.

She smiled. "I do. And when she wakes up, tell her we're all glad she survived. Come on, Papa, let's give them some privacy."

Edmund and Samantha left, closing the door on their way out. Levi stayed on the floor, one hand in Emilia's while the other brushed hair out of her eyes. She looked peaceful—like she was in a deep sleep.

"Come on, Emilia," Levi murmured. "You've got to wake up. You've just got to."

Levi stayed with her for hours, still holding her hand. But when his stomach growled in hunger, he pulled away.

"I'll be right back," he whispered. "Just need some grub. Stay here."

As he left her room, he noticed a crowd of Legionnaires outside her door. "Well? Is she awake?" one Legionnaire asked.

"Not yet," Levi replied, "but she will be soon. I meant what I said before—give her space. I don't want anyone entering her room, understand?"

The crowd nodded. In her fragile state, Levi felt even more protective of her now. He didn't want anyone around her— certainly not Cyrus and Frederic. If they tried to kill her again, would Levi be able to stop them? They'd almost succeeded on the first try. And that made him nervous.

He pushed through the crowd, walking down the stairs. He nearly smacked into Samantha who was glancing out the nearby window.

"What is it?" Levi asked. "What are you looking at?"

"Lord Tristan," Samantha grumbled. "He's outside. Again."

Levi sneered, exiting the keep. Lord Tristan was the last

person he wanted to see right now. He watched as Lord Tristan stepped off his horse, adjusting his cape. He was about to open his mouth when Levi interrupted.

"Leave," Levi said. "Right now."

"Hang on a minute." Lord Tristan held up a hand. "I heard about what happened at the ball. Will Emilia be all right?"

"I hope so." Levi crossed his arms. "Why do you care?"

"I don't, really. I'm done with that woman. I only came here to tell you I had nothing to do with the poison."

"I know," Levi muttered. "Trust me."

Lord Tristan frowned. "But...Emilia was poisoned. Although it incriminates me, even I'll admit I had the most motive at the party."

Levi sighed. "No, you didn't. There was someone else there —someone who had a reason to want her dead."

"Oh, praise the Lord. I thought you might string me up by my ankles or something. I had to make sure you knew I was innocent." Lord Tristan turned silent for a moment, then lowered his voice. "Does this...does this have something to do with the vampires?"

"Yes, it does."

"And...were they at the party? Other than you, I mean?"

"What do you think?" Levi huffed.

Lord Tristan shivered. "But...how is that possible? I thought they couldn't be out in the sunlight."

"They have their ways."

His eyes widened. "By the saints..."

"Don't tell anyone I told you that. Let me handle this, all right?"

He backed up, his hands shaking. "I think you may be the only one who can. I'm just glad you believe I'm innocent."

Levi turned his back. "Good—get out of here. I don't want Emilia to see your face when she wakes up."

"Wait," Lord Tristan urged. "There's something else I need to say."

Levi sighed. "My patience is wearing thin, Tristan. This isn't a good time—"

"I know, but I wanted to tell you that more Legionnaires will be arriving in the next few days. You convinced them. Well, Emilia did. They signed the treaty after you left." He paused. "You did what I couldn't, Levi. You found a way to stop the vampires. When Emilia wakes up, tell her I hope you two succeed."

As Lord Tristan fled on his horse, riding back to his castle, Levi still hated him for all he had done. But perhaps he had an ally in him now—and they'd need everyone to stop the vampires, especially with new ones coming into town.

Levi entered the keep again, making his way into the kitchen. He wolfed down raw meat that Alana and Peeta had prepared for him as they badgered him with questions about Emilia. He promised she'd live—a promise he hoped to keep.

As he left the kitchen, he ran into Frederic who stopped him. "Ah, there you are. May I see you in my lab, Levi? It's important."

Levi's eyes flickered to the stairs. He wanted to return to Emilia's side and check on her, but he nodded anyway, gulping at what Frederic had to show him. "Uh, of course. Lead the way."

Levi followed Frederic to the lab, spotting Cyrus as he entered. He stood along the back wall with his arms crossed. But Cyrus wouldn't meet his eyes, looking anywhere but Levi.

"What's going on?" Levi asked.

"My sunlight cure," Frederic said, gesturing around the lab. "I've searched everywhere for the vials, but they're gone."

"Oh. Oh, no. Well, did you ask the Legionnaires?" Levi

asked, pretending to be shocked. "Maybe they know where the vials went."

"We did. I spoke with Samantha," Cyrus began, still not making eye contact. "We asked around, but no one's seen them."

"Do you know where they could've gone, Levi?" Frederic asked. "Did you see anything?"

"No," Levi lied. "But don't worry. I'm sure they'll turn up somewhere—they have to."

"I hope so." Frederic scowled. "Months of work, just gone in a flash..."

"Damn, that sucks. I'm really sorry." Levi leaned against the wall, attempting to look innocent. "What will you do now?"

"I'll have no choice but to start over. I still have your blood, so perhaps I can recreate it. But that'll take some time—longer than I anticipated."

Levi looked over his shoulder to make sure no one was listening. "Will we have to postpone our attack?"

Frederic nodded. "I'm afraid so. It could take me weeks to recreate the work I lost. What a disaster."

"And don't forget the new Legionnaires are coming soon," Levi said. "Emilia's speech convinced the kingdoms to send us recruits. Will we really have a chance against them now?"

"Oh, don't worry," Cyrus said, stepping forward. He finally lifted his gaze to meet Levi's. "The attack *will* happen. Frederic just needs a little extra time. And when he gets it right, no Legionnaire will be able to stand against us."

"Well, good luck, then," Levi said to Frederic. "I hope you can work fast."

Frederic said nothing as Levi turned around, but Cyrus's voice stopped him. "Wait a sec. How's Emilia doing?"

Levi paused. "She's getting better. Why?"

"Just curious," Cyrus muttered. "Tell her we're worried about her. Make her think we care."

"Sure thing. I'll let her know when she wakes up. Well, see you later."

As Levi left the lab, he knew there was no way Cyrus didn't know he was helping Emilia. The lingering look in Cyrus's eyes seemed to tell him one thing. *Watch yourself or these vampires will kill you, Brother. And I will be forced to help them.*

His hands shaking, Levi nearly banged into Novak and Vana as he turned around the corner. He tried to maneuver around them, but they wouldn't get out of his way.

"Excuse me," Levi said, pointing at the stairs. "I need to check on Emilia."

"That can wait. There's an emergency in the stables," Vana said. "Come with us."

Levi nodded, following Novak and Vana outside into the stables. As he entered, he didn't hear anything or see anyone out of place. Frowning, he turned around to look back when Novak locked the barn door, sealing the three of them inside.

Levi crossed his arms. "Uh, what's going on?"

Novak removed his sword from its scabbard, holding it up in front of him. "I was hoping you could explain that to us."

Levi had no idea what he was talking about. Novak and Vana seemed angry, their fists balled and faces red, so Levi kept his distance.

"There's...no emergency in the stables, is there?" Levi asked.

Vana nodded. "You're right—it was a plot to get you alone. We need answers, Levi. We watched from the window as you destroyed Frederic's vials in the field. That was supposed to help us against the vampires, wasn't it? Why would you do that?"

Levi said nothing. He'd been caught.

"And another thing," Vana added. "Barbarian spies caught

you and Emilia transporting children to a pirate ship—the one that brooding sea captain commands. And then later that night, the vampires burned down the orphanage."

"I don't understand," Levi said. "What are you accusing me of?"

Novak glanced at Vana, then back at Levi. "While saving the children is commendable...we believe you're trying to sabotage Allegiant. From the inside."

Levi sneered. "What? Why would I do that—especially after saving all those kids?"

Novak narrowed his eyes. "We don't know. You still haven't explained anything, Levi. And we're getting impatient. Are you on our side or not?"

Levi thought of a cover story—fast. "Of course, I am. I heard the vampires were planning to attack the orphanage. I told Emilia, then the two of us moved the kids to Rosalie's ship. It's why she hasn't been around—she's busy protecting them."

"Why didn't you tell anyone else?" Vana demanded. "We would've helped you."

"Because we feared too many people involved would alert the vampires. It's also why I destroyed the vials—I heard rumors the vampires had tampered with them. Whether it was true or not, we couldn't risk using something that was sabotaged."

It wasn't a total lie—the vampires *had* tampered with the vials. Frederic had no intention of ever helping Allegiant.

"Please, you can't tell anyone," Levi continued. "We need to stay one step ahead of the vampires, and that means keeping some things secret. Trust me."

Novak and Vana nodded at each other, sheathing their blades. Levi breathed a sigh of relief.

"We believe you," Novak said. "But next time, we want to know the plan. We promise we'll be discreet."

"Of course," Levi said, faking a smile. "Now, if you'll excuse me, I need to see how Emilia's doing."

As he fled the stables, Novak and Vana didn't follow. Levi chastised himself for not being more careful as he entered the keep. When he stepped through the doors, Samantha ran up to him. "Emilia's awake!"

Levi's heart skipped a beat. "What? Really?"

Samantha nodded. "Really. I know you told us not to go in there, but I heard movement and wanted to check on her. She's asking for you, Levi. She won't talk to anyone else."

Levi rushed up the stairs without saying goodbye, almost tripping over his own two feet. He swung the door open to Emilia's room, noticing her sitting up in bed now. She looked much better. He closed the door and rushed to her side.

When she saw him, tears welled in her eyes. She wrapped her arms around him, pulling him close. "Levi..."

"I know," he murmured, stroking her hair. "I'm here."

She pulled away, looking into his eyes. "How did you save me?"

"It was Frederic, actually," Levi said, and he hated giving him the credit. "We rushed you to the apothecary and he made some strange-looking cure. I was afraid it wouldn't work. How do you feel?"

"Much better," she replied. "Time will tell, but I think the poison is out of my system now. I threw up while you were gone, and I think it helped. I'm not surprised Frederic found the cure so quickly—he was always smarter than me. Do you know who poisoned me? It wasn't Lord Tristan, was it?"

Levi shook his head at her steady, penetrating look. "No, he's learned his lesson. I think...I think it was the vampires."

Emilia blinked. "But how? They can't go out into the sunlight."

"I know. But I think the vampires are evolving—becoming immune to sunlight. It's just a theory, but it's possible."

"Hmm. Why would they poison me? Why not attack me outright?" Emilia frowned. "I've seen their victims—blood drained, throats slashed."

"They did this to send a message—that they can do whatever they want to us."

It wasn't the entire truth, but it would have to suffice for now.

Emilia rose to her feet, pacing back and forth. "We need to do something, Levi. These vampires are getting bolder. If they can poison me, what else are they capable of?"

"You're right," Levi said, standing up. "What do you want to do?"

"Do you remember before the party, when I said I was working on a plan?"

"I do."

"Well, I've had time to think while recovering," she said, running a hand through her disheveled crimson hair. "Between the orphanage attack and the poison, we need to act."

"I'm with you. What do you have in mind?"

"You've heard rumors of what they're up to, but I want something more concrete." She moved closer to Levi. "I propose we kidnap a vampire and torture them for information."

Levi's eyes widened in shock. "That's...quite the plan."

"I know. And before you tell me it's dangerous, I think it's our best shot. We can't afford to attack the vampires outright—not until the new Legionnaires get here. It could take days for all of them to arrive, and the vampires could be planning something right now. We must do something before we run out of time."

Levi sighed. "I...I don't know. You just recovered from

getting poisoned, Em. I don't want you putting yourself in danger again."

She scoffed. "Oh, please. This is what I signed up for when I started Allegiant, Levi. One vampire shouldn't give us too much trouble—not if we can lure them away from the others."

And if the vampire revealed what Levi was, he wondered. What if they told Emilia everything before he had the opportunity?

"You've gotten information before," she continued, reaching for his hand. "You were the one who told me about the vampire lair behind the mines. And then the orphanage attack. Aren't you tired of hearing bits and pieces? Don't you want something substantial?"

"I do, but...what about the others? Vana and Novak could handle this. Why you?"

"If something terrible happens, I won't risk anyone else's life for this—not until our new Legionnaires get here. No, it has to be us, Levi, and us alone. I can be the bait while you subdue the vampire."

"No." Levi shook his head firmly. "I won't let you do this."

Emilia ripped her hand away. "Then you don't understand. Dawn could've lived if we had a warning that the vampires were attacking the castle! A lack of information is dangerous—"

"I mean I don't want you to be the bait," Levi interrupted. "I'll be the one to lure them out. I'm confident I can subdue them too. Just find us a deserted place and I'll bring the vampire there for a torture session. The vampires shouldn't be too hard to find after sundown."

He could feel his hatred for Night Temptress rising inside of him. It would be her—she was the vampire he wanted to torture and kill. He'd already decided that when she had poisoned Emilia.

"Are you sure?" Emilia raised an eyebrow. "Don't you want back-up?"

"I'm sure. Look, I know you're worried," Levi began, "but I can handle one vamp. I fought off a bunch of them at the castle, remember?"

Emilia sighed. "Yes, I do. And okay, if you're sure. I already know of a few places behind the markets that've been abandoned for years. We'll keep our prisoner there, torture them for information. *Helpful* information. We'll leave immediately after sundown tonight, so be ready."

"Tonight?" Levi frowned.

"Yes—we'd better move while we still can. It'll be sundown in a few hours. Before we leave, I'll ask Father McGregor to come with us. He's the only person I'm trusting with this."

"Why? I thought you wanted to be discreet?"

"I do, but Father McGregor has all kinds of religious things here. We'll need those things to subdue the vampire. I don't want to take any chances."

As she turned to exit the room, Levi reached forward and grabbed her wrist. She looked back at him with a raised eyebrow until he pulled her tight to him, kissing her lips passionately. She was breathless when they pulled away.

"I thought I lost you," Levi murmured. "Never again. Don't do anything risky tonight, okay?"

"I promise," she whispered. "As long as you promise the same."

"I'll do my best to come back to you. I still haven't shown you exactly how I feel about you yet." He ran a finger up her arm, causing goosebumps to rise on her skin. "But if I think you're in danger at any time and ask you to leave...I need you to do it. Can you do that for me, Emilia?"

"Levi...I'm touched. You always know just what to say." She sighed. "If you think it's best, then I promise to listen. You have more experience with these vampires than I do, so I'll follow your lead."

Good, Levi thought. *If Night Temptress tries to reveal anything about me, I'll get Emilia out of there. It's the best I can do.*

Levi glanced outside, noticing the sky growing darker. With everything happening, Levi felt like his days were numbered—with the vampires *and* Emilia. He knew they were. And right now, he didn't want to let her go.

"Forgive me if I'm being too forward, but...can you stay with me until sundown? With you in my arms?" Levi asked, searching her eyes. "Before we risk our lives?"

Emilia nodded, smiling. "I think that's an excellent idea."

As they sat in silence with Levi's arms around her, he realized there would never be another perfect moment like this again.

TWENTY-FIVE

When sundown arrived, the Legionnaires headed to bed after another long day of training. Emilia thought it was a good idea to let them know she was all right, so Levi reluctantly removed his arms from around her waist. The Legionnaires were happy to see her and bombarded her with a million questions.

She answered what she could and bid them all good-night, telling them she needed rest to recover. Half an hour later, when most of the Legionnaires were snoring, Emilia nodded at Levi, then they tiptoed out of her room.

They walked down the stairs as Levi kept looking over his shoulder for his brother and Frederic. But Cyrus and Frederic were missing. Emilia knocked on the door to Father McGregor's chapel, trying to be quiet. He looked half-asleep and puzzled when he opened it in his nightshirt.

"Sorry to bother you, Father," Emilia said, "but this is important. May we come in?"

Father McGregor nodded, letting the two in and shutting the door behind them. Emilia explained their plan as quickly as she could, not wanting to waste another minute of darkness.

"...and we want you to come with us for extra protection," Emilia finished. "We need some crosses and holy water."

"Of course. What's mine is yours," Father McGregor replied, gesturing at the room. "But is this truly a good idea? Wouldn't it be better to involve the others, even if it *is* just one vampire? You were nearly poisoned to death, Emilia. We must not risk your safety again."

"Trust us, Father," Levi said. "We have to be discreet about this."

When Father McGregor met Levi's eyes, he seemed to understand.

"I see," Father McGregor murmured. "Very well—there seems to be no talking either of you out of this. And I trust Levi will protect us if something terrible should happen?"

"With my life," Levi said, and he meant it.

"Good." Father McGregor handed some crosses and holy water to Emilia. "Take these, then. I'll bring some with me as well."

"Thanks. Here," Emilia said, offering a cross to Levi. "You should take one too."

As Levi froze, Father McGregor cleared his throat. "We can carry them, Emilia. Let Levi focus on protecting us and luring the vampire out."

Emilia nodded, stuffing some extra crosses in her pocket. Levi sighed in relief. They turned around to give the priest some privacy as he changed back into his religious robes.

"I'm dressed now," he said. "Emilia, can you get the horses ready for us? Levi can help me with some last-minute supplies."

"Sure thing," she said, then left the chapel.

After she was gone, Father McGregor turned to Levi. "Do you have a vampire in mind for tonight?"

"The one who poisoned Emilia." Levi balled his fists. "Her

name is Night Temptress, and it was revenge on me for rejecting her. I want her dead. Tonight."

"And if she reveals what you are to Emilia?"

"Then I'll silence her," Levi said, reaching for the handle of a silver sword. "Permanently."

"I still think you should tell Emilia what you are," Father McGregor whispered. "You've wasted so much time already."

"Do you think I don't want to? Every second I'm with her, I want to confess what I am. But I'm scared, Father—scared she won't feel the same way about me when I do. And scared she'll think I'm trying to sabotage her, like my brother."

Father McGregor sighed. "I see your predicament, Levi— and I *do* sympathize. Ultimately, I can't tell you what to do, but I think the time for honesty is coming soon. And if it's your brother or one of these vampires who tells her the truth, she may never forgive you for lying to her."

The priest had a point. Before Levi could say anything, Father McGregor gathered the rest of his crosses and holy water and left. Levi followed him to the stables, considering the priest's words. He wanted to tell Emilia—but he didn't know how. He couldn't come right out and say it, could he? Tell her that she had fallen for the thing she hated the most?

Emilia walked out of the stables. She smiled at them, saddling up Margaret. "Everything's ready to go. What took you two so long?"

"We wanted to go over the plan first," Father McGregor replied. "I think we're ready now."

As Emilia nodded and hopped onto the horse, Levi spotted shadows approaching through the darkness. He prepared himself for an attack before he realized it was just the perimeter guards—Novak, Vana, and the other barbarians. Didn't they ever sleep?

Levi figured Emilia should know the barbarians had found

out, so he leaned closer. "Hey, Emilia? They know we took those orphans to the docks. They were watching."

Emilia said nothing, but Father McGregor's eyes widened. "That was you two? Good, I'm relieved to know they're safe."

"Yeah, it was us. I knew the vamps were planning to attack the orphanage," Levi explained. "I couldn't let that happen, so Emilia and I moved them all to a safe place. We couldn't keep them here, just in case…"

In case Cyrus realized what Levi had done. Father McGregor looked like he understood. A slight smile tugged at his lips. Novak, Vana, and the barbarians caught up with them a second later.

Novak stood in front of them, preventing their horse from leaving. "It's dark out, you know. You of all people should know the dangers of night. Where are you three going?"

Levi stepped forward. "Do you remember our conversation? Earlier, in the stables?"

Vana nodded. "We do. Do you suspect the vampires are planning an attack again?"

"Yes," Levi replied. "And there's a reason only three of us are going. If we brought any more than that, the vamps might see us coming. Please, you can't tell anyone about this. In times like this, being discreet is the key."

"We see," Novak replied, moving out of the horse's way. "Then we wish you three luck. If you do need reinforcements, don't hesitate to ask us for help. We'll continue to watch over the Keep while you're gone."

Levi felt bad lying to them, but he had no choice. He thanked them and hopped up on his horse while the priest mounted the third. As the three of them galloped away, Novak, Vana, and the barbarians kept their eyes on them. He only hoped they wouldn't do something stupid—like follow.

As they galloped through the countryside, heading to the

markets, Levi noticed all the homes were shuttered and locked down. No one was taking any chances anymore—not with the vampires roaming the dark streets.

"I hope one day, we won't need all this protection at night," Emilia said over her shoulder. "And maybe one day, life will return to normal."

"I know it will," Father McGregor said, glancing at Levi with a smile. "You two will make things right."

Levi crossed his fingers, hoping he was right.

Emilia led them to a secluded shack behind the markets. It looked old and run-down, with rubble and dirt outside. Emilia swung off the horse, tied Margaret to a wooden post as the others did the same, then she gestured at the home.

"When you find the vampire, bring them here," Emilia said. "It's late, so no one should hear their screams. Hopefully, they'll have some information for us. Anything at all that can tell us what the vampires plan to do next."

"Wait a moment. I have a question," Father McGregor said. "Instead of torturing this vampire...do you think their soul could be saved? That they could ever denounce their kind to help humanity?"

Emilia scoffed. "I doubt it. These vampires have one desire, Father—and that's carnage. You can't expect a wild animal to change. How could a vampire be any different? Besides, they've taken too many lives to be redeemed. The carnage they've caused is reprehensible."

Levi looked down. He couldn't believe how stupid he had been to think Emilia would still care for him when she found out the truth. Maybe it was better if she never found out—if Levi just killed all the vampires and then disappeared.

"I don't believe that," Father McGregor said, glancing at Levi. "And I'm not just saying this because I'm a priest, but I truly believe in redemption for all who seek it."

"Well, that's the problem, then. No vampire seeks redemption. They seem to like what they are. That makes them even more repulsive," Emilia muttered, shaking her head. "Come on, Father—I'll help you set up inside. I'm sure we can make a cage of some kind for the vampire."

Levi nodded. "All right, good luck. I'll be back soon. It's dark already, so it shouldn't be too hard to find a vampire."

"And if you can't separate one from the pack?" Father McGregor asked.

"Don't worry about that," Levi said, waving him off. "I know what I'm doing. And I'll bring silver with me."

"A good plan. You have until dawn to catch a vampire," Emilia said. "If you're not back by then, I'll come looking for you. Good luck, Levi—and please, don't get yourself hurt."

She pulled him in for a quick kiss, unbothered by the priest's presence. After she had pulled away, she smiled at Levi and entered the old shack. Father McGregor watched as Levi hopped back onto his horse. He made sure he still had his silver sword on him, then a black bag to put over Night Temptress's head.

And now, it was time for revenge.

"All right, I'm off. Watch out for each other, okay? If you hear something, don't take any chances. Get back to the keep," Levi said, flicking the reins. "I won't be long."

The priest nodded before Levi galloped away, following the trail that led to the mines. Since Slaughter's vampires had placed bags over their heads, when they took Cyrus and Levi to their lair, Levi used his nose to follow the scent of the vampires to their hideout. It sat on the outskirts of town, hidden away in a small cave.

He hid his horse behind a stack of rubble and waited. Ten minutes later, he watched as the group of vampires exited the cave, their fangs gleaming under the moonlight.

"Where are we going tonight?" Night Temptress asked.

"Let's stick to the outskirts. Perhaps some of the homes in the country aren't as shuttered as the ones in the markets," Slaughter said. "But curse Allegiant. They've scared off all our victims! I don't care what Frederic says. I don't like waiting."

"Patience, Brother," Night Temptress said. "It'll be worth it in the end. Frederic promised us that, remember?"

Night Temptress paused, sniffing the air. Slaughter and the other vampires raised their eyebrows.

"What's wrong, sister?" Slaughter asked.

"Nothing," she said. "Go ahead. I'll be right there."

"But sister—"

"Go," she spat.

Slaughter shrugged, taking off. The other vampires followed, their hunt beginning for the night. This was his chance—Night Temptress was finally alone.

"I know you're here, Levi," she began, glancing around. "Why don't you come out where I can see you?"

"You got me," Levi said, walking out of the shadows. "Why didn't you tell the others I was here?"

"I wanted to see what you wanted first." She crossed her arms. "If I don't like what you have to say, then I'll tell Slaughter you were poking around our lair."

"I thought I was welcome here. Frederic said so himself."

She scoffed. "After you saved Emilia, you're lucky I don't strike you dead right here. My plan was perfect—poison the bitch before she has a chance to kill us. But you ruined it!"

"Like I told Frederic and my brother, keeping her alive—"

"Yeah, yeah. Spare me," she grumbled. "Anyway, why are you here, Levi? You already said you didn't want me. You made that very clear."

He walked closer to her, growing bolder. "I was a fool.

You're the only one I want—I see that now. The reason I pushed you away is that I knew my brother wanted you first."

"And now?"

"It's simple," Levi said, cupping her face. "Now I just don't give a damn."

He pulled her in for a passionate kiss, and much to his surprise, she didn't pull away. He tried not to recoil as she lifted her arms, threading her hands in his hair. Levi felt like he'd need a hot bath afterward.

But it got him close enough. Now he just needed to strike.

She pulled away first, grinning at him. "I never could resist you, Levi. You nearly broke my heart when you rejected me. If I had a heart to break, of course."

"I know, and I'm sorry. I've come to my senses now." He leaned in. "I guess I'll just have to show you how sorry I am, hmm?"

"That you will. Come closer, Levi..." When Levi inched closer, believing he had her in his sights now, she grabbed him by the chin, her long nails digging into his face. "How stupid do you think I am? I know you're colluding with that human whore. I don't know what you're planning, but you're a fool."

So much for tricking her.

Before she could try anything, Levi punched her in the face. As she groaned in pain and staggered back, he removed the sword from his scabbard. He made sure not to touch any of the silver himself as he plunged it into Night Temptress's side. She cried out, glancing down at the sword in her stomach.

"What...what are you doing?" she asked, her eyes wide as she stared up at him. "I knew you were up to something!"

"Just taking my revenge," he snarled, twisting the sword deeper into her side. "After all, that's what being a vampire is all about, isn't it?"

Before she could reply, he tossed a black bag over her head.

He lifted her by her legs, then tied her on the back of the horse. He mounted behind her and galloped toward the markets. He kept glancing over his shoulder to make sure Slaughter and the other vampires hadn't seen anything, but they'd left already for the countryside.

He followed the path Emilia took to the shack, then jumped down from Margaret. He picked up Night Temptress before carrying her through the door. She kicked and screamed the entire way, but Levi knew none of the townspeople would come outside to investigate—not with the threat of vampires.

The shack looked even more disheveled on the inside. Broken tables and chairs lined the room while the far wall had collapsed. Father McGregor had laid out all his crosses and holy water on one of the sturdier tables, so Levi kept his distance. Emilia was adjusting the large makeshift cage she had made when she noticed him.

"You're back!" she cried. "I'm so glad you made it."

"And I brought our prey," he said. "Time to make her talk."

Emilia opened the door to the cage and Levi tossed Night Temptress inside. He realized Emilia had made the cage out of silver, so he tried his best not to touch the metal. Emilia snaked her hand inside the cage and removed the bag that covered Night Temptress's head. Levi stood behind the vampire vixen, just out of her line of sight.

"Where am I? What's going on?" Night Temptress demanded, glancing around. "What the hell have you done?"

"That doesn't matter," Emilia said. "This is an official Allegiant interrogation."

"Hmm. I should've known," Night Temptress muttered. "Where's Levi? Was everything he said a lie?"

Father McGregor stepped forward, shoving the cross in Night Temptress's face. She screamed and recoiled falling to her knees in the cage.

"You don't get to ask questions," Father McGregor said. "We are in control here, vampire—not you."

"What's she talking about?" Emilia asked, glancing at Levi.

"It's nothing," he muttered. "I had to lie to get her here. Let's not waste time—it wasn't easy getting her."

As Emilia nodded, Levi feared he'd made the wrong decision. Night Temptress could say anything—could blurt out what Levi was at any second. Although Father McGregor was trying to cover for him, would it be enough?

"There's more pain where that came from if you don't answer our questions," Emilia told the vampire. "What are the vampires planning next? What do you want from us mortals?"

Night Temptress sneered. "As if I'd tell you anything, Allegiant whore!"

Emilia glanced at Father McGregor. "Again."

He thrust the cross at Night Temptress, making her cry out in pain for a second time. As she writhed on the floor of her cage, Emilia sighed, then reached for the silver weapons she'd brought.

"This is going to be a long night," Emilia said, aiming the sword at Night Temptress, "but I've got time. You *will* tell us everything, vampire—if you want to live. I can be generous if you give me what I need."

Levi wondered if Night Temptress knew Emilia was lying, but every creature wanted to live—even a vampire. Levi just hoped Night Temptress wouldn't tell her *everything* like Emilia wanted.

Or she'd turn the blade on *him* instead.

CHAPTER
TWENTY-SIX

The minutes passed slowly. Levi stayed out of Night Temptress's line of sight just in case she saw him and decided to tell Emilia his secret. But he kept his hand on the hilt of his sword at all times, prepared for anything she might say or do.

"One last time before I get angry," Emilia began, holding up her sword. "What are the vampires planning next?"

Night Temptress spat on Emilia. She wiped away the vampire's saliva and stepped closer. Emilia slid the blade through the slots of the cage, burning the flesh of Night Temptress's arm. The vampire howled in pain and fell to the floor again.

"We're only getting started," Emilia said over Night Temptress's screams. "You haven't seen anything yet. We already discovered your attack on the orphanage and your attempt to kill me—but I want to know more."

"You...you knew we were going to attack the orphanage?" Night Temptress asked, groaning in pain. "How?"

"That's not important. But we moved the children to a safe place—one your kind will never find."

"That lying son of a bitch," Night Temptress muttered. "He was there the whole time, listening to our plans. No wonder there weren't any children at the orphanage..."

"Who was listening?" Emilia asked, pulling the sword back. "What are you talking about?"

Night Temptress opened her mouth, but Father McGregor poured holy water over her head. Her black hair steamed and made Night Temptress scream even louder. The priest glanced back at Levi for a moment.

"We're getting off track here," Father McGregor said, turning to Emilia. "If the vampires were to hear her screams, they'd come for us. We'd better stick to our main questions and be done with this."

"You're right. Sorry, my curiosity got the better of me," Emilia said, turning back to the vampire. "You've failed twice, monster—both with the orphanage *and* your poison. What you're planning next won't succeed."

Night Temptress laughed through her pain. "Oh, but that's where you're wrong, bitch. Everything we did before this? It's nothing compared to what's coming."

Emilia placed the silver sword against Night Temptress's throat, searing her flesh. "And what *is* coming?"

Night Temptress's eyes turned dark, hissing in agony. "Annihilation. Once we become immune to sunlight, this town will be ours. And when we're finished here, the rest of the world will fall. Just you wait."

Emilia pulled away, her eyes wide in horror as Night Temptress cackled. Emilia crossed the room, walking over to Levi. Father McGregor kept careful watch over the vampire as the two whispered in the corner.

"Do you hear that, Levi? Something about a sunlight cure?" Emilia shook her head. "That can't be good. So far, sunlight has been our best defense against the vampires. If they can find a way to become immune, they could attack anytime—any place. We might not be able to stop them then."

Levi placed his hands on Emilia's shoulders. "I know, but hey, it'll be all right. We have more Legionnaires coming soon, remember? Even with a sunlight immunity, they can't fight all of us and survive."

"I guess. What I'm interested in is how they're making this sunlight cure," Emilia muttered. "It sounds complex. Do you think they have knowledge of science? Medicine?"

Levi wanted to say yes—to scream that it was all Frederic's fault—but the words wouldn't come out.

"I know," Emilia said, sighing. "I'm just as speechless as you are. We'd better find out."

She walked back over to Night Temptress. The vampire had stopped laughing, but a smirk was still present on her face. Emilia bent down, pressing the sword against the vampire's arm. Night Temptress growled in pain, but bit her lip to prevent herself from screaming again.

"How are you making this sunlight cure?" Emilia demanded.

"The Bloody Doctor," Night Temptress said. "He's wise—smarter than all of us. He already figured out the sunlight cure on himself. He's been walking around out there in broad daylight without you knowing. Now he's just in the process of making it compatible with our blood."

"The...Bloody Doctor?" Emilia blinked. "Is he a vampire?"

Night Temptress nodded. "And he might be closer than you think."

"How close, foul creature?"

Much to Levi's relief, Night Temptress didn't reply. She just laughed in Emilia's face. Father McGregor stepped forward, his cross in hand.

"Why are you doing this?" the priest asked. "You behave like...like monsters."

"Because that's what we are, you pious moron," Night Temptress spat, her eyes flickering up at him. "There's no way to change us. This is what we are now—for all eternity."

That's not true, Levi thought. *I changed. But how did I change? What was the catalyst?*

"I believe in redemption for all creatures," Father McGregor said. "If one wants to change, then one can—"

Night Temptress laughed. "But vampires don't want that, fool. We like what we are. And besides, killing humans is fun. It helps to pass the time. Living forever can get tedious, you know. Too mundane. We need something to keep us entertained."

Emilia scoffed, glancing back at Father McGregor. "What did I tell you before? They enjoy killing. There's no hope for their redemption, Father. They're better off dead."

"She's right," Night Temptress said, glancing over her shoulder in Levi's direction. She sniffed the air and probably knew Levi was in the room. "No matter how much time a vampire spends with a human, they'll never be one of them— not again. It's foolish to even try."

Levi gripped his sword tight, suppressing the urge to kill her.

"Hmm. Back to this Bloody Doctor," Emilia began, changing the subject. "Is he your leader? Or is there someone else?"

"His medical knowledge impressed us, so he leads the Bloodborn Order," Night Temptress said. "But me and my brother, Slaughter, are well-respected too. Once the lesser vampires find out what you did to me, they'll never let you live. My brother will rip your throat out and feed it to the wolves. Or even better, turn you into one of the vampires. One of us." Night Temptress began laughing. "Wouldn't that be a wonderful twist of fate? To turn a vampire hunter into a creature of the night? Oh, it's so perfect—"

"Quiet. I'll make sure your kin never finds out it was us," Emilia muttered. "How many are in your cult?"

"Enough. And more are coming."

"More? From where?"

"From all over." Night Temptress smirked. "You see, we aren't the only ones who can call in reinforcements. We have what we call mercenaries—vampires from other towns who keep us updated on world events. Although the larger population is here in Osgoode, we have friends in other places. Blood-thirsty friends. No matter how many more Legionnaires you recruit, you still won't be able to stop us all."

"So, you *were* at the Ball. That's the only way you could know about the new Legionnaires coming," Emilia replied. "Give me numbers, vampire. How many more from out of town are coming?"

Night Temptress laughed. "You'll have to wait and find out, won't you?"

Emilia rose to her feet with a snarl. She grabbed Night Temptress by the front of her black dress, then smashed her face against the side of the cage. The silver burned her cheek, making the vampire howl in pain again.

"Listen, you vampire bitch," Emilia began. "Call in thousands of vampires—millions, even. The Legionnaires will still find a way to stop you."

Night Temptress chuckled, rubbing her burning cheek. "Keep telling yourself that. But a single vampire with the sunlight cure could infiltrate Allegiant—pretend to be one of you and spy on your plans. We're not just hunters, but masters of disguise too. Perhaps there's even a vampire in your midst right now—one who's been quietly by your side all this time. Wouldn't that be something?"

Emilia's face turned red. Levi hated that Night Temptress was getting under her skin, and he had to do something before she let the truth slip.

Levi stepped forward, blocking Emilia from Night Temptress. "Em, I think you should step outside for a minute."

"What? Why?" Emilia asked. "We're making progress, Levi. Slow, small progress, but still. I'm not ready to give up."

"Levi's right," Father McGregor said behind them. "You're angry, Emilia—you need a break. I'll go with you while Levi watches over the vampire."

Emilia sighed. "Fine, fine. I'll step outside for a minute. But be careful, Levi. Even tied up, a vampire is still dangerous. I'll be back soon."

Father McGregor's eyes briefly flitted to Levi before he ushered Emilia outside. Once they had shut the door, Levi turned to Night Temptress in the quiet, empty shack. She was laughing again, spit flying out of her mouth, and it made him seethe with anger. He much preferred it when she was writhing in pain.

"What are you laughing about now?" he demanded.

"You call her *Em*," Night Temptress taunted. "A nickname? How very...*human* of you. You must really love her, don't you? Shit, you're more tainted than we thought."

Levi stepped closer to the cage. "I don't have time for your mind games, Night Temptress. Let's go back to the sunlight cure. I destroyed all the vials when Frederic was out of his lab."

Levi thought Night Temptress would get angry at that, but she just shook her head. "Poor, delusional Levi. You think you're winning this war, don't you?"

He blinked. "What are you talking about?"

"It was a trap—a set-up," she replied. "Both Frederic and your brother thought something was wrong with you. That you were becoming too sympathetic to the humans. When I smelled her scent on you, I feared it might be true. But my attraction to you made me blind—I wanted to believe you wouldn't betray us. Your brother wanted to believe that too. How wrong we were…"

Levi growled. "What was a trap? Get to the point, Night Temptress, before I stake you."

"Two things—Emilia's poison, and leaving out the sunlight cure," she replied. "Frederic wanted to play a little game to test your loyalty, so he left the keep with the cure out. If you destroyed it—and then tried to save Emilia's life after she was poisoned—he'd know you were compromised. And you fell for it like a damned fool."

Levi turned silent. It was all a ploy to get him to incriminate himself—and he had played right into their hand. He couldn't trust Frederic or his brother anymore. Or anyone.

"He was willing to risk the sunlight cure's destruction to see if I was guilty?" Levi asked. "That's a big gamble. But it didn't work out too well for him, huh?"

Night Temptress shook her head. "You still don't understand. Those weren't the cure, just old vials he had lying around. The *real* cure—which is almost ready—is safe. He hid it away so you couldn't destroy it."

Levi turned around, his hands shaking. He had feared Frederic and his brother were onto him. But he never imagined they would set him up like this.

"It hurts to be betrayed, doesn't it?" Night Temptress asked. "Now you know how we felt when we found out you had feelings for that Legionnaire harlot and were trying to undermine us."

Levi spun around, a snarl on his face. "I didn't betray you! Vampires are sick—evil. If anything, *you've* betrayed your humanity."

"Keep telling yourself that. But Emilia and the others have

warped your mind," Night Temptress snarled. "Say whatever you want to defend yourself, but I see one thing when I look at you. A traitor."

"If saving lives makes me a traitor," Levi began, "then I'll gladly be one."

"Pathetic! You think you're going to win, don't you? That you're going to help Emilia kill all the vampires?" Night Temptress asked, her eyes cold. "What happens if you do succeed? Will you keep lying to her about what you really are?"

Levi paused. "No. I...I don't know. If I help her stop the vampires, maybe she'll forgive me for lying."

"We both know that isn't true. I bet that's why you haven't told her the truth yet. Because if you did, you'd have nowhere to go. Allegiant would want you dead and so would Emilia. But I can help you, Levi."

Levi sneered. "Help me? How?"

"Come back to the vampires. Fall at our feet and beg for forgiveness," Night Temptress said, reaching for him through the bars of her cage. "Perhaps I could convince Slaughter and Frederic that your lust for Emilia blinded you. You can have a place again—a place with *us*. The Bloodborn Order is where you truly belong."

Levi didn't even need time to think about his answer.

"No," Levi spat. "I realize now that I've never belonged there. I was a human first—and a human is what I'm meant to be. If you were capable of love, you know that you'd do anything to save the person you care about. I can't let you or anyone else hurt Emilia. Even if it means she finds out what I am and hates me forever."

"Fool," Night Temptress spat. "When Slaughter finds out what you did to me, he'll come after you. He'll kill Emilia in front of you and suck her blood dry. Do you know how powerful he is when he's angry? How terrifying?"

"Let Slaughter come," Levi said, stepping forward. He gripped his sword's handle hard. "Let them *all* come—even my brother. I'll kill them with a smile on my face."

Night Temptress sneered. "I can't believe a vampire would say that—not about their own kind. You may be a vampire physically, Levi, but you stopped being one mentally a long time ago. And what a disgrace. We could've had so much fun together, you know. If you weren't a weakling."

Levi said nothing, holding up his blade instead. He knew it was coming down to this. He couldn't let her live—not after what she had done to Emilia, and not after the interrogation. She was too much of a risk.

"Goodbye, Night Temptress," Levi said. "Emilia was right. There's no redemption for you."

"Emilia!" Night Temptress began, shaking the bars of her cage. "Levi is a vampire! Get in here before—"

"This is for poisoning Emilia," Levi interrupted, "and for trying to tempt me back to evil. I hope you burn in hell where you belong."

Levi plunged the sword through the slots, stabbing Night Temptress in the heart. Her eyes widened as she looked up at Levi, then fell to her knees. Violet blood sprayed across the floor of her cage.

"You can't...keep what you are a secret forever," she gasped. "The truth will come out—and Emilia will never love you when she sees your true face..."

Night Temptress collapsed, more violet blood oozing around her. Levi removed the sword from her heart and stepped back. It was over—Night Temptress was dead. But somehow, it didn't make Levi feel better, not when he knew more vampires were coming.

The door to the shack burst open. Emilia and Father

McGregor rushed inside, their eyes widening when they noticed Night Temptress's dead body.

"We heard shouting," Father McGregor said. "Is everything all right?"

"For me, yeah," Levi replied. "But as for the vampire...she's dead."

"No!" Emilia turned to Levi. "I wasn't finished asking her questions. What happened?"

"I had no choice," Levi lied. "She almost escaped. She would've killed us all if I hadn't stabbed her."

"But what if there was more she could tell us? More about this sunlight cure—or what they plan to do when they're immune?"

"Emilia, stop. I'm sure Levi feels bad enough," Father McGregor said, placing his hand on Emilia's arm. "Let's not turn against each other now."

"Father McGregor's right. And we both know she wasn't going to tell us much else—no matter how much you tortured her," Levi replied, wiping her blood off his sword. "Vampires hold their secrets close."

Father McGregor glanced at Levi. It made him feel guilty about his own secret—how far he had gone to keep it from everyone, especially Emilia.

Emilia sighed, running a hand through her hair. "You're right. I'm sorry, Levi—I'm just upset. I didn't mean to take it out on you. I thought this interrogation would tell us what we needed to know, but it raised more questions than answers. God damn it."

For you and me both, Levi thought. *Frederic and my own brother could be conspiring against me right now.*

Levi pulled Emilia into his arms, kissing her forehead. "I know everything seems scary and hopeless...but at least we have each other, right?"

Emilia smiled up at him. "Yes—and that is a blessing. Truly."

Father McGregor cleared his throat. "I apologize for the interruption, but what are we going to do with the vampire's body?"

Levi pulled away, glancing down at Night Temptress. "We need to burn her. If the vampires find her dead, they'll know it was us."

"Good point," Emilia said with a nod. "I'll gather some wood outside. We'll burn the body out back."

After Emilia had left the shack, Father McGregor looked at Levi. "She didn't escape, did she?"

"No," Levi said. "Emilia built a sturdy cage. But Night Temptress was going to tell Emilia everything. I had to silence her."

"I suspected as much. While I didn't want a vampire to tell Emilia what you are," Father McGregor began, "I think you should. At the risk of sounding repetitious, you must tell her before it's too late."

Levi looked down, remembering what Emilia had said about the vampires—that they were evil and could never have redemption. Even Night Temptress knew Emilia wouldn't come around. If he told her, he'd lose her forever.

Before Father McGregor could pressure him again, the door opened, and Emilia entered. "All right—everything's in place. Are we ready?"

Levi nodded. Emilia walked over to the cage, opening it to remove Night Temptress's body. Levi kept a hand on the hilt of his sword as she dragged the vampire to a small firepit outside. Then they dug a hole in the ground to burn and dispose of the body.

Levi helped Emilia toss Night Temptress inside the firepit,

then set it ablaze. As her body burned, the smell of flesh filling the air, Emilia sighed.

"I know she was a vampire," she whispered, "but I didn't even know her real name or background. Other than killing humans, did she have any interests? Any redeeming qualities at all? What was her life like before becoming a vampire?"

Levi paused, thinking back to his own. "I'm sure it was normal. She was human once, probably full of hopes and dreams. And then...one bite changed her forever. Darkened her soul."

Just like Cyrus had done to Levi. Everything came full circle.

Levi turned to Emilia, frowning. "But wait. Why all these questions about her background? I thought you said vampires couldn't be redeemed?"

"I don't think they can. But I'm just trying to make myself feel less guilty. It isn't easy killing something that can talk—even if it *is* spewing hate."

Levi wanted to tell Emilia she was wrong—that a redeemed vampire was right next to her—but she stepped forward. Night Temptress's body had disintegrated, leaving only black ashes behind. Emilia filled up a bucket from a nearby well and put out the fire, leaving it smoking.

"There," Emilia said, tossing the bucket aside. "One vampire down, who knows how many more to go. We'd better bury the bones before people get suspicious." After they had covered Night Temptress with dirt, Emilia gestured to the horses. "Let's get back to the keep. I want our Legionnaires training harder from now on. This sunlight cure...that'll keep me awake tonight. If the vampires can do that, what else are they capable of?"

As Levi got on the horse, helping Father McGregor up, he realized he didn't know. He was out of the loop now with Frederic and Cyrus withholding things. What were they planning for him? How were they going to stop Allegiant if they knew he wouldn't let them?

As they galloped toward the keep, they noticed Novak, Vana, and the barbarians still keeping watch. Novak rushed over to them as Emilia, Levi, and Father McGregor swung down from their horses, leading them into the barn.

"What's wrong?" Emilia asked him. "You look alarmed."

He nodded. "We've got a visitor. I wasn't expecting anyone —especially this late."

"A visitor?" Levi asked. "Who?"

"You'd better see for yourself," Novak said, gesturing at the Keep. "Everyone was eager to meet her."

"Her? She's not a vampire, is she?" Father McGregor asked.

"No—we tested her with silver. We wouldn't have let her in if we suspected she was a danger," Novak replied. "But she is... interesting. She's waiting in the kitchen, requesting to speak with the leader of Allegiant."

TWENTY-SEVEN

Emilia, Levi, and Father McGregor rushed inside, followed by some of the barbarians. Levi noticed everyone had woken up—even the children—to greet their new visitor. He spotted a flash of red hair sitting at the small wooden table in the kitchen and pushed through the people to reach her.

He almost gasped when he realized who it was. She was a spitting image of Emilia—crimson hair, green eyes, tall and slender stature. She wore a silver knight's uniform all Legionnaires had in the future with a pistol poking out of her holster. She looked worse for wear—bruises on her face and hands as well as bags under her eyes.

The woman sipped a cup of tea that Alana put on the table, then Peeta sat down next to her. When she turned to look at the three who had entered, her eyes locked on Levi's. The way they lingered suggested she recognized him—and he knew he recognized her.

This was Elizabeth Rutherford, Emilia's descendant. She had been the one who killed the Patriarch and shot Levi in the arm. Somehow, she was sitting in the keep's kitchen. Cyrus pushed through the crowd to stand beside Levi and her eyes lingered on his brother too. She began chatting with the others, giving the brothers a second to murmur.

"You're seeing this too, right?" Cyrus whispered to Levi. "I'm not going crazy?"

"Definitely not crazy," Levi whispered back. "This woman is Allegiant...of the future. She's the one who killed Patriarch. Right before we went through the blood magic portal."

Cyrus turned silent. How was it possible? As far as Levi could remember, he and his brother were the only ones the blood portal had spat out. He hadn't seen anyone else when they first arrived.

"Who are you?" Emilia asked, pushing through the crowd before sitting beside Elizabeth. "Why are you here?"

"My name is Elizabeth," the woman replied, setting her tea down. "And when I found out about Allegiant, I knew I had to join. Where I come from...vampires are a problem too."

"And where is that?" Alana asked.

"It's a land far from here," Elizabeth explained. "You wouldn't know of it. But I'll tell you, this place is very different from home."

"Hmm. That's some nice armor and weapons you got, you know," Edmund said, gesturing at her gun. "Real fancy. You ain't look like no peasant to me."

"You're right, I'm not. Where I come from, our weapons and armor are...very advanced," Elizabeth replied. "But I'm not rich or nobility if that's what you're thinking. I'm a soldier—and I'm used to fighting vampires. It's what I was born to do. It runs in my family, actually."

Her eyes lingered on Emilia. She obviously suspected Emilia was her ancestor. It wasn't a surprise—they resembled each other, and Emilia's face had gotten drawn in Allegiant history books in celebration.

"Oh, sorry. I haven't introduced myself. My name is Emilia Rutherford. Welcome to Allegiant Keep. We live here and train to hunt vampires," Emilia said. "This is my brother, Peeta, and my family friend, Alana. Other people you should know are Father McGregor, our priest; our scientist, Frederic Bors; our bard, Samantha Doyle, and her father, Edmund. We also have Levi and Cyrus Godfrey—the ones who helped me start Allegiant."

"How nice," Elizabeth muttered, glancing at Levi and Cyrus.

"You two come from far away, too, don't you?" Samantha asked, nudging Levi's shoulder. "Ever seen her before?"

"Uh, no," Levi lied. "Never."

Elizabeth said nothing. If she knew they were vampires, why hadn't she told the others yet? Or reached for her gun to kill them? And if she were in Osgoode this entire time, where had she been?

"I hope you don't find this unsettling," Emilia began, "but... you look a lot like me. Same eyes, same hair. The more I look at you, the more I feel...a connection. As if we've already met before."

"Oh, we've never met. I'd remember you," Elizabeth said. "But you're right, we *do* look alike. I guess it's true what they say—everyone has a doppelganger somewhere."

"I guess so. Say, you look injured. I'm an apothecary. I'm sure I could treat those bruises for you."

"That's kind of you, but I'm all right." Elizabeth sipped her tea again. "But I guess you're wondering how I got them, aren't you?"

Emilia nodded. "I am, but I didn't want to pry."

"No, it's all right. You deserve an explanation." She closed her eyes, sighing. "The truth is, I arrived in Osgoode about a week ago. I had a bad accident, one that left me with amnesia. I still can't remember much of what happened, but I've been slowly piecing it together. I think I came to Osgoode to fight the vampires."

Amnesia? Levi thought. *Maybe that's why she hasn't attacked me and Cyrus yet.*

"I wandered around the village for days, confused. Then, one night, I came across a vampire," Elizabeth continued, then the room gasped. "We fought—that's how I got these bruises— but I killed her with my weapon."

Levi thought back to the dead vampire he had found in the markets. Belladonna. While he remembered seeing the bullet wound in that the vampire, he never imagined Emilia's descendent had been the one that killed her.

"Killed a vampire all by yourself?" Edmund whistled. "Damn, little lady. We could sure use a soldier like you."

"I'm very good at what I do. I've practiced my whole life," Elizabeth replied. "Anyway, one day, while I was staggering through the streets, a woman found me. She took me to her home and tried to help me, but I was still dazed. I don't think I was very coherent. And her screaming children didn't help my headache."

"Was she middle-aged? Dark hair?" Emilia asked. "Always wearing an apron with yellow flowers?"

Elizabeth nodded. "Yes. How did you know?"

"Her name is Patricia. She's a midwife, one I've worked with many times. She was very distraught when you disappeared— even reported it to the constable. Levi and I were there when that happened."

Levi couldn't believe it. The thought of Emilia's descendant only a few feet away in the markets sent shivers down his spine.

If Cyrus had known about it, he would've killed her by now. And Levi couldn't let that happen—for Emilia's sake.

"I'll have to apologize to her then. I didn't mean to worry her," Elizabeth replied. "I was just so out of my mind that I think I stumbled out of her home."

"Where did you go after that?" Emilia asked.

"To the forest, I think. Yes, I remember setting up camp. I guess I hadn't lost all my wits," Elizabeth continued. "One night, I thought I heard footsteps, so I hid. I didn't want to risk another fight in my condition. A few minutes later, they disappeared."

That was us, Levi thought, *right after Slaughter and the others couldn't find any children to drink from at the orphanage.*

"Disappeared?" Samantha frowned. "You don't think those footsteps belonged to vampires, do you?"

"I believe so." Elizabeth nodded. "Who else would be in a forest after dark?"

"Huh. I wonder what they were doing there," Peeta said. "I've never heard of vampires in the forest before. They've always stuck to the markets where they can find victims."

"Your guess is as good as mine. But at least some of my memory started to come back to me then. It took about a week," Elizabeth continued. "I returned to the markets to find a place to stay when I heard the news of Allegiant. Remembering my training, I knew I had to come here. And I have nowhere else to go. Please, you must let me help you."

"How could I say no to that?" Emilia asked with a smile. "You're well-armed and dedicated, and we could always use more Legionnaires. Welcome to Allegiant, Elizabeth."

"Great," Elizabeth said, grinning back. "And I know a lot about hunting vampires. Maybe I could even teach your Legionnaires a thing or two."

Levi glanced at Cyrus who had his fists balled. If Elizabeth stayed there, she was in danger—no matter how good of a Legionnaire she was. Levi had to find some way to get her to leave.

"Um, Emilia," Levi began, clearing his throat, "we have more Legionnaires coming soon. We really don't have room for anyone else."

"She's just one woman, Levi," Emilia said, glancing back at him. "I think we can find her a room."

"And I can sleep anywhere. My people trained me to be versatile," Elizabeth replied, glancing at Levi. "Unless there's some reason you don't want me here."

"No, of course not," Levi stammered, faking a smile. "The more the merrier, right?"

"Wonderful." Emilia rose to her feet. "The barbarians outside—Novak and Vana—told me they tested you with silver. That's good—you can never be too careful when it comes to the vampires."

"No," Elizabeth replied cryptically, "you really can't."

"Well, as our guest, you can stay in my room. It's too big for me, anyway."

"Thank you, but...where will you sleep?"

"Oh, I'll find a place," Emilia replied, glancing in Levi's direction. Then she turned to the crowd. "I recommend we all get a good night's rest. Fighting vampires takes a lot of energy, and I can't have anyone falling asleep on the job. See you in the morning, everyone. Sleep well."

The crowd dispersed, introducing themselves to Elizabeth before they headed back to bed. She glanced at Levi, her mouth opening like she had something to say before Emilia led her up the stairs. In the silence, only Cyrus, Levi, and Frederic remained.

"Is that her?" Frederic asked, watching her vanish upstairs. "The one you told me about?"

"Emilia's descendant? Yeah," Levi replied. "How the hell did she make it through the blood portal?"

"I don't know, but it doesn't matter," Cyrus replied, his eyes lingering on the stairs. "She's here now. If she tells Emilia what we are..."

"You'll have to kill her," Frederic said. "Sooner rather than later."

"If you can get her alone, don't hesitate," Cyrus told Levi. "And watch out for that gun of hers. We've been lucky so far—all Allegiant has now are daggers and swords—but she's got bullets. With that and her training, she's more dangerous than all of them. Stay vigilant, Brother."

As Cyrus and Frederic walked away, heading to their rooms, Levi couldn't believe it. Did his brother *really* care about him? Even after he knew what he had done? And why hadn't they retaliated against him for saving Emilia and tampering with the fake sunlight cure?

It was tempting to confront them, but right now, Levi needed to play it safe. And he needed to figure out what their next move would be so he could stop them.

Levi sighed, trudging up the stairs to his room as his mind spun with questions. As he approached, he noticed the half-opened door. He reached for the sword in his scabbard in case it was Elizabeth coming to kill him in the night.

But when he pushed the door open, Emilia greeted him. She rose to her feet from his bed. "Sorry to intrude, but I gave Elizabeth my room."

"You're never intruding, Emilia," Levi said, removing his hand from his sword. "You can sleep in here anytime."

He turned around, closing the door behind him. Then he locked it and shoved a chair up against the door. It wouldn't have stopped Elizabeth if she tried to sneak in, but at least it would make noise and alert him.

"Expecting trouble?" Emilia asked.

"You can never be too careful," Levi replied. "Elizabeth looks tough. She's obviously not a vampire, but what if she's a thief or an assassin? She's got the weapons for it."

"I don't think so. When I look at her, I see honesty—integrity," Emilia replied. "But if blocking the door makes you feel safer, go ahead."

Levi nodded. "It does. And it's not just *my* safety I'm worried about, Em. If the vamps find out we tortured and killed Night Temptress, they'll come after you."

"They won't find out," Emilia said, placing a hand on Levi's shoulder. "And if they do, more Legionnaires are coming. We're going to win this war, Levi. I can feel it. I've never been so sure of anything before."

Emilia kept telling him that, but Levi hesitated to believe it. Between his brother's secrecy, the real sunlight cure, and new vampires coming out of the woodwork like cockroaches, he feared for Emilia's life.

"I hope you're right. I don't want to lose you, Em," Levi whispered. "Not now, not ever."

"And you won't. Look, I know I was fearful before about the sunlight cure," Emilia began, "but I'll be fine. I believe that now. And you should, too, Levi. Those vampires can't hurt us—not when we're together. And when we've killed them all and we're still standing, you'll see I was right."

Levi furrowed his eyebrows. He could've told her everything right now—what he was, what his brother was planning, why Elizabeth looked so familiar. It was all on the tip of his tongue.

"Emilia..." he whispered. "I need to tell you something."

"Shh, Levi," she said, placing a finger against his lips. "I didn't come here to talk. I came here to show you how I feel about you. If you'll let me."

He just nodded, unable to speak. And when she leaned in

and kissed him this time, it wasn't sweet or chaste. It burned with desire—and Levi had grown tired of resisting. He guided her to his bed and blew out the nearby candle, shrouding the room in darkness.

And when he entered her, he was full of love. Full of redemption.

~

WHEN LEVI AWOKE the next morning, he was alone in bed. Emilia must've slipped out when he was asleep. After he noticed the chair had moved from the door, he sprang to his feet, throwing on his clothes. He thought only of Emilia, worried Elizabeth had taken her from him.

But when he glanced out the window, he noticed the two women laughing and chatting in the training yard. Elizabeth was showing Emilia new fighting styles, and it looked like they were becoming friends.

If she told her the truth, they wouldn't be laughing, Levi thought. *Maybe everything's okay.*

As he walked down the stairs, he noticed how crowded the keep had become—more than usual. Men and women from different cultures walked through the castle, chatting and eating breakfast. They weren't simple peasants, either—they looked strong and burly, much like the barbarians and pirates. The civilians and children staying at the keep looked up at them in awe.

Samantha rushed over to him, snacking on a piece of bread. "Hey, Levi. Good morning to you. Some of the new Legionnaires have arrived. They're coming from all over the world, so they'll be trickling in over the next few days."

This isn't even all of them, Levi thought. *I wonder if Cyrus and Frederic are panicking yet.*

"The royals actually kept their word?" Levi asked.

Samantha grinned. "Yep. I think your speech really convinced them. Emilia's overjoyed. She looked pretty happy when she woke up this morning...but I'm not sure it has anything to do with the Legionnaires. I know she wasn't in her room last night. I'm happy for you two, by the way."

"You didn't tell anyone about us, did you?" Levi asked.

"My lips are sealed," Samantha said with a smirk. "If it makes you feel better, I'll tell you a secret. I had a sleepover with your brother last night, too. Though, there wasn't much sleeping involved."

Levi's eyes widened. "You...you did?"

"I did. And I think he could be the one, Levi. None of the other men in Osgoode have ever interested me, but there's something about Cyrus that I find..."

"Irresistible?"

Samantha's eyes lit up. "Yes—that's the word."

"Excuse me," Levi said, his stomach upset at the thought of Samantha so close to death. "I should go find Emilia."

Levi pushed through the crowd, making his way toward the training yard. Emilia and Elizabeth stopped laughing when they noticed him. Emilia put down her sword and wrapped her arms around Levi, giving him a passionate kiss on the lips. Levi opened his eyes slightly, noticing Elizabeth's bewildered stare.

"Sorry I left so abruptly this morning," Emilia whispered after she'd pulled away. "I heard the Legionnaires were here and you looked so peaceful sleeping. I didn't have the heart to wake you."

"That's all right. I'm just glad nothing happened to you," Levi said, his eyes flickering to Elizabeth. "Having fun?"

Emilia nodded. "Elizabeth's taught me a lot—she's a very strong warrior. I'm confident the new Legionnaires will learn fast from her. Wherever she comes from, her people should be proud of her skills."

"Oh, they are," Elizabeth said. "We were very successful in dealing with the vampires. I hope to bring the same luck to Osgoode."

"Emilia!" Edmund cried, rushing over to them from the field. "The new Legionnaires want to know where they're sleeping. They also brought some supplies for us. You should've seen them—all talking at me at once. I've got a damn headache now!"

"Don't panic, Edmund. I'll sort everything out." Emilia turned to Levi. "I've got my work cut out for me. See you later?"

Levi nodded, watching the two walk away. When he looked back at Elizabeth, she was already staring at him. It made him feel uneasy—like she knew all his secrets.

"I brought a few supplies too. Left them in the barn," Elizabeth said, breaking her silence. "Weapons and such—that sort of thing. I promised Emilia that I'd give her everything I have, and you seem pretty strong. Do you think you could help me carry them inside?"

"Sure," Levi said, though he felt nervous being alone with her. "Lead the way."

As they walked across the field and then entered the barn, Levi found it empty. Alana and Peeta were busy in the kitchen cooking for all the new arrivals, so the barn only had animals inside. Levi turned to Elizabeth as she closed the barn door behind them and shut out the sunlight.

"I left some weapons near the back of the barn," Elizabeth said, pointing forward. "They're right over there. Please, bring them over."

"Sure thing." As Levi walked to the back of the barn, he frowned. "I don't see anything—"

When he spun around, Elizabeth was aiming her gun at him. "Stay where you are, vampire. Don't move."

And that was when Levi knew his cover was blown.

"Elizabeth, please. Don't do this." Levi put his hands up in the air. "Just let me explain—"

"Fine—and you can start at the beginning," Elizabeth replied, her finger on the trigger. "Tell me how I'm standing in goddamn England centuries before I was born, while the founder of Allegiant is sleeping with a vampire?"

TWENTY-EIGHT

"Just put the gun down," Levi said, inching closer, "and then we can talk."

Elizabeth shot at a bushel of hay, scaring the farm animals. They squawked and cried out at the sound.

"I told you not to come any closer!" Elizabeth shouted. "Now start talking before I put a bullet through your ugly heart. How did I get here?"

"All right, all right," Levi muttered, stepping back. "My brother and I time-traveled here using blood magic. It's an ancient vampire ritual—one so dangerous that it's a last resort."

"Dangerous how?"

"Well, we aren't sure exactly. We haven't seen any side effects yet, but a lot of things surrounding blood magic are unknown—which is why my people don't use it. Did you use the blood magic portal too?"

"I think so. It hurts to think about it," Elizabeth muttered, using one hand to rub her head. The other remained on her gun. "The last thing I remember was chasing you and that other vampire through the bunker. Then I killed the Patriarch before some portal sucked me in and the three of us vanished. The Legionnaires screamed my name, but I couldn't move—couldn't get back to them. Everything was so bright and disorienting."

"Did anyone else come through with you?"

"No, I don't think so. It closed as I swirled around inside," she explained. "It was like being in a tidal wave. It spat me out in the countryside somewhere, a place with lots of trees and bushes. I traveled to the markets, confused as to where and when I was. Then I found and killed a vampire before that nice midwife took me in. She told me I was in Osgoode, and that was when I realized I'd time-traveled. The portal must've done a number on my head because I felt so sick and dizzy."

"Yeah—blood magic isn't supposed to be used by humans. Only vampires are strong enough for it, but I've heard some of our kind have had bad experiences with it, too," Levi replied. "Anyway, my brother and I came out in the markets. The blood magic portal must've shot us out in different places. No wonder we didn't see you."

"I see. Why would you do this?" she demanded. "Why would you use something as dangerous as blood magic?"

"Do I really have to explain it? You're from the future—you know what happens to my people. The Patriarch wanted us to go back in time to prevent Allegiant. Then a vampire empire could rise, and we'd never have to worry about Allegiant again. Only my brother and I survived and made it through, which meant everyone was counting on us."

"Now I'm starting to get it," Elizabeth muttered. "That's why you're sleeping with Emilia—so she'll let her guard down. And I remember reading that vampires looked different back in other centuries, so it's no wonder she doesn't realize what you are. Clever."

"No, no—you've got it all wrong," Levi said, stepping closer again. "I'm trying to help Allegiant. I don't want the vampires to win."

Elizabeth sneered. "Oh, really? And why would you want that?"

"I know this is hard to believe, but I've changed. Really. I've fallen in love with Emilia and want to help her. But my brother, Cyrus, and Frederic, the scientist, still want her and Allegiant dead. She has no idea they're vampires—or me."

"Oh, come on! You expect me to believe that? It sounds exactly like what a desperate vampire would say so I won't kill them," Elizabeth spat. "Vampires can't love. That's a human emotion, something they lose when they turn. Don't insult me!"

"I don't understand it either, but it's true—I *do* love Emilia. Being around her makes me a better person," Levi explained. "And if you don't believe me, listen to this. When I found out vampires were going to attack the orphanage, I convinced Emilia to move the children to safety. Would an evil vampire do that?"

Elizabeth paused. "How do I know you're telling the truth?"

"Go ask Emilia. I'll wait."

Elizabeth shook her head. "No—if I leave now, you'll run. And I've got you right where I want you, vampire. I'm not letting you out of my sight."

"Don't be stupid, Elizabeth. You're the leader of Allegiant in the future, aren't you?" Levi asked. "You're a smart woman. We should team up and stop the vampires together. What's better than turning an enemy to your side?"

"Save your breath, vampire. I'm a Legionnaire. I kill vampires—I don't work with them. And after I kill you, I'll go back for your brother and this scientist of yours. Everyone else will undergo a silver test to see if more of your kind are hiding here. It was a smart plan, you know—but you lost. And now, you'll pay with your life."

"Wait!" Levi cried, desperately. "Ask yourself this. If I wanted Allegiant to fall, why is it still standing? Don't you think I would've killed Emilia and the others a long time ago? I trained those Legionnaires myself—even told them about our weaknesses."

Elizabeth sneered. "That proves nothing. Vampires are cunning—you always have a plan. Is that lie the best you can do to convince me, vampire?"

"Emilia cares about me. You've seen the way she is around me. If you kill me, you'll only hurt her," Levi urged. "Come on, Elizabeth. You're human—which means you have compassion. Can't you find it in your heart to offer a vampire a second chance? I've done some horrible things, but this is my chance to make it right. Help me stop the vampires and I'll prove it to you."

Elizabeth paused for a moment. When Levi thought he had finally gotten through to her, a snarl appeared on her face again.

"No—I'm doing this for Emilia. She deserves better," Elizabeth said, raising her gun at him again. "Once I help Allegiant kill off the rest of you, humanity will have a better future. So many deaths will be avoided—and it's all thanks to you. Goodbye, vampire."

As Emilia fired the gun, Levi dove behind a pile of hay. The bullet grazed Levi's arm, making him hiss in pain. He crawled through the barn with a groan, hiding behind farming equipment and wheelbarrows as Elizabeth fired at him. The silver bullets bounced off the walls with loud bangs.

"You can't hide from me!" Elizabeth cried. "Get out here and face me, coward!"

The barn door was inches away. If he kept his head down,

he could make it—and rush outside to get help. It was his only chance.

The bullets stopped firing and everything became quiet. Levi could hear her heartbeat and heavy breathing, knowing she was still in there. As carefully as he could, he continued to crawl to the barn door. He raised a hand, reaching to unlock it when another bullet went off, pinging the wall beside him. He dropped his hand and looked back, watching in horror as Elizabeth walked over and towered above him. She pressed her gun against his chest and sneered.

"Crawling? How pathetic," she spat. "I'll be doing the vampires a favor by killing one as weak as you."

"Please, don't..." Levi whispered. He had only one option left—begging for his life. "Don't take Emilia from me."

Elizabeth snorted. "Hmm—maybe you do really love her. That doesn't change anything, you know. You're still a monster in my eyes. And monsters deserve nothing but death."

Levi closed his eyes, preparing for the final shot, but it never came. He opened his eyes when he heard Elizabeth gasp, hoping she had changed her mind after all. But as he glanced up at her, he noticed a sword through her chest.

Elizabeth dropped the gun and fell to her knees, her eyes wide. Then she doubled over as red blood pooled around her. Levi finally noticed who stood behind her—who had dealt the killing blow.

Emilia.

"Levi!" Emilia cried, falling to her knees beside him. "Oh my God, are you all right?"

Levi nodded, gesturing at the graze on his arm. "I think so —she barely got me. How did you get in here? She had me pinned down."

"There's another entrance around the back. One of the Legionnaires said they heard a noise coming from the barn, so I came to investigate," Emilia explained. "What happened here?"

Levi panted, looking down at Elizabeth's body. He couldn't hear a heartbeat anymore. "I don't know—she just went insane and attacked me."

"Hmm. Then you were right." Emilia glanced back at her dead body. "She wasn't a vampire, but we should've been more careful."

Levi felt awful lying to her about it—especially since it was Emilia's descendant—but he couldn't tell her yet. Not like this.

"I heard what she said before I stabbed her," Emilia began, and Levi gulped. "She called you a monster. What was she talking about?"

The truth was on the tip of his tongue. The more he held back, the more it burned. But then he pictured her face after finding out about him and gulped.

"Uh, I don't know," he stammered. "She was crazy."

"Yes, I see that now," Emilia replied, rising to her feet. "Come on—let's get that arm looked at. It looks painful. It reminds me of when I first met you. Didn't you have an injury similar to this one?"

"Uh, maybe. It's hard to remember."

Emilia frowned, glancing at the gun. "How strange. I've never seen a weapon like that before."

"Me either. But anyway, it's only a graze," Levi said as Emilia pulled him up. "It should heal fast—you'll see."

"If you say so." Emilia sighed when she looked at Elizabeth again. "I've never killed a human before—especially not one that looked so much like me. I feel awful, Levi. Like I've made a horrible mistake. Don't get me wrong—I'm glad I saved your life—but there's something inside me that wants to mourn Elizabeth."

"You're just upset, Emilia. That's normal," Levi said,

squeezing her arm to comfort her. "Let's tell the others what happened. We can bury Elizabeth later. And since I didn't say it before...thank you for saving my life."

Emilia nodded. "You're welcome. If I lost you...I don't know what I'd do."

"I feel the same way. Go ahead—wait for me outside. I'll drag the body out, so you don't have to touch her."

Emilia thanked him, opening the door to the barn. Once she was gone, Levi glanced down at the gun. He had to hide it so no one could get their hands on it. He used his sleeve to pick it up before stashing it in a barrel of hay. He knew no one would look for it there.

He dragged out Elizabeth's body next, trying to swallow the guilt he felt when he glanced at her motionless face. He met up with Emilia outside where she was busy telling the Legionnaires what had happened. Their eyes widened when they noticed the body, but no one questioned their story.

Levi spotted Cyrus and Frederic sparring in the training yard. They didn't say anything, but they looked impressed when they noticed him carrying Elizabeth's dead body, giving him a smile and a thumbs-up. He hoped maybe that would make them think he wasn't a traitor.

"Damn," Edmund muttered as he walked over, glancing at the body. "She looked like a tough soldier. Too bad she was a loony, huh?"

Levi helped bury her among the others, like Dawn, Sir Anders, and Emilia's mother. Emilia walked over a moment later and placed a hand on Levi's shoulder.

"Goodbye, Elizabeth. I wish things were different," she said, glancing down at her grave. "We know nothing about her. Where was she from—really? And was she telling the truth when she said she came to fight the vampires?"

Levi said nothing. He knew whatever he said next would only be another lie.

"I guess we'll never know," Emilia continued, sighing. "Well, the new Legionnaires have arrived. We'd better start training them."

As she walked away, meeting with the new Legionnaires in the training yard, Cyrus and Frederic walked over to Levi. They stood in silence for a few moments as the two stared down at the grave with smirks.

Cyrus clapped a hand on Levi's shoulder. "You actually did it, Brother. You killed a Legionnaire—and not just *any* Legionnaire, but the future leader of Allegiant. It feels good to see a Rutherford in the ground."

Hearing his brother celebrating made Levi angry. He kept his composure as he turned to Cyrus, shrugging. "It was no big deal. What—you didn't think I was capable?"

"Not at all," Cyrus replied. "It's just been a long time since we've seen you kill a human. Feels good to have you back, Brother."

"I never left. I've just been playing it careful—sticking to the plan," Levi lied. "Everything's working out, Cy. You'll see."

Cyrus and Frederic glanced at each other, so quick that they probably thought Levi hadn't noticed. But he did.

"Here's hoping. Anyway, we're meeting the vampires from out of town tonight," Cyrus whispered. "We want you to be there."

Levi nodded, agreeing to meet up with them later. He hoped he could trick them—make them think he was on their side again with Elizabeth's murder. He had to get in their good graces to learn their plans before Frederic unleashed the sunlight cure—and doomed them all.

～

THE RECRUITS TRAINED all day as Emilia welcomed more Legionnaires to their castle. But as Levi glanced at Cyrus and Frederic, they didn't seem too concerned. There had to be hundreds arriving from all different countries. How could they not fear losing the war?

As Cyrus and Frederic helped the others train, Levi contemplated returning to the lab to search for the true vials. Would Frederic even keep them there? Would he trust him enough for that? Levi wasn't sure.

Levi wished he *had* destroyed the real cure. Now he was afraid of what might happen next—and when. What was Frederic waiting for if he had everything he needed to evolve the vampires?

When dusk arrived, the new Legionnaires found their rooms to rest for the evening. The barbarians stayed on duty, their eyes flickering to Levi. He didn't know why they kept staring at him, but he had a bad feeling in his gut.

After dinner, Emilia found Levi in the main hall and walked over to him. "Hello, Levi. How are you holding up? I'm still upset about Elizabeth's death."

Levi nodded. "I am too. I'm sorry she isn't here."

"Tragic times for us all, I suppose. But these New Legionnaires have given me hope again. It hasn't been easy, but I think we have a good shot at winning this, Levi—with you by my side, of course. Sunlight cure or not, I'm ready for anything."

Levi didn't know what to say. How could he tell her he had his doubts—that Cyrus and Frederic's confidence frightened him?

"Anyway, it's getting late. The new Legionnaires are good, but they could always use more practice," Emilia continued, and Levi was barely listening. "We should get some rest. I hope you don't mind bunking with me again."

He spotted his brother and Frederic across the room, staring at Levi. With him and Emilia sharing a room, it wouldn't be so easy to sneak out at night.

"You're one guest I don't mind having," Levi said, faking a smile. "I'll be there soon. Some of the barbarians wanted to go over perimeter plans. I told them I'd handle it—no need to worry. You have enough on your plate."

Emilia pecked his lips. "You're so thoughtful. See you upstairs, Levi."

As she sauntered away, Cyrus and Frederic waited until most of the Legionnaires had joined her, disappearing to their cramped rooms for rest, too. They walked over, grinning.

"You manage to get away from that Allegiant bitch for one night?" Cyrus asked. "Nice work."

Levi nodded, though he hated the way they spoke about her. "I did. Let's go—before someone realizes we're gone."

"So paranoid," Frederic said with a chuckle as they walked over to the barn. "Don't worry, Levi. Allegiant might look strong now, but we have a few tricks up our sleeves."

And that was what worried Levi. He took horses from the stables, then mounted as Cyrus and Frederic swung onto their mounts. As they galloped away, Levi noticed the barbarians staring at them again from the field. They didn't stop to ask where they were going—not this time.

"I'll point the way to our lair, Levi," Frederic said. "That's where we're meeting the vampire reinforcements."

Levi followed the backroads out of the town, guiding his horse toward the one place he hated the most—the cave outside Osgoode where the Bloodborn Order lived and plotted. As he got off the horse, he didn't see anyone. Everything was quiet.

"Where are the reinforcements?" Levi asked, frowning in confusion.

"Inside," his brother replied. "Come on—they're impatient. You know how vamps can get."

As Levi followed Cyrus and Frederic inside the cave, he gasped. All the vampires were there—and a few he didn't recognize. But there was someone else inside the cave that he didn't expect to ever see again.

Rocco, the bandit Levi had helped escape. His arms and feet were bound with rope, and his eyes were wide with fear. If the vampires had captured him, that meant they had found out Levi had shown him mercy.

And that was when he knew he was screwed.

TWENTY-NINE

Levi ran through excuses in his head, trying to figure out how he was going to explain why Rocco was still alive. Just when he thought he was making himself look better with Elizabeth's death, he was sure this would get him kicked out of the Order.

Maybe even killed.

"Glad you finally made it. Tell me—does he look familiar, Levi?" Slaughter asked, circling him. "He should. He's one of the bandits I ordered you to kill. The one I made *your* responsibility."

A shadow figure stepped forward. The man looked like the vampires—yellow eyes, fangs, muscular arms—except he didn't dress them like at all. He wore leather boots and a coat made from bear skin, looking like he lived out in the wilderness.

"You two should get acquainted," Slaughter said, stepping forward. "This is Thorn. He's only some of the reinforcements we've asked to join us."

"And I brought a gift with me," Thorn said, gesturing down at Rocco. Then he motioned behind him. "And some of my friends. The other mercenaries."

Levi looked over Thorn's shoulder, noticing dozens of other vampires from out of town. They were quiet and menacing—more frightening than the Bloodborn Order. They eyed Levi carefully, sizing him up.

Rocco twisted against his binds. "Please—let me go!"

Slaughter kicked Rocco in the chest, making the bandit cry out and double over. Slaughter sneered, bending down to Rocco's level. He grabbed his chin and forced the bandit to look the vampire in the eyes.

"Do you remember me, Rocco?" Slaughter asked.

Rocco nodded. "Yes—yes, I do. We used to cause all kinds of trouble together across town."

"That was before Levi convinced us to kill you," Slaughter replied. "He said you'd attacked and robbed him on the side of the street."

"I swear to you, I didn't," Rocco cried. "I swear on my life!"

"Oh, I believe you, Rocco," Slaughter said, rising to his feet. He turned to Levi. "And I'd never thought I'd accuse one of my own of lying, but here we are."

Levi scoffed. "Why would I make that up?"

"To save innocent lives," Slaughter replied, "the same reason you helped Rocco escape. He's hardly innocent, but still. Go on, Thorn—tell our pal Levi how you found him."

"My pleasure. You see, Rocco was on his way out of town. He stopped to catch his breath in the woods, which is where I found him," Thorn replied. "He looked lost. Confused."

"I'd been wandering for days," Rocco muttered. "I had nowhere else to go. I was only doing what Levi told me to do."

"I was going to drink his blood, but then Slaughter sent me and my friends a message. He wanted all the vampires out of town to come back," Thorn replied, stepping closer to Levi. "So, I decided to bring a little present—you know, share his blood with the group—but then Slaughter said he recognized him. It's a good thing I didn't kill him at first sight, huh?"

Levi wanted to scream at Rocco for his carelessness. He had told him to run and given him another chance at life. How could he have been so stupid as to get caught by another vampire?

"If it weren't for Thorn," Slaughter began, "we never would've found Rocco and discovered what a traitor you are."

"I'm *not* a traitor," Levi lied. "I didn't let him escape. We fought and...Rocco got away. I was just too ashamed to tell you."

"Got away from a vampire? I don't think so," Slaughter sneered, turning to Rocco. "What's the real story?"

"Levi was going to kill me," Rocco began, "but then he let me go. He said he'd let me live if I quit being a bandit and got out of Osgoode."

"How generous," Slaughter muttered. "Something I'd expect from a human, but not from a vampire."

"Is this true, Levi?" Cyrus asked, stepping in front of him. "I remember that night by the docks. I watched you throw up, but I had no idea you'd let Rocco escape. Were you sick because of what we'd done to the bandits?"

Levi said nothing. He had no defense.

"Answer me!" Cyrus said, shoving Levi into the wall of the cave. He hit his back against it with a loud thud.

"Don't bother, Cyrus," Frederic said, placing a hand on his shoulder. "He's too far gone. Being among the humans has corrupted him."

"But...but you killed Elizabeth," Cyrus continued, ignoring Frederic. "I thought you were trying to protect the Order."

"I bet he was only doing that to protect himself," Frederic said. "He wasn't going to risk anyone telling his beloved Emilia what a monster he is. That would ruin everything he'd worked for, wouldn't it?"

Levi wanted to tell them they had it all wrong—that Elizabeth had died by Emilia's hand after she confronted and attacked him. But that wouldn't do him much good. He knew nothing he could say would spare his life now.

"God damn it, Levi. I'm going to ask you something, Brother, and I need a straight answer," Cyrus began. "Are you in love with Emilia?"

"Yes," Levi replied, without hesitation.

The vampires snarled, murmuring around him.

Frederic scowled. "You fool! You've betrayed your own people and for what? Something you think is love? Vampires cannot love, Levi. What you feel for Emilia is just lust mixed with the thrill of rebellion. You must be crazy. Out of your mind!"

Levi shook his head. "You're wrong. You don't understand it, but I *do* love her. And there's nothing you can do to change that. No amount of torture."

Frederic opened his mouth to argue again, but Cyrus held up a hand. "No—my brother's right. He *does* love Emilia."

Slaughter chuckled. "A vampire in love? That's insane. Don't tell me you believe his pathetic story!"

"When we first arrived in Osgoode and met Emilia, my brother kept having chest pains," Cyrus explained. "You remember that, right, Levi?"

Levi nodded. He couldn't forget that terrible pain. "But then it went away. What's your point?"

"There's an old vampire legend," Cyrus began, "that tells of soulmates. When a vampire finds the one they're meant to be with, they'll experience chest pain. It's then followed by a total change in their behavior—a transformation. When Levi first started experiencing it, I remembered the legend. But I thought it couldn't possibly be true."

"A vampire...destined to be with a vampire hunter?" Frederic chuckled dryly. "Well, isn't that a beautiful love story. Really touches my cold, dead heart."

"Most vampires don't believe in soulmates because they don't believe in love," Cyrus continued. "But it's the only explanation. It's said that true love will always find a way—whether the vampire has a conscience or not. I should've seen this coming."

"Yes, you should have," Levi spat. "I wanted to kill Emilia when we first got here, remember? You were the one who decided to play mind games. If you would've gone with my plan, we never would've ended up here. You only have yourself to blame."

Cyrus nodded, sadly. "Maybe. And maybe that's why the Patriarch made you his successor. But you still let yourself fall for Emilia, Levi. You chose to betray me and the vampires. You chose to betray what you are."

"Oh, please—you slept with Samantha. She told me that herself. You're allowed to be with a human but not me?"

Cyrus shook his head. "That's different. I don't love her—I never will. And I certainly didn't sabotage Allegiant for her either. I plan to kill her myself when we attack the keep, and that's exactly what you should be doing with Emilia."

"Never," Levi hissed. "And I won't let you kill her, either."

"You don't have a choice," Frederic said. "This ends here."

"Yes, it does. All this time, we thought Allegiant was our biggest threat," Slaughter said, coming face-to-face with Levi. "But it was you—one of our own. Cyrus, Frederic, restrain him."

Levi growled as the two vampires put their hands on him, holding him in place. "What are you going to do with me?"

"Oh, you'll see." Slaughter grinned. "Thorn, would you do the honors?"

Thorn nodded, exposing his fangs. Levi thought Thorn would kill him until he stepped closer to Rocco. The bandit looked up at the fearsome vampire, trembling at the sight of his fangs. Levi howled when he realized what was about to happen.

He couldn't save him.

"No—don't!" Levi cried out.

Thorn pounced on Rocco, sinking his fangs into his neck. The bandit cried out before he fell over, dead. Thorn wiped his bloody mouth as he stood up.

"Thank you for that, Slaughter," Thorn said. "I was starving."

"You're welcome," Slaughter said, turning to Levi. "That was the only the first part of our revenge. We're not finished yet."

Levi struggled against Frederic and Cyrus, but the other vampires swarmed him. He knew he couldn't fight them all and escape. But he could still hurt them—and hurt them hard.

"Hey, quick question for you," Levi began. "Where's Night Temptress?"

Slaughter growled. "We don't know. She vanished—probably on a hunt somewhere. Don't worry, traitor. She'll return to take her final revenge on you and Emilia. And this time, there won't be anyone to save Emilia."

Levi shook his head. "Oh, I don't think Night Temptress will be coming back anytime soon. Just saying."

Slaughter grabbed Levi's chin hard enough to leave a mark. "What do you know, traitor? Did you do something to her?"

Levi only smirked.

Slaughter punched Levi in the stomach, making him groan as he fell to his knees. Frederic and Cyrus kept a hold on him as Slaughter continued to punch and kick him. When Levi thought the beating would never end, Slaughter backed away.

"One more time, traitor," he demanded. "What do you know about my sister? Where is she?"

Levi looked up at him. "Emilia and I tortured her to death.

And you know what? I enjoyed it. Every scream she let out was like music to my ears."

"You're lying," Slaughter whispered. "She's not dead. She... she can't be!"

"Don't believe me? Head to the markets. We burned her body and buried her bones. I can take you to her grave if you'd like."

Slaughter howled and stepped forward to attack Levi again when Cyrus blocked him. "Stop! Frederic promised me *I'd* get to kill Levi. He was my brother—I turned him. Shouldn't it be my responsibility?"

Slaughter huffed, turning his back. "Fine, fine—but make him pay for what he did to my sister. She deserved better."

"You can't kill me," Levi said. "It goes against the Vampire Commandments."

"Oh, please. Don't lecture us about killing our own," Frederic muttered. "You've killed already. Does the name Loner ring a bell? I realized what you had done when Edmund mentioned the surprise attack."

Levi didn't know what to say. They knew everything—no matter how hard he'd tried to keep it all a secret.

"Before Levi's death," Frederic said, turning to the others, "I want him to see this. I want him to see what he thought he destroyed."

Frederic pulled out vials of yellow liquid from his pocket. He passed them around to the others, smirking. The vampires held the vials in their hands.

"What's that?" Levi asked.

"The sunlight cure," Frederic replied, "but stronger. Thanks to you and your brother's blood, I was able to get it finished much quicker...*and* make a few alterations to it."

"Alterations? What kind?"

Frederic grinned. "A shame you'll never find out. You'll be dead by the time it kicks in."

"Where did you keep the real cure?"

"At my shop," Frederic replied. "What you destroyed was a decoy—failed sunlight cures that I'd been working on. It was all a test to see if you would betray us or not. And you fell for it."

Then Night Temptress was telling the truth. Levi wanted to kick himself. Why hadn't he thought of checking the apothecary for the real cure?

"Bottoms up," Cyrus said, then downed the liquid.

The other vampires drank from the strange vials. After a few seconds had passed, nothing happened.

"I don't feel any different," Slaughter muttered. "You sure Levi didn't tamper with these?"

Frederic nodded. "There's no way he could have. It takes time for it to work—but once it does, you'll be very pleased with the changes."

Levi gulped. What kind of changes? How powerful had his blood made the vampires?

Frederic glanced back at Levi, sneering. "Now to disavow you so Cyrus can kill you without breaking any vampire laws. Slaughter, would you like to do it?"

Slaughter stepped forward, grinning. He reached for a silver sword on his scabbard and made sure to only touch the handle. "My pleasure."

He slashed the sword across Levi's chest, leaving a painful gash behind. Levi knew it would scar. He didn't want to cry out in pain and give them the satisfaction, so he bit down on his tongue to keep quiet, his blood pouring down his chest.

"Levi Godfrey, I hereby remove you from the Bloodborn Order," Slaughter began. "You are no longer one of us. We will treat you like any other mortal, any other prey. You have committed the ultimate betrayal and are a disgrace to our people."

And then he smeared Levi's blood on his forehead, ending the ritual. He'd heard of it in history books before—that it was only for traitorous vampires who had abandoned their people. But none of them had betrayed the vampires as much as Levi had.

He never thought he'd end up here when he thought about his future.

"Take him away, Cyrus," Frederic demanded. "Torture and kill him like the mongrel he is. Burn and bury his body, just like he did with Night Temptress. We shouldn't waste any more time on this scum."

"Wait," Levi begged, struggling against his brother's grip. "What are you planning next?"

The vampires looked around at each other. Slaughter shrugged. "I suppose there's no harm in telling you. You'll be dead by morning, anyway. When sunlight comes, we'll be attacking the keep. We have a score to settle with Allegiant. And we want to put our new powers to good use."

"You won't stand a chance," Levi growled. "Do you know how many Legionnaires have arrived? How many more are still coming?"

"We're counting on it, actually," Frederic said. "With our new powers, they won't be able to stop us. And when the keep is stained red with blood—like your precious Emilia's—we'll invade the world and build our empire, free of Allegiant forever. It's a shame you won't be alive to see it in all its glory. But you only have yourself to blame."

He heard their evil laughter as Cyrus dragged him away. When they had reached the cave's entrance, Frederic's voice stopped them.

"Oh, and one more thing, Levi. We know about the orphans. We know you moved them too."

Levi's cheeks burned. "How?"

"I figured it out, actually," Cyrus said. "After you destroyed the sunlight cure and saved Emilia's life, I figured you must've sabotaged other things too. You knew about the orphanage attack—that was where you and Emilia disappeared to that night, saying you needed supplies. No wonder you wouldn't let anyone come with you."

"And we plan to make up for the lack of spilled blood," Frederic said. "Cyrus theorized since we hadn't seen the sea captain in a while, there was only one place you would've put the orphans—their ship. It made perfect sense. While some of us destroy Allegiant Keep, others will be sent to the ship to kill the children."

"No. Please, Brother," Levi said, turning to Cyrus. "Don't let them do this. Somewhere, deep down inside you, you know killing is wrong. You were once human. Don't you remember? If I can change, you can too. Come on, Brother. Remember when we'd skip school to spend time at the mall? When we egged our neighbor's house? How about Christmas morning, waking up to presents together? We ran down those stairs so fast to get to the gifts, Mom said it was like a wild stampede of bulls."

If Levi remembered, Cyrus had to, as well. He thought those memories would work on him—would persuade him to Levi's side. But Cyrus said nothing, avoiding his eyes.

"And when Dad would hit us, you would always protect me," Levi continued. "Remember how you shielded my body with yours? That's why you became a vampire, wasn't it? To stand up to Dad and protect us? Look at me, Brother!"

"He's only trying to manipulate you, Cyrus. Do not let him. Take him away," Frederic said. "Let him die knowing his plan has failed."

Levi kicked and fought back as Cyrus tugged him out of the cave, but his brother was strong. Cyrus then pulled out a silver sword and pressed it to Levi's throat.

"Enough," Cyrus spat. "Stop struggling. Don't make this harder than it already is."

"Where are you taking me?" Levi asked. "Are you seriously going to kill your own brother? After everything we've been through?"

"Start walking," Cyrus said. "That way—far from the village. Move!"

Levi listened, walking north of the village as Cyrus trailed behind with his sword. After fifteen minutes of walking, they had ended up far from Osgoode—far from the vampire lair. When Levi looked out, he saw only miles of farmland.

Cyrus cleared his throat. "You can stop now."

Levi spun around. "You were the one who made me a vampire, Cyrus. You knew I didn't want this life. As far as I'm concerned, all of this is your fault."

Cyrus nodded. "For once, I agree with you. Sometimes, I wonder if I should've killed you with our parents that night."

"Gee, thanks. Look, we can't make up for our past mistakes," Levi began, "but we *can* prevent ourselves from making future ones. Help me stop the vampires, Cyrus. We can build a better world—maybe one where humans and vampires get along. Aren't you sick of all the fighting? All the pointless bloodshed?"

Cyrus's hand wavered on his sword. "Turn around, Levi."

When Levi did, he noticed someone had dug a deep grave into the dirt. A coffin lay inside, several feet down. "What's this?"

"You're going to get inside that coffin, just like I planned. Then I'm going to bury you and walk away."

"You...aren't going to kill me outright? Straight through the heart?" Levi spun around again. "That's how Slaughter and the others want me to die."

"Yeah, well, they're not here, so I get to make the decisions," Cyrus replied. "Now, get in quickly—before I change my mind."

"You know I can easily claw my way out of here. I've done worse."

Cyrus shook his head. "I had the coffin specially made. I ordered it myself from a carpenter in the markets when Frederic told me I had to kill you. It's lined with silver. I then wheeled it out here, careful not to touch it. It won't kill you, but it *will* prevent you from escaping. You'll be too weak to fight, and eventually, you'll die of thirst."

"You can't do it, can you?" Levi asked. "You can't kill me outright?"

"No," Cyrus admitted. "Even though you deserve it for betraying our people...I can't stab this sword through your heart and kill my own brother. But I can't disobey the others, so I'm forced to do it this way. Don't get it twisted, Levi. It's a slow, merciless death. But before you get in there, I need to know something first."

"What?"

"Do you have remorse for what you did? At all?"

"No," Levi replied. "You know I love Emilia—that I'd do anything to protect her. I only wish you could be by my side to stop the vampires. Despite everything, I still care about you, Brother. Even now."

"Damn you, Levi! If you had remorse, I would've offered you a chance to run—to get out of here. But we both know you wouldn't stay away if I did," Cyrus muttered. "I won't let the vampires do to me what they've done to you. Maybe in the new world, I can be someone. Maybe I'll even get to be Patriarch one day."

"Brother, please—"

"Get in the coffin, Levi. Don't make me force you."

With no other option, Levi jumped into the grave and stepped inside the coffin. The silver burned his skin as he lay down, looking up at his disappointed brother. He thought about fighting him, but there was a good chance Cyrus would kill him—and Levi already had a better plan in mind, one that required him to be alive.

"Goodbye, Brother," Cyrus began, reaching down. "I'm sorry it had to end this way. I'm sorry we won't get to see the empire together. I'm just...I'm just sorry."

And then he shut the coffin lid, shrouding Levi in total darkness.

CHAPTER

THIRTY

Cyrus moved fast to dump the dirt on Levi's coffin, throwing it on top with loud thumps. Levi lay there, his skin burning from the silver surrounding him.

"Brother, don't do this!" Levi cried, pounding his fists raw on the coffin's roof. "It's not too late to let me out!"

But Cyrus didn't answer. He continued shoveling dirt onto the casket, pretending he couldn't hear his brother crying out. Vampires had better vision than humans in the dark, but this far down, Levi couldn't see a thing.

I shouldn't have gotten in, Levi thought, *but Cyrus wasn't backing down. Now I'm trapped in here. How am I supposed to get out?*

The thumps of dirt stopped. Levi listened for a moment, hearing Cyrus's footsteps fade. Levi knew that if he was in his brother's place, he never would've abandoned Cyrus in a coffin. Levi wanted to call out for help, hoping a passerby would hear him, but then he remembered it was nighttime, and no one lived so far out.

I need to find my own way out of here, Levi thought. *There must be a way.*

There was only one solution, he realized. He'd have to fight.

With all his might, he used his fist to punch a hole in the casket. Dirt filtered in through the hole, trickling onto his clothes. The silver burned him the more he touched it, making him howl in pain. His arms became scratched, bruised, and bloodied. He wanted to quit—to lie back down in defeat. To let the pain kill him.

But then he remembered Emilia and the orphans. They needed him—and that gave him the strength he needed to keep trying.

It felt like it took hours, but he managed to punch a larger hole in the coffin's roof. More dirt fell inside so he kept his mouth closed and used his other hand to shield his eyes. When the hole looked big enough for his torso, he pushed his body through, feeling the weight of the dirt on him.

Just keep going, Levi thought. *Almost there.*

With his eyes closed, he used his arms to pull himself up through the dirt, grateful the silver wasn't touching his body anymore. When he had reached the top, he grabbed onto the grass and yanked himself out of the grave.

He spat out dirt as he collapsed, exhausted and shaking. Using his knees, he forced himself to stand and realized it was already dawn. It had taken him all night to find a way out of the coffin. He worried the Bloodborn Order had killed everyone by now. And with his hands almost numb from clawing his way out and the cut on his chest bleeding, he feared he would be useless against the vampires. But that didn't mean he wasn't going to try.

He glanced around, looking for his brother, but he and the vampires had vanished. He ran back to the lair, hoping to stop them, but when he arrived, everyone was gone. Which meant one thing.

The cure had worked. Sunlight didn't hurt them anymore.

He reached for one of the swords left behind, tucking it into his scabbard. Although it hurt to use his fingers, he didn't want to head into battle without a weapon. He rushed out of the cave and found Margaret still there, so he jumped on the horse and flicked the reins.

He galloped toward the markets, noticing nothing out of the ordinary. It meant the vampires hadn't attacked the townspeople—yet. Allegiant seemed like their main focus, but then Levi remembered how some vampires were heading to Rosalie's ship to feast on the orphans. And the children came first.

He rode to the docks, noticing a cluster of people up ahead. Several humans—mostly sailors and fishermen—ran past him, screaming. He jumped off his horse, grabbing the arm of a sailor that sprinted past him.

"What's going on?" Levi asked.

"Vampires—the whole lot of them! They ambushed us. Came outta nowhere," the sailor cried. "Get out of here if you want to live!"

The sailor took off, abandoning the docks. Levi scowled and raced toward Rosalie's ship, watching in horror as a dozen vampires boarded. He reached for his sword, trying to steady it in his shaking, painful hands as he walked onto the ship's ramp.

He could immediately smell the fear. He spotted Rosalie, Scrooge, and some of the other pirates battling the vampires, using their Legionnaire training. The pirates had placed all the orphans in one corner of the ship, trying their best to defend them. As the children cried and clung to each other in fear, he noticed Sister Tess's dead body on the deck of the ship and felt anger bubbling inside of him.

One vampire overpowered Scrooge, sinking their fangs into his neck. Rosalie noticed and cried out. "No—Scrooge!"

The vampire she was fighting took the opportunity to knock the sword out of her hands, leaving her defenseless. When they turned their face, Levi realized it was Thorn. The bastard who murdered Rocco.

"Although children's blood tastes sweeter," Thorn began, licking his lips at Rosalie, "I'll be happy to start with you."

"Think again," Levi said, then he plunged his sword through Thorn's heart from behind.

Thorn gasped, falling to his knees. His eyes widened as he glanced back at Levi. "And so, the traitor lives. But don't fool yourself, Levi...you can't stop us..."

As Thorn went motionless, dead on the deck of the ship, Rosalie panted and looked at Levi. "Thanks for that. You've got great timing, you know."

Levi nodded, picking up her silver sword with a hiss before tossing it at her. "Thank me later. And burn those vamp bodies when we're done."

With Thorn's death, the vampires noticed Levi had boarded and rushed to attack him instead. It gave the pirates a chance to catch their breath. Summoning all the anger he had inside him, Levi fought with his throbbing hands and bit the necks of the vampires his sword couldn't reach. He spat out their blood, loathing the taste.

Rosalie and the pirates rejoined the fight, impaling as many of the vampires as they could. Levi positioned himself so he stood in front of the orphans, defending them from vampires at every angle. When only one remained, Levi thrust his sword through their chest, killing the final vampire.

Strange, Levi thought. *Frederic said he'd made the sunlight cure stronger, but these vampires seemed normal.*

Dead bodies and violet blood coated the ship. Levi panted, flexing his hands. Some of the feeling had returned, enough that he could grip his sword. It was all he needed. Levi glanced back and noticed all the pirates staring at him—even Rosalie who hovered above Scrooge's body.

"Is he dead?" Levi asked.

Rosalie nodded, rising to her feet. "He is. I think you made them pay for it—*and* you saved the orphans. We tried to protect Sister Tess, but they came at us so fast. Poor woman. Anyway, are you okay?"

Her eyes roamed his body, probably noticing the countless wounds. Levi nodded. "I've been better, but I'll live."

"I saw it, Levi," she said. "I saw you...biting those vampires. And when you touched my sword, the silver...it burned you."

Levi stepped forward. "Rosalie, let me explain—"

"I don't care," she interrupted. "Vampire, human, or whatever you are, you saved our lives. As far as I'm concerned, you're a damn hero. I oughta buy you a pint when this is all over."

Levi almost laughed. He didn't feel like much of a hero, but it was nice to hear.

He nodded instead, turning from her. "Well, thanks. Stay here. More vampires are on their way to the keep—and they're immune to sunlight. Guard those orphans and don't let anyone onto the ship."

He left before Rosalie could argue, getting back onto Margaret. He galloped through the markets, his sword dangling in one hand as the villagers looked at him with wide eyes. As he approached the keep, he noticed three figures circling above it. At first, he thought they were just large birds—but then he looked closer.

Cyrus, Frederic, and Slaughter were in the air, flying around. They could only hover for a few seconds before they needed to set down on the roof and recharge. That must've been the alteration Frederic had mentioned. But why hadn't the other vampires received that power?

Levi left Margaret in the field, keeping her out of danger as he rushed to the keep. Some of the barbarians fought the vampires on the ground, ones who couldn't glide. The new

Legionnaires joined the fray, striking down any vampire they could find.

Cyrus, Frederic, and Slaughter watched from above, and Levi wondered what they were waiting for. He tried not to let them see him as he sprinted toward the castle and kept his head low. Novak, Vana, and the other barbarians on patrol fought several snarling vampires in the training yard. Levi assumed they could defend themselves, so he rushed inside to find Emilia and the others. The main hall of the keep was empty but stained with blood—both human and vampire. He spotted a familiar face lying on the ground and rushed over to him.

"Lord Tristan," Levi said, noticing the bloody cuts on his body. "Shit. Why are you here?"

"Someone told me they saw vampires approaching the keep. I decided to help fight," Lord Tristan said, coughing up blood. "It was my only chance...at redemption..."

Levi understood completely.

"But I never had a chance. They were...too strong for me. My guards...are dead too," he sputtered. "Save...my town, Levi. Do what I could not..."

And then Lord Tristan went limp, his eyes glossing over. Although Levi hated him, he couldn't help but feel sorry that the vampires had taken his life. And there was a bond between them, a commonality. They were two men with terrible pasts who had relented and tried to right their wrongs.

It was a tragic end, one Levi hoped didn't befall him as well.

As he shut Lord Tristan's eyes, the sounds of grunting and fighting echoed from the kitchen. He took Lord Tristan's sword, keeping one in each hand. When he made it into the kitchen, he found Samantha and Alana fighting off two vampires. Behind them, Peeta and Edmund lay on the ground, drained and dead.

With the vampires distracted, Levi had no problem stabbing each in the chest with his two swords. After they had collapsed,

Alana and Samantha's eyes landed on Levi, widening in surprise.

"Are you two okay?" he asked.

Samantha nodded, tears welling in her eyes. "Yes, but... some didn't make it. Oh, Papa..."

"Peeta, too," Alana said, looking down sadly. "He tried to fight, but...it was no use."

Levi knew when Emilia found out about Peeta's death, it would destroy her. She had no one left in her family now. He only hoped he could make the vampires answer for this.

"I'm so sorry. But what about the others?" Levi asked. "The civilians staying here?"

"All dead," Samantha said. "It happened so fast. We were caught off-guard."

"That's what the vampires were counting on. Where's Emilia?"

"She was in the barn feeding the animals when the vampires arrived," Alana replied. "We had no idea they could handle the sunlight...or glide in the air."

Levi nodded. "It's a new trick of theirs. You can thank Frederic for that, the bastard. Sam, have you seen Cyrus?"

"Only on the roof." She looked him up and down. "Does that mean you're also..."

"Yes," Levi replied. "Yes, I'm a vampire. Please, don't let Cyrus see you. He wants you dead, Samantha—trust me. Your relationship with him was a lie."

Alana cleared her throat, looking at Levi with fear in her eyes. "Was your relationship with Emilia a lie too? Were you just using her?"

"No." Levi shook his head firmly. "No, not at all. Look, I know things are really confusing right now, but if you believe anything, let it be this. I *am* on your side, and I love Emilia. Come with me now. I'll keep you two safe."

As the three rushed down the hallway, Levi passed the chapel. He noticed Father McGregor dead on the floor, the blood sucked dry from his body. He was the only one who knew Levi's secret and believed in his redemption. It felt like he had lost a mentor—maybe even a father figure.

"Oh my God, not Father McGregor too," Alana said, and Samantha placed a hand on her shoulder. "I thought Allegiant was prepared. What happened?"

"They had vampires on the inside," Samantha said, glancing at Levi. "That's how they were able to overpower us."

Levi shut Father McGregor's eyes and stood up. "Let's go—to the barn. We need to find Emilia. With everyone dead, there's nothing else we can do here."

Levi led them out a side door of the keep, shielding Alana and Samantha with his body. They wove through the battle and ran to the barn. Alana knocked on the barn door as Levi kept watch behind them. The vampires on the ground hadn't noticed them yet. They were still fighting the barbarians and new Legionnaires.

"Emilia, it's us," Alana whispered. "Let us in!"

The barn door swung open a moment later, then Levi noticed Emilia's surprised face. "I was just about to come find you! Hurry inside—you can take shelter here."

"Peeta and my father are dead," Samantha said, "as well as Father McGregor, the civilians, and a bunch of other Legionnaires. I'm so sorry, Emilia."

As Alana and Samantha entered, Emilia's teary eyes landed on Levi. "No…"

"No time," Levi muttered. "The battle needs me. Keep the others safe!"

Emilia grabbed his arm, holding him back. "The barbarians overheard your conversation with Elizabeth. They told me everything, Levi. I know you're a vampire. One of those evil, wretched things."

Levi didn't want to do this now. With his brother on the roof and the vampires on the ground, they didn't have time. But he had the feeling Emilia wasn't planning on dropping it that easily.

"I should've seen the signs. They were all there," she continued, her lip quivering. "The strange comments at the ball, how you knew about the vampires' plans. Even how cold your hands were. You were always one step ahead, and I was too in love with you to see it. Well, I suppose you got what you wanted, Levi. The vampires won."

"I'm not helping the vampires," Levi said. "Whether you believe it or not, I *do* love you. Cyrus explained it to me—my transformation. You made me human, Emilia, because you're my soulmate."

She shook her head. "I don't believe a word out of your mouth, Levi. Not anymore."

"I don't know about soulmates," Samantha said, "but I *do* know Levi saved our lives. He's all right in my book."

"Convenient," Emilia muttered, glaring at him. "Why did you only show up now? Where were you earlier when they first attacked?"

"Look at me, Emilia. I crawled out of a coffin laced with silver," he said, gesturing at his gashes. "My brother put me in there to kill me, but I came back to protect you. To protect you all. I had to."

"Great job you've done of it," she grumbled. "My entire family is dead, Allegiant is crumbling, and you lied to my face this whole time—"

Like a falling star, Cyrus landed on the ground behind him. Frederic and Slaughter landed by Levi's side, restraining him.

Emilia held up her sword to attack but the terror in her eyes was unmistakable.

"You lived, Brother," Cyrus remarked. "You must really love Emilia to risk your life by coming back here. Or maybe you're just an idiot."

"Why not both?" Frederic joked.

"We told you to kill him," Slaughter snarled, glaring at Cyrus. "What happened?"

"He lived—obviously. It isn't my fault my brother doesn't know when to quit."

"Neat little power you have," Levi muttered. "Why can't the others glide?"

"You think I'd give the other vampires this power?" Frederic snorted. "No, it's only reserved for us—those strong enough to wield it. The higher-ranking vampires. Folklore always said vampires were bat-like, so I decided to make it true. I had more time on my hands since you and your brother helped me figure out the sunlight cure much quicker. You know, if you hadn't betrayed us, you could've had this power too, Levi."

"I think I'll pass, thanks," Levi hissed. "The price is a little too high for my liking."

Cyrus turned back to the barn, grinning wickedly. Levi felt like he didn't even recognize him anymore—or maybe he had always been evil. And Levi had never realized it since he was a vampire too.

"Sammy, you in there?" Cyrus taunted. "Why don't you come out and play? We had so much fun before, didn't we?"

"Leave her alone!" Levi growled. "You want to fight someone? Start with me, you bastards."

"All in due time," Frederic said. "You've been a nuisance long enough. But since you're here...I suppose there's no harm in letting you watch."

"Watch what?" Levi demanded.

"Watch what we plan to do with your precious Emilia," Cyrus explained. "I tried to spare you this pain...but maybe it's better if you see it. Soon, you won't recognize her at all."

"Stop talking in riddles," Levi demanded, "and tell me what the hell's going on."

Emilia thrust her silver sword at Cyrus, but his reflexes had improved. He sprang into the air and hovered above her, then landed behind her to grab her arms. Alana and Samantha stepped outside with their swords, but Cyrus flew up again with Emilia in his arms, her feet dangling above Levi's head.

"No one is going to stop this," Cyrus said. "Frederic, your orders?"

"We deliberated a lot on this—but we've all decided it's for the good of our people," Frederic replied. "After all, what's better than turning an enemy to your cause?"

Levi struggled against their grip, but they were too strong— much stronger with the improved sunlight cure. He knew exactly what was about to happen as Emilia twisted and screamed in Cyrus's grasp.

"Emilia Rutherford," Cyrus began, "welcome to the life of an immortal."

And then he sunk his fangs into Emilia's neck.

CHAPTER

THIRTY-ONE

"No!" Levi cried, but it was too late.

The woman he loved was gone—a vampire now. Night Tempress's threat had come true. Cyrus floated down, carrying Emilia with her eyes closed in his arms.

"Awaken, Emilia," Cyrus whispered. "Join us."

Her eyes opened. Levi could feel the change—could sense it in her blood.

"How do you feel?" Cyrus asked her.

Emilia licked her lips. "...Hungry."

Cyrus chuckled. "Well, don't worry—we have plenty of targets. But Samantha's off-limits. I'm drinking from her."

"Emilia?" Alana asked in a shy, small voice. "Is that...is that you?"

"She's not your Emilia anymore, child," Frederic said. "She's better."

"I thought you were going to kill her?" Levi asked.

"We were," Frederic began, "but then it hit me—turning the leader of Allegiant to our side is a sweet irony, wouldn't you say?"

"It is." Emilia walked over to Levi, scowling at him. "What are we doing about this traitor?"

"Well, Frederic wanted me to kill him," Cyrus said, "but I think I'll leave that to you. A sword through the heart oughta do it."

"Emilia, no," Levi whispered, even though he knew it was pointless. "You don't have to be like them. I'm sorry I couldn't protect you, but there's still a chance to save Allegiant—"

"Save it!" she spat. "I don't want to hear from you anymore —not from someone who lied to me. I don't care about Allegiant now. As far as I'm concerned, they're all dead to me."

Cyrus picked up Emilia's fallen weapon and handed it to her. "Good. Here—strike the killing blow. They say a vampire never forgets their first kill, and I want yours to be memorable."

She took the weapon and grabbed Levi's face, making him wince in pain. Her newfound strength hurt. "My pleasure."

Levi shut his eyes. There was nothing left to do—no amount of fighting that could get him out of this. He had failed. And with his death, Alana, Samantha, and the rest of the world would die too.

"Good riddance," Emilia whispered.

Levi heard groaning and opened his eyes, surprised to find no blade had penetrated his heart. Emilia had stabbed Slaughter through the chest instead. The vampire released his grip on Levi, falling to his knees with wide eyes.

"Conniving...Allegiant whore..." he sputtered, then collapsed in a pool of his own blood. It had turned black like Levi's from the sunlight cure.

Levi didn't know what was going on, but he wasn't about to wait for Emilia to strike him next. With one arm free, he punched Frederic in the face, wrestling the Bloody Doctor off him.

As the scientist fell to the ground, Cyrus approached Emilia, but she held her sword out toward him. "Stop! Come any closer and you'll be next, vampire."

"I don't understand," Cyrus said, frowning. "You should be on our side, not his!"

Levi gasped when he realized it. "The soulmate bond. It must've saved your soul, Emilia. It must've given you a conscience."

She nodded, glancing back at Levi. "I suspected as much. I can't kill you, Levi, no matter how much you've hurt me. And I don't want anyone else to die either. I'm still me—I still have all my emotions, my conscience. And thank goodness for that."

"That's a relief. Really, Emilia, I didn't mean to lie to you," Levi said. "I just didn't know how to tell you. I was afraid you wouldn't love me anymore if you knew—"

"Um, sorry to interrupt," Samantha began, "but our people are getting killed. Look!"

Levi glanced over his shoulder, realizing Samantha was right. Even the barbarians, the best fighters they had, couldn't overpower the vampires. They had overwhelmed the keep— and when Levi looked in the distance, he noticed more approaching. Frederic had saved the rest of the vampire merce- naries for last.

Frederic laughed, rising to his feet. "You see? You can't win, not even with your pathetic soulmate bond. So go on, kiss your girlfriend goodbye. This is the end for all of you!"

Levi heard galloping in the distance and craned his neck. Rosalie rode through on a stolen horse, impaling some vampires with her sword as she approached. She stopped right in front of Levi as dirt blew upward from the animal's hooves.

"Hurry—get on!" she cried.

"Rosalie, what are you doing here?" Levi asked. "I told you to stay away!"

"Don't worry—the pirates are watching over the orphans," she replied. "Did you think I could sit out a big battle like this?"

"Stay or leave, we'll only follow you," Cyrus taunted. "You can't run!"

Levi ignored his brother, turning to Emilia. "Stay here, okay? I need to get something from the barn. Be back in a second."

"From the barn?" Emilia asked, raising an eyebrow. "What are you talking about—"

But Levi had already rushed inside, scrambling to find Elizabeth's gun he'd hidden in the barrel of hay. He sighed in relief when he found it. When he opened the weapon's barrel, only a few bullets remained, but he hoped it would be enough. Once he had it cocked, he rushed back outside to find everyone waiting for him.

"Know what this is, Brother?" Levi asked, holding the gun up.

Cyrus nodded. "Standard Allegiant weapon. How did you—"

"Emilia's descendant dropped it, and I hid it. It's fully loaded," he replied. "Follow us and I won't hesitate to fire. And I'm a good shot—whether you're on the ground or not."

"Just shoot him now, Levi," Emilia said. "While we're all still here!"

Levi lifted the gun, his hands trembling. He thought about it —he really did—but he couldn't do it. He hated his brother— and the feeling was mutual, it seemed—but he couldn't bring himself to pull the trigger. He could never force his brother into a silver-laced coffin, either. And he was grateful for that.

It meant he had his conscience back.

Levi gestured at Rosalie's horse. "All of you—get on. We're leaving."

"Leaving?" Samantha blinked. "But...but the Legionnaires need us!"

"Look around, Sam. Most of them are dead or dying. We've lost," Levi replied, his finger hovering above the trigger. "I hate to admit it, but Frederic's right. We can't stop this—and if we stay, they'll only kill us too."

Emilia scowled, still holding her sword. "I refuse to let them escape! They've burned our keep, killed the civilians and our Legionnaires—"

"I have a plan," Levi whispered. "Please—trust me. You don't want to put Alana or Samantha in danger, do you?"

Emilia paused for a moment, then sighed. "Fine. Fetch the cart. Everyone, get in. And if any of you vampires follow us, I'll be more than happy to demonstrate my new powers."

Levi helped Samantha and Alana into the cart, then he jumped on the horse. He aimed his gun at Cyrus and Frederic as Emilia sat in front of him and grabbed the reins.

"Pathetic," Frederic spat, taking cover behind Cyrus so Levi couldn't shoot him. "This isn't over, Levi. We *will* kill you all!"

Levi made a crude gesture in response. "Go, Emilia. Take us anywhere but here!"

Emilia flicked the reins and the horse galloped into the distance, Allegiant Keep becoming smaller behind them. Two vampires overpowered Novak and Vana, biting their necks and killing them. Levi turned his gaze away from the dying barbarians and Legionnaires, ashamed they had to abandon the battle. But staying meant death. And he'd come too far to let that happen.

"Are they following us?" Alana asked, glancing back.

Levi shook his head. "No, I think they're afraid of my gun. As they should be."

Samantha frowned. "Your gun? What's that?"

Levi sighed. He realized he had a lot of explaining to do it. He told them the full story as Emilia rode far from the keep—all about the future, the blood magic portal, and Cyrus's plans to sabotage Allegiant. Once he had finished, no one said anything for a while.

"I...can't believe I killed my own descendant," Emilia muttered.

"I'm sorry," Levi said quietly. "I didn't want her to die either. I tried to save her, but she wouldn't listen to me."

"And now she joins the long list of casualties. When did you realize you had feelings for me? That you could love again?"

"It was early on. I hated seeing you with Lord Tristan, and I think Cyrus realized that too," Levi said. "Speaking of which... Lord Tristan's dead. The vampires got him when he came to help."

Emilia sighed. "I'd like to say he deserved it, but...I'm not sure anyone deserves this. I still can't believe Frederic was a vampire this whole time. I shouldn't have been so naïve."

"Vampires are good liars, Em. Don't blame yourself."

"Maybe. If you and Cyrus hadn't time-traveled," Emilia began, "what would've happened? Just curious."

"Well, if I remember my brother's history lessons, you managed to run the vampires out of town, killing a lot of them. Some got away and emigrated to the United States. Frederic still evolved the vampires, but you found out his secret and killed him. When it was over, you had a child with Lord Tristan and continued to build Allegiant."

"Damn," Samantha muttered. "I prefer that ending much more than ours. Even though you deserve better than Lord Tristan, Emilia."

No one said anything as the horse continued to gallop. They had changed history, Levi realized. But for better or for worse? He didn't know yet.

Rosalie pulled the reins when they reached a farm in the distance, stopping the horse and cart. "Well, we've hit the outskirts of Osgoode. I don't think the vampires followed us here. What now?"

"Your plan had better be good, Levi," Samantha said as she stepped out of the cart. She reached back, helping Alana out. "We left a lot of good people behind back there."

Levi nodded, jumping down. "I know, I know. Do you remember when I told you about the blood magic portal?"

Emilia's eyes lit up. "You're not considering—"

"It's the only way," Levi interrupted. "I know it's dangerous —using blood magic always is—but I have to try. If we can go back into the past, maybe I can stop all this from happening."

"How?" Alana asked.

Levi sighed, lifting his gun. "By killing me and Cyrus. In the past, I mean."

"Won't that kill you now?" Emilia asked. "And affect us in the future?"

"I don't know, but it's a risk we have to take. The vampires have defeated Allegiant, Em. Do you know how fast they'll spread to other parts of the world now?"

Emilia shuddered at the thought.

"Exactly. It's why the five of us need to go back—again— and stop me in the past," Levi said. "It's my only hope at redemption. What does everyone think?"

"I think all this vampire and time-travel stuff is giving me a headache," Alana muttered. "So confusing."

"I think I understand it all. And if Levi thinks it's best...then I'm with him," Rosalie said. "He saved my life today. I'll do whatever he says. And if going back to the past means Scrooge lives, then I'm in."

"Good, thank you. Sam?"

Samantha nodded. "If we can save my father...then yes, we have to try. Succeed or fail, at least we did something."

"Yeah, same," Alana said. "Peeta deserved to live. Dawn too."

"Agreed." Levi turned to Emilia. "It's just you now, Em. Are you in or not?"

Emilia turned silent for a moment, sighing. "It seems I have no choice. How do we use this blood magic? Do you even know?"

"I think so. I'll just copy what Patriarch did. I remember him telling me the ingredients." Levi picked a lily from the field, then used his silver sword to cut his hand. A drop of blood fell onto the flower before he turned to the others. "Good. Now we just need the blood of a virginal human to complete the ritual."

Alana blushed. "That, um, would be me."

Levi handed the sword to her. "Just a tiny prick. Let it drop onto the flower."

Alana took a deep breath as she pricked her finger with the sword. When it dribbled onto the flower, the blood combined to turn the petals black. The five waited with bated breath, but nothing happened.

"Come on," Levi muttered. "It worked for the Patriarch. This can't be how it ends—"

The flower burned up in his hand. A second later, a giant red portal opened in front of them like a door. It sucked in all the plants around them like a vacuum, and the five of them backed up so it wouldn't catch them in its pull.

"This is it," Levi yelled over the loud wind. "We have to jump in—together!"

"How do we know it'll take us to the right place in time?" Samantha asked.

"I'm not sure. I think we all have to be imagining it at the same time. Picture the markets at night, a little over two weeks ago before my brother and I got here. Are we ready?"

"Wait," Emilia said, turning to Levi. "You said before you

feared telling me the truth because you thought I couldn't love you. Not as a vampire."

Levi nodded. "Yeah, that's right. I've done terrible things in the past, Em. Being with you helped make me a better man, but it doesn't change what I've done—"

Emilia wrapped her arms around his neck, pulling him in for a passionate kiss. He almost forgot the eyes on them or the noisy portal a few steps away. When she pulled back, she smiled with her new fangs.

"I couldn't stop loving you, Levi. Not for anything in the world," she said. "That much is true by how strong the soul-mate bond was—by how it saved my conscience. No matter what happens, I will always love you. You *are* redeemed in my eyes."

Levi smiled sadly. "I love you, too, Emilia—and I only wish we could've had more time. If we succeed at killing me and my brother, then...this timeline might not exist. We could vanish—all of us."

"I know," Emilia whispered. "If that's true, then...I'm just glad we're together now. And I forgive you for everything that's happened."

That gave Levi some comfort, even if he knew this was the end. He held onto Emilia and gestured at the others. "Grab onto me. We want to jump into the portal at the same time!"

Samantha, Rosalie, and Alana reached for them, holding onto Emilia and Levi for dear life. Levi took a deep breath. "Good. Ready?"

Everyone nodded. Alana snapped her eyes shut, trembling with fear.

"Now—jump into the portal!" Levi cried. "Come on!"

They sprinted into the swirl, and Levi felt the familiar feeling of his body becoming weightless again. But something was wrong—it felt different than the last time. The blood magic portal turned black, and Levi had this sinking feeling as though they weren't heading into the past at all. That maybe they had played around with blood magic too much and done something terrible.

"What's going on?" Emilia asked. "I...can't see anything!"

"Something isn't right," Levi said, losing his grip on the others. "Emilia!"

"Levi!" Emilia cried, falling out of his grasp and slipping away.

And that was the last thing he remembered.

ALSO BY DANA GRICKEN

The Vampire Empire

Blood Oath

The Maidens of Fairhaven

Modern Fairytale

Enchantingly Yours

Spellbound Heart

The Soulless War Trilogy

The Dark Queen

The Dark Evolution

The Dark Cage

The Dragonwitch Chronicles Trilogy

The Girl Who Walked Through Fire

The Girl with the Invincible Blood

The Girl and The Silver Mark

The Hearts Companion

Ten Years: A Poetry Collection

Reverie: A Poetry Collection

Short Stories and Novellas

Whispers in the Woods: A Short Story Collection

Little Things: A horror novella

Drifting Darkly: A sci-fi novella

ABOUT THE AUTHOR

Dana Gricken is an author from Ottawa, Ontario, Canada. The Dragonwitch Chronicles was her first series. Since then, she's published THE DARK QUEEN, THE DARK EVOLUTION, and THE DARK CAGE—the full trilogy in the Soulless War series. You can find those books at online retailers in both e-book and paperback forms.

In January 2020, she signed with Jessica Reino of the Metamorphosis Literary Agency. Please stay tuned for announcements on new books! In the meantime, if you've read and enjoyed her work, please don't hesitate to reach out to Dana on Twitter and Instagram—both @DanaGricken.

In her spare time, she enjoys watching Star Trek with her cats, reading, and playing video games. She hopes her books bring joy to people and wants to write over a hundred novels in her lifetime.

A small press bound by the belief that every voice matters.

Sign up for our newsletter to learn about new releases and more.
https://oliver-heberbooks.com/subscribe/

Follow us on social media:

facebook.com/oliverheberbooks
instagram.com/oliverheberbooks
amazon.com/oliverheberbooks
youtube.com/@OliverHeberBooksPublisher